"The Cr... bloody i... tin, you'... usurper ha...

Andy Rem...

"*The Crown of the Blood* should ... ... a warning sticker on the front... it's one of those books that are almost impossible to put down."

SFBook.com

"Well written, cunningly plotted and above all else a combat story of survival that shows that Thorpe is more than prepared to slaughter a world to establish his own rule. Great stuff."

Falcata Times

"Gav Thorpe writes war as it should be written: brutal, dark, bloody, treacherous, confusing, and insane. The novel is well-written, with a complex plot that promises additional books, ruthless, fully developed characters, and a penchant for psychological realism that makes the book an adult read rather than a childish escape."

Red Rook Reviews

"The setting and story are well thought out and are remarkably logical for a fantasy novel. If you enjoy military or historical fiction, you will enjoy *The Crown of the Blood*. Action, intrigue, conquest, and charismatic generals are waiting for you here!"

James Atlantic Speaks

GAV THORPE

The Crown of the Usurper

THE CROWN OF THE BLOOD
BOOK III

ANGRY ROBOT

ANGRY ROBOT
A member of the Osprey Group

Lace Market House,
54-56 High Pavement,
Nottingham,
NG1 1HW, UK

www.angryrobotbooks.com
As you rise, so shall you fall

An Angry Robot paperback original 2012
1

A catalogue record for this book is available
from the British Library.

ISBN: 978-0-85766-132-6
eBook ISBN: 978-0-85766-134-0

Set in Meridien by THL Design.

Printed in the UK by CPI Group (UK) Ltd, Croydon, CR0 4YY

JUBILEE WOODS.ORG.UK

This book is dedicated to Gordon.
Frankly, one was going to be sooner or later,
so it might as well be this one.

CARANTATHI
Autumn, 213th Year of Askh

I

The sound of hammer on stone ringing outside the window matched the pounding of Ullsaard's head. He lay on the bed and looked at the dawn light creeping across the ceiling. He had not slept, not since he had suffered the strange vision of Urikh, his eldest son, placing the Crown of the Blood on his head.

The King of Greater Askhor was left in no doubt that what he had seen was genuine. The experience had been so visceral, and so like the sensation he himself had felt when he had put on the Crown and the ancient king, Askhos, had attempted to possess him. For some reason – and Ullsaard suspected he knew which one – Urikh had travelled to Askh and delved into the vaults of the palaces to retrieve the Crown that Ullsaard had hidden there.

Of this much Ullsaard was certain, but there questions too, that he could not answer; most pressing amongst these was why his son had taken it upon himself to wear the Crown. Had it been idle curiosity, trying it on for size like a child wearing his father's boots, or did Urikh really intend to take the Crown and the kingship for himself? This second possibility froze

Ullsaard's heart. He and Urikh were not close, and his eldest son's ambition had never been in doubt. Yet for all that, he knew Urikh was a patient man, a thinker too. His mother, Ullsaard's middle wife Luia, was also a schemer, a seeker of prestige above all things, but would she risk destroying her family in a hasty lunge for power?

Ullsaard also did not know whether Urikh had felt anything of the connective moment that had bound the king to the Crown. Did his son know that the Crown had properties beyond being a badge of office? And in this matter Ullsaard needed to know what had happened, if anything, to Askhos, whose essence or spirit had been passed down the generations of the Blood through the Crown. Was Askhos still trapped? Was he in Urikh's head as well as his own, or instead? Ullsaard's claiming of the Crown against the rightful succession had thrown Askhos' plans into turmoil, putting him to a limbo state between the Crown and Ullsaard's mind. What effect would his son's interference have?

These questions and others had plagued Ullsaard since the early hours of the morning and driven away any chance of sleep. The shadows on the wall deepened and the light brightened. The sound of crowing cockerels and the increasing clamour of domestic life intruded upon Aegenuis' halls.

He pulled himself out of bed, wearily splashing water from the bedside bowl onto his face. He dragged his fingers through his beard, which had become somewhat long and bedraggled over the last stage of the campaign to conquer Salphoria.

Throwing on his shirt and kilt, leaving his armour and weapons on the floor where he had dropped them, Ullsaard opened his travelling chest and pulled out a pair of simple sandals. He put these on, his lower back protesting as he bent over to lace the thongs together, and shuffled to the door. Opening it a little, he saw the two legionnaires who had come to his assistance during his episode the night before.

"I thought you two would have been relieved by now," he said, startling both of the soldiers.

"We turned down our relief, king," said the legionary on the right hand side of the door. "We thought it best that we stay on hand, stop any rumours spreading."

"Rumours?" Ullsaard remembered dismissing the two men with a tale that that he had been suffering from a vivid dream, but he could not recall anything else he had said beforehand.

"You know, king, about Urikh and the Crown," said the other soldier. "Talk like that can set some men's tongues flapping."

"Not us, though," the other legionary assured Ullsaard with a stern nod.

"I appreciate your attention to duty," said Ullsaard. "What are your names?"

"Codurin, king," said the first.

"Nesthor Kabad, king," answered the other, placing his hand to his breastplate in salute.

"I'll be sure to mention your names to General Anasind, to bear in mind when he is looking for some sergeants."

Their words of thanks died out as Ullsaard's expression grew grimmer.

"And I'll also know who to look for if it ever comes to my ears that someone has been gossiping about Urikh," said the king, looking meaningfully at each of the men. They nodded nervously. "Good, we understand each other. My armour and weapons need cleaning and polishing – see to it while I have breakfast."

"Yes, king!" the legionaries said in unison, nodding their heads in deference.

Ullsaard stepped out into the bare hallway. The floor was of grey slabs of stone and the walls covered with crumbling plaster painted a subdued red. He looked left and right, trying to

remember the way back to the hall where he had feasted with
Aegenuis. A cough behind him attracted his attention to Codurin. The legionary flicked his head to the right, not meeting
his king's gaze. Ullsaard gave a wordless grunt of thanks and
set off.

II

After startling the cooks by an unannounced and unintended
visit to the kitchens, Ullsaard eventually found his way back
to the main hall. Thick ceiling beams held up a thatched roof,
hung with shields and banners. A deer leg roasted over the
firepit dug to one side of the hall, a chimney above it drawing
off the worst of the smoke, and a table made from lacquered
planks split from a single massive tree trunk ran for two-thirds
of the hall's length.

At the far end, seated in a throne made of the same deep
red wood, was Aegenuis. Older than Ullsaard by several years,
the former king of Salphoria was still an imposing figure, and
must have been a feared and fearless warrior in his prime. He
had dark red hair and a thick beard, now streaked with grey,
and the swirling tattoos on his arm matched his hair in colour.
A lionskin cloak hung across the back of his chair. He had on
a shirt of fine, bronze mail links, and his hair and beard were
braided with gilded beads, so that the Salphor leader glinted
in the gloom.

To Aegenuis' right the chair was empty. His son, Medorian,
had been responsible for the attack on Ullsaard's army as the
Askhan king had marched to make peace at Carantathi. Ullsaard did not know whether Medorian had been slain fighting,
though many thousands of Salphors had, and Aegenuis had
received no word. On the left of Aegenuis sat three of his advisors, most important of these the aged chieftain, Aghali. The
senior counsellor was saying something to Aegenuis, his wiry

frame swathed in a cloak far too big for him, wizened fingers tapping out his points on the tabletop.

The smell that filled the hall both swelled Ullsaard's hunger and made his stomach turn; there had been much Askhan wine and Salphorian beer consumed the night before. The ache of emptiness and the fragrance of the deer leg roasting over the firepit won over the nausea.

"It is not so bad to be a king that breakfasts on venison," Ullsaard called out, attracting the attention of the Salphors. Aegenuis grinned, though his counsellors seemed less pleased to see their new Askhan ruler. Ullsaard paid it no heed; conquered peoples were never happy to begin with.

"Necessity, not luxury," replied Aegenuis. "It is winter. There are no farms here and all my grain stores are feeding your bloody army. We hunt when we cannot farm, and so we eat venison for breakfast."

A maid brought a wooden platter of meat and small potatoes to Ullsaard, laying it at a seat a little down the table on Aegenuis' right. Ullsaard looked at the scene and grimaced.

"You are in my seat, friend," said the Askhan king.

Aegenuis frowned, confused for a moment. One of his advisors said something angrily in Salphorian, but Aghali hissed a reproach. Aegenuis stood up and bowed, before stepping aside to wave Ullsaard to the throne.

"The king of Salphoria sits at the head of the long table, you are right," said the Salphorian lord.

"It's not personal," said Ullsaard as he pushed past Aegenuis and flopped down into the large chair. The maid looked between the two kings, unsure what to do. Aegenuis walked around the table and slid Ullsaard's platter of food in front of him.

"And where does a king without a kingdom sit?" asked Aegenuis. "By the firepit?"

"Here," said Ullsaard, rapping his fist on the table in front of the chair to his right.

Aghali said something else, and Aegenuis translated the old chieftain's protest.

"That seat is for the king's heir. It should remain empty."

Mention of his heir set Ullsaard's nerves on edge. He kept his demeanour calm on the outside, even as the questions that plagued him returned.

"Sit," said Ullsaard, slapping a hand on the table. "My heir is all the way back in Okhar, running the province for me; seems a waste to let a chair go empty on his account."

Aegenuis nodded and sat down. He reached across the table and pulled a goblet over the wooden planks. Wine spilled onto the table.

"Drinking early?" said Ullsaard, plunging a knife into the thickly cut slice of venison on his plate. He sawed away, glancing at Aegenuis out of the corner of his eye. "Never had the stomach for drink before Noonwatch."

"I have just lost a kingdom, I need a little comforting," said Aegenuis. He took a mouthful of wine and drank it ostentatiously, smacking his lips. Placing the goblet purposefully on the table, he fixed his stare on Ullsaard.

"So, my king, what happens now?"

"Lots of things," replied Ullsaard. "None of that matters for the moment. I am not staying in Carantathi. You will be left in charge."

Aegenuis' surprise was apparent as he sat back in on the bench, eyes widening.

"Don't get carried away, it is only for the time being," Ullsaard continued. "Salphoria is too big to be one province, but until I can find some governors and build some proper provincial capitals I need someone to be in charge, and that's you."

"What makes you think I want to be?"

"The fact that you murdered your own father to be king gives me an idea that you like being the top dog," Ullsaard said with a cold smile. "I killed my father too, you know. We have more than that in common. You know that there will be resistance, there always is. You know also how to persuade most of your people not to fight against me, but to accept their new future."

"My reputation is worth less than a piss in a pot these days," said Aegenuis. "If I work for you, there are some that will think I am a traitor."

"They can think what they fucking well like," snapped Ullsaard, quickly tiring of the Salphor's objections. To the Askhan king it made sense for all of the right reasons and was a done deal. Aegenuis knew this too and was being awkward for the sake of being awkward. "You'll be working with my general, Anasind. Believe me, we have a lot of practise at this sort of thing in Askh, and it will be painful at first but the people will settle down. Your son, and any other headstrong chieftains, need to be dealt with swiftly."

"I know you think I must agree to this, but what if I refuse?"

"You can get the fuck out of my hall, for a start," said Ullsaard. "You don't have a choice. If it's not you, I can't trust anyone else. My first captains will be a lot more brutal than your words. You may be an arsehole, Aegenuis, but I know you wouldn't wish that on your people."

"And why such a speedy departure?" asked Aegenuis. "You have been in Carantathi less than a day."

"Other things to do, better things," said Ullsaard. He needed to get back to Askh to find out what Urikh was up to, but he could not tell anybody that all might not be well in Askhor. If the Salphorians caught even the slightest whiff of weakness in the Askhans they would rise up. Aegenuis was no different. He knew he was being bought off and if he had the chance to play the part of glorious liberator he might just seize it, rather than drift through his final years in peace, safe but lonely and despised by his people.

"Better things than establishing control of your new territories?" Aegenuis looked curious rather than suspicious, but it was impossible to tell if the Salphor suspected any deeper motivation behind Ullsaard's unwillingness to stay.

"I'm a conqueror, not an administrator," Ullsaard replied with a smile and a shrug. "I've got places to go, people to kill; those bastard Mekhani, for a start. I've definitely got unfinished business with them."

"So you'll be withdrawing some of your legions from Salphoria?" said Aegenuis. His expression was of innocent inquiry, but Ullsaard knew better.

"Mother of a bitch, you are a sharp one, aren't you?" exclaimed the Askhan king. "Don't get any stupid ideas. The legions are here for a good while yet. When I need them for other duties, I'll let you know."

Ullsaard dropped his knife and spoon onto the plate and stood up. He waited patiently, finger tapping lightly at his belt buckle, until Aegenuis realised his was meant to do the same, by way of obedience to his new king. With an apologetic nod, the Salphorian got to his feet and waved for his counsellors to do likewise.

"Thank you," said Ullsaard. "I'll see you again before I leave. And expect a visit from Anasind too."

The King of Greater Askhor left the hall by the main doors, squinting as he was met by bright sun, low on the horizon. Two ranks of legionnaires were standing guard along the steps outside. They raised their spears in salute to their king as he walked quickly down the wooden stairs to the rutted road that wound down the mountain through Carantathi.

From the road Ullsaard could see the cause of the early

morning banging. Legionnaires from his army were busy on the wall of the city, reinforcing the towers with blocks taken from several houses demolished near the gateway. They had been in Carantathi less than a day and already his Askhans were treating it like home. Wooden scaffolding encased the gatehouse and five massive tree trunks had been dragged into the square behind, where axemen, sawmen and carpenters were setting to work creating planks for an inner gate.

Ullsaard turned to his left and looked hotwards, along the range of the mountains. He took a breath of cold air tinged with dung and smoke. The peaks stretched away into the distance, becoming paler and more insubstantial until they were swathed by mist and cloud altogether. It was a harsh land, but had some of the majesty of Askh. To dawnwards he could look down across the plains and forests and hills of Salphoria, his view extended by many miles by the altitude. All of these were his domains now – in name, at least.

The hall and surrounding houses blocked the view to duskwards; the unconquered lands that lay beyond the mountains were as much a mystery to the Salphors as they were to the Askhans. Ullsaard longed to find a vantage point from which he could see what lay that way, but that would have to wait for the moment. For reasons not of his making he was forced to look back to dawnwards, to the palaces of Askh. It felt like a kick in the gut, to have come so far and achieved so much, only for his son's stupidity to draw him the thousands of miles back to the empire's capital.

Hooking his thumbs into his belt, he collected his thoughts. The conversation with Aegenuis had left him with some doubts. In truth, it was too early to leave Carantathi, as much as Ullsaard had faith in Anasind and trusted that Aegenuis' self-interest would prevail. The hasty departure would raise questions, no matter what excuses Ullsaard gave. It occurred to him that if he could stay for just a few days his departure would not raise as much comment.

He wondered if he was over-reacting. In the cold light of day it seemed more and more likely that the tale of a dream he had spun for his guards might be the truth. Had it been a convincing dream, brought about by fatigue and a deeper fear of his son's ambition?

It could be foolishness to race back to Askh, preparing for a confrontation that existed only in his mind. The more Ullsaard thought about it, the more he considered the whole episode to be fantastical. Urikh was not stupid enough to make a bid for the Crown at the moment, no matter how much he disliked Ullsaard and how hungry he was for power. His son had no base for such a claim, in terms of legions or other resources.

It was too quick to make sense. Urikh could not even know whether Salphoria had been secured or not. More than three thousand miles separated father from son, the only tenuous connection between them was the Crown itself. Urikh could put it on his head as much as he liked, it would not make him king in anything but his daydreams.

Unless he has the support of the Brotherhood.

Ullsaard felt his knees weaken and he stumbled back towards the steps, the voice of Askhos ringing loudly in his head. The dead king's presence felt stronger than before, his voice somehow closer. It took a little time to recover from the shock of feeling Askhos inside his mind after so long enjoying the silence.

"How do you know?" Ullsaard hardly moved his lips as he spoke, his voice a whisper. He had never been able to just think his words to Askhos; with two voices in his head it became confusing. "Do you see anything? Are you in Urikh too?"

Something struck Ullsaard, an unsettling feeling that rose up from the pit of his gut to make his chest clench tight with concern.

"How is it that I can hear you, when we are so far from the Crown? What has Urikh done?"

I know nothing more than you, Ullsaard, other than that where I was once in the Crown, now I am not.

"What does that mean?" Ullsaard's legs felt weaker and weaker, and he sat down on the bottom step in front of the long hall. He was talking out loud, but did not care. "What do you mean you are no longer in the Crown?"

It is as I say, Ullsaard. I was in the Crown, only dimly aware of you. When Urikh placed the Crown upon his head there was heat and pain, and then darkness. I woke – or think I woke, it is hard to explain – in your head; only in your head. I know nothing of what happened to the Crown. I cannot feel it any more.

Ullsaard tried to absorb this despite the ache that was pulsing up and down from the base of his skull to the top of his head.

"Is it possible that Urikh, somehow, learnt of the Crown's power, and managed to drive you from it?"

There is only one man that I know of that can separate me from the Crown. He is the man that bound my essence to it in the first place.

"Lakhyri," muttered Ullsaard, as if the word was the vilest curse ever devised by man.

ASKH
Autumn, 213th Year of Askh

With golden eyes, the high priest of the Eulanui looked at his latest puppet ruler sitting on the Askhan throne, the Crown of the Blood perched uncomfortably on Urikh's head. The Crown was unimportant now, just a symbol and nothing more. Lakhyri had reversed the rites that had placed the spirit of his brother Askhos into the iron and gold, rendering the Crown inert. It meant nothing to Lakhyri that he had set his brother's spirit adrift from its anchor; Askhos had not only failed to deliver the empire the Eulanui desired, Lakhyri was beginning to suspect that his brother had secretly reneged on the deal that had granted him virtual immortality.

The rare blunders, the mistake with Cosuas that had allowed a pregnant court whore to give birth to Ullsaard, and the slowing of the empire's expansion pointed to either growing sloppiness on the part of Askhos, or a desire to forestall the inevitable day when he would have to hand over his dominions to his true masters.

That day was now fast approaching and Lakhyri could not afford to suffer any more delays. He had laughed at how easy it had been to manoeuvre the other pieces into position. First Ullsaard, then the true heir Erlaan, and now bringing forth his secret piece in the game, Urikh, each had gone through the motions of rulership, but soon it would be time for the pretence to end. The Eulanui would return, and Lakhyri would be their regent on this world, for time eternal.

Parchment-like skin etched with scars and faded tattoos creased as Lakhyri allowed himself a slight smile; an almost unheard-of indulgence for the high priest.

"You sent for me, King Urikh?" asked Lakhyri. He bobbed his head a fraction in mimicry of a bow, but nothing more.

"You are sure that my father is aware of what we have done?" asked Urikh. He was dressed in a simple tunic and light kilt, his skinny arms wrapped about by golden torcs and bracelets, his slender fingers now adorned with jewelled rings. He far more resembled his mother in slightness and elegance than he did his father. She, Luia, was sat on a chair beside the throne, like a queen, although to Lakhyri it seemed the son's dedication to his mother had waned immediately he had come to the palace to claim what he saw as his birthright.

"Though I have removed the curse that had been placed upon the Crown, my king, the act of doing so was immediately made known to Ullsaard. The moment you placed the Crown upon your head, he was aware of what you had done. I expect he is returning to Askh as we speak."

"And what will he do when he arrives?" demanded Urikh.

"You know what he will do," answered Luia, before Lakhyri could say the same. It had been centuries since Lakhyri had had any sensation approaching an interest in the female flesh, but there was something about Luia's keen intellect, ruthless attitude and straightforward manner that reminded Lakhyri of his long-dead wife. "He will try to take the Crown from you."

"As your mother says, so I concur," said Lakhyri. "It is my hope that he underestimates the resistance he will meet here."

"And the Brotherhood, they spread the word across the

empire that my father has been slain. How do we stop rumour of his return from spreading equally fast? If we wish to maintain the fallacy that he has been killed campaigning in Salphoria, it will be no good having him strolling into Askh."

"Do not fear on that account, my king," said Lakhyri. "Ullsaard is a marked man. He will no sooner approach Askh than a man can touch the moon. The eyes and ears of the Brotherhood seek your father, and I have located just the man to turn the myth of your father's demise into a reality."

"This man, who is he?" asked Luia. As she leaned forward, her pale blue dress parted at thigh and breast, revealing white skin. Lakhyri ignored the distraction and looked into her calculating eyes. "Can we trust him?"

"It is better that you do not know who it is," replied Lakhyri. "And no, we cannot trust him at all, but I already have that matter in hand also. One of my most dedicated Brothers is handling the situation."

"The details of Ullsaard's death cannot be public," declared Urikh. "If you cannot trust this assassin, why use him?"

"I use this man because there is not a man alive, including those in this chamber, who have a greater reason for wanting Ullsaard dead. Assassins can be paid, but this man will kill Ullsaard for revenge. No money brings that sort of dedication."

THEDRAAN, ERSUA
Autumn, 213th Year of Askh

The crowds parted for the black robes of a Brother, allowing Leraates to pass easily though the marketplace. The town of Thedraan was heaving, the market one of the last opportunities for families and business to set in stores before the winter snows came down from the Altes Hills that rose from the Ersuan farmlands less than a dozen miles to duskwards.

Animals alive and dead, cereals and vegetables, pots and pans, timber and furniture, all were on display. Thedraan had grown in the last half-year from a small summer town to a bustling market junction, benefitting hugely from the traffic that was pouring into newly conquered Salphoria. Leraates' overt reason was to talk to the headman and headwoman – a welcoming, aging couple named Rainaan and Thyrisa – about the construction of a Brotherhood precinct to attend to the rapidly growing town's administrative and judicial demands. This provided an explanation for the presence of Leraates, a senior member of the brethren, in a backwater like Thedraan.

His real reason was to find a man. Lakhyri had been very specific, and his message-dream had brought Leraates back from Salphoria to hunt for this fellow. His face had been fixed in the Brother's thoughts since he had received the dreamcall from his master, and he spied the chubby features of his goal across the stalls of the market. He did not know the man's name – the dream-image had been too vague for such details – but he was important to Lakhyri's plans.

The target was selling garments for women from a handcart about fifty paces away, his voice louder than all of the other traders as he yelled his seller's banter. He was wide of girth, dressed in a strange mix of Salphorian and Ersuan clothes – a bright red shirt that was clearly made in the empire, over checked woollen trousers woven on the handlooms of the Salphors. On his head he wore a black and white bandana, darkened with sweat from his curly blonde hair. The man was constantly looking around and his gaze fell upon Leraates for a brief moment. His reaction was immediate, his spiel coming to a stop and becoming apologies to disappointed customers as he swept a canvas cover over his cart and started to waddle off through the crowd.

Leraates quickened his pace, but the throng of people meant that he lost sight of his quarry on a couple of occasions. After the second time, the man was nowhere to be seen. Leraates broke into a jog, heading up the main road from the market, following the direction he had last seen the fleeing man. Though the town had seen high fortunes of late, Thedraan was still smaller than many settlements in the empire, and there was no warren of roads or maze of back alleys that could provide shelter for a fugitive.

Darting down the gap between two buildings, Leraates came upon an upended handcart. He pushed it out of the way and rounded the corner in time to see the fat man, or at least someone in a similar scarlet shirt, entering one of the food tents pitched up on the town's outskirts for the duration of the market.

Leraates had spent much of his life walking from one precinct to another across the length and breadth of the empire, but he was no trained runner. He was short of breath by the time he reached the tent. The door flaps were open to let smoke and the steam of kettles and cauldrons seep out. He ducked into the fume, the sweat-sodden collar of his robe itching against his neck.

The light was poor beneath the canvas roof, despite the window openings in the sides of the tent, and the eating area showed no sign of the red-shirted man. Leraates saw that there was another doorway opposite and headed towards it. He stopped a couple of paces later as he heard raised voices from behind the reed screen that separated the dining customers from the kitchen fires. There was an angry shout and the noise of a large pan being dropped.

Leraates headed around the partition and almost ran into a red-faced woman picking up chopped onions from the floor.

"Have you seen a large man in a red shirt?" he demanded.

The woman looked up with a scowl, about to unleash abuse for this further disturbance. Her expression became one of surprise and then contrition when she saw the Brother's robes. She pointed to a door flap behind set of shelves laden with dishes.

"He spilt my onions," said the woman, her frown returning. "I hope you cut off his balls."

"Thank you for your help," said Leraates. He made no comment on the suggested punishment, and stepped past the woman to head for the exit.

The opening from the cook tent led out onto a small stretch of grass surrounded by the two-storey houses of Thedraan's small but distinguished nobility. Leraates had been here earlier in the day with the headfolk and all looked as before. There was no sign of the man in the red shirt.

Walking across the cropped grass, he searched for a sign of where his quarry had gone. The man certainly moved nimbly for someone of his size. With this came a thought that caused

Leraates to stop. He looked over the closely trimmed grass of the lawn. Sinking to a crouch, he looked again. To his right was the telltale darkness of bent grass blades, a line of footprints cutting straight across the grass, heading towards the right-hand corner of the little courtyard.

Leraates covered the lawn at a quick trot. On arriving at the pavement, he was gratified to see a few droplets on the paving slabs. It had not rained in Thedraan for several days and the stone was otherwise dry. The wetness had to be sweat from the fat man.

Looking around the corner of the end house, the Brother saw that the path led down a short hill to a cobbled street. It took him no time at all to jog down the street, but as he reached the junction, he came to more traffic. Three wagons were rolling past, and there was a boy herding a flock of geese across the road behind them, causing a small crowd to gather as the birds ambled past.

There was no sign of red shirt or large man. Leraates stepped back and leaned against the timbers of a merchant's store behind him, catching his breath. Lakhyri had been exceptionally insistent that the man in the red shirt had to be the one to kill Ullsaard. Leraates was not sure why this had to be the case, he himself would happily slip a knife between the usurper's ribs if given the chance, but he had not become a senior Brother by second-guessing the high priest or his motivations.

"Excuse me, Brother?" Leraates looked over his shoulder at the sound of a man's voice. There was a wiry, middle-aged man standing with his felt hat in his hands, a slightly apologetic look on his stubbled face.

"Yes?"

"I saw you all running there, Brother, and I thought that perhaps you might be chasing the large fellow what came dashing across the road not more than ten heartbeats before you turned up. Had I known he was running from a Brother, I would have tried to grab him for you. Am I right?"

"You are right, citizen," said Leraates, patting the man on the shoulder and offering him a smile of genuine gratitude. "I need to speak with him."

"He went into the drinking den across the road," the concerned citizen said, pointing to a wooden building with bright yellow paint liberally washed across its boards. Serving maids moved about the fenced enclosure beside the tavern, bringing trays of drinks to thirsty market goers sat on benches that had been pulled out to make the most of the dying autumn sunshine.

"Thank you, citizen," said Leraates. He reached into the breast of his robe and pulled a Brotherhood token from an inner pocket. It was made of dark wood, carved in the shape of the Crown. He dropped it into the man's palm and curled his fingers around it. "When the next Brother comes for your half-year's taxes, give him this and tell him why you have it. It will stand in lieu of your payment."

"A half-year's taxes?" The man stared at the token as if it was made of pure iron, and then stuffed it into the fold of his cloth belt with a surreptitious glance around. "Thank you, brother. Thank you!"

"It is you that have the gratitude, of the Brotherhood and the empire," said Leraates. Having regained both his breath and his composure, the Brother gave the man another pat on the shoulder and stepped out into the road at a more even pace.

When he reaching the drinking establishment, he inquired of the large man's presence with one of the maids, and was informed that the red-shirted fugitive was renting rooms upstairs. She was kind enough to furnish Leraates with directions, and like the man in the street was rewarded for her dedication to Imperial service with a half-year tax token.

Leraates had to suppress a rebellious smile as he walked into the dark interior of the tavern and turned towards the stairwell to the left of the main doors. If Lakhyri's plans came to fruition, there would be no tax collections in the spring. In fact, there would not be very much of anything at all.

When he reached the top of the stairs, Leraates orientated himself. To his left the corridor ran for a few paces. There was room enough for one door before it ended at the outer wall, where a small window looked down over the courtyard by the road. To the right, the passageway contained three more doors and then turned to the right again. There was light from a window at the far end too, but no lamps or candles in the sconces on the walls. It was a dingy little place, and Leraates wondered how the manner of man that took such rude lodgings could be of any interest to Lakhyri.

He took a few steps down the corridor and stopped as he heard the creak of the door by the stairs opening. He heard a heavy thump on the floorboards and had half-turned when something large slammed into him, sending him face-first into the floor. Before he had time to think, Leraates was pinned down by a massive weight.

He smelt old sweat and heard deep breathing as the point of something sharp nicked at the side of his throat.

"The man in the red shirt, yes?" said Leraates.

"Ullsaard can go fuck his ailur," said a voice beside Leraates left ear. The man spoke good Askhan, but with a Salphorian accent. "Sending assassins dressed as Brothers after me now, is he? He'll have to do better than that."

"I assure you, I am a Brother," Leraates managed to wheeze. The man on top of him really was quite heavy and the breath was being crushed from the Brother's lungs. His ribs were starting to ache. "Please could you let me up?"

"You're a polite one, I'll give you that," said the big man.

"Manners are all well and good, but I don't take kindly to folks that want to see me dead. Luckily, lovely Haanah downstairs told you exactly what I wanted her to. You see, a man in my position doesn't take chances. I've got enough money to make sure everybody in this building wants me to stay alive and well."

"That is very good, but I do not wish you dead," said Leraates. He was beginning to feel quite faint from lack of air.

"Everybody wants me dead, Brother." Leraates felt the man shift and the point that digging into his throat was withdrawn. "Don't try to deny it. I'm the most wanted man in all of the empire. Ullsaard would give away two of his wives to have me caught and killed."

"Really?" Leraates was genuinely surprised. "I was not aware that the empire wanted anybody quite that much."

There was a strangely high-pitched giggle and the weight lifted slightly from Leraates' back.

"Well, if anyone knew who I was and that I am alive, I'd be the most wanted man in the empire," said the stranger. "Now that I see your face, I recognise you. You might not know it, with your creeping about while you conspired against me, but I marked you early on. You knew Furlthia."

Leraates knew the name well. Furlthia had been one of the cabal led by Leraates dedicated to halting Ullsaard's expansion into Salphoria. There was only one other man still alive who could have known anything about the conspiracy: Anglhan Periusis. The former Governor of Magilnada had somehow escaped the utter destruction of his city. Here he was, as real in the flesh as anything, and Lakhyri wanted to hire him to kill Ullsaard.

"Well, fuck me," was all Leraates could say.

ASKH
Autumn, 213th year of Askh

I

Allenya stood looking duskwards at a window in the palace, a crumpled, tear-stained tatter of parchment in her hand. The bustling city below seemed muted, the colours faded and the noise distant. Her gaze lingered on the mountains in the distance, but she did not see them. Her mind was much farther away, in the wilds of Salphoria, where somewhere her husband's body lay.

The letter in her hand had arrived twenty days ago, but it still seemed unreal. Ullsaard could not be dead, she had told herself again and again. He was too full of life, too stubborn and too good at fighting to be dead. She knew the words of the letter by heart, but she opened it again and read them, tears welling up in her reddened eyes once more. The script was formal, the ink strokes crisp and precise. The words were sharp too; a simple message declaring that the king and his bodyguard had been ambushed by Salphors whilst on campaign, and all had been slain.

Allenya tried to take some comfort from the assumption that had been made. Nobody had seen the king fall, because nobody had returned to the camp. It was possible that Ullsaard had escaped or been captured.

It was false hope, and Allenya despised herself for clinging to it.

"Come and sit with me, sister," said Meliu. Allenya's youngest sister sat with her needlework in her lap, on one of the couches arranged on the carpet at the centre of the chamber. Vases of wilting flowers stood on tables around the room, and a bright blue bird perched in a cage close to the other window.

Moving without conscious volition, Allenya walked slowly across the room and sat on the couch opposite Meliu. Her sister's hair was shorter, she realised. Allenya wondered about her own appearance for a moment; she had sent away her handmaids when the letter had arrived and they had not been allowed to attend her since. She had dressed herself and brushed her hair, but she knew that she probably looked a sorry state.

She did not care.

"What are we now?" Allenya asked quietly. "Useless widows of a dead fool."

"We are still queens, my sister," replied Meliu. "And Ullsaard was never a fool. Urikh needs us now."

Allenya could not find it in herself to condemn Urikh's swift coronation, though it pained her that Ullsaard's heir had moved so quickly to install himself as king. Luia had spoken much of the need for continuity and stability in a time when the empire was still recovering from upset. The Blood were still on the throne, and Greater Askhor would continue to grow and prosper. All sound reasons, and yet they left Allenya hollow, as if Urikh did not care in the slightest that his father was dead. Even Luia had cried at the news, and she had been less than an ideal wife to the king. Urikh had been solemn and dignified as he had praised Ullsaard's achievements and ac-cepted the Crown of the Blood, but Allenya could sense the delight hidden beneath the veneer of decorum.

"We should go for a walk later," said Meliu.

"Why?" Allenya picked up her own embroidery and looked at it. In one corner was a lake, and the start of a garden, green grass and trimmed trees petering out into whiteness. Not a stitch more had been made for twenty days, and the creased linen was spotted with stains from her tears.

"We cannot stay in here forever, sister," said Meliu. "We need to get out and breathe fresh air. It will be winter soon. We can go to the markets and pick out woollen dresses and thick gloves."

"Perhaps," said Allenya without enthusiasm. The simple thought of looking at dresses, Meliu gushing about new designs and beadwork, sent a shudder through her. It was so false; so pointless. "He was always away for so long, but I always knew he would come back."

"Yet we always lived with the knowledge that this day might come," said Meliu. Crossing the room to sit next to Allenya, Meliu gently stroked her sister's brown curls. "Ullsaard was a warrior when we met him, and he died a warrior-king."

"And Jutaar…" Tears came again as Allenya thought of her son, slain by the treachery of Anglhan, who had kept Allenya and Meliu hostage without their knowing. The tears were hot with anger as well as grief. She buried her face in the shoulder of her sister, wetting the cloth of her pale yellow dress. "Salphors took my two beautiful men from me, Meliu. They've taken both of them."

Meliu continued to run her hand over Allenya's head, whispering words that meant nothing.

II

The chamber was well-furnished, with carpeted floor and tapestries on the walls, but it was no less a cell than if there had been bars and bare stone. Sitting on a bench constructed to take his huge bulk, Erlaan-Orlassai fumbled at the pages of his book with multi-jointed, taloned fingers. Eyes etched with golden runes tried to focus on the words of *Sanctities of Lawmaking*, but he could not concentrate. He needed to stretch, to run, to fight. His immense body was eating away at his resolve, demanding platters of food every day to be sustained. If he wanted, he could have drained the life force from the blind Brother that brought the tray of meat and bread every few hours, but Lakhyri had warned him against such behaviour.

Erlaan-Orlassai put the book on the table in front of him and flexed arms as thick as tree trunks. His muscles rippled beneath iron-hard skin scarred with more of Lakhyri's runes. Bronze plates were riveted into his flesh, creaking as he moved and scratching him. There was nothing physical stopping him from leaving his chamber; not a Brother nor a door could bar his path if he really wanted to leave.

It was no way to be treated, he thought. He was the true heir of the Blood, and ruler of the Mekhani tribes. The empire was his by right, and there was not a day that passed without the temptation to quit the Grand Precinct and take the Crown for himself.

He daydreamed a lot; of the time when he had led a horde fifty thousand-strong, and brought Ullsaard to the brink of defeat. The humiliation gnawed at him. He had so much time to himself, without distraction, that he relived the moments again and again: the spears that had pierced wrist and ankle and arm and leg, pinning him to the ground; Ullsaard's sword a hair's breadth from his throat; the chains that had bound him and the thick cord that had stitched his lips together.

For nearly a year and a half he had been confined in the Grand Precincts, at first in genuine bonds, and later by promise to Lakhyri to bide his time. The High Brother's plans were coming to fruition. Erlaan-Orlassai had to believe that. When

the time came, when Urikh's mock rule had served its purpose, Erlaan-Orlassai would ascend to the throne as he should
have done before.

A growl escaped from Erlaan-Orlassai as he contemplated
the future. It was with a mixture of happiness and disappointment that he thought of Ullsaard's death; happiness for the
fact, blighted by the knowledge that it had not been by Erlaan-
Orlassai's hand. He contented himself with dreaming up the
ways he would visit pain on Ullsaard's heir, and inflict misery
on Urikh to match the misery Erlaan-Orlassai had suffered at
the hands of the former king.

With a sigh, Erlaan-Orlassai reached for his book and started
reading again. He would not be a tyrant, he told himself, as he
tried once more to understand the principles of Askhan prop-
erty law. He would be a proper king and the people would
accept him as such, despite his monstrous appearance.

RUINS OF MAGILNADA, SALPHORIA
Early Winter, 213th year of Askh

I

A few scattered stones and hillocks were all that remained of the once-mighty city of Magilnada. The ground was still bare, turned over and salted by the vengeful legions of Ullsaard. Dark earth spread like a bloodstain from beneath the white cliffs at the coldwards extent of the Altes Hills. A few miles to duskwards were the blackened mounds of the pyres, where the bodies of thousands of men, women and children had been burnt. Their bones littered the grassless hills, broken and picked clean by scavengers.

Gelthius was confronted by a slew of memories as he looked across the barren lands, and none of them particularly happy. There had been a short time when the Thirteenth had been stationed in the city, before the big thrust towards Carantathi, when he had been amongst friends and family, and there had been laughter and drink and comfort.

In all, Magilnada had become a place of misery. It had been built by dissidents to rival Askh, but the Askhans had long memories and the Salphors had coveted the prize, so that the city had a bloody history. Now all of that was ended. No chieftain would ever rule Magilnada again, and no children would run through its streets. The ghosts of the dead haunted this place, and the good spirits shunned it.

Two hundred years of life and death, politics and culture, brought to ruin by the decision of one man.

That man, King Ullsaard, sat astride his ailur a short distance away, gazing to dawnwards. The rest of the guard company, one hundred legionnaires including Third Captain Gelthius, was breaking the night's camp. Their trek across Salphoria had been swift, and Gelthius' early departure from Carantathi had been a disappointment. After nearly fifty years, he had finally seen the capital of his former king – albeit as an Askhan legionnaire rather than a Salphor – and he had been chosen amongst those who would leave just two days later.

Carantathi had been a bit of a letdown, in reality. After seeing the cities of Greater Askhor, including glorious Askh itself, the wood and stone huts of Aegenuis' city had seemed rather ordinary. It was a nice enough place, set high in the mountains that gave unrivalled views of the surrounding landscape, but Gelthius knew that within a year it would look no different from the dozens of Askhan towns he had passed through in his travels. Building by building, thatched roofs would give way to tiles, and crudely hewn stone would be replaced by painted brick. The wall itself, the labour of thousands of Salphors, would be pulled down and a new, higher, stronger barricade built.

The same would be happening all over Salphoria, Gelthius realised; at least to those towns and villages that had survived the invasion. He was a trailblazer of sorts, he concluded; one of the first of a new generation of Salphor-Askhans. The Ersuans and Nalanorians and Enrairians and Anairians and Maasrites and Okharans had all gone through the same painful inclusion into the empire, and now it was Salphoria's turn.

He had made third captain without trying, and it would not

be long until a Salphor was made first captain, perhaps even before he died, if the spirits granted him enough years.

He chastised himself for thinking of the spirits. He had been careful not to talk about them with his legion comrades, but it still rankled at Gelthius that the Askhans destroyed the spirits wherever they went. They called it superstition, a distraction from the civic duties of the people. The Brotherhood espoused dedication to the empire above all other things, and to pledge money and time to bodiless entities that – they insisted – did not exist was considered foolish.

Nobody had ever told Gelthius outright that the spirits did not exist, and as far as he could tell there were no laws, legion or otherwise, that said a man could not offer praise or appease-ment to them. There was just an assumption that the spirits did not exist and any man who thought otherwise was not right in the head and likely to be shunned.

The men he had sent out to draw water from the nearby river were returning and Gelthius would have to go back to the camp. A small, rebellious part of him did not want to go back. None of his men paid any heed to the notion that Gelthius might have feelings about the occupation of Salphoria. In a way it was good that they saw him only as Third Captain Gelthius, bringing him into the faceless homogeny of the legions. On the other hand, their crude jokes about Salphorian women and their graphic stories of the Salphor warriors they had killed bit deep.

Gelthius was forced to content himself with the knowledge that he had managed to save his family, bringing them to safety before the ire of the Thirteenth had fallen on the village of Landesi. They had not passed back through the lands of the Linghar, and he was glad of that. It would test his new loyalties to the limit to see the blackened remains of his own house and the crow-gnawed bones of his cousins and former friends. His wife, Maredin, had been set up in a new home in Thedraan, close to the border. Gelthius hoped that he would have a chance to see her and his children on the way back to Askh, though it was the lot of the legionnaire to be far from his family for years at a time.

A call attracted his attention. Looking back towards the camp, Gelthius saw that the abada carts were being filled. He raised a hand to acknowledge the shout and took one more look at the waste of Magilnada and the king who had ordered it.

For all that he was saddened by the fate of Salphoria, it was better to be on the winning side than not.

II

As the small column of men and carts headed along the road – now a paved, Askhan road instead of a packed dirt trail – Ullsaard sat to one side of the men on Blackfang and considered his plans. It was two days to the border with Ersua and the empire proper. If Urikh really had made a grasp for the kingship, it would be now that his son would have to strike. Ullsaard had considered bringing all of the Thirteenth back with him, and several other legions too, but the risk of giving the Salphors cause to rebel outweighed the king's concerns for his own wellbeing. There was little point in returning to Askh to restore his authority if it lost him his greatest conquest.

It reminded Ullsaard very much of the last time he had crossed back into Ersua, avoiding Anglhan's Magilnadan legions. Many of the men he had taken with him on that journey were with him now. There was no hiding this time. Urikh was expecting him and would have schemed accordingly if Ullsaard's worst suspicions were correct. It was just a question of getting one step ahead of the usurper. If Ullsaard could reach Askh he would be able to deal with the matter quickly and quietly, and the rest of the empire could carry on as it had been. The great drama of the war against Lutaar did not have to be repeated.

Slapping the reins against Blackfang's shoulder to urge her into a walk, Ullsaard fell in behind the last group of legionnaires following the carts. Within two days, Ullsaard would have to choose a course of action and a route.

He could march straight to Askh, relying on speed to get him to his goal. There was much to be said for haste, but Urikh's first concern would be the speedy appearance of the true king. He would have patrols, or at the least spies, on the border looking for Ullsaard. The most direct route would be the most closely watched.

An alternative was to take the road coldwards towards the Ersuan capital at Marradan. Once there, Ullsaard would be able to take control of the Ersuan legions belonging to Asuhas, the governor. With some military clout behind him, Ullsaard could rely on support from his old friend Allon, the governor of Enair to coldwards, and that would pretty much be all he needed to return to Askh and demand the surrender of his son.

Which was why it was also an obvious plan, and one that Urikh, being a devious son of a bitch, would be expecting. Ullsaard considered the possibility that his son might have Asuhas on his side already. The ruler of Ersua owed nothing to Ullsaard as a man, and could easily be swayed by promises from Askh. Yet to simply give up on a potential ally on the chance that he would be an enemy was not in Ullsaard's mind. The governors' and their support, or their apathy, was key to the power of the empire. If they united, there was not a king that could tame them to his cause. Ullsaard had managed to cajole, threaten and basically bludgeon the governors into lending him their support, and several of them were still sore from the experience and no doubt looking for a little payback. Asuhas was one of those who had come quite willingly, and that in itself made Ullsaard suspicious. Asuhas had changed master once without too many qualms, he could do it easily again for Urikh.

All of which pondering did not help Ullsaard reach a decision. He had dashed back, filled with a deep fury at his son's treachery, but a long march had tempered his anger with patience.

Menesun, Ullsaard thought suddenly.

In hotwards Ersua, barely fifty miles from the scrub of Near-Mekha, Ullsaard had a villa and estates from his time as a general. Like his lands in Apili, he had not thought about them since he had set out for Askh, but now they might have a use.

Menesun was about six days' march to hotwards from the Magilnada gap. From there he could find out more concerning the state of play in the empire. Those garrisons and companies he had questioned in Salphoria had known nothing was amiss at home, but if Urikh wanted to exercise power as king the knowledge had to become public. A few days within the borders would tell Ullsaard a lot more about the situation than he knew now.

He passed the word for his bodyguard to turn hotwards across the plains, feeling more confident about the next few days than he had been when he had woken up. With a bit of luck and some hard work, it would be possible to curtail Urikh's rule before it had even begun.

With his immediate plans settled, Ullsaard allowed his mind to wander a bit further ahead as he contemplated the punishments he could mete out on his wayward son.

GENLADEN, ERSUA
Autumn, 213th Year of Askh

Built out of timbers taken from the woods in the Ersuan High-lands, the houses and stores of Genladen seemed rustic and peaceful, set against the foothills of the mountains. Smoke drifted lazily from the chimney holes in the roofs and the streets were home to goats, chickens and other small livestock, which roamed freely between the two dozen or so buildings that made up the village. A narrow stream cut through the centre of the hamlet, crossed by a wooden bridge wide enough for two carts to pass abreast. There was one stone building at the heart of the Genladen, which from a distance seemed to be both a tavern and some kind of official residence.

From the road overlooking the valley in which Genladen nestled, Ullsaard and his men watched the village. It had been more than fifty days since they had left Carantathi and in that time they had barely seen a night under a roof. Ullsaard could feel the anticipation of the soldiers as they looked down at the alehouse, with its brightly painted red benches in the main square.

"I want good behaviour from all of you," Ullsaard warned them. "We are entering my lands now. I will pay for lodgings and legion ration, anything else comes out of your own pockets. And you will pay for everything. There will be no foraging here. Am I understood?"

There was a chorus of "ayes" from the fifty soldiers.

"Right, let's get on then."

It was early in Low watch, mid-morning, and the only inhabitants to be seen were women and children attending to the chores of the day. They stopped to gawp at the soldiers and their leader, the peasants' attention fixated by the ailur of the king. Smaller infants raced off with terrified yelps and screams, while the older children shied away or grinned moronically.

"Shouldn't they be paying homage or something?" asked Sergeant Muuril, marching not far behind Ullsaard. "This ain't no way to welcome a king."

"I'll not be causing a fuss, sergeant," replied Ullsaard. "These people don't know me from their cousins, much less know I'm the king."

"They know you're important, right enough," added Gelthius. "Ailur and a bodyguard makes you out to be someone special."

"All right, let's make this official then," said the king, holding his hand up to halt the short column while he reined Blackfang to a stop. He turned in the saddle to look at Muuril. "You're good at shouting. You have the honour."

"Yes, king!" replied Muuril with a broad smile. He stepped out from the front rank and paced a short distance ahead of Ullsaard. Quite a crowd of women and older children had gathered on the edges of the muddy road. Chickens squawked and goats bleated, adding to the hubbub of the villagers' speculations.

"All citizens of the Greater Askhan empire, make homage to your ruler!" declared Muuril, lifting up his spear in salute to his king.

The peasantry's muttering grew in volume, and there was some shaking of heads and frowning. Muuril took some paces towards them, his expression thunderously angry, before Ullsaard's call checked him.

"Sergeant, remain where you are." Ullsaard motioned Blackfang into a walk and approached the crowd, singling out a gaggle of the oldest women: three crones in black dresses and headscarves that regarded the king with ancient eyes.

"I am your king," Ullsaard said, fixing the women with a glare. "You should show respect."

The old women looked at each other and then Ullsaard. One of them took a step forward and gave an awkward bow. She looked back at the other villagers and nodded and bowed at her signal.

"Forgive us, but we aren't used to such company, our king," said the woman. "And we wasn't expecting a visit, neither. We never had no king come here before, and specially not one so new."

"These are my lands," said Ullsaard. "I own the villa at Menesun. You have been my people since before I became king."

"Well, maybe that's true of your father, but we ain't never had you visit from what I remembers, and I remembers before your father took over," said the elder.

"My father? King Lutaar? What has he got to do with anything?"

"Oh, my mistaking, much apologies, our king," said the woman, hunching over again in a deeper bow. Ullsaard winced as her back cracked several times when she straightened. "It gets confusing sometimes. I thought it was King Ullsaard that was your father."

Ullsaard blinked at the woman, her rambling almost incomprehensible. He realised that there was most definitely some confusion clouding the conversation.

"I am King Ullsaard," he said.

"You are?" The old woman's wrinkles deepened as her eyes

opened wide with surprise. She gaped, showing off more gaps than teeth.

"I tolds you so!" snapped one of the other elders. The woman, her skin more like leather than human flesh, pushed her way past the spokeswoman. "King Ullsaard it is! Like the first time I laid eyes on you, if you pardon my familiarity."

"Who else would I be?" Ullsaard's patience was rapidly running out.

"King Urikh, of course," replied the first elder. "You're the very image of your father, you know."

"Quiet!" Ullsaard snapped, turning to glare at his legionnaires, who had started whispering and chuckling at the old woman's mistake. He returned his attention to the villagers. "I am King Ullsaard, why would you think otherwise?"

"Because we heard you were dead, our king," said the first elder. "Only four days ago, from a Brother no less. Came through here saying that King Ullsaard was dead, and King Urikh was now in charge of the empire."

"We even had a feast in your honour," added one amongst the young women who were listening intently to the discussion from a short distance away. "I cooked game pie in your memory."

Ullsaard suppressed a growl of annoyance, directed not at the women but at Urikh. Of course he would announce Ullsaard's death before he took the throne.

"And how did I... I mean, what did the Brother say was the cause of King Ullsaard's death?"

"Dirty Salphors done for King Ullsaard," said another villager.

"An exaggeration," announced Ullsaard. He stood up in his saddle and raised his arms. "As you can see, I am alive and well. My death has been misreported."

As soon as the words had left his lips, Ullsaard regretted them. He had not been thinking straight, and it had been another mistake to announce his presence. It was too late now.

One villager would talk to another, and they would meet folk from other towns at the next market, and word would spread. This was gossip-worthy news. Twofold, in fact, for not only was King Ullsaard not dead, they had heard it from the mouth of the great man himself who had stayed at their inn. Such news would spread like wildfire and soon would come to the ears of the Brotherhood. As such, they would pass on the report of Ullsaard's return and it would come back to Urikh, or at least it would come to the attention of Lakhyri.

The king muttered a collection of his least eloquent swear words as he tried to think of some way to salvage the situation. He could think of nothing to take back the words that were already rippling through the gathered villagers.

"Enough of this chatter," he declared. "Now that we are properly introduced, I insist that I stay for the night. Warn your innkeeper and find food for my men, tonight there shall be another feast."

II

The smoke from the fireplace was backing up, spilling from the chimney into the room. Gelthius' eyes stung, but he stood to attention as best he could while ignoring the fumes choking his throat. He also ignored the smirks from the bartender wiping a cloth across his counter just in the eyeline of the third captain. The man busied himself cleaning the kegs and demijohns arrayed on the shelf behind the bar, while a younger woman swept old straw from the floor. She was probably his daughter; both of them had raven black hair and startling blue eyes.

From outside came the clatter of hammers on nails and the rasp of saws as the people of Genladen made ready for the king's festivities. Inside the tavern, groups of boys and girls sat at two of the long tables garlanding what flowers, leaves and berries they had been able to find in the foothills; given the lateness of the season there was more gold and brown than yellow and blue.

The door behind the counter was propped open by a barrel, letting out a steady cloud of steam, and the smell of roasting meat caused Gelthius' stomach to grumble loudly. Rabbit, fish and legion rations had been his fare since the late summer. Even on the night they had taken Carantathi there had been too much to do to secure the city, and he'd eaten only sparsely. Gelthius had probably been better fed on Anglhan's landship. His stomach rumbled again as another waft of roasting pork reached him. This was greeted by chuckles from his companions.

Beside Gelthius Sergeant Muuril waited with Gebriun, Loordin and Faalin. All five of the soldiers turned their gazes diligently straight ahead as King Ullsaard entered the common room. The king wafted a hand in front of his face, scowling at the smoke. He turned towards the innkeeper and called out in his best parade ground bellow.

"I can't see my hand in front of my fucking face in here! Get that chimney cleaned before I return."

With that simple instruction, Ullsaard gestured for his men to follow him out into the courtyard behind the inn. There were a few stools arranged in the shade of a tree – not that the sun had much strength left to it. The king sat on one of the stools and signalled for Gelthius and the others to do the same on the others.

Gelthius had no idea what the king wanted them for. He had approached Gelthius at the second hour of Dawnwatch as he was taking up the lead of the guard, and had asked that he attend him at Noonwatch with four of his most reliable men. So here they were, all of them eager to know what Ullsaard had in store for them.

"You're leaving the Thirteenth," said the king, much to the surprise of the legionnaires. Ullsaard noticed the disappointment on their faces and smiled. His voice dropped a little. "Not to worry, lads, it won't be forever. I have a secret mission for the five of you."

Gelthius leaned closer, intrigued, and the others exchanged half-knowing glances.

"I know you have all been in some scrapes for me, and in each of you beats the heart of the Thirteenth," the king continued. "I am going to ask you to do something for me that will seem strange, and I cannot tell you exactly why."

"Excuse me, king, but is this because of that mix-up with the crones?" said Muuril. "Only, it was a bit off-putting to hear that you'd be declared dead. Do you need us to settle the matter?"

"In a way, sergeant, but not the way you think." The king took a deep breath, his expression soured. "All right, no secrets at all. If I can't trust you, I'm fucked anyway. Urikh has tried to take the throne from me."

"Told you," said Loordin, folding his arms. "I fucking said so, didn't I?"

"You said no such fucking thing," answered Gebriun. "You just said 'I bet that little bastard Urikh is mixed up in this'. You never said he was trying to be king."

"Are you finished?" Ullsaard's growl cut through the chatter.

"Sorry, king," said Gelthius, glaring at the others. "What do you need us to do?"

"Urikh is going to find out that I have returned, and I need to know what the lie of the land is," the king explained. "At the moment, I need to know what Governor Asuhas is doing, and whether he is in the pocket of my son."

Gelthius nodded, though he was not sure he understood what was required of him. Ullsaard waited and when there were no questions, continued quickly.

"I need some good men inside Asuhas' palace to keep an eye on things. All of you were inside the walls at Magilnada, and I remember the work some of you did for me in Ersua after the city fell. It's dirty, secret work, but you can handle it."

"Begging your pardon, king, but how are we going to get into the palace, like?" asked Gebriun. "Without giving away that we're with you, anyhow."

"Asuhas is still recruiting heavily. Since he lost..." The king stopped, swallowed hard and looked away for a moment. His fists clenched in his lap and he straightened, jaw clenched, before carrying on. "Since the First Magilnadan were destroyed, Asuhas' legions took the brunt of the fighting against the Free Country Salphors. Asuhas is still raising a new legion as his garrison. You will be joining the recruits. Experienced men like you should have no problem."

"One problem," said Muuril. He drew up the sleeve of his tunic to show the symbol of the Thirteenth tattooed on his arm. The other men did likewise. "How do we explain these, king?"

Ullsaard looked at the marks, one hand rubbing the scar on his lip.

"I'll have release papers drawn up," Ullsaard said after some thought. His smile was lopsided, eyes mischievous. "We'll date them to last year, before the march to Carantathi. Congratulations, you've all served your minimum term in the Legions. You'll be entitled to your pensions and a quiet life."

There was a glance between Muuril and Faasil, which Gelthius did not understand but Ullsaard seemed to recognise with a knowing nod. The two of them were both nearly thirty years old and coming up to their legitimate ten-year service.

"Yes, I'll hold true to the papers, if that's what you're think-ing," said Ullsaard, eliciting nods of gratitude from the two veterans. The king looked at Gelthius, Gebriun and Faalin. "That goes for all of you."

It took a little while, and the nudge and smiles of Gebriun, for the import of this announcement to sink in to Gelthius' brain. The king would be signing their release papers, legally guaranteeing their legion pension, allowing them to leave the legion and get on with the rest of their lives. Though they had all chosen to be members of the Thirteenth, Gelthius under a little more duress than the others admittedly, they would be free of their oaths if they did as the king wished.

"It'll just be paperwork, of course," said Muuril. "We'll know that we're still part of the Thirteenth, right?"

"If that's what you want," said the king. "Any of you would be welcome back to the legion, or you can take the offer as it has been made."

"Yeah, but it's just for show," Muuril continued, looking at the others. He rapped a fist against his breastplate. "We're still Thirteenth, where it counts."

The others nodded, though none of them seemed as adamant as the sergeant.

"How can we be sure that we'll get into the palace?" asked Faalin. "Garrison legions are stationed all over the province."

"As returning veterans, you'll be given first choice for home duties," said Ullsaard. "Say you have family living in Marradan and you'll be guaranteed posts at the palace. Trust me, Asuhas will need veterans in his new legion; you'll be his first captain's dreams come true. I wouldn't be surprised if you were all made third captains, at least."

"One other thing, king," said Muuril. "It's a good seven days between here and Marradan, eight more likely. How are we going to communicate with you?"

"I'll be in Menesun, so it will be closer to ten days," said Ullsaard. "I'll set up shifts of runners, from Marradan to Menesun, they'll be able to carry messages between us. I'll pick five men, and I'll give you a list of the names before you leave. Also, before you head out, you'll have to agree where you'll meet the runners in Marradan. I'll leave it up to you to sort out, I don't need to know the details."

"And when do you want us to get going?" Gelthius asked, thinking about the pig roasting in the kitchens and the other festivities being planned. It looked like he would be leaving again before he had time for a proper meal and a drink. He glanced towards the inn and Ullsaard must have read his gaze.

"Tomorrow morning," said the king with a grin. He slapped a hand to Gelthius' shoulder. "Pork and crackling for you tonight, and be sure to get some cold cuts to enjoy on the way to Marradan."

"Thank you, King," said Gelthius. He stood up and nodded.

"We'll not let you down," said Muuril, as the others got to their feet.

"I know you won't," said King Ullsaard. He turned his gaze to the tents that had been erected on the hillside just outside the village. "Best get back to camp, you have preparations to make."

They waited until they were out of earshot, heading up the road towards the campsite, and then all five men started talking at once. It was Muuril, largest and loudest of them all, that prevailed.

"Did you get that, lads?" he said. "King's chosen men, we are now. And pensioned too, if you slackers want that. I tell you, forget tonight, it's going to be pork and crackling all the way for us."

"Unless Asuhas finds out we're spying on him and has us killed," said Gebriun

"Ah, don't spoil it you miserable cunt," said Muuril.

"Eight days until we get to Marradan," said Loordin. "That's enough free time for me. After that, it's not worth worrying about. "

"I think I'm going to enjoy retirement," Faalin said with a wink. "I hear that Ersuan women are very hospitable."

"Welcoming enough, if you don't mind shagging something with more stubble than you," laughed Loordin.

"You're quiet, captain," said Muuril, noticing Gelthius' solemn mood. The third captain had become something of a talisman for the group, his journey from debtor to officer seen as a sign of good luck by the other men. The others quietened, ready to absorb the sage words of their officer-mascot.

"You're all forgetting why we're off to Marradan," said Gelthius. "Urikh is claiming to be king and Ullsaard has been declared dead. Unless Ullsaard handles this situation quick, it'll mean war again. "

"It won't come to that," said Loordin, though there were doubtful looks from the others. "It can't come to that. Folks have only just got used to having Ullsaard as king, they won't take kindly to Urikh. And most of the legions are in Salphoria, there's nobody here to fight a war."

"If war breaks out, we might find ourselves on the wrong side in the Twenty-first when we should be in the Thirteenth," said Gebriun. "I don't reckon our new commander's going to be as trusting as King Ullsaard."

"*If* Asuhas is for Urikh and not Ullsaard," said Muuril.

"We'll know soon enough," said Gelthius. "Let's just make sure we get everything in order before we set out."

"Yes, captain." The dutiful response was given by the legionnaires without any mockery or irony, and Gelthius realised that the others would be looking to him to continue being leader once they reached Marradan.

He walked in silence as they started to chatter again. It was one thing to be a third captain in a legion, basically chasing the legionnaires to make sure the second captain's orders and rota were put into practice. Now they would be looking for real leadership, and Gelthius had no experience of that.

I'm in charge, he thought. Spirits help us.

MARRADAN, ERSUA
Late autumn, 213th year of Askh

I

Marradan was home to a strange atmosphere, and it pervaded the legion that was stationed there; or perhaps it was something about the Twenty-first that had an effect on the city. It was hard for Gelthius to put his finger on, because the city itself was a dismal place. Grey clouds unleashed a constant drizzle on grey, cobbled streets that wound between grey, stone buildings with grey, slate rooftops. The people wore drab clothes of grey and brown and beige, perhaps so as not to stand out in their grey world. The only colour Gelthius had seen since arriving was the green that was paired with a light grey on the flags flying from the walls and the shields of the growing Twenty-first Legion; grey and green being the colours of Ersua.

Gelthius and his companions had been welcomed into the ranks as soon as they had presented themselves and their papers to First Captain Lutaan. The legion commander was young for his position, animated and enthusiastic to welcome the men of the Thirteenth under his command. Gelthius had seen him before, though only from a distance. Lutaan was nephew to Donar, first captain of the Fifth who had campaigned alongside

Ullsaard in his bid for the throne and had fought frequently
next to the Thirteenth during the invasion of Salphoria. It had
been the Fifth, along with the Seventh, that had been caught
in a Salphorian ambush with the Thirteenth during the march
to Carantathi, and who had been with the king when he
reached the Salphors' capital.

From personal experience and reputation, Gelthius knew that
Donar was a sound, sensible commander and though Lutaan
lacked age and experience, the men of the Fifth had spoken well
of him during his time as a second captain. To Gelthius that
boded well, and he hoped that Lutaan would be loyal to the
king rather than the governor. Lutaan was certainly facing a
challenge, having to create a legion from nothing in the face of
local apathy.

Gelthius and Muuril had been kept together, to form the core
of a new company being added to the legion; Gebriun, Loordin
and Faasil had been made sergeants in other companies. The
first impressions of the Ersuans who made up the bulk of the
legion – nearly all of them from Marradan and the surrounding
towns – was of a surly, tight-lipped bunch. They were not outright hostile to the newcomers, but there was no obvious
comradeship or extension of friendship from the locals either.

In the first couple of days after arriving in Marradan, Gelthius picked up on one reason for the cloud that hung over the
newly re-formed legion. If legions were destroyed or disbanded their number became available for the next body of
men to be founded. The last Twenty-first legion had been renamed the First Magilnadan by the traitorous governor
Anglhan. The stigma of the Magilnadans' treachery – including
the murder of Prince Jutaar who had led the First Magilnadan
– would remain with the legion even though there was no
connection between the men who made up the Twenty-first
now and those who had sided with the Salphors. At least for

living memory, the Twenty-first would be known as oath-breakers and mutineers, though it was no fault of theirs.

Worse still, in a way, and a further reminder of this ignominious past, was the fact that the legion had a newly forged icon of Askhos. No legion had ever lost its battle standard in over two hundred years of the empire, but the icon of the First Magilnadan had disappeared when the legion turned rogue. Gelthius had placed his hand on the new icon, which was kept in the first captain's headquarters at the barracks, and had noticed the cleanliness and shine of the gilding, and the pristine condition of the sculpted face of Askhos. The icon of the Thirteenth had been kept clean and polished but countless battles had left a history of dents, scratches and chips that were worn by Askhos like proud battle scars.

With no company of their own as yet, Gelthius and Muuril were attached to the palace guards on a semi-permanent basis. While this gave them easy access to Asuhas's dwelling, it meant they could only see the others in their little band every four days, as the watch rotations brought around the companies of the rest to the palace.

Their day-to-day routine was much as would be expected by a garrison, split between patrolling the palace and its grounds and drilling at the barracks. Four days after arriving, Gelthius met Ullsaard's first runner, Haaldir, in a small winehouse far from the drinking holes of the legionnaires. There was not much of remark to tell the king's messenger, and so Haaldir departed with only the news that the king's spies had been accepted into the Twenty-first and that Gelthius and Muuril were within the palace walls keeping an eye and an ear ready for any news of Urikh.

While many provincial palace buildings were situated outside their capitals, the palace of Asuhas was an imposing, five-storey building that formed one side of Marradan's central square. The square was large enough for ten thousand legion-naires to drill in rank and file, and opposite the palace rose the three-tiered ziggurat of the Brotherhood precinct. The houses of the Ersuan nobility and richest traders completed the square, which was reached by three roads; one through the palace itself, which was built as an arch over the thoroughfare, two others from either side of the Brotherhood precinct.

The interior was divided between the main audience hall and adjoining chambers, and two wings that accommodated the governor and various other important noble families of Ersua. The patrols of the garrison legion covered all of the areas that were used by the public and staff, and most of the private chambers, but it was odd to Gelthius that the Twenty-first were not responsible for the governor's chambers. These were protected by legionnaires with black shields and helmet crests denoting that they were attached directly to the Broth-erhood. Usually these soldiers oversaw punishment work groups, protected the precincts and manned the few prisons where convict-labourers were housed overnight.

The blackcrests, as they were referred to outside of the Brotherhood, were part of no formal legion, answering instead to the senior brother of the precinct to which they were at-tached. For practical purposes, they were usually stationed in their own enclaves within the camps and barracks of the provincial garrison legions, sharing armouries, kitchens and other facilities. Gelthius had spent no time at all with the blackcrests in his time with the Thirteenth, but he could tell from the reactions of Muuril and the others that they were considered a bit strange for swearing loyalty to the Brother-hood and king rather than legion and king.

"I know the Twenty-first ain't no veteran legion, but I never heard of no governor being protected by Brotherhood troops," remarked Muuril, when he and Gelthius met at the end of their guard shift at the palace. The two of them walked back to the main barracks together, while most of the other legionnaires on their shift visited family or drinking holes. The walk took less than half an hour, but it gave them some chance to speak to each other in privacy.

"Wasn't always like that, neither," Gelthius answered. "I heard from Captain Anadlin that the blackcrests were only brought in as guards in the summer. It put Captain Lutaan's nose right out of joint, it did. Like he was being told his legion wasn't up to the job. Reason given was something about how close Marradan is to the Salphor border. Something about the Twenty-first might be needed for the campaign and so they had to be free to leave without abandoning the palace."

"Fucking blackheads," snorted Muuril. "And ain't that about the same time that Urikh decides to have a go at being king?"

"If the Brotherhood have been convinced that King Ullsaard is dead, they might want to ensure the governors remember who is in charge," said Gelthius. "Nothing like a few dozen blackcrests standing around your bedroom door to remind you where your loyalties lie."

"And that's why I can't see Asuhas agreeing to it, not freely," said Muuril. The two of them fell silent as they passed a group of legionnaires sitting on the benches outside a brothel, wine cups and ale tankards on the tables between them. Half-naked girls sat on their laps whispering compliments and offers, while two men with heavy cudgels stood to one side, watching the proceedings with bored expressions. Gelthius shared nods with a few of the customers he recognised.

"You know what we need to do?" said Muuril. "About them blackheads, I mean."

Gelthius was afraid that he did know, but he shook his head and made Muuril spell it out all the same. If Muuril said it out loud, it was the sergeant's fault.

"We've got to get into the governor's chambers," said Muuril and Gelthius silently cursed, his assumption confirmed. The sergeant did not notice and continued. "They've got to be hiding something in there. We have to have a look at what it is."

"Why?" said Gelthius, knowing the answer but feeling like he needed to raise the argument anyway. "Why can't we just tell the king that there's a bunch of blackcrests guarding Asuhas, and we can let Ullsaard decide what to do. If we go poking around and get caught, it's gonna raise suspicions, right enough. And then what if someone makes the connection between us and the king, what with us being from the Thirteenth and everything?"

Muuril considered the third captain's protest for some time, until the walls of the barracks were in view at the bottom of the street.

"Because the king trusts us to do what is right by him," the sergeant answered, patting Gelthius on the arm, "and you and I both know that finding out why a bunch of the Brotherhood's muscle is guarding the governor's chambers is what we need to do."

"Yeah, I know," Gelthius conceded, "but it ain't gonna be easy."

"Sure it is," said Muuril, his stubbled face split by a grin. "I've already figured out how we do it too. All we need is some time to talk to Loordin."

"Why Loordin?"

"Because he's a mouthy gobshite, that's why." Muuril's grin stretched wider as Gelthius shook his head and gave the sergeant a doubtful look. "Trust me, captain, it's a great plan."

II

"This is a shit plan," snapped Loordin.

"Shut up and keep walking," said Muuril, waving his spear, "or I'll jab you with this for certain."

It was just after the Noonwatch change of guard and Gelthius and Muuril were advancing down the main corridor to Asuhas's chambers with Loordin between them. Loordin was off-duty and dressed in the tunic and hose of a servant, a crudely tied scarf around his arm to hide his legion tattoo. To complete the disguise, Loordin had a silver tray purloined from First Captain Lutaan's quarters earlier that morning, on which had been artfully arranged several apples and other fruit.

Ahead of them two Brotherhood legionnaires barred the passageway, standing to attention, their spears held behind their shields. The corridor was in the heart of the palace wing, with no windows, and so it was impossible to see the faces of the soldiers in the lamplight – they were in shadow from the lanterns hanging from the ceiling behind them.

The two Thirteenth legionnaires and mock servant were stopped by the lowered spearpoints of the blackcrests, about half a dozen paces from the two soldiers.

"What's this?" asked the blackcrest standing on the right.

"Food," replied Loordin, in the sarcastic tone he had perfected over many years of making his fellow legionnaires pay for every slip of the tongue and stupid question asked. Loordin also had a peculiar slouch of the shoulders that cried out insolence without a word being said. Gelthius had been on the receiving end of the slouch several times when he had assigned Loordin to Gravewatch sentry duty or some other onerous task.

"Who for?" said the other blackcrest, stepping forward.

"It's fruit. It's for the fucking monkey, who do you think?" said Loordin.

Gelthius could feel Loordin trembling, and could also sense Muuril trying hard to stifle a laugh. Gelthius was filled with dread by the entire scheme, but Muuril's slightly reddening face and clamped tight jaw was infectious and the third captain could feel the laugh building up in his gut.

The suppressed amusement of the two legionnaires no doubt added to the shortness of temper of the two blackcrests, who were not happy with Loordin's explanation.

"Monkey? What monkey?" the one on the left demanded.

"I don't know, I just arrived," said Loordin, adding a petulant sigh to further antagonise the blackcrests.

"There ain't no monkey here," said the right-hand blackcrest.

"Really?" Loordin was really shaking now, though Gelthius could not tell whether it was from nerves or excitement. The legionnaire straightened and looked the closest blackcrest in the eye. "You see, I was told the governor's quarters was full of fucking monkeys."

Gelthius bit his lip fiercely to quash an outburst as what Loordin had said sunk in to the minds of the blackcrests.

"You little bastard!" The closest blackcrest pulled back his spear, ready to use it as a club.

Loordin tossed the platter and fruit into the face of the blackcrest and bolted as the second lunged at him. The legionnaire's tittering laughter acted as further bait, and the two blackcrests could not resist. With a clatter of dropped shields, they set off in pursuit of their tormentor with shouted threats.

"Fuck me, it actually worked," said Muuril, glancing at Gelthius and then behind at the three men running down the long passageway. "Come on, they won't chase that little runt forever."

The two of them headed down the corridor, checking the doors and archways to either side. Most of them were empty storerooms, a few had mops, buckets, brushes, and other materials and equipment for the servants to clean the floors and walls. The sound of running petered out entirely and they looked back down the passageway. There was no sign of the blackcrests but they knew time was short.

"It has to be one of these," said Muuril, "I've seen it before, when we was in the palace in Askh. One of these has to be the baths. Gotta be on the ground floor for the lava to heat the water, right?"

Gelthius shrugged his ignorance. The next door they found was locked and the one after opened onto a stairway up to the next storey. With anxious looks back down the corridor, they continued along the passageway until they reached an archway on the right. With a sigh of relief, Gelthius caught the scent of bathing oils and felt heat from dissipating steam on his face. Stepping through the archway the two legionnaires came into a tiled space with shelves stacked with jars of unguents and powders. They cautiously passed through another archway at the far end of the narrow chamber, checking that the room beyond was empty first.

Wooden partitions separated out a dozen curtained spaces, each with its own small chair, low shelves and row of hooks, where bathers could hang their belongings. A quick search revealed that nobody was using the baths at the moment, which was not unusual for the middle of the day. It would likely be several hours before anybody would, and that gave Muuril and Gelthius the opening they needed.

Stripping off their armour and uniforms, the two men hung up their gear in the two partitions furthest from the entrance, leaving them in the tunics they had been wearing underneath their regulation clothes. Gelthius unravelled the slender hose he had wrapped around his waist beneath his armour and put them to one side while he removed his sandals. He pulled the hose on, the sensation odd after wearing his legion kilt for so long; he remembered when the kilt had felt new and strange too.

Searching through the cupboards opposite the partitions, Muuril found pairs of backless slippers used by bathers and tossed a pair to Gelthius. He pulled them on, to find they were a little big for his feet. He searched through the cupboards for something a bit smaller, but they all seemed to be of a similar size. He shuffled about in the slippers for a few moments to make sure he could walk in them, and then stowed his sandals with the rest of their uniforms. The two men went back out to the previous room and grabbed two jars of coloured salts each. With these under their arms, they moved into the main bathing chamber, where two pools were filled with water, separated by a narrow walkway. One pool steamed heavily, heated by a lava pit beneath the palace; the other was a cold plunge pool.

Cutting between the baths, they found another doorway to the private chambers; the servants' entrance. This arch led into another storeroom, filled with towels and tongs, empty braziers, scrapers and other cleansing tools. Nobody saw them emerging into the corridor beyond, and a quick scout around assured the two infiltrators that there were no blackcrests in the immediate vicinity.

Carrying their salt jars as if they were badges of office, Gelthius and Muuril set off in search of the governor's chambers.

III

Gelthius was not sure how one man and his family could use so many rooms. As well as the audience chambers, feasting halls and gardens where he met with citizens and officials, Asuhas had more than two dozen private rooms: lounges, dining areas, banqueting suites, a personal kitchen, seven bedchambers, wardrobes, a cold bath and an indoor garden filled with exotic plants sent up the Greenwater from near-Mekha and Cosuan.

It was the middle of the day, and there were very few servants around. The majority of the governor's staff were attending to their master as he went about his official business in the public areas of the palace. The lack of activity in the apartments meant that Muuril and Gelthius were able to wander freely through them. They had abandoned their bath salt jars on the second storey when it became apparent that they would attract more attention with them than without.

Near to the stairwell on the fourth storey they came across a locked door, which Muuril reckoned to be a personal office of some kind.

"Should we break it open?" he asked, taking a step back, readying for a kick.

"No!" replied Gelthius, standing in front of the sergeant before he could put his foot to the door. "A busted door is a sure a way as any of saying that somebody has been sneaking around looking for things that they ain't meant to find. Beside, the noise might bring someone."

"Do you know how to pick locks?" asked Muuril, his face showing more hope than expectation. Gelthius shook his head.

"The only robbing I done was stealing goats and chickens, and they wasn't locked up."

"Let's have a shufty down here," suggested Muuril, jabbing his thumb over his shoulder at a side corridor they had yet to explore.

Gelthius nodded, and the two of them sauntered under the archway and into the small passage. There was another arch at the far end, and Gelthius could see benches and cupboards. Entering, the two found themselves in a guard room, with holes in the wall overlooking the stairs so that defenders could see an attacking enemy and jab at them with spears or shoot arrows through the narrow gaps. Peering through the holes, Gelthius realised that they had been artfully fashioned; he had quite a view from the mid-storey landing but had noticed nothing of the murder holes when he had been coming up the stairs.

"Hey, these would be better than servants' gear," said Muuril. Gelthius turned and saw the sergeant standing next to the open door of a tall cupboard, a black shield in one hand, a black-crested helmet in the other. "There's five sets in here, bound to find some that fit."

"What if we run into other blackcrests?" said Gelthius. "They might not know all the faces of the servants, but sure they would think it odd not recognising one of their own?"

"We can walk around as free as birds in this gear," said Muuril. He tossed the shield to Gelthius, who caught it awkwardly, snatching at the rim before it cracked on the varnished wooden boards of the floor.

"Fine," said the third captain, placing the shield to one side. "Let's see what they've got."

It took a short while to find helmet and breastplate that was not outrageously large for Gelthius' small frame. Muuril, being considerably larger than most men, also had a hard time, but managed to squeeze into a set of armour too. Swapping leggings for kilts and slippers for sandals once more, Gelthius somehow felt properly dressed again, even though his new gear chafed a little as he moved.

"We'll split up and have a quick look around this floor, and then head up to the top, right?" said Gelthius. "No point spending too long, eh?"

Muuril nodded and headed out the door, Gelthius just behind him. Gelthius turned right at the main passage, while Muuril headed back cross the landing to the left. The apartments that the governor occupied were self-contained, linked by three guarded corridors – and it did not take Gelthius long to check the three rooms he found; another dining room next to a reception chamber with low couches and tables, and a wide-windowed sun room overlooking the palace grounds to hotwards. Returning to the stairs, he met Muuril, who shook his head.

"More bedrooms," said the sergeant. Gelthius sighed. It was

beginning to look a lot like their risky adventure would prove to be pointless. There was nothing here except old tapestries, poorly polished silverware, unused crockery and mouldering furniture.

Moving to the uppermost storey, Gelthius and Muuril discovered a set of double doors that led to a large hall, the floor decoratively tiled, the walls covered with embroidered hangings showing the Askhan legions conquering the Ersuan kings' armies. The pair walked around the walls, looking at the detailed threadwork.

"That's got to be Salacis Pass," said Muuril, pointing to the next hanging. It depicted a legion in a narrow mountain valley, advancing into a storm of arrows and rocks unleashed by barbaric, bearded Ersuans on the slopes above. "That was a fight and a half."

"Looks like it," said Gelthius. Muuril said something else but the third captain did not really hear it; he was sure he had heard a noise on the stairwell outside the main doors.

"Did you hear that?" said Gelthius, convinced he heard feet slapping on stone.

"I can't hear anything," said Muuril. He took a few steps towards the next tapestry and then stopped. "Hang on, yes I did."

The two of them jogged to the door and stopped. Gelthius held his breath as he listened, trying not to hear the thump of his heart in his chest.

There were definitely voices drifting up the stairwell. They were speaking quietly, and Gelthius could hear the slow slap of sandals on the steps. He darted a look at Muuril, who shrugged and took a step into the corridor before shrinking back. There were shadows on the stairway, at the bottom of the last flight.

Gelthius jabbed his thumb back into the room and the two of them stepped out of sight, as quietly as they could manage in the ill-fitting wargear. The voices were very close now and came straight towards the open doors.

The two legionnaires hurried to stand beside the nearest wall, about ten paces apart. Gelthius muttered a call to attention and the pair brought their spears down with a thump, keeping their gazes fixed ahead. Trying not to turn his head to look, Gelthius moved his gaze sideways towards the door as the conversation suddenly silenced and the sound of feet on stone became the thud of steps on the wooden floor of the great hall.

"We're running out of places to speak." Gelthius heard a reedy voice. Out of the corner of his eye he saw a small, thin man pacing into the hall, wearing white robes of office: Asuhas. His hair was oiled back across a balding pate, and his top lip and chin were darkened by a wispy covering of hair. The man's fingers fidgeted constantly, playing with the creases in his robe and the rope of grey and green cords that served as a belt. "I don't know why they have to be here, the Brotherhood made their position very clear and I agreed with them."

"This lot are everywhere, don't pay them any heed," said the governor's companion.

Gelthius already knew the voice before a large man in a bright red shirt and checked Salphorian trousers strode into view. Gelthius choked back a gasp as he laid eyes on Anglhan Periusis. The former landship owner stuck his thumbs between his belt and his generous gut and turned towards the two legionnaires.

For a moment Gelthius was like a rabbit paralysed in front of the hunter's bow. He could not stop himself meeting Anglhan's gaze, and the two looked at each other straight on. Swallowing hard, Gelthius managed to look away, staring blankly ahead, though his hands were sweating profusely on his spear and shield grip. He heard Muuril shuffle his feet, obviously recognising the traitorous governor as well.

The third captain continued to feel Anglhan's stare on him for a few moments, as his heart started beating quickly, hammering against the inside of his breastplate. It was impossible that the former governor would not recognise him; Gelthius had spent nearly twenty years in the man's service.

"How odd," said Anglhan. The boards creaked under his heavy tread as he took several steps towards Gelthius. The legionnaire forced himself to relax the grip on his spear, ready to lunge forward and drive the tip into Anglhan's face. He noticed Muuril shifting his weight slightly out of the corner of his eye.

"What's odd?" asked the governor.

"This tapestry shows a legion being defeated," Anglhan said, pointing at the hanging behind Gelthius. "They're being massacred!"

"The Battle of Sulunnin. Out of the way, there," said Asuhas. He flapped a hand at Gelthius and Muuril, who moved aside. "Step out of the way so we can see properly. Yes, that was a rough one for the Sixteenth and Eighteenth. Early snows caught them by surprise, and they were ambushed by a tribal coalition in the foothills before they could build a proper winter fort."

"But why celebrate a defeat in this way?" said Anglhan. Gelthius was not sure, but he thought for a moment that the old landship captain actually winked at him as he walked past.

"It is a memorial, not a celebration," said Asuhas. "We Askhans learn from our mistakes as well as our successes. Something you Salphors are not so good at."

"You are referring to the unfortunate loss of my city?" Anglhan spoke lightly of the massacre of thousands of Magilnadans, as if he had played no part in its downfall. "As you see, I have returned and I am better placed than ever."

"I don't see why the Brotherhood would tolerate you at all, Periusis, much less make you the king's prime agent in Ersua."

The two men wondered down the hall, their voices growing fainter, but Gelthius could still hear what was being said. Muuril shook his head, obviously displeased by what he was hearing.

"Stay calm," whispered Gelthius.

"Fat goatfucker should be dead," growled Muuril. Gelthius could see the sergeant's knuckles turning white from the tight grip on his spear.

"Not now," said Gelthius. "Ssh, listen!"

Muuril said nothing though he glared at Anglhan's broad back as the conversation between the traitor and the governor drifted down the hall, carried by a slight echo.

"I can confirm that he hasn't been seen coldwards of Thedraan or dawnwards of Caprion," Anglhan was saying.

"So he is definitely not coming to Marradan? You are sure of that fact?"

"He has not come any closer, so he has to have headed hotwards, or turned back into Salphoria ," Anglhan assured the governor. Gelthius decided that the two men had to be talking about King Ullsaard. Either news travelled far more swiftly than the king had anticipated, or Asuhas and Anglhan had been keeping an eye or ear out for the return of the king. "It makes no sense for him to go back into Salphoria, so it has to be hotwards. I can't think that he'd return to near-Mekha, so what else is down that way?"

"He has an old villa, at Menesun on Lake Temerin," said Asuhas. "Why he would go there, I don't know; nothing but hills and goats and peasants."

"Exactly," said Anglhan, slapping a hand to a wobbling thigh. "If you wanted to lie low, where would be better?"

"So, are we going to tell Leraates? That he's in Menesun, I mean. It's your responsibility really, not mine."

"I don't think Leraates needs to know just yet, does he?"

said Anglhan. He chuckled as he clasped his hands to his belly. "Certainly from my position I have no desire to make myself dispensable. If I were you, I would think long and hard before saying anything."

"I see what you mean." The two had reached the furthest extent of the hall and turned back towards Gelthius and Muuril. The governor raised his voice. "You two, leave us."

"Aye, governor," said Gelthius, lifting his spear in salute. Muuril followed suit and the two of them tramped from the hall.

"We could go back in there and gut both of those traitorous cunts," snarled Muuril, stopping at the top of the stairway. "We'd be doing the king a favour and no mistake. Those treacherous sons of a pig's arse!"

"Not now, not yet," said Gelthius, ushering Muuril down the first few steps. "First priority is to tell the king what we heard. We'll let him decide."

Gongs and bells sounded the third hour of High Watch as the two men of the Thirteenth descended to the ground floor. They reached the main corridor where they had entered and almost walked straight into a group of ten blackcrests turning towards the stairwell.

"Where have you two been?" barked the sergeant. "Haven't you heard? We've got intruders."

Gelthius met the man's stare with eyes wide with surprise. The sergeant's eyes narrowed.

"Hold on," said the sergeant, reaching out with his shield to stop Gelthius as he tried to step past. "Do I know you?"

Muuril answered for Gelthius, ramming his black enamelled shield into the side of the sergeant's helmet. Gelthius was already sprinting into the corridor when the sergeant's unconscious body hit the ground with a clatter. He tossed aside his shield and spear and pumped his arms, darting a look back to see Muuril jabbing the butt of his spear into the throat of another blackcrest.

A shout of alarm echoed down the passageway as Muuril followed Gelthius, the blackcrests only a few paces behind. Gelthius ran and ran, passing through archway after archway as he headed towards the main entrance of the palace. He ripped off his helmet and let it drop from his fingers as he skidded on a rug laid across the smooth floor. Muuril had caught up with him and the two almost fell down in a tangled heap, the sergeant hurdling Gelthius' skidding body at the last moment.

Barging through a door to their left, they burst into a small garden between the wing and the main palace. There were four legionnaires in the green-and-grey of the Twenty-first guarding an open gate on the far side of a pond. Gelthius and Muuril splashed through the water and reached the legionnaires, panting heavily.

"Fucking blackhead cunts want for us," gasped Muuril as he pushed between the bemused legionnaires. "Do the captain and me a favour, eh?"

Gelthius did not wait to hear agreement as he pushed on through the tunnelway beyond the gate. At the far end an archway led into the main palace and his sandals slapped on the marble of the grand foyer. He had never seen marble before he had gone to Magilnada, and when he had first set foot inside Asuhas' palace he had been astounded to see an entire greeting hall made out of green-veined stone. Now he didn't pay it a second look as he hurtled through the crowds of petitioners and functionaries milling between two curving sets of steps leading up to the main audience hall.

He aimed for the sunlight streaming through the row of open doors and reached the threshold as sounds of shouting and fighting erupted behind. Crashing into one of the doors he looked back, expecting to see Muuril in the altercation, but the sergeant was hot on the captain's heels. Beyond him, soldiers from the Twenty-first and the blackcrests fell brawling into the foyer. The legionnaires stationed at the entrance heard the ruckus and piled across the entrance hall to help their comrades.

"Let's ditch this weight," panted Muuril, pulling open a buckle that kept his breastplate in place. The two quickly shed the bronze armour while a crowd of amazed onlookers gathered around; nobody tried to interfere.

Thus lightened, Muuril and Gelthius ran out onto the broad steps that led down to the city square. The clamour from inside faded as they sprinted down the steps, taking them three at a time. The square was thronged with the noble's market; stalls with expensive jewellery, clothes, pets and all manner of luxuries were laid out in rows; the high born and aspiring rich of the city and their entourages glided slowly between the stalls and soon Muuril and Gelthius were lost in the throng.

IV

Anglhan stood looking at the tapestries while Asuhas received a report from the captain of the Brotherhood guards. The governor of Ersua had been less than pleased to become an acquaintance of Anglhan but was too afraid of Leraates and the Brotherhood to do more than complain about the situation. Asuhas' weakness had made it easy for Anglhan to present himself as an ally, a conspirator that would help Asuhas loosen the grip of the Brotherhood on his office. The former governor was reminded of the boast Asuhas had made earlier: "We Askhans learn from our mistakes as well as our successes. Something you Salphors are not so good at."

Perhaps Anglhan did not think like a Salphor, and had never thought like a Salphor. He was not about to repeat his previous mistakes. Some men might give up on lofty goals after a disaster

like Magilnada, but to Anglhan it was just another lesson in life
to be heeded and built upon. A man not as driven as Anglhan
might have concluded that he had become greedy and should
have been content with the governorship of an Imperial city
rather than manoeuvring to become ruler of his own kingdom.
Anglhan pitied this theoretical man, for it had not been greed
that had overthrown Magilnada, nor had it been ambition that
had been the cause of Anglhan's downfall. The only mistake
Anglhan had made in his attempt to become his own man was
that he had been too obvious in his approach.

As he watched the governor of Ersua arguing with the
blackcrest officer, Anglhan was certain that this time he had
made the right choices. When he had been approached by Leraates, Anglhan had been offered overt power: agents and
legions, money and an army of Brothers to do his bidding. It
had been a foolish move on the part of Urikh – or whoever
was acting on Urikh's behalf – because it showed Anglhan how
necessary he was.

This other, fictitious Anglhan, might also have been swayed
by the desire for revenge against Ullsaard, for upsetting his earlier plans. The real Anglhan sneered at the sentimentality of
revenge. If Ullsaard was to be killed, that was one thing and a
pleasurable step on the road back to a superior fate, but Anglhan would not allow such sentiment to drive him. Of course,
he had not let Leraates know that; the Brother was convinced
that Anglhan hungered for Ullsaard's blood as a hound
hungers for a bone. It was convenient to let Leraates think that
Anglhan would stop at nothing to see Ullsaard slain, and to
also think that in Anglhan he had found the perfect man to
blame when news of the treachery against the king finally
came to the surface. Anglhan knew perfectly well what Urikh
had in mind. The new king wanted his hands clean of any involvement in Ullsaard's killing, and to be able to claim that he

had acted in good faith on the news of his father's death, which would be revealed at a later time to be the machinations of the faithless, treacherous Anglhan Periusis.

Anglhan wanted to laugh at the naiveté of Urikh's ploy. It was more obvious than a ten-thousand strong army marching down a road. The lure of gold and soldiers was not tempting at all, because Anglhan had no desire to leave his mark anywhere near the death of Ullsaard. In becoming governor of Magilnada, Anglhan had put himself into the view of the powerful and the ambitious men around him. That had been his mistake, not greed. This time he would work through others – Leraates and Asuhas for the moment, and ultimately the king. They would be the public face of Anglhan's private power.

"There has been a disturbance in the lower halls," announced Asuhas, having dismissed the blackcrest captain. "It seems there has been some fighting between the Brotherhood guards and the Twenty-first."

"As I understand it, the blackcrests are not very popular," said Anglhan. "This hardly seems to me to be pressing news."

"While it is true that there is always tension between the Brotherhood troops and traditional legions, it is also normal for legion discipline to be maintained. There was a particular event that triggered the animosity into confrontation, and that is the cause for my concern."

"A trigger?" asked Anglhan, not really interested. The bully boys of the Brotherhood and Captain Lutaan's men could slaughter each other for all the difference it made to the former governor.

"It seems that some of the Twenty-first, and it is unclear how many, were masquerading as members of the brotherhood detachment. I cannot fathom why that would be the case."

"Just stirring trouble, no doubt," said Anglhan, although

now he was convinced that earlier he had not been halluci-
nating. That legionnaire *had* been old Gelthius. He hadn't seen
the former debtor since Thunder Pass, but he could now see a
connecting line going from what had happened between the
Twenty-first and the blackcrests through Gelthius and back to
Ullsaard. It was just a suspicion at the moment, but there
would be records at the Brotherhood precinct that would confirm or dispel those suspicions.

"I'm sorry, were you talking?" Anglhan said, realising that
he had not been listening to Asuhas for a short while. "Please,
forgive my insolence."

"I asked you what you planned to do about this situation with
the Brotherhood," the governor said. "You know that I have
pledged every assistance to you, but I cannot aid you with these
damned black-crested enforcers looking over my shoulder. You
must speak to Leraates and have him pull back his hounds."

"I'll see what I can do, but Leraates doesn't answer to me,
friend," said Anglhan. He patted Asuhas on the shoulder.
"Please excuse me, I will go and speak to Leraates now."

It was time, Anglhan had decided, to set the fox amongst
the chickens and see what would happen. Asuhas was already
clucking madly. How would Leraates react?

V

Anglhan crossed the square at a fast walk, cloak wrapped
about his body, one hand holding his hood over his head. The
market traders were packing away their stalls and heading off
with wagons and handcarts, as the last buyers had all been
driven back to their homes by a resurgence of the autumn
rains. In front, the rain glistened from the grey slabs of the
Brotherhood precinct. Its arched tiers were just a little lighter
than the cloudy sky, which was growing darker every moment, hiding the setting sun.

The hour did not matter to Anglhan; the precincts of the Brotherhood never closed their doors. Day and night the courts and tax collectors worked, keeping the empire sailing smoothly along like a galley on the Greenwater.

Reaching the cover of an awning stretched over the upper steps leading to the precinct, Anglhan untied his cloak, shook it out and bundled it under one arm. He wiped his sleeve across his face, soaking up the rain that had reached his skin. A soft but pointed cough halted Anglhan as he took a few steps towards the dark opening of the doorway.

The small, leathery-faced man who sat behind a table at the precinct's main portal had seen Anglhan come and go more than a dozen times, and yet the clerk's officious nature could not allow him to let the Salphor past without comment.

"Name?" said the clerk.

"Karoom Karaa, said Anglhan, earning himself a scowl and pursed lips.

"That is not the name you gave to me before," said the clerk, laying down his stylus and wax tablet to fix Anglhan with a scrutinising stare.

"If you know my name, why do you keep asking me what it is?"

"It is my job to ascertain the identity of everybody who enters the precinct. It is not my duty to assume I know that identity." The wiry official glanced over his shoulder, towards the two blackcrests standing at sentry beside the open doorway into the building. He returned his gaze to Anglhan. "Name?"

"Daefus Maron," said Anglhan, using the alias he had established for himself in Thedraan. He and Leraates had been in agreement that it made no sense for the name of Anglhan Periusis to ever be entered into any official records of the Brotherhood.

"Purpose?"

"Crown business," said Anglhan. He fished into the pouch at his belt and brought out a Brotherhood token. It was much like the tax tokens Leraates and others often gave out as rewards and bribes, except that it was made of silver and marked with a series of numbers on the reverse.

The clerk took the token and inscribed the numbers into his wax slate before pulling out a roll of paper from a box beneath the table. Anglhan folded his arms while he waited for the door warden to verify the numbers against his list.

"Host?" said the man, handing back the token.

"Brother Leraates," said Anglhan, tapping his fingers on the bulge of his arm.

The clerk produced a ledger and turned the pages until he came to the one he wanted. Running a finger down the page, the man tutted and shook his head.

"You have no appointment to see Brother Leraates."

"Is he here? He will see me regardless of appointment."

The clerk consulted his book again, brow furrowed. He gave a quiet snort and darted a dirty look at Anglhan. The same had happened on every previous occasion, and Anglhan was starting to enjoy the charade.

"Very well, it appears you have open privileges," said the clerk. He gestured to the blackcrests and one of them came over. "Arrange for someone to escort this visitor to the meeting chambers of Brother Leraates."

Anglhan was forced to wait, during which the city rang in the second hour of Duskwatch. The sun was almost set and the steps of the precinct were lit by four massive lamps hanging to either side of the doorway. Eventually a black-crested legionnaire emerged from the open door and nodded for Anglhan to follow.

Inside the precinct was dry and dusty, unlike the rest of the city which was almost permanently damp. Anglhan had no idea how the Brothers managed to keep out the rain all of the time, and he had not seen any evidence of fireplaces during his visits. While the outside of the precinct was clad in the grey stone that made up most of the city, the inside showed exposed walls of light orange brick. The floor underfoot was of the same, and Anglhan wondered how the Brothers could work in such monotonous environs. There was not a mat, carpet or hanging to be seen; not in any of the parts of the precinct he had been.

"This place could do with a mural or two," he said to his escort. The man shrugged with indifference. "Or perhaps a mosaic?"

He tramped after the blackcrest, heading along low steps that led up into the heights of the ziggurat, slowly winding around themselves, doorways and archways and branching passages to either side. There was the muted murmur of conversations through some of the doors, and clacks of counting beads moving from bowl to bowl. Aside from the jingle of the blackcrest's armour, Anglhan thought he could also hear the barely audible scritch of stylus on wax and nib on parchment. The Brothers made no sound as they shuffled from room to room in their black robes and slippers, and twice he had to stop suddenly as one of the silently-moving civil servants emerged from an archway just ahead of him.

"Lava, it must be," Anglhan said out loud. Rather than echo his words, the bare walls absorbed the noise, stilling Anglhan's voice.

"What's that?" said the legionnaire, looking over his shoulder for a moment.

"The heat and dryness, it must be lava in origin. You know, heated from underneath, like bath houses."

"You might be right, I've never thought about it before," said the blackcrest. "I know they must make it here somewhere."

"What about ailurs? Do they breed them here?"

The soldier shook his head.

"Just at the Grand Precincts in Askh, I hear. Maybe they used to at Oorandia as well, I don't remember. Certainly not seen any ailurs around here, not even Asuhas has one."

"And who is your commander?" They turned and took a steeper flight of stairs, which narrowed quickly, almost to the point where Anglhan's bulk would not fit between the brick walls and the legionnaire had to hold his shield edge-on in front of himself. The tapered stairwell opened out a short flight later, into a high-ceilinged chamber that ran from one side of the precinct to the other; Anglhan could see the palace through the windows to his right and the distant Ersuan hills to his left.

It looked like a storage area, filled with barrels and cupboards and crates, but Anglhan had been here before and knew that it was the precinct's hall of records and not some menial store room. Somewhere in here would be the recruiting papers of the Twenty-first. If Gelthius had been with the legion for some time, that would put paid to Anglhan's suspicions. If he was a newer recruit, that would mean he spent plenty of time with the Thirteenth after Thunder Pass, and was likely one of Ullsaard's men.

It might be coincidence, but Anglhan would never take coincidence for granted. Besides, it worked in Anglhan's favour if the tale was true.

"You didn't answer my question," said Anglhan.

"Don't have a commander, as such," said the blackcrest. "We've got second captains and third captains, a few of them around, but the senior Brother is Leraates. Before him, it was Brother Sangaal."

"Seems a bit odd, having Brothers in military positions. Impractical."

"It's not like a Brother's ever going to be leading us into

battle, is it?" said the blackcrest. "We just guard stuff, for the most part. The regular legions are for fighting wars."

"You can leave me here, if that's all right," said Anglhan. He flicked a finger towards the curtained doorways that led to the offices of the senior Brothers. "You can tell Brother Leraates I'm here."

"Tell him yourself, I'm supposed to be off-shift," said the blackcrest. Anglhan watched the soldier turn on his heel and stride back to the stairs.

When the thump of the legionnaire's tread on the stone steps was distant, Anglhan set about looking through the records. He did not know the intricacies of the Brotherhood's system, but had been observant when he had made previous visits. To aid him, there were signs hung at regular intervals on the shelves and cupboards, and wax slate logs were also attached to each shelf and drawer.

It was simple enough to find the section that was concerned with the latest raising of the Twenty-first. A sheaf of parchments were tied together with cord, and on them were listed the names of all of the recruits so far. Reading from the end of the list backwards, it was not long before Anglhan found Gelthius' name, and a notation to the effect that he had been dismissed from the Thirteenth for serving his ten year term and re-signed with Captain Lutaan.

That was all the proof Anglhan needed. Gelthius had been on his landship ten years ago, and so the documentation had to be fabricated. It was possible that Gelthius had forged them himself, but it made no sense to desert one legion in order to join another. Looking at the record, Gelthius saw that there were four others who had signed on to the legion rolls at the same time – all of them veterans of Ullsaard's Thirteenth.

"You sly bastard," said Anglhan, shoving the papers back into their drawer.

GAV THORPE   77

"Who is a sly bastard?"

Anglhan's blubbery body wobbled as he straightened with shock. Stumbling around, he found Leraates standing just behind him, hands at his stomach, tucked into the sleeves of his robe. "Did you find what you were looking for?"

There was something about the precinct – maybe the dim light or the colours – that made Leraates seem more menacing than when Anglhan had first encountered him. His eyes had pinpricks of light reflected in them, stabbing into Anglhan like inquisitive, distrusting daggers. Leraates had more confidence here too, Anglhan was certain. Like a predator on home ground, the Brother was more certain of himself, and his authority, when surrounded by the trappings of his position.

"I was just about to tell you," said Anglhan, recovering from his fright. "It is not good manners to sneak up on a man like that."

"I heard you rustling about and came to see what had so intrigued you," said Leraates. The Brother waved a hand to the doorway of his chambers, where the red curtain had been pulled back, revealing the lamp-lit room beyond. "I assume some discretion is required?"

"Yes, that would be good," replied Anglhan.

He followed Leraates across the room, sweat pickling on his forehead and jowls.

"Why is it so hot in here?" he asked, dabbing at his face with his sleeve. He glanced outside to see rain sleeting down on the rest of the city.

"Airflow and lava vats," said Leraates, standing to one side of the doorway, inviting Anglhan to enter with a waved hand. "Heat rises, so the upper levels of the precinct get warmer. However, the very top of the building is exposed to the elements more, which chills the air. This is about the hottest storey."

"And you can work here, like this?"

"Better than some," said Leraates. "At least the climate here keeps the air moist. Further to hotwards, the upper floors can be like kilns. Really, the wax melts on the slates and the clay ones bake in your hand."

Beyond the curtain was a small antechamber with a few stools and little else. A solid door barred the way to the next room. It opened to Leraates' touch as he stepped past Anglhan and entered his private domain.

Following on the heel of the Brother, Anglhan found himself in a spacious chamber, with three narrow windows opposite the door and an archway to his right. The first room was informally furnished, much to his surprise, with a white-and-green patterned rug on the floor and low couches upholstered with the same design. The room was lit by candles in sconces on the walls, and the windows were shuttered with dark wood, giving the room a strangely homely feel despite the bare bricks.

"Let us discuss this in my workspace," suggested Leraates, continuing through the archway. The next room was also furnished with stuffed chairs and a carpet, but there were no windows and much of the available space was filled with more shelves, and racks of scrolls and tablets.

Anglhan lowered himself into one of the chairs, as Leraates moved behind a desk whose top was covered with neatly arranged styluses, pens, wax and clay tablets, seal rings, trays of Brotherhood tokens and parchment sheets. Under a weight made of a polished piece of grey and black marble were several documents, which Leraates swiftly covered with a blank piece of paper.

"Something you don't want me to see?" said Anglhan.

"I do not wish you to know anything I do not tell you," Leraates replied, sitting down in a plain wooden chair, resting against its high back. "I am certain that you understand why."

"Ullsaard is definitely back from Salphoria," Anglhan said. He was excited and in no mood for verbal sparring.

"It still seems a little early," said Leraates, though his expression was one of shock, indicating that he believed Anglhan. "We know from other reports that he reached Carantathi, more than two thousand miles away. For him to have returned so soon indicates that he would have left not long after the city fell."

"Which means that he did not set out on his return because of Urikh," said Anglhan. "There is no way that he could have known what his usurper of a son had done. Well, not until he got back to Greater Askhor. Let's be generous and say that he met a messenger heading into Salphoria with the news of Ullsaard's demise. He cannot have had more than thirty days to react, but he has done well so far."

"Done well with what?" Leraates leaned forward, hands steepled to his chin.

"He has five men inside the Twenty-first Legion. They have had access to the palace of Asuhas for the last ten days."

"That is of little concern to you," said Leraates. "Asuhas is not important. Where is Ullsaard?"

"I do not know," said Anglhan. "He may have decided not to cross into Ersua if he learnt of what Urikh has done."

"That would be problematic," said Leraates. "He could be anywhere."

"Not so much of a problem for me," said Anglhan. His chair creaked in protest as he shifted his bulk forward to lean an arm on his knee. "If Ullsaard is still in Salphoria, he's in my territory. His legions are spread thin, it will take some time for him to muster any force worthy of a battle."

"You want soldiers?"

"Five hundred, that is all," said Anglhan. "Make them black-crests, and send along as many Brothers as you like to stop me from doing anything bad with them. I promise, with my contacts as a Salphor, I will have Ullsaard rooted out before his beloved Thirteenth or anyone else will be able to help him."

"Do you really think I am going to let you head off into Salphoria with five hundred of my legionnaires? You must think I was kicked in the head by an abada."

"You are welcome to lead the search yourself, Askhan." Anglhan almost spat this last word, and he saw Leraates' lips twitch in irritation. The Brother was a pure-born Askhan, probably of some noble family or other, and although he spoke of duty to the empire and Greater Askhor, Anglhan knew that deep down the Brother was as arrogant about his superiority as any other man born behind the Wall.

"I have my own connections in Salphoria, and considerably more resources," said Leraates, speaking one of the dialects of duskwards Salphoria before switching back to Askhan. "Why would I risk letting you off the leash at this delicate juncture, to do something I am more capable of completing myself?"

"As you like," said Anglhan, looking crestfallen, although inside he wanted to sing. Leraates could not help but try to take the credit for himself, just as the clerk on the door could not stop himself from quizzing Anglhan on every visit. "To every man his station", was one of the phrases from the Book of Askhos that Anglhan liked a lot, and men of power did not reach such lofty positions by being nice or being humble. Leraates was just like any other power-grabbing Askhan, and that was the weakness Anglhan would exploit.

"You will remain under the guard of Governor Asuhas while I look for Ullsaard," said the Brother, standing up. "You are not to leave the city. I shall send instructions to that end immediately, so do not think to slip away now."

"As long as I get to see Ullsaard's head at some point, I have no intention of going anywhere else," said Anglhan. He curled

his lip in derision, for added effect. "I am happy to be enter-
tained at the palaces, at the cost of the governor. It is certainly
better than having to sell jewellery and such for a few
askharins."

VI

Having arranged for one of his soldiers to escort Anglhan all of
the way back to his rooms in the palace, Leraates headed down
into the depths of the precinct. It was here, hidden behind
doors that most of the Brothers did not know existed, that the
true bulk of the building extended. Beyond the lava vats and
the storage rooms, in dark corridors of yellow stone carved with
sigils brought from the first Temple, Leraates advanced with
quick strides, his path lit by the yellow glow of a small lantern.
The air here was as dry as a desert, and not a creature lived; no
spiders in the cracks and no flies on the walls.

The rasp of voices echoed along the passage, coming from a
lit chamber ahead. Within were five men kneeling naked in a
circle, flesh etched with lines and runes and astrological devices, their black robes hanging on pegs on the sandstone wall.
Between them was a hexagon of stone, into which had been
carved thousands of tiny sigils. They whispered the words of
their incantation and reached out to stroke bony fingers across
the marked stone. Their rune-carved backs undulating as they
made their supplication, the men paid no heed to Leraates as
he circled around the group, heading for an archway opposite
the one by which he had entered.

Beyond this portal was a series of rooms linked by more archways, each chamber the same size and shape – a square roughly
twenty paces across – with slab-like beds, benches and tables.
Plain clay crockery was arranged ready for eating, with bronze
knives and spoons. A fine layer of dust covered everything, for
it had been a while since the lower precinct had been home to

men who required normal sustenance; of late only true acolytes of the Temple had stayed in the catacombs.

Past these cells was a chamber much like the stone room where the men mumbled the words of power to the Eulanui. It was domed, two window-like openings flanking the doorway. Bronze mirrors and carefully fashioned lenses in small passages above brought down light; a strange yellow light that never dimmed or brightened whether it was day or night in Marradan.

On a small stool sat a youth, perhaps thirteen or fourteen summers old. His skin was well-tanned, cut with a few of the sect's runes but otherwise bare, the first curls of adult hair showing under his arms and above the loincloth he wore around his waist.

Unlike the rest of his body, the boy's face was covered in fleshy etchings. Every piece of skin was scored or marked in some way, creating a tracery around his eyes and lips that seemed to delve into itself, forever spiralling into smaller and smaller patterns until one could not follow the miniscule cuts any more. When he blinked there were more runes on his eyelids, and there was a delicate tracery of white scar tissue inside his ears.

"Greetings," said the youth, bowing forward on his stool, his supple spine allowing him to place his forehead on the floor between his feet. "I have expected your return with excitement, Brother."

"Greetings, Herikhil," said Leraates, pulling up a stool so that he could sit facing the youth. "Can you reach Lakhyri for me?"

"Oh, the high priest himself!" The boy clapped his hands in delight, his sigil-scribed face splitting with a toothy grin. "I am blessed."

"Yes, you are," Leraates said patiently.

Herikhil closed his eyes and sat with his hands on his knees, his feet together on the floor, back straight. His breathing

slowed and deepened, until it seemed to Leraates that the
youth had fallen asleep. The Brother knew better and watched
closely as Herikhil's eyes began to move back and forth beneath the closed lids, as though scanning the room for
something only he could see.

"He is away from the precinct for the moment, but he hears
me," said Herikhil. "He will return shortly."

"I will wait," said Leraates. He pulled out a roll of parchment
from the inside of his robe. The Brother hummed tunelessly
to himself as he unrolled the sheet, revealing a coloured map
of dawnwards Salphoria. It covered his lap and folded over his
knees, and the detail was remarkable. The map was Askhan,
of course, and so showed every track, stream and village
within three hundred miles of the border. The map was so recent that Magilnada was not on it.

Leraates began to trace his finger along the grey lines of
newly built Askhan roads and old Salphor trails, trying to figure out where to start his search for Ullsaard. The Brother was
going to proceed on the assumption that the true king had
learnt of his son's action and would assemble a fighting force
before crossing into Greater Askhor. From what Anglhan had
said, this made the most sense.

Looking for somewhere from where it was possible to march
swiftly into Ersua left only half a dozen places within easy
reach of the main turnpike that had been laid in the wake of
Ullsaard's advance. The Salphors did not have the right sort or
number of ships to bring the troops into Ersua by river, so the
road was the only option. Once the Brother knew where to
find the former king, it would not take much to convince Ullsaard that Leraates was working against Urikh, and once he
had wriggled into Ullsaard's confidence he could get close
enough to slay him; settling Lakhyri's problem and dispensing
with the need for Anglhan at a single stroke.

Leraates glanced up at Herikhil's face, but the youth seemed to be in a pleasant slumber, his lips half-raised in a gentle smile. Returning to the chart, Leraates procured a wooden framed tablet of wax and a stylus, and started to write names and directions and distances onto the tablet.

A moan from Herikhil attracted his attention. The boy's face was twitching, every muscle moving of its own accord, his eyes roving around unseeing behind closed lids. Thin rivulets of blood seeped from the wider scars, and soon Herikhil's face was a mask of blood. He made no cry and showed no signs of pain, but beneath his fair skin bone and muscle contorted, reshaping to lengthen his cheeks and narrow his mouth, eyes sinking deeper into sockets that broadened even as his brow became sharper above them.

"What news from Ersua?" Though the voice was Herikhil's, the tone – the hard words and lack of preamble – was totally Lakhyri's. "Has Anglhan found Ullsaard yet?"

"The former king is still in Salphoria, to the best knowledge of the traitor," said Leraates. "I have said it before, but I do not know why you let that venomous, verminous man live. If I spent half as much time looking for Ullsaard as I have keeping an eye on Periusis we would have him by now."

"Your objections have been noted before, and discarded," said Lakhyri. "The Salphor is not only the means by which we can deny involvement in Ullsaard's execution, he will also be the bait that lures the old king out of hiding."

"If so, that is likely to happen soon," said Leraates. He looked at Herikhil's faces and saw displeasure wrinkle the boy's brow.

"What has happened?"

"Spies of Ullsaard, I believe, were found in Asuhas' palace today. I have checked the information with the captain of the guard and he confirmed that members of the Twenty-first legion disguised themselves as Brotherhood legionnaires. We do not know what they intended or if they succeeded, but Angl-han has shown me the records that link newly recruited members of the Twenty-first to Ullsaard's favourite legion, the Thirteenth."

"And these new recruits, have you found them yet?" Though Herikhil's eyes were the same bright blue as before, there was just a flicker of gold in their pupils, and the stare was penetrating.

"I have my soldiers searching the barracks and palace grounds, and Asuhas has ordered First Captain Lutaan to also find the infiltrators amongst his ranks."

"Lutaan is not to know that Ullsaard may be alive."

"Of course not," snapped Leraates. He calmed his manner, knowing that it was not wise to be too aggressive, despite Lakhyri's abrasive manner. "Forgive my outburst, but you seem short of temper today. Do I not have your trust anymore? I can handle this situation."

"It is not you, it is Urikh," replied Lakhyri. "Our new king forgets which powers placed him on his throne, and summons me to his court like a common chamberlain. Tomorrow he will receive a reminder of his place in the grander scheme."

"You are not going to tell him about Ullsaard, are you?" said Leraates. He regretted the question as soon as he asked it; Herikhil's boyish face screwed up into a derisive snarl.

"Though it is of no concern of yours, you are right. The less Urikh knows about the current situation, the better. The first he hears of Ullsaard's discovery will be seeing his father's corpse. If not, there is a chance that he might well decide to imprison Ull-saard or something equally counter-productive."

"I do not think that Urikh would be sentimental towards his father," said Leraates.

"That is highly unlikely. A more probable cause of interfer-ence by the king would be a desire to handle the matter personally. If Urikh decides that he wants to be in charge of his father's death it could threaten the successful outcome of our efforts. Regardless of Anglhan, Ullsaard, Urikh or any other distraction, you must stay focussed on the ambition we share."

"To see the rightful ruler installed, and the new empire created," said Leraates. He dipped his head in deference to the high priest. "I shall not forget."

Herikhil's features squirmed and changed again, dripping more blood down his bare chest, until his face resembled the youth once again. There was a beatific smile on the boy's lips as Lakhyri pulled away his presence. Eyelids fluttering, Herikhil regained control of himself, eyes slowly focussing on the senior Brother.

"Such light and sweetness," murmured the youth. He turned to a bowl and rag on a table next to him and washed his faces, splashing the floor with water and blood. Wiping his hands and brow, Herikhil looked at Leraates. "I am tired. Do you wish for me to contact anybody else today?"

"No, Herikhil, you may rest," said Leraates, gesturing towards the bare slab that served as the boy's cot. "You have done well."

Leraates left the youth as he lay down on his stone bed. Lakhyri had not said anything against Leraates' plan of action, and he assumed that he had the high priest's consent to search for the king in Salphoria. There was still much to organise – legions, bribed Salphor chieftains, Brothers – but he was spurred on by the thought that he was nearing his goal. In a matter of days, perhaps two dozen at most, he was sure he would have Ullsaard in his grasp.

VII

The rain was pouring down, the clouds blocking all light of moon and stars. The lights of Marradan could be seen a few miles to coldwards; thousands of torches on the city wall and lanterns lighting the streets were enough to create a glow on the horizon.

In a dell a little more than hundred paces from the main hotwards road another much smaller light glowed in the darkness.

The shuttered lantern, almost closed tight against wind and rain, only shed enough light to illuminate a circle no wider than a man's outstretched arms. In that dim glow, three men huddled behind a handcart turned on its side, their cloaks hitched over their heads on spears to create a rough awning. The three men sat on rectangular shields, arms crossed over bronze breastplates to keep warm. All three were sodden wet, their tunics sticking in folds to their flesh, leather kilts glistening in the lamplight.

"Should've grabbed our bedrolls," said Loordin, his teeth chattering.

"Wasn't time," replied Muuril.

"What's keeping Gebriun and Faasil?" asked Gelthius. Not long ago he had heard the distant ring of bells in the city. "It's past Gravewatch by now."

"We should go," suggested Loordin. "If they ain't here yet, they've been caught. Simple as that. They could be leading them blackheads right here."

"Give them a few more hours," said Muuril. "They might be hiding out until the gates open again at Dawnwatch."

"Right enough," said Gelthius. "We'll start off second hour of Dawn, before the road gets too busy. Should put a few miles between us and the city."

"I'm off for a shit," said Loordin.

"In this?" said Muuril.

"Don't figure you want me dumping it in your lap, big man," replied the legionnaire. "I went to the place that puts all them Maasrite spices in the food last night and it ain't biding its time no longer."

Loordin disappeared into the darkness, already hitching up his kilt around his waist before he was out of sight.

"Can you sing?" asked Muuril.

"Not really," said Gelthius. "Why?"

The sounds of Loordin's evacuation erupted through the rain, causing both men to grimace. It was followed by a string of swear words and curses.

"Too late," said Muuril. "I've already got an image now."

"What do you reckon the king'll do next?" Gelthius asked, to take his mind away from the sounds of bowel movements and mild distress emanating out of the darkness.

"Ullsaard? Not sure. Perhaps you can help me figure this out. We go marching off to conquer Salphoria, and while we're away that little fuck of a son gets big ideas and decides to be king for himself, right?"

"So far, I think."

"We ain't in Carantathi more than two days before Ullsaard decides it's time to go home for a little reunion."

"Yeah, that seems to be what happened."

"So do you think the king got wind of what Urikh was up to?"

"Maybe heard a rumour or had a feeling," said Gelthius. "He couldn't have been certain, otherwise he would have come back with the whole army. That would put Urikh in his place, right enough."

"Well, he couldn't abandon Carantathi, could he? Pull out the legions and the Salphors would be back to their old tricks in no time at all."

"Bit of a shame, really. Being king is more of a pain in the arse than you think, isn't it?"

"It is when you've got a bitch's cunt like Urikh for a son. Hold up, the rain's dropping off."

Gelthius pushed himself to his feet and leaned out from under the cloak roof with a hand outstretched. Just as he was doing this, there was a yelp from the direction of Loordin. The legionnaire came stumbling back into the dell, a brown stain down the inside of his right leg.

"Fucking arsehole, you should've cleaned up!" snarled Muuril, standing up to grab Loordin's breastplate in preparation for shoving him back into the dark.

"Someone's coming!" Loordin hissed, slapping away the sergeant's arm. "Shut your holes!"

They all looked to where the legionnaire pointed, at a spark of light in the night. It was a lantern swaying on a pole by its pendulous movement, and soon the sound of the rain drumming on canvas pulled taut could be heard. As it approached, the light resolved itself into a lamp, hanging on the side of a cart coming up the road. The tramp and splash of an abada's tread became audible. There was a man in heavy robes and hood on the driving board, and Gelthius took the driver to be a Brother.

"Put out the lamp," he said, not looking at the others. The darkness around him deepened as one of them complied.

The cart stopped on the road, almost level with where the dell was. It was easy to find because there was a pair of trees flanking a broken gate; the landmark the five men of the Thirteenth had agreed would be their mustering point in the event of discovery.

"Something not right about this bastard," said Loordin. There was a scrape as he drew his knife from its sheath. Gelthius' hand went to his own knife and pulled it out; it would be too difficult to untie the cloaks from the spears in the blackness.

The cart driver stood up on his board, one hand on the reins, the other pulling back his hood. The light from the lamp was not enough to show his face as he turned left and right, staring into the gloom. Hitching the reins, the robed man jumped down onto the road and walked towards the gate.

"You pig fuckers had better be here!" a voice called out, revealing the hooded figure to be Faasil. Turning, he stepped into the light of the lantern, revealing his distinctive jutting chin and broken nose.

"You're late, you lazy cunt!" Muuril called back with a laugh.

The three of them forged out of their shallow hiding place towards the wagon. They were halfway there when Muuril stopped and grabbed Loordin by the arm.

"You," said the sergeant, propelling the legionnaire into the night, "still have shit on your legs. Show some self-respect."

"Yes, sergeant," Loordin called back. His following words were a lot quieter as the dim outline of the man disappeared, but still unintentionally loud enough to be heard. "What about all that shit in your head, you bossy bastard?"

"Leave him be, sergeant," said Gelthius as Muuril took a step after Loordin. He hated pulling rank sometimes, and even having any rank to pull, but it was amazing the effect it had on the others. Legion obedience was so ingrained, Muuril stopped immediately and turned back, despite being much larger and more experienced that the Salphor. "You can deal with him when we're back at camp with the king, right enough."

"Right enough," said Muuril, his voice low with menace.

They reached the light from the wagon lantern and found that Faasil was around the back of the cart, pulling something off the back.

"Here you go," said the legionnaire, tossing a rolled blanket to Muuril. The sergeant caught it with a grateful smile. He flapped out the thick woollen material and flung it around his shoulders as another blanket came arcing towards Gelthius.

"Where'd you get these?" asked the captain.

"Stroke of luck, to be honest," said Faasil. He climbed up under the wagon's awning and dropped something else over the side to Muuril. "Have a ham, sergeant."

Muuril caught it in one hand and held it to his chest like a babe to stop it falling into the dirt. Gelthius could smell the smoke and herbs from several paces away and his stomach growled, reminding him that they had not eaten since they had fled the city just after dusk.

"What luck?" Gelthius asked.

"Never mind that, where's Gebriun?" said Loordin, coming out of the darkness, legs now cleaned.

"Climb aboard," said Faasil, glancing coldwards up the road. "There could be blackcrests coming for us."

"Where's Gebriun?" snapped Gelthius, agitated by the man's evasiveness.

"I had to leave him," Faasil said quietly. His voice became louder, more defiant. "It was that or we'd both get caught. I feel like a right arsehole, I really do, but I had to run out on him, there was nothing else to do."

"Blackcrests?" said Muuril, heaving himself over the side with one arm, the ham still cradled in the other.

"Nope, it was our own, the Twenty-first," explained Faasil, as Gelthius pulled himself up to the driving board. It was an old instinct; as an officer he didn't have to drive if he didn't want to. Faasil stepped over from the back to sit beside the captain and offered to take the reins.

"I've got it," said Gelthius. "You just tell us what happened to Gebriun."

"We picked up Loordin's message just before we were due on at Howling, and so we were able to skip off from that and make our way to the barracks stores. Figured you three would be leaving in a hurry, but that we would have some time to get prepared for the trip to Menesun."

Gelthius slapped the reins across the shoulder of the abada and the wagon lurched as the horned beast took up the strain in the traces. With a creak of the axle, the cart started to move down the road.

"We were still loading up the wagon when word must have reached the barracks from the palace. Gebriun sensed something was wrong when he saw the off-watch company coming back together. He went off to find a captain to ask what was going on and I carried on getting blankets and rations."

With the abada plodding along, Gelthius was able to turn around and examine the contents of the cart. Muuril and Loordin lounged between piles of sacking, blankets, flour bags and meat cuts. There was a small keg stowed just behind the driving board. Loordin seemed to notice it for the first time just as Gelthius saw it.

"Since it hasn't stopped pissing on us since we got to Marradan, I'm hoping that isn't water," said the legionnaire.

"Oh? Right you are. Gebriun found it by the company kitchens. Dunno what's inside, but I figure on mead or wine."

"Let's have a tap and find out?" said Loordin, leaning across the cart, his knife appearing in his hand. Muuril's fingers closed around his wrist and pulled him back.

"Let's find out what happened to Gebriun first," said the sergeant. "No drinking until tonight."

"What does it matter?" said Loordin. He tried to snatch his arm from Muuril's grip but failed, wincing as he painfully twisted his shoulder. "Let go of me, you great big arsehole."

"Stop it," said Gelthius. "Not now."

"Not ever," growled Muuril, thrusting Loordin back against the side of the wagon before letting go. The sergeant leaned close to Loordin's ear. "I'm still the sergeant, and you still do whatever the fuck I tell you to do."

"Really?" said Loordin. "Says who?"

"Says the captain," replied Muuril holding up his thumb. He curled his fingers into a fist. "And his four mates."

Gelthius tossed the reins to Faasil and turned around further as Loordin met Muuril's stare. The third captain wasn't sure what to do. Muuril was right, but threats of violence were not the same as real discipline. In Salphor any chieftain could throw his weight around while he was in his prime or the best warriors gave him their support, but the authority of a sergeant, or a captain like Gelthius, had to stem from the whole weight of the legion being behind him, not just personal prowess and friends with muscles. Out in the late hours of the night, with not another legion soul within miles, Gelthius found that authority hard to summon up.

The sergeant and the legionnaire were still fixing each other with dagger glares, slowly leaning towards each other until there was only a hand's span between the tips of their noses. In the shadows made by the lantern on the awning pole Gelthius noticed that each man had a hand on the hilt of his knife, though neither had drawn their weapons.

The captain had to say something. He cleared his throat, but Loordin spoke before Gelthius had the chance.

"The captain and his four mates?" said the legionnaire, eyebrows raising. There was a twitch at the corner of his lips.

"Not my best," answered Muuril, talking out of the corner of his mouth in an attempt to still look grim and determined.

"That's as bad as 'The king and the four princes'," said Loordin, as the twitch became a smirk, which broke Muuril's resolve. The sergeant chuckled and sat back, shaking his head. Gelthius let out the breath that he had been holding and turned his attention to Faasil.

"Gebriun?" asked the captain, gesturing for the reins. Faasil handed them over and continued his story.

"I had the abada all hitched up and the wagon by the gate

when he comes running through the store yard, all panicked. 'They're after us, all the Thirteenth boys!' he yells at me, and there's Captain Daasin and twenty lads running after. The men on the gate hears this and start coming out of their little tower, shields and spears up and looking to mean business, and I know that unless that abada starts moving now, they're going to be on me and dragging me off that cart in a heartbeat."

"So you left Gebriun behind?" said Muuril.

"I had to!" Faasil's voice dropped to a pleading whisper. "I had to go, sergeant, otherwise they would have us both."

"You did right," said Gelthius, darting a look at Muuril, who twisted his head left and right with a couple of cracks of his neck, a sign of irritation, but said nothing to contradict the verdict of his captain. Gelthius patted Faasil on the arm, knowing that the legionnaire was feeling as sick as anything for leaving his friend behind. The man was hunched, shoulders and jaw tight with tension. "Gebriun will be fine. He wasn't even in the palace. He might get locked up, but he'll be fine."

"We can hope," said Loordin.

"More than hope, right enough," said Gelthius. "All Gebriun's done is get signed up with us. Nothing against him."

"Except attempted desertion and aiding a deserter," said Muuril, his voice low, his expression grim. "Flogging and company punishment, at best."

"Good news is they won't kill him," said Loordin. All of the men looked at him, surprised.

"It is a killing offence, aiding a deserter," said Gelthius, his heart heavy. "What makes you so sure?"

"Because they'll be needing him for information, won't they?" replied Loordin. "He's one of us, so they'll be interrogating him instead, not just slitting his throat."

Faasil moaned as if in physical pain, struck by the thought that he had abandoned his companion to torture.

"Better than both of you," said Muuril, "like you said. Anyhow, ain't like the Brotherhood to be that crude. More than likely Gebriun has been offered a chest of askharins for his troubles and is putting us right in the shit."

"What makes you say that?" Faasil said sharply. "You don't think Gebriun would turn on us. I thought we was tight."

"I'd sell you out for a hundred askharins," Loordin told the legionnaire. "Maybe fifty."

"But not the king," said Gelthius. The others looked at him with surprise and he shrugged. "That'd cost a thousand, at least, to turn on Ullsaard, right enough."

The three other men contemplated this for a little while, and it was Muuril who spoke first.

"I figure if you're going to drop the top man in the shit, you better make it worth your while," said the sergeant. "Three thousand askharins."

"Why stop at three?" said Loordin. "I'm sure the brotherhood could afford five."

"You lot are wrong, just wrong," snapped Faasil. "Stop joking about it, okay? Gebriun isn't going to turn on us, right?"

"Just saying, is all," said Loordin.

"Get some sleep, you look like you need it," Gelthius told Faasil. As the legionnaire jumped over the board into the back of the wagon, Gelthius looked at Muuril and Loordin. "You two as well."

"I can drive, if you're needing to close your eyes for a while," said Muuril, leaning an elbow on the board.

"No, I'm not tired anymore," said Gelthius. "I need to think; figure out what we're going to do next, right enough."

"That's easy," said Loordin, lying down with a flour sack as a pillow, his sodden cloak pulled over him up to his chin. "Keep heading hotwards until we reach Menesun. Then we tell the king's what happened, and leave it up to him."

"They'll be after us," said Faasil. "Can't take the main roads, they'll catch up with us for sure."

"Right enough," said Gelthius with a nod. He reached out to Muuril. "Still got that Ersua map?"

The sergeant ferreted around in his stuff and produced a tarred canvas envelope. He shook water droplets from the map case and handed it to Gelthius, who pulled the map from its cover and handed the envelope back to the sergeant. By the light of the lamp he could see the carefully painted greens, blues and reds of forests, rivers and roads.

"I'll figure it out, you lads get your sleep," he said.

Between the hectic, exhausting day, the sleepless night and the rocking of the cart, it was not long before the captain was accompanied by the snoring of the three men. Gelthius studied the map, but finding a safe route to Menesun was the least of his concerns.

MENESUN, ERSUA
Late Autumn, 213th year of Askh

Although he was still confident that he could resolve Urikh's challenge without bloodshed, Ullsaard was not taking any chances. While there was nothing in the report sent by his men in Marradan to suggest imminent conflict, there was always the possibility that if Urikh learnt of the true king's whereabouts he might persuade Asuhas to send a force to deal with matters.

The king's lakeside villa a few miles outside of Menesun was looking more like a legion fort than a summer retreat now that he and his small company had spent some time there. The main wall was surrounded by another made up of an earthen ramp set with sharpened logs about which was dug a ditch as deep as the embankment was tall, also filled with stakes. The side gate had been bricked up, and the flimsy main gate replaced with a barrier of heavier timbers riveted with bronze to break axe heads.

On the lakeside, which formerly had been a gentle white pebbled beach, Ullsaard had placed more stakes just beneath the surface of the water, to hole any boat that came within a quarter of a mile of the shore. That had been a laborious task of planning and careful execution. The king had, more by fortune than intent, brought Naamas Dor amongst his contingent, and the engineer was enjoying the chance to exercise his inventiveness in the fortification of their new encampment. Dor had devised timber-framed squares of tarred linen that could be lowered into the soft bottom of the lake to create a sort of lock system, allowing water to be pumped out and the lake bottom to be dug for the insertion of the spikes.

The landwards wall of the villa itself covered with scaffolding at the moment, surrounding the wooden skeleton of a new tower overlooking the approach from Menesun. Meanwhile Dor had teams of legionnaires working in the courtyard sawing and chiselling pieces of wood and twining thick rope into springs, to make a spear thrower that would be hauled up to the tower when complete.

The engineer had other plans too, and had spent the afternoon explaining them to Ullsaard as the pair had watched the unfolding works.

"It's not like we'll be able to hold off a legion or anything, but we can sleep a bit safer at nights," said Dor as the two of them walked along the stone beach. He had just been explaining his idea of tar-filled pits behind the walls, which could be set alight if the enemy tried to break through or climb over.

"I don't want another Askhan wall," said Ullsaard, glancing at the engineer. Dor was a solidly built man, though much shorter than the king. His face was constantly darkened with stubble, and his scalp was the same. As he spoke he gestured frequently with grime-stained, knobbly-knuckled hands with broken fingernails. He walked with a slight limp; a pale scar ran along his right shin from foot to knee as evidence of some accident or battle injury in the past.

"I don't understand, king," replied Dor. "The Askhan Wall is a marvel; even more of an achievement when it was built."

"And completely pointless," said Ullsaard, stopping. "If

someone comes here looking for a fight, I want to be ready, not half-prepared to weather an attack from the whole empire. We don't need to be legion-proof, just able to defend ourselves.

"It would help if you were to tell me who might be attacking, king," said Dor, not meeting Ullsaard's eye. "The Mekhani are the closest threat, do we need to dig behemodon traps?"

"Are you taking the piss?" snapped the king.

"Not at all!" Dor replied hurriedly, and Ullsaard could tell from the shock on the engineer's face that his suggestion had been serious.

"I don't think behemodon pits will be needed," said Ullsaard. Dor was still looking crestfallen at the king's accusation. "If it comes to it, I'll just punch them, eh? Look, these works are just precautionary. I am going to be spending a bit of time here, so I want to feel secure."

"I understand, king," said Dor, though he could not wholly mask a dubious look. The engineer quickly looked away, across the lake. Ullsaard followed the man's gaze, seeing the black sails of a few fishing vessels in the distance. The lake was not quite so big that it stretched to the horizon, and the surrounding hills on the duskwards side could be seen, dotted with small crofts that were home to a few scattered goatherds and peat diggers.

It was a nice, semi-wild spot, and that was why Ullsaard had originally chosen it. He and Cosuas had driven Mekhani invaders back across the hills from here and by ancient right of the conqueror the lands had been given to Ullsaard as first captain of the Thirteenth. It had been that victory that had secured his elevation to General of the Blood, and aside from a brief visit before his attack into Mekha Ullsaard had not been back.

There was a muted beauty about the place. Ullsaard was not one for landscapes usually; he was too practical. However, the pale blue-grey of the lake, the washed-out purples and greens

of the heather-covered hills and the dark canopies of the lakeside woods had an undeniable appeal.

"Do you need me for anything else, king?" Dor broke into
Ullsaard's short reverie.

The king looked at the distant slopes and followed their line
around the lake to where they were split by the Menes river,
from which the local town took its name. There were rough
pastures on the slopes, where pigs and goats were driven out
to feed.

It was quaint and reminded Ullsaard of the wooded hills of
Enair where he had been raised. It was also too easy for an
enemy to ford across the mouth of the Menes and attack along
the shore.

"How would you widen a river?" he asked, the question
eliciting a smile of approval from Dor.

COLDWARDS OF THEDRAAN, ERSUA
Late Autumn, 213th Year of Askh

Nonchalantly leaning against the gatepost of a farmstead, Gelthius bit into the dark red apple in his hand. He chewed slowly, watching the column of Legionnaires disappearing into the distance, heading duskwards along the new Salphor road. Ranks after rank of black-crested soldiers marched in ragged lines, a veritable company of Brothers in black robes to accompany them.

"Ah, the bastards are going the wrong way," said Muuril, standing on the wagon by the gate, one hand held against the watery afternoon sun. The weather had turned fair for the last couple of days, drying puddles that dotted the paved the road the men from the Thirteenth had been following.

It had been a close run thing for the first two days since their escape from Marradan. They had been only a few miles away from the city when the five hundred blackcrests had marched out. With the Brotherhood's soldiers close behind, Gelthius had stayed on the main road, pushing the abada for a couple of extra hours each evening to open up some distance on the following column. Heading for Thedraan, where he hoped to lay low with his family, the third captain had been torn between avoiding the pursuing force and warning Ullsaard.

It had been Loordin, unusually, who had convinced the captain to head for the king's villa as quickly as possible, even though they risked being caught by outriders on kolubrids, or by a garrison that might receive word ahead of them. The legionnaire had put it succinctly: "If they get to the king, we're all fucked one way or the other."

So they had kept to the road and made the best time they could, and had reached the brow of a hill crested by the road a few miles from the streets of Thedraan. The town could be seen to hotwards, almost empty now that the last market had ended and the farmers had gone back to their holdings, and the nobles back to the larger, comfortable towns and cities.

Gelthius moved back to the wagon, and saw Faasil staring intently at the column of legionnaires heading dawnwards. Even when Gelthius pulled himself up to the driving board beside him, Faasil's gaze was fixed on the departing troops.

"What now?" asked Muuril. "They clearly ain't heading for Menesun."

"I reckon Gebriun gave them the run around a bit," said Gelthius. There was a small but noticeable flinch from Faasil when Gebriun was named. "Must have told them the king was in Salphoria."

"We head back to the king, fast but not reckless, and let him decide, right?" said Muuril. "No attracting attention or anything."

"Sounds good to me," said Gelthius.

"We can't see our folks in Thedraan," said Muuril. "Got to keep going past."

"Why not?" asked Loordin. "My wife won't be happy about that, and I've got a two year-old boy I haven't seen since he were born. She finds out I was only a mile away and didn't come by, she'd tear my balls off."

"They'll want to come with, won't they?" said Muuril. "If the king's expecting a fight, and it looks like he'll get one, we don't need a bunch of women and kids at the villa."

Loordin directed a plaintive look at Gelthius.

"Right enough," the Salphor said with a sigh, admitting the truth of the sergeant's words. "And if word gets out that there's men from the Thirteenth back, it could cause other problems too."

"Right, well you can tell Maagri that when I do get to see her, right? It'll be your balls, not mine, right?"

"If she's as understanding as my Maredin, I'm sure your balls'll be fine," said Gelthius. He met Loordin's stare with a straight face for as long as he could, which was not long, and then the pair of them burst out laughing.

"I'll take Maagri over Maredin, any day," said Loordin. He stood up and clapped a hand to Gelthius' shoulder. "You don't have need for that pair of hairy prunes anyway, do you? You haven't used them in years."

Gelthius smiled but said nothing. Faasil had been quiet throughout, making no mention of his sister and two daughters in Thedraan; his wife had died after the birth of their second child. He wore the same determined stare he had been directing towards the legions.

"Get us on, right enough," said Gelthius, pointing at the reins that hung beside Faasil. "Five days at least until we reach Menesun."

There had been less clatter and clamour around the villa in the past few days. Dor was running out of improvements to make to the defences, and Ullsaard was running out of patience with Dor's more outrageous suggestions for defensive fortifications and devices. Work was still ongoing on the outer rampart of earth and stakes, and walls were being built further up the road leading to the villa, to provide rally points and cover for archers defending the approach. The spear thrower had been finished and hauled into position to the roof tower, mounted on the same system of wheels and gimbals as the ones of the Askhan Wall, apparently. It could traverse almost all of the way around a circle, leaving only a small blind spot to duskwards where it could not point. The tower itself was sparse, made of wooden beams and rope, with no real cover for the men at the top – anything more substantial might prove too heavy for the villa walls, Ullsaard had been informed.

Dor was currently in Menesun commandeering the small forge that the locals ran. He needed to make bronze heads for the bolts, and there was no way of doing that properly at the villa. He had also commissioned a large number of clay pots from the brickworks outside Genladen, which he intended to fill with oil and stopper with wicks to create firebombs. There was also a need for more arrows, though they would have sharpened, fire-hardened wooden tips rather than proper arrowheads because there was not enough bronze for everything.

Standing on the balcony of the main bedchamber, Ullsaard could see the gate, the courtyard and down the hill towards Menesun. If he looked to his right, he could just about see a loop of the lake shore. The largest part of the villa was three storeys high, and the king's chambers were on the top floor; the other two floors had been turned into dorms and additional storage for his company of men. On the coldwards end of the villa, to the king's right, a single-storey wing jutted out from the front of the building, inside which Blackfang was housed in a dark pen.

The villa itself was made of stone blocks, heavily plastered, capable of withstanding even a direct hit from a catapult. The paint was cracking in places, the plaster's off-white showing in patches through the dark ochre and patterns of red and blue spirals. The roof was not so secure, being made of red clay tiles. Dor had been into the attic space under the roof and secured heavy canvas sheets between the tiles, toughened with strips of leather to prevent shrapnel scything down into the upper storey, but there was nothing to stop a well-placed boulder plunging down through every floor.

There were smaller, timber-built structures inside the wall of the compound – a storeroom, tool shed and other outbuildings. To hotwards, about fifty paces outside the wall, was the abada corral. Three of the beasts plodded about inside the reinforced fence, munching on the long grass. The road leading from the gate bent sharply left about a hundred paces from the compound wall, turning to Menesun that lay three miles to hotwards. Everything else was a mixture of grassy pasture, and gorse and heather-covered hills, until Ullsaard could see only a green and purple blur in the distance.

The wind was strengthening, bringing a chill off the lake, and he had a cloak wrapped around his shoulders, over a shirt, jerkin and breastplate. He remembered complaining to Cosuas about the scorching heat of Mekha, but a long and cold campaign across Salphoria, and the dampness in the air now, made that seem like a lifetime ago. It was less than two hundred miles to the official border with near-Mekha, where the plains of Ersua eventually gave way to the sun-baked lands of the Mekhani.

He had never felt the cold like this before, and wondered if he had caught something in Salphoria, or if it was just his age. He would be fifty at the start of the next year. Askhans did not celebrate birthdays, but reckoned their age from the midsummer new year after they were born. It was a good age, not the longest lived, but older than many he had known. Longevity was most likely another gift of the Blood.

Although everything was shaping up nicely, the king was beginning to regret his course of action, as sensible as it had seemed at the time. There had been no runners from the men in Marradan for nearly eight days, which meant that either something bad had happened to them, or there was nothing worthwhile to report. This latter possibility made Ullsaard wonder if he should have gone directly to Marradan instead of scurrying down to Menesun to make a bolthole. It had been the cautious, sensible option, and that almost made it the bad choice in Ullsaard's eyes.

He had been burnt too many times to not watch his back though, and the present situation required a delicate approach; not Ullsaard's strongest trait. This was not war, not yet, at least. They were still in the realm of pure politics, and that was a world that was muddied and vague, and still something of an undiscovered territory to Ullsaard. He wished he had Noran with him, to be that voice of calm and caution, to weigh in against the king's natural desire to act.

You have me.

"When you choose to interfere," Ullsaard replied quietly. It was the first time since leaving Carantathi that the ancient king had made his presence known. "Where were you before I crossed into Ersua? Advice might have been helpful then."

Without the Crown as my anchor I... drift, and it is hard to settle in your thoughts. For the first time, Ullsaard felt that he not only heard Askhos' words but could feel something of the man within him; he felt the old king's uncertainty. *I admit, I do not know what is going to happen to us now. The Crown was the lock and the key, the ship and the anchor. I think Lakhyri sought to cast me out altogether.*

"Where? Where would you be cast out to?"

Do you remember when you dreamt you were in my tomb, Ullsaard? The king shuddered, which was all the answer Ullsaard needed. *That is right. It was in endless nothingness of stars and dust, you said. The Crown was my tomb and my womb. The only beacons I have left in that emptiness are your thoughts.*

"How can the Crown be a place?"

Do you really want to know the answer to that question? Ullsaard did, and the old king knew it. There was the mental equivalent of a sigh. *When looked at from the top of the hill in front of you, this villa might seem solid, yes? That what you can see is everything there is to see?*

"Like a box, with its lid closed?"

Exactly. You have a good mind, Ullsaard. Something else I gave to you through the Blood. It is a shame you use it so sparingly.

Ullsaard's impatience flared and he felt a reaction from Askhos, as if the king had flinched. The current king did not mention what he had felt, and Askhos continued his explanation without remark.

All things are like this house. They seem to us solid because we look at them from far away. We do not have eyes powerful enough to see inside the little windows and doors. In that space, between the smallest pieces of what a thing is, you can hide entire universes. The Crown appeared to be a thing of gold and iron, as solid as the floor or your head, but it was a gateway into another place, filled with nothing save for my consciousness and… Well, it does not matter what else is in there.

It was there again, the hesitation and fear Ullsaard had felt before. There was a lot that Askhos had never told him, and never would, but just as the ancient king could see Ullsaard's thoughts, Ullsaard now had a sense of what Askhos was thinking.

"There are other things in the void between, aren't there?"

None of this is relevant to your present predicament. Do you wish to have my help or not?

"You might have something to say that is useful," said Ullsaard, resolving that he would return to the subject of the place in-between when he had the opportunity. If Askhos' grip on reality was as bad as the king claimed, it made sense for Ullsaard to take what he could from Askhos' knowledge and experience while he could.

You fear that through inaction you have surrendered the advantage to your son.

Ullsaard watched as the guard was changed below. The men at the gate sloped off towards the kitchens while the new legionnaires on duty took up their positions. It did not matter whether they were in the mountains of Salphoria, the deserts of Mekha or a well-appointed village in Ersua, soldiers were always the same; the first thing on their minds after getting off duty was a bite to eat and something to drink.

Are you ignoring me? You haven't asked me what I would have done in your position.

"I don't want to know what you would do; I'll make a decision for myself."

I would have brought the legions back with me. You've conquered Salphoria once, you can always do it again if you are forced, but you only need to lose the empire once.

"Maybe you're right, but that doesn't matter now. I made my decision, now I have to live with it."

It's not too late. Send messengers to Salphoria and bring back the legions.

"And do what with them? Start another war?"

You are a general, one of the finest to have ever lived, and you keep hiding from that fact.

"I'm not going to turn this into a war, not again," said Ullsaard. "I'll not have thousands of my men dying because of Urikh's vanity."

Then give up your claim to the Crown. Disappear and become an ordinary man, and let Urikh rule. One day, not too distant, you will die of old age anyway, and your son will be the true king. Ullsaard could not allow that, and it was more than just pride that stopped him from slinking away to Cosuan or Salphoria. *Of course, the lovely Allenya, pillar of your life.*

"Don't even think about her!" snarled Ullsaard. A couple of men in the yard below glanced up at the balcony; the king's anger had added volume to his voice. Keeping his words quiet, Ullsaard continued. "I'm not going to abandon her, or let her think I am dead."

So, what you mean to say is that you'll not have thousands die by your vanity, but you will for the love of your wife.

"Allenya would not have it, so neither can I," said Ullsaard. He turned around and leaned back against the balcony rail, closing his eyes. "I would drown Greater Askhor in blood to be with her again, but she would not take a man who could do that."

You are a man who could do that, and still she loves you.

"None of this is helping," said Ullsaard. He opened his eyes and crossed his arms. "I do not have my legions to hand, and I am not going to start a war. Accept that, and tell me what you think."

You must make embassy to the governors, as you have already concluded. Urikh cannot command the direct loyalty of any legion except perhaps the First and the soldiers of the Brotherhood. As you robbed me, as Lutaar, of my forces, you must have every other legion loyal to you. The threat of force will be enough to bring Urikh to his knees, without having to spill a drop of blood.

"That's it? You tell me what I already know and call it advice?"

Go in person, do not send messengers.

"Why not? It would take a long time to visit all of the provinces."

When I sent heralds to the tribal chieftains, they ignored my pleas and demands. Some of the chieftains even slew my messengers because what I asked of them was so outrageous. My heralds having failed, I went to the chieftains myself. No ambassador, no herald, can ever argue with the full weight of your authority, nor give concession or make demand like a king in person.

Ullsaard considered this. His primary concern had been to keep his return secret. He had failed in that goal, even if Urikh was not yet aware of his father's homecoming. The only course of action left to Ullsaard was to control, as best he could, the way the news of his survival was spread. The more people that saw him, the harder it would be to deny his return as a baseless rumour.

Now you are using that brain of yours. Ullsaard felt a moment of warmth, of genuine pride from the shade of his ancestor. *It is a shame that I had to take control of all my sons, I am sure they would have made me very proud as kings.*

Hearing excited voices for below, Ullsaard returned his attention to what was happening in the courtyard. The main gate was being opened for a man in kilt a tunic – Ullsaard recognised him as the runner he had sent out the previous evening, Kaathan. The soldier was talking with the men at the gate as he came in, and they turned and pointed to the balcony.

"What is it?" Ullsaard shouted. "Why are you back so soon?"

The legionnaire hurried across the yard and stood beneath the balcony. Ullsaard could not tell if the dampness on the man's skin was moisture from the air or sweat, but he was breathing quite heavily and took in a gulp of air. His black hair was cut short, like all legionnaires, and the wet made it clump into haphazard spikes. Kaathan bowed his head until Ullsaard called for him to stand up.

"I was leaving Genladen this morning, my king, just a few miles further up the road, when I met with Captain Gelthius and the others." Ullsaard absorbed this information without comment. "He sent me back, to tell you that it might not be safe here. Governor Asuhas definitely knows where we are, or thinks he does."

"What else?"

"Governor Asuhas is definitely in league with Urikh, my king. Captain Gelthius said he heard as much with his own ears. Ersua might not be safe for us, he told me."

"And why is Captain Gelthius not telling me this himself, and why haven't I heard earlier?"

"I don't know that, he never said. Him and the others are making their way here as quick as they can. They'll be here before High watch at the latest. The captain said he would be telling you everything else he knows when he got here, but it was best if he told you himself."

Sounds suspicious. I don't know why you trust that Salphor mongrel. And you made him captain?

"He's honest and loyal, and that's better than most of you pure Askhans," said Ullsaard, although the truth was that as one of the Blood he was about as Askhan as could be possible, even if he had been raised in Enair.

"I'm sorry, my king, what did you say?" said Kaathan. "Did you want me to go to Askh?"

"What? No, I don't want you to go to Askh. Since there's no point you going to Marradan, I want you to head off to Thedraan instead. See what you can find out about Asuhas' business lately. Find out if word of my return has spread to there yet."

"Yes, my king," said Kaathan, bobbing his head and lifting a fist to his chest in salute. "I shall leave within the hour."

Ullsaard flexed his fingers on the balustrade of the balcony, squeezing the wood with calloused fingers. He had known that Asuhas would learn of his return soon, but it was still slightly unsettling for it to be confirmed so quickly. If Asuhas knew, then there was every reason to expect that the Brotherhood knew as well. Runners moving from precinct to precinct could make the journey from Marradan to Askh in as little as fourteen days, if they could get a swift ship down the Ladmun to the Greenwater.

Tonight, not fourteen days.

"What's that?" said Ullsaard, moving into the sparsely furnished chamber adjoining the balcony. This had been a room appointed for receiving visitors, with many chairs and sofas. Ullsaard had turned it into his command office, removing all but one chair and two tables. He sat in the chair behind the largest table and sorted through the pile of papers for a map of Greater Askhor. "If we leave tomorrow, we can cut around the hotwards side of the lake and head towards my Apili estates in Okhar. We'll be into Nalanor before Urikh hears we're in Ersua."

If the Brotherhood knows that you have returned, and wish for your son to learn of the news, he will either know it already or he will know it by tonight.

"They would have had to have sent a runner the moment I reached the border," said the king. "Impossible."

There are other ways to communicate.

"A carrier bird? Kolubrid rider? Even that takes time."

Listen to me! It was the first time the old king had ever filled Ullsaard's thoughts with such urgency. The king's head throbbed for a moment, but he caught a backwash of anxiety from the trapped spirit that added venom to his demand. *The Brotherhood have means by which they can pass message from precinct to precinct in a matter of hours. Think of it as speaking across that gap between real things that we spoke of earlier. The Grand Precincts receive all of the messages sent between the lesser precincts, and Lakhyri will be monitoring them for any mention of your return.*

Ullsaard groaned and rested his head in his hands, elbows on the papers in front of him.

"That fucking Brotherhood! You told me they would be loyal to me as the new king. They are nothing of the sort. I wish I had never reinstated the bastards."

Most Brothers are honest, dedicated servants of the empire, Ullsaard. If they are told that Urikh is the rightful king, they will believe it. Why would they not? Lakhyri must keep a lid on the lie he has created about your death. While he masquerades as Head Brother he has full authority from the king, but if the falsehoods he has used to install Urikh begin to spread, his control will crumble.

"You seem quite keen to help me, all of a sudden. I thought that you and Lakhyri shared the same goal?"

Perhaps once, though I was never as dedicated as he was. That is why I chose to be immortal in spirit but not body, as he is. Our masters were

*a means to an end for me, and if I am honest, for the past hundred years
I have dedicated less and less effort towards fulfilling their demands.*

"What masters? Who does a king serve?"

*Nobody, and that's my point. Let me just assure you that Lakhyri
and I have diverged in our objectives, and in seeking to achieve his,
my brother tried to kill me – kill me forever. I knew that he would, as
soon as he saw me in your dream. He realised that I like the physical
life too much, and that cannot be countenanced by those I once served.*

Ullsaard could feel obstinacy in Askhos and chose not to
pursue the point for the moment. Until Gelthius arrived and
reported in detail what he had unearthed there was little else
Ullsaard could do for the moment. He crossed the room to a
set of shelves where his maps were held, and pulled out one
covering Ersua and Okhar. If he needed to move to his estate
at Apili, it was best that he started the preparations now.

Yet even as he moved back to the table, Ullsaard returned
to the words of Askhos. Pulling a leaf of blank parchment towards him, the king flicked open the lid of an ink pot and took
up a quill.

He had a couple of letters to write first.

II

The king was sitting at a broad table poring over maps when
Gelthius entered at his call. The third captain had decided to
come alone to make his report; there was no need for Muuril,
Loordin and Faasil to complicate matters further. The Salphor
knew that it had been a mistake for the spies to draw attention
to themselves, and he was regretting the decision to back
Muuril's plan as he looked at Ullsaard. The king's brow was
knotted in concentration, and he did not look up when he spoke.

"What is Asuhas planning to do, captain?"

"I can't say, King," said Gelthius. He decided that short, honest answers would be his best policy. There was no point trying

to get away from what he had done. "He didn't talk about that when we was listening."

"I see." The king grunted and sat back in his chair, directing a fierce stare at Gelthius. "Later you can explain why you are back here so soon, without that information. First, tell me what you did manage to find out. Leave out nothing."

"Yes, King," said Gelthius. He took a deep breath and held it for a moment, telling himself not to rush his words, even though he was as nervous as he was when he went into battle. He slowly let the air out of his lungs and began. "There is a detachment of blackcrests looking for us. They think you must be in Salphoria, or leastways we watched them going towards Salphoria a few days ago."

"A few days? Be more specific, Captain. When did you see them, and where?"

"Just a few miles coldwards of Thedraan, King. They took the new road duskwards, towards Magi... towards the ruins. That was five days ago."

The king grunted and pulled out a map. From where Gelthius was looking it was upside down, but even so it was easy to recognise the Magilnada Gap. An idle thought entered Gelthius's mind as the king studied the chart, his finger moving along the main road: would the Magilnada Gap be renamed now that the city no longer existed? If people started calling it something else, other people wouldn't know where they meant, but it seemed stupid to name an area after a city that wasn't there anymore.

"And you're certain that they did not double-back?"

The king's question caught Gelthius off-guard.

"No, King. I mean, yes, King, I'm sure. Or at least, when we met Caaspir, one of your runners, in Thedraan, I told him to keep an eye out for them blackcrests and he never caught us up with any news, so I figure they've kept on into Salphoria, right enough."

"So you sent Caaspir to scout the blackcrests?"

"Yes, King." Gelthius nodded hard, though judging by the king's expression, Ullsaard was not too happy about that course of action.

"You did not think it would be better to send him back here with your news?"

"I did think about that, but I thought that some news was best delivered by me, in person, right enough. Caaspir's a young man, I'd have to have written everything down and to be honest, King, writing is not my strong point. I thought speaking to you would be more accurate."

"I see," said Ullsaard, though still his frown was saying otherwise. He checked a wax slate. "And what about the runner in Marradan? Josstin? Did you not think to send him ahead of you?"

"We had to leave in a hurry, a right awkward situation it was. There wasn't no time to send word to Josstin, and we only just warned Faasil and Gebriun in time."

"I noticed that Gebriun was not with you when you returned," said the king. Gelthius knew that nothing got past Ullsaard, and he had been unsure how to raise the topic. "Did you find some other use for him on the way back?"

"Bad luck it was, that they got to him before he could get out of the city. The Twenty-first, I mean."

"All right, it seems that we'll have to start at the beginning, to make everything clear."

And so that is what Gelthius did, narrating everything that happened between the group's departure from Genladen to the moment Muuril and the captain encountered Governor Asuhas. Ullsaard listened to it all without comment or question, occasionally nodding or shaking his head. When it came to mentioning the appearance of Anglhan, Gelthius hesitated. The king had razed an entire city to get revenge on the traitorous governor – rumour had it that Anglhan had threatened Ullsaard's family – and Gelthius was not sure how Ullsaard would react to the double blow of Anglhan's survival and his continued connections to the king's enemies. It was news of the worst kind and Gelthius sincerely wished he had brought Muuril now, for some support and perhaps to let the sergeant pass on this turd-like nugget of information.

"What is it?" said the king. "What are you muttering to yourself about? You heard voices on the stairs coming up and you stayed in the great hall. What happened next, captain?"

"The governor weren't alone, King. It was him, Asuhas, coming up the steps, and there was another man with him. It was Anglhan, King. Anglhan Periusis, my old debt guardian. The governor of…"

Gelthius' voice trailed away as he abandoned trying to fill the silence left by his announcement. The king had gone very still, like an ailur about to pounce. His eyes were looking at something else, straight through the third captain. There came the scratch of fingernails on wood as the king's hands formed fists on the table.

"Anglhan?"

Gelthius might have expected the king to snarl or hiss or shout the name, but instead the word was uttered with no emotion whatsoever. It was a dead sound; disbelief, rage, despair and many conflicting reactions countering each other to create an utter lack of feeling. It was worse than any bitter snarl or angry bellow that Gelthius had heard before.

"Yes, King," Gelthius managed to say. And because the king said nothing further, he added, "I'm positive, King; saw him with me own eyes."

"Good," said Ullsaard. "That's good."

"Is it?" Gelthius' surprise made his voice rise sharply in pitch. He coughed in embarrassment and tried hard to keep his tone even. "Why's that good?"

"If Anglhan isn't dead, that means I still get to kill him," said Ullsaard, looking properly at the captain. The king's eyes were narrowed and there was a twitch in his jaw.

Not wishing to stay any longer than necessary in the king's presence, Gelthius chose to continue with his story, detailing what he remembered of the conversation between Anglhan and Asuhas. When the captain mentioned that the two of them had agreed to keep a man called Leraates in the dark about Ullsaard's possible whereabouts, the king regained his animation.

"Leraates is one of the highest ranking members of the Brotherhood, and if Anglhan and Asuhas are working against the Brotherhood we should exploit that split," said Ullsaard.

"Right enough, King," said Gelthius. "I should mention that, at this point, Sergeant Muuril made the suggestion that we should kill both the traitorous cunts; his words. I thought that we would get caught for sure if we did that, and then you're be none the wiser."

"A difficult decision," said Ullsaard, "but as I mentioned, you leave me the pleasure of killing that bloated pile of shit. Your appreciation of the strategic overview is welcome, captain."

"Thank you, King. Erm, though I'm not rightly sure I know what for."

"You were right to think of the big picture, Gelthius. Getting caught would not have helped me in the slightest. Now that I know Asuhas is working against the Brotherhood, I can drive a wedge between them and maybe get some leverage on both."

Ullsaard's words brought to mind how a tree was felled, with his talk of wedges and leverage, but Gelthius wasn't quite sure how they applied in the current situation. Determined to finish his story and get back to the others, he pressed on with his explanation.

"The Twenty-first answers to Asuhas, of course, so when we

was discovered, it was them that came looking for us as well as the Blackcrests. Faasil and Gebriun was getting supplies but Gebriun was caught."

"Unfortunate for Gebriun," said Ullsaard.

"Right enough, King, right enough. It was hard to leave knowing that them bastards have got him, but we had to do our duty first."

"Commendable," said Ullsaard. "I knew I had picked the right man, and that you had picked the right men, as soon as I had spoken to you. I like you, Gelthius; loyal, dependable, sharp enough in a tight spot. The men like you too."

Gelthius bobbed his head in thanks and chose to say nothing. Ullsaard stared at him, in the way a man stares at a whore or a meal, trying to decide if he finds what he sees appealing. Realising that king was thinking, the captain kept his tongue and endured Ullsaard's scrutiny by studiously looking at the line of a shelf just past the king's shoulder.

"I know that at the moment my favour isn't what it ought to be, but I'm going to make you a second captain. Also, I think it fair reward for your actions in the last few days. Also, pass the word to Muuril. I'll make him third captain."

Gelthius was not so sure about promoting Muuril, and his expression must have betrayed that fact to the king.

"No? Don't you want to be a second captain, Gelthius?"

"It's not, that. No, King, I'm very thankful for that, right enough. No, it was Sergeant Muuril I was thinking about."

"Doesn't he deserve some recognition? It was his idea, you said, to break into the governor's quarters."

"Oh, it was his idea, for sure, and he should get credit, just like Faasil and Loordin for doing their part too. It's just that I don't think Muuril would want to be a captain. I mean, he'd say yes and all, cause he wouldn't want to let you down, but in his heart he likes being a rankman, and sergeant suits him better than being an officer. The men wouldn't follow him the same if he wasn't one of them."

"I see." Ullsaard dragged his fingers back and forth across his bearded cheek, eyes straying to look out of the window. "I think you are right, captain. I remember when I moved from sergeant to third captain; that was when I knew I wanted to become first captain. You start to look up at the other officers, not across to your men."

"Not me, King," said Gelthius, wanting to quickly quash any hint that he would put his promotion before anything else. Ullsaard looked at him with a doubtful expression.

"I just made you second captain, and you tell me you wouldn't want to be first captain?"

"No, with all respect, King. Seems like a lot of work, and I ain't the brightest. I thank you for the credit you've given me and the favour you've shown me, but I wouldn't want a legion. I mean, in my experience, it's them sort of thoughts that starts getting you into trouble, isn't it?" Ullsaard's eyebrows raised a fraction further and Gelthius realised what he had said. "Begging your pardon, but I meant that some folks are suited to being on top and some aren't, and I'm one of them what isn't. Suited to being on top, I mean. And those that ain't suited but try to get to the top anyway are setting themselves up for the biggest fall. If I fall, I'd rather it weren't from such a height, if it's all the same."

For all the time he had spent in close proximity with the king, he still felt horribly intimidated by the man every time he was near him. Ullsaard had a feral power that overawed lesser men, and Gelthius thought of himself as a man who was easily impressed. His life had not prepared him for conversation with governors and generals and kings.

"Well, second captain, you've not even got a third of a company here, so your dreams of conquering the empire will rest for the moment," said the king. Ullsaard seemed to catch up with what he had said and his good humour disappeared. "Isn't that just what I'm trying to do? Take on my son and Greater Askhor with fifty men? I must be mad."

Sometimes Gelthius wasn't sure if the King was talking to him or to himself, and at that moment, Ullsaard's attention definitely seemed to be focussed elsewhere. The Blood had given Ullsaard great strength, charisma and resolution, but in Gelthius' view it had brought some less desirable traits with it. He wondered if a susceptibility to madness was one of them.

"Do you have any orders, King?" asked Gelthius.

"Yes, I do," replied Ullsaard. The king nodded, seeming to agree with himself. He pulled a chalk-covered slate from under some parchments on the table and held it out to Gelthius. "I need forage parties to go out and get supplies from Menesun and Genladen; everything's on this list."

Gelthius took the list and gave it a quick look: wagons and abada, rope, firewood, dried food, water butts, timber, shovels. The list filled the whole slate in the king's small script, and on the other side too Gelthius discovered when he turned it over. He had seen lists like this before.

"Are we leaving, King?" Gelthius glanced out of the window. "And just as we were settling into the place?"

"Two days, captain," Ullsaard said briskly, standing up. "I want to speak to each of the men that went to Marradan with you. Send Muuril in first, and tell Loordin and Faasil not to get themselves lost or put on guard duty."

"Right enough, King," said Gelthius, relieved to see Ullsaard back to snapping off orders, full of confidence. The captain lifted a fist to his chest and turned towards the door. He took a step and then turned back. Ullsaard was already walking towards his shelves. "Excuse me, King, but you hadn't settled on what to do with Muuril."

"It'll wait, captain," said Ullsaard. "I'll tell him myself."

"Right enough," said Gelthius. He walked to the door as quickly as would be polite and breathed a huge sigh of relief as he stepped out onto the landing.

He caught a glimpse of Muuril on the floor below, ducking back behind a corner. A moment later, the sergeant stepped out onto the lower landing, a nonchalant expression plastered across his face.

"Oh, all right there, captain?" said the sergeant, affecting surprise at their encounter.

"Enough shitting about, sergeant, I know you've been waiting for me," said Gelthius as he trotted down the stairs. "Find Loordin and Faasil, the king will want to speak to all of you, so be ready for when he sends word."

"Yes, captain," said Muuril, his smile fading. There was shouting down below, on the ground floor. Both men turned as someone came up the stairs, taking them three at a time. His face was drenched with sweat, his tunic also soaked with perspiration. Gelthius' stomach tightened as he recognised Caaspir, the runner he had left in Thedraan.

"Where's the king?" the legionnaire demanded, his voice a hoarse rasp. He was as red as a Mekhani, his chest heaved in and out and his arms and legs were trembling like a newborn goat.

"Whoa there," said Muuril, putting a hand on the man's chest to stop him going past. "Take a moment before you see the king. Get freshened up and catch your breath. Show some fucking respect, you look like you've run all the way from Thedraan."

"I fucking have," snarled Caaspir, knocking aside the sergeant's arm.

"The blackcrests?" said Gelthius, meeting Muuril's concerned look with one of his own.

"I fucking wish," said Caaspir. "It's the Twenty-first."

"How many?" said Gelthius, his heart pumping harder, sending a flush of heat through him. His stomach did another turn. "Where?"

"Coming here. The whole fucking legion!"

III

"What a fucking shambles," said Ullsaard. His words were pitched just loud enough to be heard by the men in the house behind him and the courtyard below; and the comment would be quickly passed to those by the shoreline and keeping watch down the road.

"Very slovenly," replied Muuril, the newly-named King's Companion. It was a title that had not been used since the chieftains had been turned into governors, but bestowing it upon Muuril had had the desired effect; the rangy man's chest was puffed out with pride and his breastplate was shining with more polish than ever before. It was the name that had been given to Askhos' original bodyguard, who had been the chieftain Ansarril. The Book of Askhos claimed Ansarril had personally killed forty men in one battle and saved the First King's life seven times during the conquest of Askhor. It was a rank without command, and Muuril was clearly loving the prestige of being the king's chosen man.

The two of them looked out across the fields at the lines of legionnaires marching from dawnwards, dividing into three lines. One column headed across the road leading up to Menesun, another to occupy the crest of a hill overlooking the villa from coldwards and the last was setting up a defensive line between the buildings of two farms about a mile apart from each other. What should have been a straightforward manoeuvre had been turned into a joke by the simple fact that two of the companies trying to head coldwards had been placed too far down the line of the march and had run into a company that was digging in next to the road.

"I reckon we shouldn't have too much trouble kicking in these bastard's cunts," said the Companion. "Hardly a veteran among them."

"You don't have to lift my spirits, Muuril," said Ullsaard, dropping his voice. "Save that for the men. We're heavily out-numbered and unless you think you can knock up a ship or boats for fifty men in the next two hours, we've got no line of retreat."

"I know it's not really for me to ask, but why did we stick around? We've had two days, we could have been sixty miles away and more. This lot would never find a small band of men over rough country."

"I'm the king, I have to make a stand," said Ullsaard, repeat-ing the exact words that had started his speech to the company the night before, when he had announced that they would be defending the villa rather than leaving. Most of the men had known about the coming of the Twenty-first before the king, and it had quickly become common consensus that Ullsaard wouldn't let them stay to get butchered. When the first day had past, the king had heard some rumblings and, independ-ently of each other, both Muuril and Gelthius had reported that the legionnaires were getting anxious. Ullsaard had filled them with the beer and food meant for the march to Apili and fired up their courage with a short but stirring speech.

"I thought we was saving the bullshit for the men," Muuril replied. Ullsaard smiled at the sergeant's attitude; there would be captains, never mind kings, who would have taken such words as insubordination. Ullsaard had never been that type of officer, and as long as there was respect for him and his position, he had never punished bad language or plain speaking. Oddly, he had noticed that often it was men who had been promoted from the ranks who came down hardest on that sort of thing, as if they were trying to balance out some deficit in their authority.

"If it wasn't the Twenty-first here, it'd be the Seventeenth at Apili," Ullsaard told his Companion. As he thought about the situation, the king's mood became fiercer and he gritted his teeth. "I'm not going to be chased all over *my* fucking empire. And I will not be bullied by a fucking governor."

Ullsaard noticed Muuril nod approvingly out of the corner of his eye, but his bodyguard said nothing for a few moments.

"Wish we had the rest of the Thirteenth with me, all the same," added Ullsaard, calming down.

"Too fucking right, for sure. We'd have given these bastards a good kicking at Marradan and you'd be in Asuhas' palace having choice words with the slippery little snake."

"The slippery snake comes to us, luckily," said Ullsaard. He pointed down the road, towards a line of five ornate wagons, each pulled by a team of four abada. Each wagon was the size of a small house, trundling along on five axles. There was a small contingent of kolubrid riders to either side, bearing pennants of grey and green; the golden icon of the legion was mounted on the side of the wagon at the front of the group.

"I don't understand why Captain Lutaan would march against you," Muuril said. "Donar and him have been loyal to you almost from the start of everything. And you've been good to him, approving him as first captain."

"Donar was loyal to Askhos before he joined me, and so was his nephew," said Ullsaard. "A lot of people were. Maybe Asuhas convinced Lutaan that when everything's finished, he'll be on the right side of this dispute if he stays with the governor."

"We're all loyal to Askhos," said Muuril, trying to hide his surprise, but doing a poor job of it. "You mean loyal to Lutaar."

Ullsaard recalled what he said and suppressed a grimace. He hadn't been contacted by the dead king since Gelthius had returned from Marradan. In a way Ullsaard was grateful to be free of the distraction, but he was also curious to know what Askhos would have made of his current predicament. Despite the ancient ruler's absence, he was still preying on Ullsaard's mind.

"Loyal to Lutaar, yes," Ullsaard said. He quickly saw an opportunity to change the topic of conversation. "I need you to bring the abada into the villa courtyard. Have them stabled by the hotwards wall. If we have to retreat back to the house, I want them roused up and running through the enemy."

"As you say," Muuril said with a salute.

When his Companion had left, Ullsaard continued to scrutinise the manoeuvres of the Twenty-first. He already knew from the information gleaned by Gelthius' mission that the legion was barely above half-strength: three thousand men at most. Weighed against this was the fact that he only had fifty, so mattered not whether it was three thousand, five thousand or fifty thousand. The enemy definitely had the advantage of numbers.

The Twenty-first were also, as Muuril had so eloquently pointed out, a bunch of inexperienced youths for the most part. With the exception of Captain Gelthius, every man inside the compound had been in the legions for at least five years, most of them seven or more; and even in his short time Gelthius had seen nearly a dozen battles, three of them big ones. Ullsaard had said as much to the legionnaires. "If there was a group of men who are going to hold their nerve, trust in their king and go down fighting, it's the battle-hardened bastards of the Thirteenth." Sentiments that would soon be tested to the limit, but Ullsaard really had no fear on that account.

He tried hard to concentrate on other advantages to his credit, rather dwell on the number of men ranged against his tiny force. He could hear the distant noise of the approaching army; the jingling of armour and tramping of feet was unmistakeable, even though it was barely audible yet. It was a noise that brought back so many memories; thirty years of fighting, in the ranks and as a commander.

The king remembered something Muuril had said to him after the men had been dismissed to their duties in the morning: "They'll fight for you, and they'll die for you. You've never been beaten, and they ain't ready to start losing now."

It was true that Ullsaard had succeeded time and again, when defeat had seemed likely, if not outright certain. Gelthius had said something similar when the king had been sneaking back into Greater Askhor, avoiding the army of Anglhan. Whatever happened, history would not forget King Ullsaard, he was sure of that; the man who had defied a king and conquered the most powerful empire in the world. What was fifty men against three thousand compared with that?

You did not achieve that greatness by blind faith in yourself.

"I wondered if you would show up," said Ullsaard. "You show your usually perfect timing."

In moments of heightened emotion, your thoughts are stronger and I can latch on to them, like a rope thrown to a drowning man. Askhos seemed less bombastic, and when he spoke of drowning men Ullsaard had a flash of recollection; of that endless gulf of stars and dust that swallowed everything. *Yes, my disassociation from the Crown is beginning to wear on my good nature and optimistic outlook. If you die, I shall be set adrift in the abyss, until madness consumes me and eventually my will to live can last no more and my essence evaporates into the void. It has been many years – longer than the two hundred and twelve since I founded this empire – since I feared death. Now oblivion seems certain, and I find that I do not wish to accept it meekly.*

"There is nothing certain about death today," growled Ullsaard. "I'm not finished yet."

I did not say today would see our deaths, but it will come one day.

"You've picked a bad time to rediscover your mortality, you old bastard. If you haven't got anything useful to add, keep quiet. I'm thinking."

What is your enemy's axis of weakness?

"I see none," said Ullsaard. The axis of weakness was a concept passed down by the Book of Askhos; the flaw in the enemy's organisation or deployment that had to be exploited for victory. "If we leave the sanctuary of the compound, we will be surrounded and annihilated. Even though they perform their manoeuvres like Mekhani, I cannot seize upon their inexperience."

You are missing my point. How can you forget so many hard-learnt lessons when you really need them? The axis of weakness here will not be military, it has to be personal. What are the weaknesses of the men you face?

"They are inexperienced, scared. They have drilled but only a handful will have seen actual battle and bloodshed."

Not the legionnaires, their commanders! Asuhas is a coward at heart; what about Lutaan? Will he give in if he does not have the easy victory he expects?

Pausing to consider this, annoyed that it had taken Askhos to point out how narrow Ullsaard had allowed his thoughts to become, the king considered the measure of the men leading the Twenty-First.

"Lutaan is innovative, brave. Donar trained him well, but he is not the most organised and has no experience of battlefield command; not of a whole legion. It could be that he will panic if he becomes flustered. Asuhas will want nothing to do with the fighting; he'll stay as far away as possible in his wagons."

Good. So how do you make Lutaan flustered? What pressure can you apply?

"Myself," said Ullsaard. "He was on my staff for a long time in Salphoria, before I sent him back with my recommendation to Asuhas. If he can look me in the eye and still order the attack, I'd be surprised."

Not when you start talking about how loyal his uncle is, and how well Donar has been faring under your patronage.

"That counts for nothing though, if Lutaan thinks he is up against the whole empire. When I toppled you, it was the first link in the chain to break that was the hardest. The fact that his legion is so dismal counts against me – I can't pretend that with the Twenty-first I have a chance of taking on Urikh."

Then let us consider something that you can control. What do you hope to achieve by fighting?

A flippant answer sprang to mind, but Ullsaard let it die before it reached his tongue. Whether of its own accord or prompted by Askhos, his mind lurched back to a sleet-filled sky and a narrow mountain road leading to Carantathi. He thought of Aegenuis, a king who had been a vain, proud man, and a man fuelled by drink, but who had sense enough to sacrifice his own rule for the protection of his people. What would Ullsaard achieve by resisting Asuhas? The death of fifty men? He had ruled for less than three years, his legacy would be a footnote in the chronicles.

I did not seek to sow doubt, but to ask a genuine question.

Ullsaard looked at the men by the road, their arrows in small bundles in the grass next to them; on the step built inside the wall and at the murder holes cut into the gate. Muuril had said they would die for their king, but did they have to? He saw the King's Companion walking back across the compound, followed by a dozen men leading the abada.

"Companion!" Ullsaard called out. It took a moment for Muuril to realised the shout was meant for him

"Yes, King?" the sergeant bellowed back.

Ullsaard considered his next words, for he was taking a risk, but he trusted his instinct.

"This battle does not have to be fought. Do you think I should give myself to Asuhas peacefully, Companion?"

"Not fucking likely, my King! That arsehole Asuhas means you harm, and as your Companion I can't let it happen. These men would rather die than spend the rest of their lives with the shame of knowing they laid down spear and shield to let their king be killed."

"Bollocks to Asuhas!"

Ullsaard was not sure where the shout had come from, but it was followed by several more colourful declarations of loyalty. Then someone, somewhere called out the king's name and this too was answered. The men on the wall turned and lifted their spears in salute, and the shouts were even heard by the archers up the road, who rose up from their places and waved their bows.

The chant then changed, led by a voice from up on the spear thrower tower.

"Thirteen! Thirteen! Thirteen!"

Leaning forward, Ullsaard craned his neck and could just about see Captain Gelthius raising his spear in time to the shouting. It echoed from the walls of the villa, and rang inside the chamber behind Ullsaard. The king grinned as he straightened.

"It doesn't matter what I want, these men will never let me surrender. I suppose I better win this battle for them."

Despite his bravado, Ullsaard was much of the opinion that winning or losing would not be down to his actions but those of his opposing commander, Lutaan. Ullsaard would have a better chance to get a measure of the man as a first captain soon – there was a delegation of soldiers advancing up the road beneath the icon of the Twenty-first. Ullsaard had a runner take a message out to the archers that the embassy was to be allowed to approach unmolested.

It was better that Lutaan did not get to see just how few men Ullsaard had; though if the other commander was worth his rank he would have got a fair idea from questioning the folk in Genladen. To ensure that Lutaan did not use the pre-battle pleasantries as a means to spy out the villa's defences, Ullsaard would meet him on the road, some distance from the compound. He called for Blackfang to be made ready and then put on his cloak, picked up his shield and golden spear and headed down to the courtyard.

Muuril was waiting for the king at the main doors, another legionnaire next to him holding the ailur's reins while a third tightened the cinch on her saddle.

"How many in the bodyguard?" the Companion asked.

"Just you," replied Ullsaard. "Lutaan really isn't going to try anything underhand."

"Are you sure? I'm handy with a spear, and you're no slouch, King, but the report is that Lutaan's got twenty men with him. If he wants to grab you, there's nothing we'll be able to do to stop him."

"We'll wait for him with the first line of archers. That'll give him something to think about."

"Aye, King, that'll suit me."

Ullsaard pulled himself up into Blackfang's saddle and signalled for the men at the gate to pull it open. With Muuril striding on his right, the king rode out of the compound. They walked about a quarter of a mile down the hill and then waited for Lutaan and his entourage to reach them. Ten men were crouched within a three-sided enclosure beside the road, their bows in hand, bundles of arrows laid out on canvas mats behind the stone wall of their redoubt.

"Lutaan's going to know you're here anyway, might as well show yourselves," Ullsaard said to them as he reined Blackfang to a stop next to the fortification. The men stood up and nocked arrows to the strings of their bows, watching the group of legionnaires marching in time up the hill. Their golden standard was shiny in the dull autumn sun, bright against the drab stone of the road. A glance up showed Ullsaard a sky filled from horizon to horizon with low, grey cloud. It was dim and miserable, and the wind was picking up. There was rain in the air and he hoped it would break before too long; an assault on the villa would be much more precarious on muddy ground and over slick stones.

Beside his icon bearer, Lutaan was garbed in his full regalia. He wore a long green cloak with a grey fur trim. His spear was iron-tipped and tied with a pennant of the same colours, and his shield was silvered, crafted into the snarling face of an ailur, the edge rimmed with more iron. The first captain had profited well from his exploits before returning from Salphoria, that much was obvious.

Lutaan held up a hand to halt his guard and carried on alone, quickly covering the remaining fifty paces to where Ullsaard waited. The King watched carefully and next to him he felt Muuril stirring, ready for action. The Companion's head turned left and right as he scanned the hillside pastures and scattered trees and bushes for signs of foes.

"I wish we had our icon," Muuril said quietly.

Ullsaard did not reply, but was glad that the icon of the Thirteenth was nowhere near Menesun; there was enough hinging on the next few hours without the future honour of the Thirteenth being put at stake. He dismounted from Blackfang and led her to a bare tree hanging over the road. Tying her reins around its slender trunk, he rejoined Muuril just at the other commander was reaching the sergeant.

"Hail Ullsaard," said Lutaan, stopping about ten paces away; well clear of a lunging spear thrust.

The king had seen Lutaan dozens of times before, attending to Donar, but this was the first time he really paid the man any attention. The first captain of the Twenty-first was lean, with tight muscles. His face had little fat and was clean shaven, his nose also thin, leaning slightly to the right from an old break and there was a short, ragged scar under his right eye. Eyes as grey as flint regarded Ullsaard solemnly. Lutaan had the same weathered flesh as most men in the legions, but a spray of freckles across his nose and cheeks betrayed a once-fair complexion.

"You remind me of your uncle," said Ullsaard, hoping that a reminder of the ties between the king and Lutaan's family would count in his favour.

"I'm taller," said Lutaan. "And smarter."

"And more arrogant," said Ullsaard.

"Perhaps," replied the first captain.

"You're, what, thirty summers old? It takes longer than that to get more wily than Donar."

"Thirty-five, I look young for my age," said Lutaan.

"Before we carry on, I should point out your first mistake."

"Well, yes, that would be useful, thank you," said Lutaan. The man was surprised and seemed genuinely intrigued by what Ullsaard was going to say.

"When you greet me, you should say 'Hail King', or 'Hail King Ullsaard'. You forgot my title."

"I see. That was intentional, not an accident. You are not the king now."

"I remember you swearing an oath to me when I sent you to Asuhas. By the way, where is your paymaster?"

"Urikh is king now. Times change. You should know that more than anybody. It's not personal, it's just that with you off in Salphoria, you took your eye away from the prize and it has been snatched from under you. Urikh has the Crown and sits in the palace in Askh. The Brotherhood proclaims him king. That's good enough for me."

"Donar wouldn't have been threatened by that. He wasn't, in fact."

"I'm not Donar, and though he's a good commander, don't think I respect him so much that I would throw away my future to emulate him. He guessed you had the beating of Lutaar.

I've seen you do incredible things, Ullsaard, but there is a new power in Greater Askhor now and you can't beat it."

Ullsaard absorbed this, pleased and annoyed by Lutaan's bluntness. On the one hand, Lutaan was proving to be of strong character, straight talking and focussed. On the other hand, he was setting himself against Ullsaard, and that would not be tolerated.

"Is this the point when you ask for my surrender? To save us the trouble and protect the lives of our men?"

"You've already considered it, I hope," said Lutaan. He took off his helm and placed it under his arm. His hair was dark brown with a hint of bronze about it and was cut at shoulder length. The first captain wiped sweat from his forehead. Ullsaard answered with a cold stare and Lutaan sighed. "I will ask you to reconsider, for the lives of my men."

There was a cough and a scuff of feet from Muuril. Ullsaard looked at the sergeant and then turned his attention back to Lutaan with a smile.

"My Companion, Sergeant Muuril," said Ullsaard, nodding towards the man. "You had something you wished to say, sergeant?"

"How many?" Muuril asked quietly, looking at Lutaan.

"How many what?" replied the first captain.

"How many of your men do you think you'll save if we surrender now?" The sergeant was fearless, glaring at Lutaan from the shadow of his helm's brim. The commander of the Twenty-first looked up at the villa and then turned to gaze back at his army, still marching into its positions.

"Three hundred," said Lutaan. His assessment was delivered in a deadpan tone. "Most of the people in the village couldn't count past their fingers, but a conservative estimate from what they said would place your numbers at a hundred. Probably less. I think you could take down three times that number before I have control of that building."

Muuril nodded and Ullsaard could sense the veteran's respect. The Companion stepped closer and his voice was still quiet and level.

"What if I make it my personal duty to make sure you're one of those three hundred?"

"Personal threats are worthless, sergeant," said Lutaan, unflustered as he looked up into the Companion's rugged face. "You know that the battle will have long been decided before I approach the compound."

"I would serve a captain like you, but for one reason," said Muuril, chuckling to himself.

"You *can* serve a captain like me; you'd be welcomed back to the Twenty-first, Sergeant Muuril. It was a shame you had to leave."

"And that's the problem I have, you see. I couldn't fight for a traitorous, arse-licking, honourless cunt."

This finally garnered a reaction from Lutaan, who stepped back, lips twitching. It took a moment for the first captain to compose himself, and he then directed his gaze to Ullsaard.

"There's no need to hurry this," said Lutaan. "I'll be attacking tomorrow, probably about the third hour of Dawnwatch, I reckon. I'm sure you'll still be waiting for me."

"Take all the time you like, we're not going anywhere," replied Ullsaard. "Be sure to look your men in the eyes when you get the chance, and tell them why they'll be dying tomorrow. See if you can guess which three hundred are going to fall."

"This is not my first dance, Ullsaard. The men in my legion aren't like the Thirteenth. They fight because I pay them to, and I have promised them a healthy reward for their victory tomorrow." Lutaan held open his cloak, showing the fur lining. He held up his other hand, gold rings set with rubies and emeralds on his fingers. "Remember when you offered us Askh? You gave the legions the capital to make their whore and their payday, and we conquered the empire for you. Remember when you promised the empire all of the wealth of Salphoria? Well the Fifth did their share of conquering there too. I've done very well for myself. Certainly well enough for a few thousand askharins for my men. It doesn't matter a fuck to them who wears the Crown."

Lutaan turned and strode back towards his retinue, cloak and crest flowing in the wind.

"Stupid bastard don't understand at all," said Muuril. "Loyalty, honour, the pride of a legion. He thinks it's just about the pay and the loot?"

"No, he's right," said Ullsaard as he untied Blackfang and swung himself into the saddle. "This is my doing, I have to fix it."

Muuril darted a questioning look at his king, but Ullsaard offered no extra explanation. He was not in the mood, because Lutaan, intentionally or not, had made the king realise what he had done over the past few years. It reminded him of words spoken by his old mentor, Cosuas, not long before Ullsaard had killed him. The king had not paid them much heed at the time, or since, but now they rose up from his memories as a form of moral indigestion.

He could remember Cosuas, his old, lined faced streaked with rain, standing in a puddle at the gate of a farm. Ullsaard had asked what Cosuas owed to Lutaar and the aging general had replied that he owed the king his allegiance.

"All you've done is reduce the empire to a bauble that men can scrap and claw at each other over."

Damning words, ignored for so long, but they came back to haunt Ullsaard. How had Cosuas been so prophetic? Were Urikh's treachery and the negotiable loyalty of Lutaan simply the saplings of the seeds Ullsaard had sown when he had usurped the Crown?

He rode up the hill, noting how long it would take Lutaan's men to cover the same distance en masse. Ullsaard looked up

at the men of the Thirteenth visible on the tower and at the
gate. They would give their lives, not altogether gladly but of
their free will and for a purpose more than just financial, to
see him victorious come the battle. The Thirteenth, and the
Fifth and so many others who had stuck with Ullsaard
throughout the civil war and the Salphorian campaign, would
slowly become something else.

He had to win, to stop the decline that he had started. Ullsaard had not appreciated the true consequences of his actions
when he had cut the head from Lutaar, but the discovery that
the old king had simply been a physical vessel for the spirit of
Askhos had just been the start of Ullsaard's woes. He had dealt
a wound to Greater Askhor; it was festering and would kill the
empire if he did not do something to stop the spread of the
taint. As king he could ensure the legions remained true to
their origins, and that the governors and the people found a
new respect for the authority of the Blood. Ullsaard would
make the Crown mean something again, and restore the pride
that his actions had tarnished.

IV

Under the cover of darkness, the men of the Twenty-first had
been busy during the night. As Captain Gelthius lit another
watch candle and Sergeant Muuril called out the second hour
of Duskwatch, flickers of flame sprang into life in the fields
lying to coldwards and duskwards of the compound. The pre-
vailing winds came down from the mountains and swept out
onto the plains, and this morning was no different, bringing
the first smell of smoke to the villa.

Climbing up to the spear thrower gantry, Gelthius could see
in every direction. He stopped counting the fires at thirty.
Green branches and leaves make the smoke dark and thick,
and it was coming in thicker and thicker clouds as the bonfires

grew in ferocity. He turned about and looked hotwards at the lake. It was impossible to see anything in the darkness, but the lamps of the sentries were still lit, shining yellow along the shore. If they saw or heard anything amiss, they would sprinkle firedust into the lanterns, turning the light to a warning red. It was not a perfect system – an arrow from the darkness might fell a guard before he knew there were enemy close at hand – but it was better than having a man trying to yell the alarm from half a mile away.

In the light of their fires, the Twenty-first were forming up. Hearing feet on the ladder behind him, Gelthius glanced down and saw King Ullsaard heaving his heavy frame up into the scaffold tower. The king gave the captain a nod as he squeezed onto the platform, stepping between the spear thrower and the rope fence that was all that kept a man from falling to his death on the courtyard slabs below.

"Wind's too strong," said the king.

"Aye, we can see them, right enough," said Gelthius. "They'll not get the drop on us that easy."

"That's not what I meant," said Ullsaard. "The smoke isn't to hide them now, it's to get in our eyes and throats, and make it hard to see when they reach the wall. Trust me, I've done it myself, at Khar. It'll be plenty thick enough by the time they're ready to attack. I meant that the wind will blow those fires out of control soon, and being in fields and everything we can expect the blaze to spread. If Lutaan's men don't get through or over the wall, they'll be trapped against it by the flames."

"Perhaps that's what Captain Lutaan intends, King," said Gelthius. Ullsaard turned an inquiring glare on the captain. "You know, by way of an encouragement."

"Maybe," said Ullsaard, the smile on his face appreciative of the notion rather than humoured by it. "Potential death is a great motivator."

"Works for me every time, King," said Gelthius. He fell quiet as Ullsaard surveyed every direction from the tower, spending some time looking Dawnwards to where the bulk of the Twenty-first were camped.

"Expect the attack at the third hour of Dawnwatch," said the king.

"Will do, King," replied the captain. He wondered how Ullsaard could predict the time of the attack with such accuracy and put it down to experience – there had to be something about the way the enemy were moving that suggested they would be ready in an hour, or maybe something in the Book of Askhos that recommended it as the ideal moment to launch an assault.

Without any further explanation, Ullsaard swung out to the wooden ladder and disappeared out of sight, leaving Gelthius alone with the men manning the spear thrower.

"Mark the position of the gate now," said Gelthius, worried by the thickening smoke.

"Captain?" The three other men looked at each other. Confused and amused in equal measure. The one who had spoken pointed towards the gate. "It's there, captain."

Gelthius produced a piece of charcoal from his belt pouch and handed it to one of the crew.

"Aim the thrower just over the gate and make a mark on the ropes and spindle," explained the Salphor. It was trick he had seen used on the landship, when the fog was so close you could not see all the way up to the top of the mainmast. "When the smoke's thick, you'll be able to tell you're still pointing at the gate."

"That's real clever, captain," said the man who had the charcoal. When the other two had rotated the spear thrower to the required direction, he drew thick lines on the ropes and the wooden disc that formed the main turntable. "Let's do it for a few other places too."

Gelthius agreed on three other set elevations and directions
– towards the corner of the stable block, the jetty on the lake
and between the two outbuildings by the hotwards walls – so
that he could shout out a command and they would know
where to point the war engine.

With this small measure taken, Gelthius had nothing else to
do except wait. His promotion to second captain notwithstand-
ing, with Ullsaard present and so few men there was no need
for intermediaries between the commander and his companies.
Gelthius was not a sophisticated man, and his experience of the
world was coloured by his lowly ambitions, but it was not without some sense of pride that he thought of his new rank.

It was, of course, utterly meaningless, he told himself as he
looked out at the three thousand soldiers of the Twenty-first
getting ready to kill him. Within a few hours – starting at the
third hour of Dawnwatch if Ullsaard was correct – being second captain, legionnaire or a general would not make any
difference. The last time Gelthius had checked, being a second
captain hadn't made his shield and breastplate any thicker or
his spear any longer.

So he waited, feeling no different as a second captain then
he did before his first battle with the Thirteenth. His stomach
was tight and aching, and yet he was simultaneously hungry,
having been unable to force any breakfast into himself earlier.
There was sweat on his face and hands, despite the fact that
the wind was cold, save for the heat of the smoke, which was
thickening as the flames grew stronger and stronger in the pre-
dawn light.

About half way through the second hour of Dawnwatch, the
Twenty-first started their attack. Like a serpent uncoiling to
strike, the massed companies of the legion emerged from their
marching forts, lining up along the road to dawnwards and to
coldwards. The three-headed serpent would strike from every

direction, splitting the defenders. Gelthius knew nothing of siege warfare and wondered if this was a costly strategy or the most prudent. He supposed that there were only so many ladders in the enemy army, and the walls would allow only so many men to climb over, that it was pointless having everybody advancing together; they would simply get in each other's way.

Gelthius wondered where he should fight, if he received no specific instruction from the king. Part of him wanted to be in the battle close to Ullsaard. He had seen the king fighting and there would be a certain amount of safety being nearby. Against this was the suspicion that Ullsaard was a lodestone for danger – it followed him around and he was always at the centre of trouble. A small, treacherous but vocal part of Gelthius also wondered if he could get away with positioning himself down by the lake, where he could quickly lose himself in the reed beds or, in a desperate situation, swim out to safety.

The sound of drums sounded out a marching beat; one that Gelthius knew well. He saw the icon of Askhos being raised by the First Company at the head of the snake slithering up the road, like a single golden eye reflecting the reddish light of the dawning sun.

It was hard to just wait and do nothing while the enemy advanced. The walls around the compound did not look so much like protection as they did a barrier to keep Gelthius in. They would be trapped once the Twenty-first broke through the gate or had a foothold over the walls. Then that high wall of stone and the rampart of stakes beyond would be a hindrance, not a help.

As much as Gelthius wanted to tell that selfish part of himself to shut up, the voice grew stronger. All he really wanted was to be with Maredin and his children. That was all that he had ever really wanted since he had been taken away on Anglhan's landship. He had been days – only two days, he dimly remembered – from freedom when he had been caught up by Aroisius the

Free's men and Anglhan had pitched them all into his insane plans. If Gelthius could send a message to himself back then, he would tell himself to keep his head down, wait to be assigned as driver to the herald, Noran, and then when they were in the middle of the Free Country, make a bolt for freedom.

Betraying Ullsaard felt wrong, but the situation looked hopeless. Before he even knew what he was doing, Gelthius was climbing down the ladder to the ground. He saw Muuril standing by the main doors of the villa and turned away sharply lest the sergeant see something in the captain's expression. Feeling heavy with guilt but unable to stop himself, he walked around the stable block and headed towards the rear of the villa. There were several legionnaires between the building and the wall, standing on piled crates, one on a chair, to peer over at the advancing enemy.

"Aye, here's the captain!" one of them, Anjoor, called out.

Gelthius tried to think of something funny to say but his mind was too filled with fear for wit. All he could think of was making sure he survived to see Maredin and the children again. He just about managed to raise a hand to wave in acknowledgement and then hurried on, heading directly for the gardens at the rear.

The sun was just about strong enough for light to creep around the villa and bathe the shore in dim greyness, the occasional fleck of red catching on waves and ripples. Gelthius was aware of the six men down by the water's edge, their lanterns gleaming bright in the darkness. It might be good to make a quick inspection of the sentries, the captain told himself. He tried to ignore the sounds of marching men rising beyond the walls as he made his way down the stepped pavement towards the quayside.

He was halfway to the water when he heard a shout from a man to his left. Gripped by guilt, thinking that somehow the guard had guessed his cowardly intent, Gelthius stopped immediately. He realised he was still in the light spilling between the slats of the shutters on the rear windows, and so easy for anyone to see, silhouetted against the house. He was about to turn back and seek shelter inside the building when he heard his name being called from the man at the lakeside.

"Captain! Captain Gelthius! Something in the water."

The smoke from the fires was drifting across the surface of the lake, making it impossible to see more than two dozen paces, but Gelthius could hear distant splashing as he scampered down the last steps and reach the shouting sentry.

"Boat?" he asked, bringing up his shield in case a vessel was to suddenly emerge laden with men of the Twenty-first.

They listened for a while, during which the quiet was broken by the slap of the spear thrower firing and a cheer for the men atop the tower. Even with the advantage of elevation, that meant that the lead ranks of the Twenty-first had to be well within half a mile.

Trying hard to push aside all the other noises he could hear – the crackle of the fires, the noise of the men reloading the spear thrower, the crunch of small stones under his sandals – Gelthius strained to hear the splashing.

"That way," said the sentry, pointing coldwards along the shore. Some of the other men were heading along the lake path, drawn by the commotion. Gelthius ignored their shouts of inquiry and looked out across the lake as best he could.

Sure enough, there was something in the gloom. The dawn light was catching on more ripples and there was the sound of slow but steady splashing. It was not enough noise to be a body of men but Gelthius could not relax.

"Who's out there?" he demanded. There was no reply and Gelthius' eyes were stinging from the smoke.

"We'll take out a boat," he said, pointing back towards the short stone jetty. There were two boats, one with four large sweeps, the other with sweeps and a sail. Deciding that if things came to the worst, he could probably shove the legionnaire over the side and sail to freedom, Gelthius told the other sentries to go back to their posts.

Between the two of them, they managed to get the sail lifted. Untying the rope on the jetty, Gelthius stopped for a moment, his attention attracted by a concerted shout from outside the compound: the sound of men charging. He turned to call out to the men on the tower, but stopped himself. He was too far away for them to hear or reply.

"One thing, just one thing at a time," he muttered, pushing the boat and jumping over the widening gap to land next to the sentry, Aduris.

"What's that, captain?"

"Never mind." Gelthius took a quick look around the small deck and pointed to a rope attached to the yard arm. "Fasten that to that hook there, and I'll man the tiller."

Under the ex-fisherman's directions, Aduris trimmed the sail and Gelthius managed to get them underway, heading in the direction of the faint noise. Away from the shore, Gelthius felt a calm descending on him. He could barely see the villa in the smoke and the jetty was fast fading from view as well. Soon the two men were cocooned in a grey mass, barely able to see twenty paces.

Aduris was a good soldier, and as tempting as it was to leave Ullsaard and the Thirteenth to their fate, Gelthius couldn't bring himself to kill the man in cold blood; either by spear or drowning. And on top of that, there was no point making a break for freedom if he was going to sail into a fleet of enemies out on the lake.

"It'd be quicker if we rowed as well," said Aduris.

"And noisier," replied Gelthius. "Got to listen, ain't we?"

So they kept quiet and listened. Gelthius heard splashing to his left, closer to the shore, and Aduris pointed and nodded.

"Something that way," said the legionnaire.

Gelthius moved the tiller and had Aduris trim the sail again. As they glided across the water, the slosh of small waves against the hull did not mask a louder splashing coming from ahead. Further out on the lake the smoke was thinner, but still Gelthius could not see anything. The captain tied the tiller to keep them on a straight line and prodded Aduris with his foot.

"Get to the prow and keep a sharp eye," Gelthius told Aduris. The soldier moved to the bow and almost immediately looked back at Gelthius, animated.

"Just to the left a little," said Aduris, fetching his spear from where he'd stowed it in the bottom of the boat. Gelthius adjusted the course and peered ahead. There was a shape in the gloom, low in the water. As they came closer, Gelthius saw arms rising and falling in powerful, slow strokes. The swimmer was about thirty- five or forty paces away, almost perpendicular to the boat's heading.

"Ho there!" the captain called out, getting to his feet. "Stop where you are!"

The swimmer complied immediately, a head bobbing into view, arms moving back and forth as the man treaded water.

"Captain Gelthius? Is that you?"

Now that he was closer, and with the aid of the voice, Gelthius recognised Gebriun. He had a short beard, several days' worth, but the face was unmistakeable. Gelthius called out with wordless delight, but then realisation hit him and his stomach knotted and his joy died.

"You're alive?" said the captain as Aduris helped the naked legionnaire into the boat. "But Faasil said th–"

"Faasil's been paid off," gasped Gebriun. The four words

struck Gelthius like hammer blows, each a punch that made his gut spasm. The captain looked back at the shore as Gebriun continued, between deep breaths, but could see nothing in the gloom. "He tried to turn me too, and when I said no he had the Twenty-first come for me. I managed to escape, ran for it and hid out in the country hoping to find you or one of the others, but the legion was already days ahead of me. When I got here, I saw that there were soldiers in Menesun and the villa was surrounded. I've had to swim about three miles."

"We have to get back, warn the others," said Aduris, grabbing one of the sweeps. He held it out to Gebriun. "Have you still got enough breath?"

"You steer, I'll row," said Gelthius. Not less than a quarter of an hour before, Gelthius had been ready to run out on the men of the Thirteenth, but now he grabbed the oar and sat down, nodding for Gebriun to take the tiller. Gelthius had planned to quit the villa if things turned badly, but now that Faasil had been revealed as a traitor it somehow meant more to Gelthius that Ullsaard won. It somehow made it more real that his comrades, men who had been good to him, were about to die, and he couldn't let that happen without being with them, even if it meant he would die too.

V

It had always been one of Ullsaard's principles that he only started fights that he was sure he would win. Of late that principle had been tested several times, but none more so than now. He had not chosen this battle, and had certainly not desired any kind of confrontation, but he was forced to deal with the situation as he found it.

The archers along the road had done little to buy the time Ullsaard had hoped for; twenty men with bows could do nothing to hold back several companies of soldiers in full armour and with shields raised. Without proper bellows-bows the men had difficulty penetrating the defences of the oncoming legion and so Ullsaard had quickly sent word for the bowmen to withdraw to the villa; there was no point risking them being killed by   Lutaan's archers.

Though his force was outnumbered six-to-one, Ullsaard was not despondent about his chances of victory. A good wall counted for a lot, and in their desire to bring Ullsaard to battle swiftly, Lutaan and Asuhas had not brought siege engines with them. Assault was the only option, and that was the easiest kind of attack to face. Bombardment would have been far more effective, forcing Ullsaard to either sally out and be butchered, or reduce his newly fortified home to rubble around him.

A hard fight across a well-defended obstacle was not the most desirable engagement for a legionnaire, and if Ullsaard's men could hold the wall long enough, and inflict enough casualties, the ranks would take matters into their own hands. It only took a few to decide that the risk was too great, the reward too little, and others would soon follow. And once one assault failed it was all the harder to have the men try again.

Ullsaard prowled the small area of the balcony like Blackfang padding back and forth in her pen below. The king could see the three columns advancing on the villa and he wanted to do something other than sit and wait for them to land the first blow. He had racked his brains for some action that he could take to even the odds in his favour, and he had dismissed them all as too risky for uncertain gain. He had considered sneaking out in the night and setting fires in the legion camp, but a quick scouting party led by Muuril had returned with the news that the Twenty-first had double sentries on duty; Lutaan had not trusted his inexperienced officers and soldiers to keep good watch and had taken precautions.

The smoke was also a good ploy on the part of Ullsaard's

opponent. Even in the rolling clouds of fume the columns could be seen and heard, but their exact numbers were hidden. It made the most sense for the gate to be the target of the strongest attack, but Lutaan knew this also and might instead try to overwhelm one of the other walls. It was a matter of bluff and double-bluff. The best Ullsaard could do was keep a careful watch and be sure to respond quickly as the battle developed.

He wanted to be down in the courtyard, spear and shield in his hands, ready to fight himself, but reason told him that he needed to maintain a loftier view. If his presence would make a difference, he would fight where needed, but he would not know where his presence would have the greatest impact unless he kept a proper overview of the battle; and that meant being on the balcony, and keeping one ear cocked for a shout from one of the men tasked with bringing reports from the lakeward side of the compound and the wall to coldwards.

Swirls and shadows in the smoke showed the snaking lines of the three-pronged attack. The company coming up the road was closest, but only by fifty paces or less. Lutaan had timed the assault well and all three columns would arrive at about the same moment. Ullsaard was certain that there were more men to coldwards than dawnwards.

He looked for Captain Gelthius, but the Salphor was not in the spear thrower tower and not in the courtyard. Irritated, Ullsaard swept an eye over the men, looking for someone else who could be trusted with the orders. Leaning over he saw his Companion almost directly below the balcony, on the steps of the main door, ready to defend the entrance if the enemy should break through the gate or come over the walls.

"Muuril, move ten men to the coldwards wall," the king called down. "And stay there yourself."

"Aye, King," replied the sergeant, lifting his spear in acknowledgement. Ullsaard watched as names were called out and ten men were brought back from around the gate and on the wall behind the hotwards outbuildings. The group trotted out of sight around the corner of the stable wing.

Despite the smoke, Ullsaard could see ladders being carried over the heads of the lead companies. They were not tall ladders – the compound wall was not even twice the height of a man – but there were lots of them.

"Archers, target the ladder carriers!" Ullsaard shouted. "Slow them down."

The twang of bowstrings and hiss of arrows slicing air disturbed the quiet. The king could also hear the tramping of the Twenty-first, getting louder and louder on the road. He fancied he heard the voices of the officers calling out, shouting words of reproach or encouragement. The crackle of the flames was not so loud as it had been, and though the light from the fires had died down, the rising sun was more than making up for the loss.

"Duskwatch, third hour," came the shout from somewhere below, follow by the clang of a knife pommel hitting a bell. "Third hour!"

Ullsaard smiled. Lutaan had told the king to his face exactly when the attack would reach the walls, and he was out by only a matter of a couple of hundred paces. Ullsaard admired that sort of boldness, even as he also respected the organisation it had required to get three thousand men into position at such a precise time.

"At the wall!" The shout was from the spear thrower crew. Ullsaard turned around and looked up at the men, who were swivelling their machine to coldwards. One of them saw the king looking and pointed. "Hundreds of them, king, at the coldwards wall."

The rope of the spear thrower snapped as the bolt was loosed into the smoke. Ullsaard could hear the shout of an officer giving the command to charge and the insults being hurled back by Muuril and others.

It was a relief, in a way, that the fighting had started. Ullsaard was committed, and all he had to do now was what he knew best – fight and win.

VI

Pulling at the sweep reminded Gelthius of his time on Anglhan's landship. He fell into the rhythm quickly, grunting the stroke to Aduris. Gebriun sat down by the tiller, shivering.

"Take my cloak," said the captain. "Water's nearly freezing."

Gebriun did as he was told, unfastening Gelthius' cloak and wrapping about his shoulders as he returned to the stern. Gelthius glanced over his shoulder now and then to see how far away they were from the dark blot in the smoke that was the shoreline. He could see the villa rising up against the lightening sky, perhaps four casts away, maybe less ; more like two hundred paces.

"Keep going, almost there," said Gelthius. The muscles in his lower back were already protesting; just a couple of years ago Gelthius would have worked all day at the landship's crank without a problem. On the other hand, when he had first been brought into the Thirteenth Gelthius had been hardly able to walk a couple of miles before his shins were agony and his feet were numb. Times had changed his body.

He rowed in silence, teeth gritted, until he heard the scrape of the keel and felt the boat shudder and then tip sharply to the right.

"Shit," said Aduris. "The underwater stakes!"

"What?" asked Gebriun as Gelthius locked his sweep and moved to the front of the boat. He peered over the gunwale and saw a log not far beneath the surface of the lake, its sharpened tip wedged between two planks.

"The king has the shoreline covered with stakes to stop boats."

"And you thought you'd just mention this?" snapped Gebriun. The legionnaire looked at Gelthius, body quivering. "I can't swim no more, captain. If I get in that water again, I'll drown."

"I can't swim," said Aduris as Gelthius' gaze fell on him. The sentry shrugged apologetically.

"Right, we'll lever off," said Gelthius, returning to his sweep to pull the oar from its place. "Grab hold of this and push down when I say."

He managed to guide the flat of the paddle between the stake and the hull, where he thought it would lift the boat away from the spike.

"Go on, with all our weight," said the captain, grabbing hold of the sweep and leaning on to it. Nothing happened and Gelthius tried harder, spitting as his arms, already sore from rowing, started to tremble. The haft of the sweep was bending dangerously, and Gelthius worried that if it snapped he would get dagger-sized splinters in his face.

There was a crack of wood and the boat lurched again. The sweep had held, but the hull had not been so strong. Gelthius saw water gurgling through a hole below the waterline. On the positive side, the boat was drifting again, turning in the wind.

"We've got a leak," said Aduris, staring in horror at the water dribbling into the bottom of the boat.

"Best row quick then," said Gelthius, pulling the sweep from the legionnaire and sitting down. "We'll get to shore before we sink if you get your arse down here and start rowing!"

Aduris complied and the two of them found their beat soon enough. The boat started to get a bit heavier in the bow as more water came in, and as it became more sluggish progress became harder.

"I'll bail, keep rowing," said Gebriun. He snatched off Aduris' helmet as he stepped along to the bow, and used it as a pail to eject water back into the lake.

Using his sweep to steer now that Gebriun was not at the tiller, Gelthius managed to keep the boat pointed at the shore-line, despite the wind trying to push the boat around and the anchor-like effect of the water still coming into the prow. It was with some relief that he heard the scraping of wood on stone as they reached the shore.

Panting, he leaned on the sweep, grateful to be back on dry land. It was only after a few moments that he remembered that they had been hurrying for a reason.

"Come on, we have to find Faasil before he can do any-thing," said Gelthius, hauling himself from his seat, pushing the oar aside. He jumped from the boat, sandaled feet landing in the shallow water. His shield and spear he left behind; he knew that if he was too slow they wouldn't help at all. Splash-ing to the bank, the captain called out, bringing the other sentries hurrying through the smoke. The noise of bronze crashing against bronze echoed from the villa and walls; the battle was in full fury and the shouts of both sides joined with screams of the injured.

"Faasil? Where's Faasil?" the captain demanded. Behind him, Gebriun and Aduris did the same from the boat.

"In the courtyard, I think," said one of the sentries, appear-ing with lamp in hand. "I think he volunteered to be at the gate."

"At the gate?" Gelthius lost his footing for a moment, and the sentry grabbed his arm to keep him upright. The captain's chest felt heavy and his stomach shrank into an even smaller, tighter ball. He stumbled towards the villa, shouting, but his voice was lost in the tumult of the battle.

VII

Lutaan seemed determined that he would force his way in over the coldwards walls. It was the longest line to defend, running down to the lake, and the Twenty-first were coming again and again. At the middle of the line, Muuril had a good vantage point to see what was going on, though his opportunities to do so were few and far between as the intensity of the fighting waxed and waned.

The enemy legionnaires approached under cover of their shields. The spear thrower took a toll of the advancing men, but not enough to break their ranks or determination. On reaching the wall, the men of the front and third rank used their shields as a roof while the second rankers pushed the ladders into position. The spears of the fourth rank were used to drive back the men behind the wall and then when a gap had been opened the officers would give the order; the men of the front rank would open up their shields and the second rank would surge up the ladders with swords and knives, trying to get too close for the defenders to use their spears.

It was a tactic the legions had used for decades, probably more than a century, and Muuril had put it into practice a few times during the advance into Salphoria. If the men were coordinated, brave and trusted in their officers, it was a sure way of taking a low wall such as the one that surrounded the villa.

Fortunately for Muuril and the rest of the Thirteenth, the warriors of the Twenty-first were neither experienced nor disciplined enough for the manoeuvre to be carried out flawlessly. The ranks did not close together properly when a man fell to a lucky arrow shot or the spear thrower, and so the defenders were able to throw stones and loose more arrows into the exposed ranks. Without complete protection from above, the second rankers would push up their ladders to be met by a row of jagged speartips thrust down by Muuril and his men. When the fourth rank attacked, they presented a wavering, broken line of pikes rather than a thicket of spearpoints to drive back the men at the wall, which left the second rank in even more danger when the order came to make the assault.

As much as he wanted to see the traitorous bastards of the Twenty-first made to pay for their actions, part of Muuril was pleased to see that more than half the time the officers had seen that the defenders were still in position and had called the companies back, ready to attack again; it was good to see captains prepared to keep their men alive.

"Come on you useless cunts!" Muuril roared, leaning right out over the wall to plunge his spear one-handed into the shoulder of a man who had been left unprotected by the shield of the legionnaire to his right. The soldier fell back, blood gushing from the wound, which left the man to his left exposed to a second jab from the Companion.

The company beneath him weren't even trying to scale the wall; Muuril could see the bodies of the dead from the first three assaults being dragged back through the ranks to clear the footing at the base.

"You picked the wrong side, you shit-stinking, wet-nosed whoresons of bitches." Muuril rammed his spear against the side of a legionnaire's helm, sending the man sprawling into the muck that had been churned up from rain, blood and the tread of hundreds of men. "You think you can beat the Thirteenth?"

The sergeant knew he was bleeding from a few small cuts – one on his chin was particularly sore, and he had a gash on his right hand that would need a few stitches later. The men around him were also bearing their injuries without remark; four men had been killed and about twice that number had been carried away to the side of the villa to pass away or re-cover as their injuries dictated. There was no dedicated surgeon, only an orderly, and he was too busy fighting to look after the wounded.

The coldwards wall stretched for about seventy paces and was now manned by thirty of the defenders, shoulder-to-shoulder along its whole length. Down by the lake, a high rampart thick with stakes extended outwards for a quarter of a mile, ensuring nobody could slip around to Duskwards. The staked ditch around the wall was angled in such a way that the men struggling out of the trench were ripe targets for the spear thrower and bow men. Unable to keep their shields in front of them as they negotiated the slope, the soldiers of the Twenty-first had lost dozens of their number in the first moments of their initial assault.

Looking to Dawnwards, Muuril saw that the fighting extended around the corner of the wall and towards the gate. Not far away, about twenty paces from where he was standing on a brick step behind the wall, the sergeant saw a knot of about twenty legionnaires with their shields covering them from every direction like a protective shell. Their armoured carapace was butted up against the wall and the sergeant couldn't tell was happening beneath; but he had a very good idea. Under the cover of their shields they were scraping and chipping away at the stones and mortar, hoping to weaken the wall enough that they could pull it down with grapples and line.

"Picks!" he shouted, pointing to the cluster of shields. "They're trying to break the wall. Fetch the oil."

The defenders of the villa had no lava, but they had secured as much lamp oil and animal fat as they could, and now a clay pot of the bubbling, searing liquid was manhandled to the top of the wall, the spears of the carriers thrust through the pot's handles. Muuril grimaced as the scalding contents of the pot were poured over the attackers; thick, hot sludge splashed onto the other men around the defensive shell and seeping through the gaps in the shields. There came howls of pain and shrieks as the men beneath the shield roof broke apart, some dropping weapons and shields to clutch scalded arms and faces, some fleeing back through the press of bodies behind them as the rest of the legionnaires on the wall thrust down with their spears into the disorganised mass of warriors below.

"Grim," muttered the sergeant, returning his attention to the immediate vicinity.

The company that had been attacking his position withdrew, stepping backwards with shields raised. Here again the inexperience of the Twenty-first made them vulnerable. A veteran legion like the Thirteenth was able to part ranks enough to allow one company to pass through another, providing a seamless and constant reserve to the fighting line. The Twenty-first could not manage such a thing, especially with one company retreating in some disarray, and so it took some time for another company to come forward and take the place of the one that had left, giving Muuril a chance to reorganise his defenders, sending some more men down towards the lake where he had seen a few attackers actually getting to the top of the wall, and generally giving the defenders time to catch their breath.

Muuril was doing just this when he heard his name being shouted from down the side of the villa. He saw Gelthius limping towards him as fast as he could, and behind him ran a man naked save for a cloak wrapped around his body.

"What happened to your leg?" the sergeant asked. He turned and jumped down to the next step of the rampart behind the wall.

"Cramp," growled Gelthius. "Faasil's a traitor, where is he?"

Muuril took this in with a blank stare, and then his gaze drifted over to the naked man. It was Gebriun. Muuril stared for a moment, not sure he believed what he saw, and then the words of his captain sank in.

"Shit," said the Companion. "He's at the gate. Follow me, captain."

Muuril vaulted down to ground level. He pointed to where about half a dozen men were clustered at the front of the compound, adding their weight to the timber braces that had been wedged behind the gate. The wood of the gate was splintered and broken in many places and shook again from the impact of a ram. Muuril set off across the courtyard, looking to see which of the men was Faasil; all of the legionnaires had their back to him.

Gelthius shouted out Faasil's name and one of the soldiers turned. Seeing the captain and sergeant advancing across the yard, Faasil panicked. He thrust his sword into the throat of the man next to him and barged away the supporting strut he had been holding. The other legionnaires were too busy with what they were doing to see what had happened and two more were cut down by the traitor. Faasil then dragged himself up the steps to the right hand platform built as a temporary gate tower overlooking the wall. Two more legionnaires toppled from the scaffold, blood trailing from their guts as Faasil shouldered his way to the wall itself. With a last glance at Muuril, the legionnaire jumped, disappearing from sight.

"At least he didn't…" Gelthius' words died away as the timbers of the gate cracked again, sending splinters flying through the air, the remaining men at the braces sent sprawling. With a screech of tearing metal, one of the gates twisted on its hinges, and Muuril stared through the widening gap, right at the face of a young soldier of the Twenty-first, who seemed to be as surprised as Muuril that the gate had fallen.

The sergeant glanced at the press of men piling against the remnants of the gate; they would be through in a matter of moments. He looked at Gelthius, hoping that the captain would say what to do, but the Salphor just stood there staring

in horror as the first legionnaires pushed through the gap between the gates. One of the Thirteenth grabbed his spear and
lanced it through the attacker's thigh, blood splashing onto the
timbers of the shattered gate.

"Fall back!" roared Muuril, taking matters into his own
hands. His voice rang out as he grabbed Gelthius and pushed
him towards the main doors of the villa. "Back to the villa!
Pass the word! Fall back!"

VIII

Ullsaard could not totally comprehend what had happened as
he watched the men of the Thirteenth streaming back across
the compound. The battle had been hard-fought, but the king
had not expected such a reverse barely an hour into the fighting. He had not seen exactly what had happened at the gate,
but from his vantage point on the balcony it had seemed as if
one of the Twenty-first had somehow slipped over the wall
and attacked his men.

As legionnaires ran back towards the main building, Ullsaard
saw Muuril on a divergent course, heading towards the teth-
ered abada. Behind him trailed a limping Gelthius, who kept
looking over his shoulder as the gates were heaved apart,
while more soldiers of the attacking legion clambered over the
undefended walls.

Muuril used his sword to slash through the ropes holding
the abada struck the beasts with the butt of his spear, waving
for Gelthius to get out of the way. The Salphor officer hobbled
towards the villa's main doors as the abada snorted and started
to move. The Companion's high-pitched shrieks and the crack
of his spear on grey flesh made the lumbering creatures pick
up speed.

The men pouring through the gate did not realise their
predicament, as more of their comrades pushed in from behind

and stormed over the walls. There were at least fifty men in the courtyard when the closest abada broke into a thundering run, head lowered, snorting with anger. The other three followed, a mass of muscle and horns charging out of the smoke into the legionnaires of the Twenty-first. Cries of panic and pain rang around the courtyard as men were gored and trampled. Bones were crushed and flesh punctured and torn as the abada tried to push their way out of the gate, stamping on the men that had fallen, slashing left and right with their horns.

A bolt from the spear thrower slashed through the smoke, passing above the stampeding beasts to cut down three men in the gateway. The impetus of the abada charge had slowed and those of the Twenty-first forced to confront the beasts by the press of bodies behind stabbed out with their spears, opening up cuts on the bodies of the abada. This only enraged the creatures more and they started to rampage again, shoulder-to-shoulder, two in front of the other two, sweeping away everything between them and the gate.

Arrows from the upper floors of the villa started to pick off the soldiers that had come over the walls or somehow managed to avoid the rampaging abada. Ullsaard checked on Muuril and saw the Companion helping Gelthius, the captain with one arm over the sergeant's shoulders, heading towards the rear of the villa.

Ullsaard was not the sort to ask questions of why something had already happened when there were still consequences to deal with. He had known the outer wall could not hold forever, and had made contingency for a retreat back to the villa. Looking back from the balcony, he saw a dozen men in the command room already, bows in hand, firing into the back gardens as well as through the front windows. Most of the men would be on the ground floor, barring the doors and guarding the windows.

When the abada had finally charged their way clear of the men at the gate, the Twenty-first advanced again to support those who had already climbed into the compound. There seemed to be some confusion though, and Ullsaard heard laughter from his men as two companies tried to pass into the gate at the same time. A bolt from above scything down one of the rank sergeants did not help the concentration of the attacking soldiers.

Ullsaard then heard horns blowing the withdraw order. This caused more anarchy as the companies that were entering the compound had to turn around, while the men inside were only too happy to fall back, having been the target of concerted and persistent bow fire since they had entered. As well as the carnage at the gates, another dozen or more bodies littered the flagstones of the yard by the time all of the Twenty-first had retreated back beyond the wall.

"What the fuck are they up to?" asked Muuril, joining Ullsaard on the balcony. A glance showed the king that captain Gelthius was sitting on the floor in the room behind them, massaging his left leg.

"I have no idea, sergeant," said Ullsaard. "It seems that Lutaan did not make himself very clear to his officers, whatever he intends."

"Sorry about Faasil, King," said Muuril. "I should've spotted he was wrong."

"What are you talking about, sergeant?" Ullsaard glared at his Companion, annoyed by the distraction. The king was trying to study the movements of the Twenty-first through the smoke, to discern what Lutaan's next move might be.

"Faasil, he was a traitor," explained Muuril. "Gebriun escaped and brought word."

"Gebriun escaped? From where?" As he asked the questions Ullsaard realised that the answers were irrelevant, especially in the heat of battle. What had happened could not be changed. What was about to happen was very much in the balance. "Never mind, just check you've got trusted men at every door and window, we don't need any other mishaps."

Chagrined, the Companion saluted and left Ullsaard. The king could see something being pulled up the slope towards the villa, and could hear the rumbling of wheels on the stone road. When it came into sight, he heard murmurs from the men around him, and he felt a momentary twinge of fear too; it was a lava thrower.

"Spear thrower!" Ullsaard bellowed up to the tower. One of the men leaned over the rope fence and raised a hand.

"Already on it, my king!" the soldier called down. "We'll aim for the bellows, that'd be easy enough to pierce."

Ullsaard waved a hand of approval and turned his attention back to the war machine being dragged along the track. It was larger than those he had used in the desert, with curved bronze plates protecting the thick wooden barrel that served as the lava reservoir. Ten men hauled at ropes and the same number had their backs bent, hands clasping handles set into the structure of the engine.

Something blurred past the machine and sent up a shower of shards from the stone of the road; the spear thrower's first shot. Arrows arced over the wall from the windows to the left and right of the king, and one of the men at the ropes stumbled as he was hit. There was no shortage of manpower though, and as two legionnaires darted in to pull the man clear of those following, ensuring he was not crushed by the wheels of the engine, another took up the place of the injured soldier.

The murmurs and whispers from the Thirteenth became louder and more worried as the large engine turned the bend in the road, and could now be seen directly through the gates. It was about a hundred paces away, and Ullsaard tried to work out what sort of range it might have. A normal lava thrower could fire about fifty paces, so a conservative estimate would say seventy-five for such a beast of a machine. Well within bow range, although several dozen archers from the Twenty-first were now gathering just outside the wall, doubtless to target any archers inside the villa that showed themselves for too long.

All the effort to take the coldwards wall had just been a feint; the gate had been Lutaan's target since the first attack. All he needed was a clear line of fire for that monstrous engine. Ullsaard had not guessed; during the campaign in Salphoria he had taken no lava throwers and they had completely slipped from his thinking.

Another spear launched from the thrower clanged off the metal casing, leaving a score across its surface but doing no serious damage. The crew had the engine about sixty paces away now and a flurry of arrows sailed into the air from the archers outside the compound, forcing Ullsaard to retreat inside the villa. The missiles clattered against the walls and on the balcony, and from below he heard a cry of pain as a shaft found someone unfortunate or stupid enough to still be at a window.

The crew of the lava thrower had detached their ropes and four of them were using hammers to drive pitons through metal loops attached to the wheels to make the whole engine stable. Ullsaard could see the lighting rags being stuffed down the flared muzzle of the machine, while a safe distance away a long torch was lit. When the pegs had been secured, three men set to work on the bellows, stripped to the waist, the sweat glistening on their bodies as they built up the pressure inside the engine.

The soldier with the long torch suddenly flew backwards, a spear from the tower jutting out of his chest. The brand tumbled from his grasp and a ragged cheer went up from the men of the Thirteenth. The joy was short-lived though, as another soldier stepped up and seized the brand. The man with the burning rod looked back and Ullsaard saw a second captain a short distance behind the machine raising his arm in preparation to give the order.

They had no defence against this. Though stone and brick, the villa was not impervious to lava. It would pour through windows and set fit fire to the doors, clinging to everything. Water just served to spread the flammable liquid, so sand and dirt were the only way of extinguishing flames that burned an unsettling dark red and black, and there was nothing inside the villa to douse such a blaze. Ullsaard was not sure how many shots would be held in the reservoir, but he expected four or five at least – more than enough to have the villa blazing from one end to the other; the smoke would kill the men inside before the flames got to them.

Ullsaard watched with narrowed eyes as the captain in charge of the engine turned his head. Following the man's gaze, the king saw Lutaan just a few steps away, half-hidden behind a body of men. It seemed a cowardly way of winning the battle, but Ullsaard admired the ruthlessness of the plan; never have a fair fight, he reminded himself.

He saw the captain nod and his stomach clenched, as did the king's fists at his sides. He heard swearing from the legionnaires behind him; they had backed away from the windows and some were edging towards the door leading to the landing and stairs.

With a growl, Ullsaard ran out onto the balcony.

"You show them cockless pigs!" shouted Muuril, reading the king's actions as a sign of defiance. The sergeant's assumption could not have been any further from the truth.

"Parley!" bellowed Ullsaard. "Parley for surrender!"

IX

It was the looks of disappointment and shame on the faces of his men that bit into Ullsaard's heart. There was resignation in the look of some, fear in those who were not sure what would happen to them next. There was condemnation from others; Muuril was seething, the men holding the rope that tied the sergeant's hands struggling more than their companions who had brought Blackfang out of the stables. The ailur sensed something was wrong, and at a word from Ullsaard would rend and bite anything nearby, but he stayed silent for the same reason he had ordered his men to disarm themselves; unleashing Blackfang's fury would only get the ailur slain.

The judgement in the eyes of Muuril and a few others was justified. The Thirteenth had never surrendered; not under Ullsaard's command and not before. They were one of the Unbreakables, the seven legions who had never been defeated nor disbanded since their founding. Although it was less than a third of a company present, each man represented the legion as a whole, and each man knew the full weight of what Ullsaard had done, and the burden of their failure was great indeed. The First had traditionally been the legion of the king's bodyguard, but the Thirteenth were Ullsaard's favourites and they had not protected him. A few of the men were openly crying, more stifled tears.

Ullsaard carried his spear and shield with him, and the ring of soldiers waiting in the courtyard widened as the king stepped out of the door.

"Who will take the weapons of his rightful king?" Ullsaard asked.

"I will," said Lutaan. The first captain stood next to the icon bearer of his legion, a little way off to Ullsaard's right. Light rain was falling and Lutaan had sought the shelter of the stable doorway. Now the commander of the Twenty-first strode towards Ullsaard with a hand held out.

"Take it," said the king, tossing his golden spear to the first captain, who caught it easily enough. Ullsaard threw the shield to the floor at the captain's feat. "More riches for you, gifted by my endeavour."

Lutaan hefted the spear and smiled. He stooped and picked up the shield, assuming the guard position.

"A little heavy for me, I have not your build, Ullsaard," admitted the commander. A third captain approached at a gesture from his leader and took the captured wargear away. Another followed, a length of rope in his hands.

"I'll not be bound like an animal," snarled Ullsaard, bringing up his fists. The officer with the cord stopped and glanced at his commander.

"You will, unless you want every man in this compound butchered here and now." This declaration came from the direction of the gateway. Ullsaard knew the voice of Asuhas and saw the man standing between two burly legionnaires just inside the courtyard. "I don't trust you not to do some harm to me or one of my men."

"Come and bind me yourself, if you're so insistent."

"Don't make this worse," said Lutaan, his voice too quiet to carry to the governor. "I will have my men beat you insensible if I have to. I'm here to take you in, and I will."

"What made you think I wouldn't go up in flames with the villa?" said Ullsaard, glaring at Lutaan. The first captain met the king's stare with a smirk and a shrug.

"I didn't," Lutaan admitted. "Asuhas wanted you alive, but the king's order was alive or dead. Now, come on, I just need to tie your hands like the rest of your men. Or are you too important to surrender under the same conditions as you laid upon your soldiers?"

Saying nothing, his eyes enough to convey his murderous thoughts, Ullsaard held out his hands, wrists together. The officer with the rope came closer and threw a few loops around the king's wrists and then tied a complex knot. A length of the cord was left dangling and Lutaan took a step and bent down, one hand reaching towards it.

"If you try to lead me around on a leash, I will kill you, right here, right now, and fuck the consequences," growled Ullsaard. Lutaan's hand stopped with his fingers a short distance from the rope.

"I understand," said the first captain as he straightened. With a nod, Lutaan turned towards Asuhas and waved him to approach. "He's secure."

The governor showed no pleasure as he looked up at Ullsaard's face. When he spoke, it was in a matter-of-fact way.

"I think it is more fortunate that we have claimed you, rather than Brother Leraates and his blackcrests. We will treat you decently enough."

"Why?" Ullsaard's question hung answered while Asuhas considered his answer, the governor toying his bottom lip with a fingertip. The king felt no need to elaborate.

"Urikh has the Brotherhood, which means he has the power to depose me should he wish," said Asuhas. "They have been recruiting blackcrests like you would not believe, and with most of the fighting legions in Salphoria, we governors have had little choice but to accede to your son's demands. Even so, I think he may carry through Leraates' threat."

"What threat could cow all of the governors of Greater Askhor?" said Ullsaard, his anger not dissipated but his raw fury diminished by genuine interest. "Even with all of the blackcrests in the empire, the brotherhood could not overthrow every province."

"They don't have to," said Asuhas. "The Brotherhood have learned since you disbanded them. Between military muscle and the ability to shut down all commerce, taxes and the general running of the empire, the Brotherhood has all of the high dice in their favour. As Leraates pointed out, does Greater Askhor really need governors?"

"There is something else, something you aren't telling me," said Ullsaard. He could sense fear in Asuhas; a tremor in the voice, a shake of the hands when he mentioned the Brotherhood. It was more than potential loss of privilege and position that kept him in check.

"They have their means," the words coming quickly, propelled by the governor's eagerness to speak of something else, "and it was Murian who folded first, and as soon as Anrair was loyal to Urikh, what choice did I have? Divide and conquer, I'm afraid. Urikh learnt from your successes there, Ullsaard."

The former king was not about to take his son's deviousness as a compliment.

"And what are you planning to do with me?" said Ullsaard. "You speak of me as if I'm some kind of prize to be fought over with Leraates."

"You are a prize, the most valuable in the empire." This answer came not from Asuhas, though Ullsaard recognised the Salphorian-tainted accent well.

"Anglhan!" The word was snarled between gritted teeth as Ullsaard shouldered aside Asuhas to confront the fat man walking across the compound. The former governor was smiling, his podgy, beringed fingers splayed over his gut, thumbs hooked into the pockets of a sleeveless jerkin worn over a bright red shirt.

Ullsaard lowered his head and charged at the treacherous Salphor, but Anglhan was nimble for his size and dodged aside. Grabbing a spear from one of the nearby legionnaires, Anglhan swung its haft into Ullsaard's knee as he awkwardly tried to turn for another attack. Already off balance, the king tumbled to the floor. Two more blows, to his shoulder and the side of his head, dazed the king sufficiently for Anglhan to feel confident enough to approach.

"Thought you had seen the last of me, didn't you?" the former governor asked with glee, slashing the end of the spear butt into Ullsaard's ribs. Ullsaard heard a shout and sounds of fighting, Out of the corner of his eye he spied Muuril being forcefully put down by his guards. Several others from the Thirteenth were also sent to the ground with clubbing blows. "You destroyed my fucking city, killed thousands of people who had done nothing wrong. I may have been a traitor, but you are a monster."

"I'm going to kill you, and when I do I'm going to make sure it is drawn out and painful," replied Ullsaard, getting one leg underneath him. He was sent sprawling again as the spear shaft rapped against his knee, sending pain surging up the king's leg and spine.

"You're not going to kill anybody," said Anglhan. "You're going on a journey, all the way to Askh. And when Asuhas and me present you to King Urikh, he will be pleased and he will see that we are men of value to him."

"You bargain me to buy favour with my son?" Ullsaard twisted to glare at Asuhas. The little man nodded morosely and shrugged.

"It is an unsafe world, Ullsaard. I need all of the allies I can get, especially the king."

"I am your king!" roared Ullsaard, but in his heart he knew it was no longer true.

"You are nothing," said Anglhan. The Salphor knelt down next to Ullsaard, lips not far from the king's ear. His next words were a whisper. "But I will make you great again, have no fear. You don't trust me, but I am your best hope of staying alive."

Anglhan then spat in Ullsaard's face and rose up, his massive form dark against the cloud-filled skies. Anglhan kicked Ullsaard hard in the face, heel connecting with the king's jaw, and the sky spun into darkness.

CARANTATHI
Winter, 213th year of Askh

I

It was bitterly cold and snow was falling again, but despite the weather Anasind made his daily rounds of the wall, checking on the new fortifications and the men on duty. He trudged along the frost-covered stones – the first job of each watch rotation was to clear the snowfall of the previous Watch – checking the mortar on the ramparts and to ensure that the stones weren't cracking. In such cold conditions, it was easy to overlook small flaws in the construction only for them to turn into much larger problems within a few years. It was the Askhan way to do a job properly and Anasind was not going to hand over a city that was unfit to defend or was a terrible drain on resources to maintain.

He had no idea what had possessed the Salphorian kings of old to build their greatest city so far into the mountains, but the freezing conditions were certainly a discouragement to anybody who wanted to rule from here. He had a pair of gloves fashioned from sheep hide and stuffed with wool, and still his fingertips were numb. Like all of his men, he did not wear the traditional legion kilt; woollen Salphorian trousers kept the snow and biting wind from his legs. Some of the men

168

grumbled, particular the Enairians who were no strangers to inclement weather, and Anasind had even caught a few wearing their kilts over their trousers in silent protest at the concession made to the climate. As the winds had strengthened and the snows had fallen more heavily, the sense of the Salphorian clothing was made clearer and the complaints had stopped.

He received raised spears in salute from the men at their posts, and nods from those at the braziers in the timbered shelters every two hundred paces. There were only four proper towers, one at each corner of the walls, and the main gatehouse, so Anasind had quickly supervised the erection of palisades and wind breaks, which served as cover from both attack and frostbite.

The city had gone into a kind of hibernation once the snows had started falling every day. Most of the people stayed in their homes, and the city was covered in a layer of smoke from their fires. The livestock that had been put out on the mountain pastures had been brought into the city, accompanied by the extended families that tended the animals, and so the half-empty streets had bustled with beasts and people for a short while, but now all but breeding stock had been slaughtered, the carcasses salted and put into the natural caves beneath the hill on which the long hall was built.

Most of the legions had been despatched across Salphoria, to make winter camp overlooking the rivers and roads that would be the lifeblood of the new territory of Greater Askhor. The Askhans had done their fair share of burning and pillaging on the advance duskwards, and now they did their best to organise, ration and distribute the food stores that remained, supplemented by forage and game taken by the legions themselves. Anasind had impressed upon his first captains the need to be even-handed, and although the legions would not go without proper meals, where once the favour of chieftains had decided who would feed and who would starve, now the Askhans would show that all were to be treated equally.

Only six companies of the Thirteenth remained in the city, about as many soldiers as the food stores could supply on top of the condensed populace, supplemented by a local militia overseen by Aegenuis. Some of the sergeants had, on their own initiative, started to take Salphorian recruits into their drill sessions, while the elders of Carantathi passed on what they knew about surviving the cold of the mountains, urged on by Aegenuis. The deposed king of Salphoria had been good to his word to Ullsaard and did his best to accommodate the needs of Anasind, and to tamp down any flames of resentment amongst his people. In all, the winter forced Salphor and Askhan to work together.

Anasind was just completing his rounds, coming up to the guard tower on the right hand side of the gate, when he saw a figure approaching up the road. The snow drifts were high, and the man was swathed in furs, wading as much as he was walking. Perhaps the shutdown of the city had made Anasind doubt anybody ventured outside the walls, but he rubbed his eyes and looked again, fearing some kind of snow-blindness was affecting him. Despite this, the man was still forging his way through the whiteness.

As he came closer, it was clear that the approaching man was dragging a bundle behind him on a small sled – easier than carrying it on his back, Anasind realised. Bundled up in furs, his head wrapped about with the same, it was impossible to tell the age or build of the man. However, there was something distinctive about him. On his sled were stowed a spear and a shield; the gear of a legionnaire.

There were encouraging shouts echoing down the pass as some of the men on the walls saw the new arrival, but Anasind knew that a lone legionnaire braving the terrible winter mountains was not a good sign. He wondered which of the possibilities it represented: a legion camp attacked; a town starving; a column ambushed. Another thought occurred to the general as he signalled for some men to go down to the ground and open the small door within the main gate – the death of the king, perhaps?

Worried by this sudden thought, Anasind followed the men despatched to the gate, and waited with them while the man hauled himself and his sled through the gateway. Ice crystals had formed around the brim of his fur-lined hood and his cheeks and chin were hidden by a bushy beard. Long straggles of hair escaped from the confines of his headgear; a man the opposite of a neatly presented legionnaire. Anasind was instantly suspicious and put a hand to the hilt of his sword. With a thud, the other men closed the gate door.

"Whoa general, don't gut me yet," the stranger said, throwing back his hood. Black hair, tousled by the wind, flowed from the man's scalp, but as he swept it away from his face, Anasind recognised him. "It's me, Caaspir. The king sent me."

II

After relinquishing Caaspir of his sled and harness, Anasind had the man taken care of and then brought to his quarters in one of the old noble's houses on the mound by the long hall. The general's neighbour was Aegenuis, and sometimes Anasind overhead the man when he was drunk, lamenting his demise or arguing with his family. Occasionally there was also noisy sex, but he had learned the warning signs that the former king was feeling amorous, and would find excuse to visit the long hall or one of his officers for the night.

Having been given something hot to drink and some food, Caaspir arrived half an hour later, a small waterproofed packet under his arm and a grim look on his face. Anasind met him in one of the dining chambers, where the fireplace was largest. Timber was scarce, though there was coal in the mountains, and it was prudent to have the least number of fires burning at any time, so the dining room and the main bedroom were the only chambers in the house that were warmed.

Caaspir's sudden arrival and pensive expression reminded Anasind that something was amiss so the general dismissed his attendants from the room.

Caaspir looked grateful for the privacy. He still had his ragged beard and hair, but had swapped his smelly furs for some properly-made Salphorian trousers and jacket. He looked more like one of the barbarian chieftains than a member of the king's favoured legion.

"The last I saw of you, you were heading to Askh," said Anasind. He poured mulled wine for the legionnaire, who took the drink in his free hand and stayed at attention. "You've come back a long way."

"Yes, general, I have," said Caaspir. He proffered the package, which Anasind took. "Missives from King Ullsaard, general. I was to deliver them to you personally, nobody else."

"What if I was dead?" said Anasind. He knew the way Ullsaard thought, and such an outcome would have been considered.

"Then I was to burn them and, according to the king, we'd all be fucked worse than the cheapest whore visiting the barracks."

Anasind wanted to laugh but it died on his lips; he sensed no humour in the messenger.

"Do you know the contents of this?" He waved the packet in one hand. It was light, most of the weight from the tarred leather.

"Letters, general, penned by the king. Nothing else."

"So what could be so important, I wonder?" said Anasind.

"The king said I were to answer any questions what you might have, general, and if you have a mind, I could tell you what's been happening. Before you read the letters, I mean."

"Go ahead. Sit down, if this is going to take some time."

Caaspir sat on the opposite side the table, the cup of mulled wine clasped in both hands. He fixed Anasind with a sincere look.

"King Ullsaard's son, Urikh, has taken the Crown for himself. The king's holed up in his villa at Menesun, in Ersua. Well, he was when I left. Before that happened, he gave me the letters in that package and said you was to read the one with your name on first. The other is for the Salphorian, Aegenuis."

"Why would he write to Aegenuis?" Anasind wondered aloud, unbuckling the strap that held the packet together. Two waxed parchment envelopes slipped out onto the table, one with his name on it, the other marked for the former Salphorian king.

"I don't know, but King Ullsaard said it was important that you fulfil his wishes as outlined in his writing to you," answered Caaspir.

The letter began:

If you do not receive another message from me in five days' time, I am probably dead or a prisoner, so here is what you must do.

III

Aegenuis had to read the first lines again. His spoken Askhan was coming along well, but his people did not have a history of writing. It was unfamiliar, because in writing Ullsaard had a fluid, rounded script and his words were less functional than when he spoke. Some of them Aegenuis had to guess at the meaning, but the context made the message clear.

I find myself short of friends. Oddly, of all the people I have known, there is only one I have taken a nation from and yet I hope to count

*you among my allies. I have no other choice but to trust you. If you
are reading this letter, it means that General Anasind has received no
message from me to rescind his orders.*

*Urikh has tried to oust me from power and I have no legions to fight
him. I have never been anything than forthright and honest with you,
and though I have Salphor blood on my hands, a river of it, I have
never held any malice towards you as a person or towards your people.
Urikh will be a despot, and he will be corrupt. He is able to usurp me
because he has unleashed the full power of the Brotherhood. The
Brothers will be heartless. They will take what they need from your
people and crush everything that remains of your culture and tradi-
tions. I grew up in its wake in Enair, so I know of what I speak. If you
trust me and wish no extra woe upon come to Salphoria, please cooperate with General Anasind. He will tell you what I need you to do.*

Shocked, Aegenuis looked sharply at Anasind, who was
standing by the fire, watching the former king carefully.

"You know what this says?" asked the Salphor. The general
shook his head. Aegenuis grunted and rubbed his bearded
chin, thinking through the possibilities. He sat down at the end
of the table and reached for a beer jug. Taking a mouthful direct from the ewer, Aegenuis reached a decision. "You know
that Urikh has kicked out your friend?"

"Yes, he told me that in his letter," said Anasind.

"If word of that was to get out, it could spell the end of your
occupation of Salphoria. News like that spreads quickly. Winter's a bad time to be in a hostile land."

"Ullsaard likes you," Anasind said, half-turned towards the
firepit, eyes reflecting the light of the lamps hung from the
beams overhead. "That is why I have given you that letter, five
days after receiving one myself. Because I like you, I'm going
to tell you another of the things the king has instructed me to
do today. I am to stay by your side, day and night, from this
moment forward. If I think you are betraying Ullsaard, in any

way at all, I am to put my sword in your gut or slit your throat. He leaves it entirely to my judgement. If you choose to make a veiled threat again, I will kill you. The situation is too serious for niceties."

"Well then, looks like I don't have much choice," said Aegenuis. He raised the beer jug in toast to Anasind. "For better or worse, it seems I'm Ullsaard's friend. What does he want us to do?"

ASKH
Winter, 213th year of Askh

I

A look from Allenya parted the two black-crested soldiers standing at the main doors to her sister's apartments. One of them growled something and the door opened, swinging inwards to reveal a mosaic-floored entrance hall and a Maasrite serving maid with head bowed.

Allenya strode through the door, paying no attention to the servants that were gathering like a flock of hungry starlings. She headed down the hall and then took an archway on her right, which brought her into a dining hall. Passing through this, the queen walked briskly into a lounge, where a stretch of coldwards-facing windows showed a view out across the capital city. It was mid-afternoon, the sun touching the peaks of the mountains to duskwards, leaving much of the city in shadow. Lights from windows and torches illuminating the streets were spreading out from the dawnwards gate, bringing light back to Askh as the darkness of winter's night crept from one side of the city to the other.

"What is Urikh up to?" she demanded of her sister, Luia, who was sitting in one of the chairs by the window. Luia was staring thoughtfully out of the window, her long black hair obscuring one side of her face, reddened lips pursed. Slowly the king's mother turned, as if in a daze.

"Whatever he wants to do, I'm sure," said Luia, not looking up at Allenya. "He is the king, after all."

"There are legionnaires all over the palace, and he's ordered that Ullnaar be brought back from the colleges." Allenya stood over Luia, arms crossed, glowering at her sister. "It feels like I am being kept prisoner. What is he afraid of?"

"Nothing," Luia said, sharpness returning to her voice and her eyes. "The palace has always had guards. Why does it concern you so much, sister? He just wants to make sure we are protected."

"The task of guarding the royal palace is for the First, not the thugs of the Brotherhood. And it reminds me of Magilnada. You were not there sister, but you would feel the same if you thought for a moment you were being held hostage. I wanted to visit Pretaa, but Urikh has informed me that I should not travel to Enair, or leave the city at all. He would not even see me, he sent me a letter!"

"So it is your pride that has been bruised?" Luia swivelled in her chair to look at Allenya properly. The queen knew what her sister saw; the grey ash of mourning daubed on her cheeks and forehead still; dishevelled clothes and unkempt hair. Luia gave Allenya a look of pity and stood up, one hand reaching out. "It is the middle of winter, sister, now is not the time to head coldwards. In the spring, we will visit Ullsaard's mother and pay our respects. Meliu can come too. It will be just the three of us; Urikh can stay here with his musty Brotherhood friends and we will be able to forget about what has happened."

Allenya saw empathy in her sister's face, though she was not convinced it was wholly genuine. As comforting as Luia's words were, they did not answer Allenya's question, so she spoke it again.

"Why does Urikh feel he needs to increase the guard of the palace? And why has he brought in these Brotherhood blackcrests?"

"Why do you assume I am party to the reasons for all of his decisions?" replied Luia. She shrugged. "The empire has been in a fragile state since Ullsaard killed Lutaar, and this latest disruption has been unsettling for many people, especially the nobles. I am sure my son is doing his best to protect his family, and his position. I am grateful for his diligence."

Though there was bravado in Luia's words and tone, Allenya knew her sister well, and could tell when she was perturbed. There was a shadow around Luia's eyes that testified to sleepless nights, and not caused by the procession of lovers Luia invited to her bedchambers. Hearing the scuff of feet, Allenya looked over her shoulder and saw a black-robed figure entering, his face covered by a silver mask inscribed with delicate swirls, patterns and sigils. She felt Luia stiffen beside her, then unconsciously step slightly back to stand behind the eldest sister.

"Brother Aalek, I was not expecting a visit today," said Luia, regaining her stern demeanour. "I do not recall saying that you could enter my apartments."

"Apologies, my queens," said the Brother, though he made no bow or gesture to back up his words. Bright blues eyes regarded the two sisters from the rectangular slits in the mask. "It is fortunate that you are both here. I sought Queen Allenya in her chambers and was disturbed to find that she was not present."

"I am at liberty to go where I wish within my own home," said Allenya, though as the words departed from her lips she could feel the force of the Brother's stare and knew the emptiness of them. She continued defiantly. "I am entitled to visit my sister whenever I wish."

"No injunction was intended, my queen," said Aalek. "I meant merely that I have disturbing news to deliver and I feared I would not deliver it properly before you heard a dangerous rumour."

"Rumour? What rumour?" said Luia.

"An imposter has entered Greater Askhor, claiming to be the previous king," said Aalek. He clasped his hands in front of him and gazed down at the floor. "This man attempts to rally an army against King Urikh, asserting he is your dead husband."

The thought of someone masquerading as Ullsaard filled Allenya with horror and disgust, and Aalek's warning served as a further reminder that her husband had been killed. Lightheadedness threatened to make Allenya faint. Noticing her sister's distress, Luia took her by the arm and guided her to a chair, pushing gently but insistently until Allenya sat down. Brow furrowed, Luia turned her attention back to Aalek.

"How could anyone claim to be Ullsaard? It is ridiculous."

"Any man with a few soldiers can claim to be a king, my queen," replied the Brother. "Who would dare to argue otherwise? The common folk, even many captains in the legions, do not know what your husband looked like. They have only the coins minted during Ullsaard's reign to judge the imposter, and any passing resemblance would satisfy doubt. If a man acts like a king, he is likely to be believed by the ignorant and ill-educated."

"This imposter cannot be too clever himself, if he thinks he can topple my son with such a laughable ploy," said Luia.

"Indeed, the threat is minimal, but King Urikh wished that you be made aware of this plot, lest word of it came to your ears by less sympathetic means. I would not wish to raise the hopes of my queens, to see them rudely dashed when the bald truth is revealed."

"Your consideration for our feelings is noted," murmured Allenya. She looked out at the roofs of Askh, the mix of grey slate and red-grey tiles slicked with moisture. Looking at the dismal scene and thinking on the words of Aalek, she felt a sudden chill and pulled her shawl tighter around her body.

"Bring hot tea," said Luia, and a moment later two silent handmaids left the room. She laid a hand on Allenya's arm. "Do not worry, my sister. Urikh will not throw away the legacy bequeathed to him by our late husband. This charlatan will find that his support grows thin once word is spread of his treachery."

Allenya stood up abruptly, pulling away from the grasp of her sister. The queen looked at Brother Aalek and clenched her hands into fists at her sides.

"Find this man who pretends to be Ullsaard, and punish him for his insolence," Allenya said, her voice and fists trembling. "I want him to know pain for the insult he visits on the memory of my dead husband, and for the hurt he causes to me and my sisters. Kill him, Aalek, and make him pay."

The silver mask hid the Brother's reaction, except for the sudden widening of his eyes betraying surprise. He collected himself in a heartbeat and bowed his head.

"It will be a pleasure to do the queen's bidding," said Aalek. "This villain will be apprehended and he will be made to repent the error of his decision, of that you should rest assured, my queens."

After Aalek had departed and hot honey-sweetened tea brought in, Allenya walked to the windows and stared down at the city. The largest houses clustered around the Royal Mound like piglets suckling at a sow, eager to share in the wealth, power and prestige of those who lived in the palace. The dwellings became less grand the further they were from the mound, gradually giving away to the homes of traders, then shrinking further and mingling with industries such as tanneries, until the least desirable dwelt in the shadow on the walls, wedged in the spaces between the towers and the barracks and the training grounds of the First Legion. The curtain wall of the city was almost lost in the dim light, seen only by the braziers and torches that lit the stones.

"Ullnaar will return soon," Allenya said eventually, as servants closed the shutters to keep out the raw breeze. "I should return to my rooms, Meliu will be looking for me."

II

Watching her sister depart, Luia had a lot to think about. She paced back and forth across the chamber while servants banked up the logs in the fire and brought in an incense-burning brazier to lighten the smell. Luia barely registered their presence as they dodged and sidestepped from her path.

The arrival of the Lakhyri – the queen paused in her step for a moment as she thought of that etched, withered creature – had coincided with the news of Ullsaard's death. At the time she had thought it fortuitous that Urikh had such an experienced aide on hand to take care of the ascension to kinghood, but now the convenience of the situation was beginning to nag at her credulity. She suspected that perhaps Urikh was being manipulated by the High Brother in some way that she had not discerned. Part of her even wondered if the Brotherhood had somehow been complicit in the death of her husband. It was not the first time such thoughts had occurred to her, but the strength of the Brotherhood was in Greater Askhor, and their reach did not stretch far into Salphoria yet. It would be unlikely they could engineer the attack that had slain Ullsaard, as much as they might have desired it.

Her worries were mounting. The loss of Ullsaard had been a bitter blow to Luia's hopes of securing the future of her family. Urikh was clever and able, but he was too young to be king; especially with the likes of Lakhyri trying to take advantage. She had tried her best to steer her son towards the correct decisions, but he was determined to be a man alone, disregarding her advice out of hand.

Urikh had once listened to everything his mother had taught him, but since taking the Crown he had become more and more distant from her. Luia suspected that Lakhyri was inserting himself between mother and son, to bring the king to his own agenda. It certainly appeared that the High Brother's plans were bearing fruit; Urikh was keen to strengthen the power of the Brotherhood. The king claimed that a bold and dynamic Brotherhood was a symbol of a bold and dynamic empire, but Luia was not yet convinced of the wisdom of offending the governors and nobility. Under Ullsaard, the Brotherhood had proven that their support was invaluable to a king, but there had to be balance. Soon the Brotherhood would not need the authority of the king at all.

With this thought, Luia stopped mid-step, so abruptly that a servant who had been looking to step behind her was forced into a flailing spin by his drastic attempt to avoid her. She glanced down at the youth as he sprawled on the floor, the corner of her mouth rising in a sneer.

Dismissing this distraction, Luia sat down in a chair beside the fire. She could not believe that Urikh did not see that he was making himself redundant to the power of the Brotherhood. Luia knew that he had a plan; her son was too canny and too careful to let his power be given away piece by piece without some objective in mind.

If only Urikh would take her into his confidence as he once did, Luia would be reassured that all was well. At the moment, she was frustrated, able to speak to her son only in the presence of others. That had to change.

"Naami, please convey my regards to my son, and have my staff attend to me," the queen said to her chief handmaiden. "We have a feast to arrange."

GERIA, OKHAR

Winter, 213th year of Askh

I

There was a light frost on the ground, covering the terraced hill-sides with its pale blanket. The early morning sunlight glittered from the empty vine frames and frozen cisterns. Everything seemed sparkling and fresh, even the clear blue sky above. The air was crisp with the cold, but not unpleasant, and Noran took a moment to watch the cloud of his breath dissipating. He took in another deep breath, enjoying the sensation of clean air in his lungs, and let it out in another burst of vapour.

The view to hotwards was stunning, showing the Greenwater carving its way through landscaped hills and dark fields. Turning his head just a little, Noran could see the wood and stone buildings of Geria clustered around the dock piers. Even now there were ships coming and going on the great river, the latest cargoes being carried to and from the colony of Cosuan at the end of the Greenwater. Cranes and teamsters were in constant action, loading the final harvests and winter wares, or unloading the strange fruits and spices that had started to come coldwards along the river. Out on the water, pilot boats guided ships to and from their berths, the strokes of their oars leaving faint trails like the footprints of insects on blue earth.

A little further inland stood the palace of the governor, Urikh. The grey stone building looked more intimidating than ever with its new barracks block built to dawnwards, overlooking the river. Noran had not seen Urikh since paying the governor a courtesy visit on his return in the spring. He had received neither summons to the governor's house nor had Urikh deigned to visit his father's old friend at his villa.

The arrangement suited Noran well. He had harboured no desire to spend time with Urikh in the past, and Noran's self-imposed exile from Ullsaard benefited greatly from the lack of contact with the king's family. It was possible for Noran, now and then, to forget everything that had happened to him since he had journeyed to near-Mekha to summon Ullsaard back to the capital.

The time in Geria had been restorative, both physically and mentally. He was even on speaking terms with Anriit, his eldest and only surviving wife. They were not intimate by any means, but they could now spend time in a room with each other without their conversations devolving into insults and accusations. The relationship was helped somewhat by the fact that Anriit was currently in Askh, spending the winter months in the capital with her family.

"It is a very pleasant day, Artiides," Noran declared to his chief steward, who was standing a little further up the slope with his master's coat folded over his arms. A former second captain in the Seventeenth Legion, Artiides was the same age as Noran, with wiry muscles and a keen mind for organisation.

"Very pleasant, yes," Artiides replied dutifully. "It is also cold, and you should be careful not to chill your blood."

"Thank you," said Noran, holding out his arm so that Artiides could slip on the long coat over his master's shirt and jerkin.

"We'll be getting company soon," Artiides remarked as he straightened Noran's collar. The steward pointed down the hillside to the road, where a detachment of legionnaires was marching towards the villa. Their green and red shields marked them out as men of the Seventeenth – Okhar's garrison legion.

"I see a second captain with them," said Noran, staring down at the approaching troops. "Some message from Urikh, no doubt."

"I am not so sure," said Artiides, laying a hand on Noran's arm to guide him back towards the villa. "Why send a captain to do a herald's job?"

"What are you doing?" Noran demanded, pulling his arm from his servant's grip.

"There are more soldiers in the fields to coldwards," said Artiides, indicating the direction with a flick of his eyes. "Best not show that we have seen them."

Noran looked out to the fields and saw several dozen legionnaires, in two groups standing at junctions on the road leading coldwards. They were formed up in ranks, not idly lounging.

"I see," said Noran, his heart sinking. He nodded to Artiides and the two of them set off back towards the villa at a quick but not untoward pace. "Have you any idea why they might be here?"

"None at all," said Artiides. "I still have friends in the Seventeenth. If there had been anything brewing I would have heard it."

"It will still be half an hour before they arrive, let us not waste any time," said Noran.

"I'll get everything ready, have no fears," said Artiides. "If there's any trouble, leave it to me."

II

Noran stood just inside the doorway of the villa, at a vantage point where he could see and hear what was going on at the main gate. He watched Artiides, sword at his belt, gathering a handful of the men, who also carried weapons from the stores. Artiides opened the small postern gate, bowed his head and stepped back to admit a tall, rangy man in the uniform of a second captain.

"Captain Juutan, Seventeenth," announced the officer.

"I know who you are, Juutan, why the formality?" replied Artiides. "And why the heavyweights out there?"

"I bear news for the master of the villa, Noran Astaan," Juutan said stiffly.

"And I'll make sure he hears it as soon as he is back from his morning walk," said Artiides.

"Please, friend, don't be awkward about this. Just take me to Astaan now."

"What news?" Artiides said. "What news is so important that it needs fifty men to escort it?"

"Ullsaard is dead, Urikh is now king," said Juutan, shaking his head. "Now, take me to Astaan."

"Urikh is king?" Noran could not tell if Artiides was playing for time or genuinely shocked. "Since when?"

"I have orders, all right. Let's do it the simple way, eh?" Juutan's hand strayed to the hilt of his sword, and Artiides took a step back. There was the sound of unsheathing blades around the courtyard as the other servants bared their weapons.

"Let's not get hasty," said Juutan, holding up his hands. "I just have a job to do."

"What job?" demanded Artiides. "You've delivered your news, now piss off."

"That is not the only reason I am here," said Juutan. "Along with the news of King Urikh's accession, First Captain Harrakil received orders that Noran Astaan be detained and escorted to Askh to attend the new king and renew his oaths as his herald."

"I see," said Artiides. The steward stepped closer and Noran could not hear what was said next. When he stepped back, Artiides raised his voice again. "Very well, you leave me no choice. I will fetch my master here."

Noran shrank back from the doorway as Artiides turned and strode back into the shadow of the villa. He grabbed hold of the steward as he crossed the threshold.

"What is happening, Artiides?" Noran said, his grip tight on the other man's arm. "Why do they want me to go to Askh to renew my oaths?"

"I don't know, but the orders came from Urikh himself," Artiides replied tersely, pulling free from Noran's grip and leading him further into the entrance hall . "He claims that Ullsaard has been killed, and he has taken up the Crown."

"Ullsaard dead?" Noran shook his head, disbelieving, but sense prevailed after a moment. Ullsaard had been waging war; it was not beyond the realm of possibility that he had been slain in battle or else killed by his Salphor enemies. "I am surprised that Urikh wants me though."

"I don't know what it is, but it doesn't sit right in my head," said Artiides.

"Why send an armed guard?" said Noran. "What reason does Urikh think I might have for refusing a command to attend him? It sounds to me like the action of a man unsure of himself. If Urikh thought he had a legitimate claim to be king he would just send for me and not worry about escorts."

"So you think that Urikh is acting like a guilty man? You were a friend of his father, perhaps he thinks you're a loose end. It might not be safe in Askh."

"It might not be safe getting to Askh," added Noran. "Accidents happen on board ship and on the road. What should I do?"

"Run like fuck. We'll hold them as long as we can."

There might have been a time when Noran would have demanded to know if there was cause for such panic, and would have stopped to ask Artiides why the need for alarm. The past years had taught Noran the folly of inquiring too deeply during life-or-death situations, so he simply accepted the veteran captain's assessment and bolted back into the villa.

There was no time to pick up any belongings of note, but Noran did make a quick detour via the kitchens to snatch up some bread and a bag of fruit; he had no illusions about his ability to forage even in fertile Okhar.

With these provisions secured, Noran darted back through the villa and into the main feast chamber, which opened out onto the gardens through wide screens. The weather had not yet turned cold enough for the screens to be erected, and so Noran had an unparalleled view of the land to dawnwards and coldwards. A hasty look confirmed that one group of legionnaires were still out in the fields; the other could not be seen.

There were angry shouts from the front courtyard, and a cry of challenge from Artiides. His few retainers would not hold long against a fifty legionnaires, and so Noran ran into the gardens, turning hotwards.

He knew he needed to have a plan, but for the moment his only concern was to get away from the villa and Geria. Hotwards seemed the most likely route, angling to dawnwards to take him away from the patrols along the Greenwater. His family's estates covered quite a large slice of Okhar, and he would be able to spend the night in one of his tenant's farms. There were too many little farmsteads and holdings for a company of legionnaires to search in a day. After some time to think, he could set out on the following morning for a more certain destination.

With this in mind, Noran ran across a lawn and ducked through the archway of a wall between the ornamental gardens and the kitchen garden. Plunging across lines of herbs and vegetables, Noran headed straight for the high hedge at the back of the villa, beyond which was a wall and then the open fields. There were scattered woodlands almost directly to hotwards; he could hide out in there.

He stopped before he reached the hedgerow, realising that up on the terrace he could be seen by the legionnaires on the roads below. His progress would be easily marked. From the kitchen gardens he could follow the wall around to the front of the villa, and make his escape back down the road towards Geria.

It was a daring plan, sneaking out behind the soldiers that had been sent to take him. It depended on whether the captain leading the contingent had posted any men on the serving entrance through the coldwards line of the wall. In all likelihood it would be clear, but that did not mean there would be nobody watching the road.

Knowing that he was dithering, and such hesitation might be the difference between living and dying, Noran made a decision. He headed out through the hedge and found the gate in the wall that led out to the vine terraces. With a last glance back at the villa, he opened the gate and stepped out, shouldering his bag of bread and fruit.

Something hard hit him in the gut almost immediately, sending him crumpling to the ground. Noran looked up to see five legionnaires standing over him, the butts of their spears pointed in his direction from behind a short wall of shields.

"Come quietly now," said one of the men, passing his spear to his shield hand and then reaching out to help Noran to his feet.

Noran threw a punch, badly. The soldier ducked back away from the blow, which was fortunate because had it landed Noran realised he would have broken his knuckles on the man's helmet.

"Grab him, gag him!" snapped the man Noran had swung at, and moments later, Noran was bundled back to the dirt, a rag shoved into his mouth. His wrists were bound in front of him and he was lifted to his feet once more, this time with less decorum.

"Wriggly little bastard, aren't ya?" laughed one of the soldiers as Noran's arms were grabbed and he was half-led and half-dragged away from the gate.

Noran stumbled a few steps, trying to make himself as much of a deadweight as possible. When this did not work, he dug his heels into the soft earth as best he could, but was heaved on regardless. They were coming to the end of the wall and would be turning around the corner to the road in moments. Noran had no time left, he had to act now.

Lifting a foot, he kicked the legionnaire to his right in the back of the knee as the man took a step, sending him sprawling face first into the mud. Dragged down by his fall, Noran twisted to land on his shoulder. The other soldier who had been holding him had to release his grip to stop himself being pulled down. In the moment this afforded Noran, he managed to get his feet under himself and push up, launching himself to the left, crashing through the vine fence to plunge sidelong down onto the next terrace.

Getting to his feet again, he ran as fast as he could along the row of winter-dead vines as the soldiers burst down onto the path behind him. They did not shout, but pounded after him, slowed by their spears and shields while Noran's tied hands prevented him running freely. Already panting hard from exertion and fear, Noran hurled himself down to the next tier of the terrace, landing awkwardly. Pain flared through his ankle as he pressed on, and within a few strides he was limping heavily.

His ankle gave way completely a dozen paces later and sent him sprawling into the dirt once more. Gritting his teeth, Noran rolled around, trying to get back up again. Rough hands grabbed his arms and tunic, pinning him to the ground.

The soldier who had first spoken to him stood over Noran, spear held ready.

"I was hoping it wouldn't come to this," said the legionnaire. A heartbeat later he smashed the end of his spear into Noran's temple.

III

A dull throbbing and a sharper pain around his ear signalled to Noran that he had regained consciousness. The first thing he did was to flex his arms, and to his surprise found that he was not tied. His legs were free too, and from the crunch of wheels, the rocking of something hard beneath him and the stink of abada dung, Noran guessed his was on the back of a wagon.

Opening his eyes as he sat up, the noble confirmed his assessment. He couldn't have been out cold for long, the rooftops of his villa were still visible in the distance as he trundled down the hill towards Geria.

Immediately behind the wagon trooped Noran's servants, each of them showing cuts and bruises. He counted only eight, meaning that two were missing, Artiides amongst them. Each man had his hands bound in front of him and there was a detachment of legionnaires behind them with spears lowered. The retainers looked up as Noran righted himself.

"Where's Artiides, and Kapul?" asked the noble.

Faaduan, who was closest of the men, shook his head and said nothing. Glancing over his shoulder, Noran saw that he was on the only cart in the column, two legionnaires on the board at the front. More soldiers marched to either side of him, and he remembered the face of the man walking just beside the abada.

"Captain Juutan?" he called out, and the man turned at the sound of his name. Falling back, the captain looked at his charge, examining him from head to foot.

"Sorry about that bash on the head there, but you should've just come quietly," said Juutan.

Noran lifted a hand to the bruise on the side of his head, nodding slowly.

"It is an instinct, highly honed, you see," he explained. "I have learned to my constant regret that I do not mix well in the company of armed men. You seem like a civilised man though, captain; diligent and attentive, no doubt. Please, speak with me for a moment."

Juutan hauled himself over the side of the cart and sat down on the bare boards next to Noran, his scabbard across his lap, shield propped against the side. As Juutan adjusted his breastplate, Noran was able to study him for a few moments, running an experienced eye over the man's dress and features. Seeing the man more closely, Noran realised he was older than he had first thought, crow's feet marking the corners of his eyes and his forehead lined under the rim of his helmet. Given his age, Juutan was very likely a career soldier, sworn into the legions until death; a younger man might still be in his ten year tenure. There was also a certain cast to his skin and hook of the nose that suggested Okharan-born, and on the balance of probability from Geria itself. That made him a bit of an oddity; most Gerians whether common or noble were brought up with the Greenwater in their blood, not service to the legions.

"What's the point of being captain if you cannot ride while your men walk?" Noran said airily.

"I like marching with my men," replied Juutan. "I do not think of myself as better than them because of my rank."

And the captain's words confirmed what Noran had suspected: Juutan was a commoner who had made his way up through the ranks. That made Juutan both dedicated and poor, because the camp costs of an officer, especially one of a garri-

son legion in a provincial capital, would soak up almost all of
his wages.

"You know," Noran began, leaning closer, "my family have
considerable estates across the whole empire."

"I've heard of the Astaans," replied Juutan, with a hint of
reproach. "There's some say your father has more money in
his vaults than there is in the Okharan treasury."

Noran smiled, taking this comment as a hint that Juutan
was aware of Noran's wealth. The nobleman folded his hands
in his lap as he swayed from side to side in time with the cart's
motion.

"If you and your men were to return me to my villa, I could
help you conduct a thorough search of the premises," Noran
suggested. He kept his voice low; Juutan might be one of those
officers who would take a bribe for himself but not if it was
known by his men.

"My orders contained no mention of a search," said Juutan
with a shrug. "It is just my job to get you to the wharfs. There's
a ship waiting to take you up the river."

"I am not certain such a journey would be agreeable at this
time of the year," said Noran, hiding his surprise at the captain's naiveté. "Winter is coming and travelling to coldwards
will bear heavily on my constitution, which has been taxed in
recent times."

"That is not my concern," said Juutan.

Noran bit his lip, unsure whether Juutan was being stupid
or coy. He decided it must be the latter; nobody was that
callow.

"While I am sure that King Urikh is a fine fellow, I really
have no desire to travel to Askh at this time," Noran continued, convinced his persistence would pay off. "I could happily
pay you to convey my regards to the king."

"That's not my orders."

"All right, I understand, but you have to play fair," said Noran, his voice dropping to a whisper. "How much will it cost me?"

"It won't cost you anything, the king is paying for the ship's commission," said Juutan.

"For the love of… How much will it cost me not to be put on that ship?"

Sitting back, his face showing conflict between surprise and disappointment, Juutan shook his head.

"Not for all the money of the Astaans," exclaimed the captain. "My honour is more important than your wealth. If I let you escape I would never live it down. First Captain Harrakil picked me personally for this."

"I bet he did," Noran mumbled, "I just bet he did."

MARRADAN, ERSUA
Winter, 213th year of Askh

With shovels over their shoulders, the line of prisoners marched down the road with sullen expressions, two dozen armed legionnaires of the Brotherhood to escort them. They reached the snow drifts that marked where the previous days' labours had ended, and without any order needed to be given, they set to, digging through the snow to open the road to the Ersuan capital.

There were seventy men in all – not all of them legion convicts. Thirty-two were the former soldiers of the Thirteenth, seven others disgraced members of the Twenty-first, with the rest being made up of general thieves, vagabonds and, most heinous of all in the eyes of the Brotherhood, tax dodgers.

Some dug away at the snow, while others hauled it into the fields on handcarts. It was back-breaking work, even for men hardened to a life in the legions, clearing mile after mile of roads to keep the arteries of the empire clear for commerce.

"Leastways we're not up in Enair," said one of the men from the Twenty-first, Linnir, whose facial hair hid his mouth, the dark brown of his straggly beard and hair streaked with grey. None of the prisoners were allowed a blade of any kind, so all sported hair growth depending on the amount of time they had been in the punishment company.

"I don't think they even bother clearing the snow up there," said Loordin, plunging his shovel into the snow. He lifted it out and turned the white pile onto the handcart in front of Muuril. The King's Companion, face obscured by a ragged fringe and a great bush of a black beard, grunted but said nothing.

"He doesn't talk much, your friend, does he?" said Linnir.

A group of prisoners trudged past them, moving further along the road. They clambered up a bank of snow that had piled up against a compound wall, almost as tall as a man. Tools were passed up to them and they started to dig into the white mass.

"He hasn't got much to talk about," said Gelthius. Dressed in fur-lined boots and woollen clothes, the former legionnaire was not cold, despite the wind and the snow. His heavy gloves made handling the handle of the shovel difficult though, and he dropped as much snow as he managed to load onto Muuril's handcart.

What Linnir said was true, though. Muuril had barely spoken half a dozen words since they had been told to surrender by Ullsaard. It had been a hard blow to all of them, but being appointed King's Companion had meant a lot to the sergeant. To have not only the title but his honour ripped away so cruelly just days later had almost broken the big man.

"I don't know what you lot was thinking," said Linnir, stamping on his shovel to force it deeper into the snow. He gave the handle a twist and turned to Muuril with the laden shovel. "Fifty men against a legion? If that'd been me, I would have handed Ullsaard over first thing. Might've gotten a reward instead of spending the rest of your lives clearing snow, shovelling shit from sewers and eating hard bread and gruel."

"Doesn't work that way, does it?" said Loordin. "Ullsaard's been our commander for nearly ten years now. You don't walk away from a man that's done good by you."

"Ullsaard's done fuck all except get your mates killed and you lot up to your necks in shit." Linnir turned back to the drift. "And what thanks do you get? None. Even when you're willing to lay down your lives for that bastard, he goes and turns out to be a coward after all."

Gelthius opened his mouth to shout a warning out of instinct, but Loordin's shovel hit Linnir in the side of the head before the words came out. The man pitched forwards into the snow, blood spewing from a ragged gash above his ear. The drift turned pink as more life fluid pumped from the deep wound, the hot liquid melting a red valley through the snow.

Loordin stepped towards the injured man, shovel raised for another blow. A gloved hand closed around the handle of the tool and wrenched it away. Gelthius saw Muuril toss the improvised weapon back along the road, and slapped a hand into Loordin's chest when he made to take a step towards it.

"He's still alive," growled Muuril, nodding towards the groaning Linnir. "Murder gets your throat slit."

"I thought you of all of us would understand," said Loordin. He glanced at Gelthius, who had to look away. "You heard what he said about Ullsaard."

"He's right," said Muuril. He pushed Loordin back and hauled Linnir to his feet. The man's furs were soaked with blood and Gelthius could see the white of bone poking through the rip of flesh caused by the shovel. Muuril hauled Linnir over his shoulder and then strode off towards the group of blackcrests hurrying down the road to investigate.

"No, Ullsaard was never a coward," said Loordin. The blackcrests stopped Muuril and inspected the injured man over his shoulder. Spears lowered, three of them closed in on

Loordin. "He was a bastard, but never a coward. We're his men. Thirteen!"

His rallying cry went unanswered and Gelthius focussed his attention on the wooden blade of his shovel.

"I just know that, thanks to Ullsaard, I'm never seeing Maredin or my children again," said Gelthius, turning his back on Loordin. "Fuck the Thirteenth."

ASKH
Midwinter, 213th year of Askh

I

The palaces of the king had many audience chambers and feasting halls, but none of these were as grand as the domed Hall of Kings. Large enough to seat seven hundred guests, the chamber was built from blue-green marble from Maasra, and had been erected in celebration of the inclusion of that province into the empire. Several hundred lamps hanging on gilded chains illuminated the evening's proceedings which were, considering the size of the venue, somewhat smaller than the grand occasions for which the hall had been built.

Present at the king's midwinter feast were his mother and two aunts, his younger brother Ullnaar, his wife Neerlima, and daughter Luissa, who was seven summers old. The rest of the hall was taken up with numerous dancers, acrobats, fire-breathers, contortionists, stilt-walkers, puppeteers, and several pipers, drummers and hornblowers. The musicians had begun the feast but were now silent, having worn thin the king's patience with their parping, banging and tweeting noises; Urikh had never been fond of music in any form and was not going to tolerate it while he was eating.

Sitting at the centre of a long table arranged crosswise in the hall, the king had to look left and right to see his family, and spent most of the meal gazing down the length of the hall, over the heads of the performers.

It had been a wise decision by his mother to host a proper midwinter's feast. The whispers and looks Urikh had received from the members of his family had grown more obvious with the passage of time, and the chance to bring everybody together and create the impression that all was well had been soundly argued by Luia.

A company of servants attended the table with silver platters and gilded carafes, though there was little in the way of actual consumption or celebration. Urikh did his best to set a good example, filling his plate with roasted fowl and broiled venison, winter cabbages and succulently prepared stuffed fruits; he had never had much of an appetite and picked at the small mountain of food that sat in the trencher in front of him.

"The goat's cheese is perfectly ripe," he declared, prodding a knife towards the head-sized ball of dairy produce. A wedge shape had been cut into the side of the cheese by the king, most of which was now sitting on a small plate by his right elbow. It sat there with a bunch of grapes from Maasra, gently going softer in the heat of all the lanterns. Urikh was sweating almost as much as the cheese, dressed as he was in four layers of robes and a cloak, his sash of office over the top; he was still governor of Okhar as well as king.

"Salphorian mead?" Luia ventured, gesturing for a servant to approach, a jug the size of a baby cradled in his hands.

"Yes, why not?" said Urikh, beckoning to the serving boy with a gilded goblet. "It is all part of the empire now, we should not be prejudiced. It will be all the fashion amongst the nobles next summer, I am sure."

There was a choked sob from Allenya at the mention of Salphoria and Urikh suppressed a sigh. The powdered drugs that Lakhyri had recommended be placed into the queen's food were certainly keeping her docile, but at the expense of a terrible depression and bursts of near-catatonia. The smallest mention of anything that reminded Allenya of Urikh's father would bring tears to her eyes at the very least. Urikh considered whether he needed to instruct the Brothers overseeing his aunt's meals to lessen the dosage; the queen's emotional frailty was becoming embarrassing and would cause suspicion if it continued for much longer.

"Performers, leave us!" announced the king. The less people there were to see the queen distraught, the better it would be. He could rely on a certain level of discretion, if not absolute silence, on the part of the servants; singers and actors from the streets would have no compunctions about spreading royal gossip.

Legionnaires moved forwards to usher the dawdlers out of the hall.

"Will you visit Carantathi yourself?" asked Ullnaar. Urikh's brother had undergone something of a growth spurt in the last year, probably the last he would have, and was now the tallest man at the table. His hair was curled like his mother's but was losing some of its lightness; as a student of law he spent more time in dusty libraries and old cellars than in the sun and his pallid skin looked slightly unhealthy. His blond hair was cut to shoulder length, a floppy fringe covering his face, which every now and then he brushed back with a toss of the head and sweeping hand.

"In the spring, I will," said Urikh. "I am eternally grateful that father was able to complete the conquest of the new territories before his unfortunate death. I believe there is not another man in the empire that could accomplish what he did."

"I think you underestimate your own abilities," said Luia. "You handled the Greenwater pirates magnificently, and the men of the Seventeenth look up to you as much as the Thirteenth adored your father."

Urikh knew such praise was unwarranted – his victory on the Greenwater had been exaggerated in the telling, and the loyalty of the Seventeenth was secured more by coin than reputation. However, Urikh appreciated the loyalty and dedication his mother was displaying. Catching the look of Allenya, he chose his next words carefully.

"There is not a man that can replace my father, as a king or a general. He was gifted beyond many who came before him, and the blood of Askhos ran thick in his veins. I shall try to emulate his achievements, but I do not think I will match them."

There was a grateful smile from Allenya, and Urikh was genuinely touched by it. He held no malice for the rest of the family, and in truth it had not been malice but ambition that had made Urikh turn on Ullsaard. Lakhyri's promises had simply been too rich for Urikh to turn down.

"There are grumblings that you will supplant the Book of Askhos with the Covenant of the Brotherhood as the central text of the law," said Ullnaar. "It is argued that what you have done will undermine the power of the legions and the governors, and further increase the standing of the Brotherhood."

"The grumblers are correct" said Urikh. Ullnaar was too astute to fall for a dishonest answer, so Urikh chose absolute honesty instead. "Ullsaard showed that the legions and governors had become too powerful and I have rectified that oversight. The Brotherhood are the bedrock of Greater Askhor, and with Salphoria brought into the empire they will need every resource to impose the imperial way of life on the barbarians. The empire has gone through turbulent times and she needs a steady hand now, not more warmongering."

"But is it the hand of the king that will guide the empire, or

the hand of the High Brother?" Ullnaar continued. Urikh
would not rise to the bait being laid before him.

"Both, as it has been since Askhos first wore this Crown,"
said the king. "Greater Askhor has never been ruled by the
whim of a single man, and that is its strength. Each province
must be as the empire, but on a smaller scale. The governors
have been too free to do as they wish; I know this from my
own experience. Had our father not fallen victim to the murderous intent of the Salphors, I could have amassed my own
wealth and soldiers and made a challenge against him."

The fact that it had taken no military effort and very little
expense to oust his father was not lost on Urikh. The Brotherhood held the key to the empire, something Ullsaard had
never really appreciated even after he had become king and
reinstated the institution.

"You risk dividing the empire, sundering the Crown from
the provinces," said Ullnaar. He pointed accusingly at Urikh
with his knife, which still had a piece of chicken on the end.
"Say what you like, you need the provincial legions and that
means you have to keep on good terms with the governors."

"The Salphors fell to our father because they could not
unite. Every Askhan knows that is why we will always be
stronger than our enemies. When you and the other lawyers
have finished tearing apart my proclamation and putting it
back together again the governors will see that it is for the benefit of all that we centralise the power that was discarded by
Ullsaard. At the moment we waste so much potential, stealing
from one province to pay another. It cannot be right that the
people of Nalanor or Okhar labour so hard only for their taxes
to be spent shipping the cereals they have grown to Anrair and
Enair. Every province must be able to sustain itself."

"And you would have our grandmother starve for want of
bread because Enair has poor farms and a cold climate?" Ullnaar

204 THE CROWN *of* THE USURPER

dropped his knife onto his plate in disgust. Urikh noted something of a melodrama about his brother's performance and wondered whether Ullnaar's display was merely practice for court rhetoric and posturing. Urikh smiled thinly. Meliu did not quite understand the argument, and turned a ferocious frown towards her nephew.

"You will do nothing to harm your grandmother," Meliu insisted, wagging her finger. "Or anybody's grandmother, for that matter."

"Even if she were not of the royal family now, and even if she had not been kept well these years by our father's money, Pretaa would not starve. Like anybody, she is free to choose where she lives. If Enair cannot provide for her, she can live in Ersua or Nalanor, or wherever she likes. That is a liberty everybody enjoys, and with Salphoria now open to our people, I see nothing but a better balance of people in the provinces. As it can provide, so each province shall find its own level."

"Your father would not have agreed with such a sentiment."

Urikh had been smiling to reassure his aunt that all would be well, but the smile faded at the sound of the voice that echoed down the hall. The king looked towards the doors and saw Noran standing there, two men of the Seventeenth to either side of him.

II

As Meliu let out of a laugh of delight, Noran fought down a wince. The queen was already on her feet and running around the table, but the herald really did not desire an emotional reunion. Ignoring his one-time lover as she ran down the hall, her white and blue dress flowing behind her, Noran looked at Urikh. He wore the Crown and robes of office, but there was something hunched about his posture, something in him that could be seen from this distance that set him apart from the other kings Noran had known. The current ruler of the empire did not sit easily with its burdens upon his shoulders.

"My father is dead, and his wishes now irrelevant," said Urikh, standing up.

Before Noran could reply, Meliu had reached him. He turned just in time to open his arms and catch her in an embrace. Her hair smelt of winter flowers and her skin was cold as she pressed her cheek against his, but the sensation of her soft body against his dispelled the unease he felt at being brought to Askh, though only for a moment. She kissed him on the neck, once, and then stepped back, her words reminding Noran of why he was at the capital.

"It is so good of you to come," said Meliu. She glanced at Noran and then her gaze fell to the floor and she shuddered a little. "I suppose you came because you heard... Because of what has happened."

Noran did not say anything in answer, not immediately. The eyes of Urikh were fixed upon the herald, and Noran noticed that the king still held his knife in his hand, somewhat symbolical of his mood. He had to be careful with his words in the presence of Urikh, and making life difficult for the new king by making accusations of abduction would not endear the herald to his dead friend's son.

"It is right that I offer condolences to the family of the king, and share with them the sadness they must feel at the passing of his father," Noran said, the words coming a little stiffly. The years spent with Ullsaard had softened his grip on courtly language and it felt stilted and unnatural now, when once half-truths, flattery and obfuscation had been second-nature.

"You are almost as family to us, Noran," said Allenya. The queen stood and beckoned him to approach the feasting table. Meliu slipped her arm under Noran's and the two of them walked up the hall.

"My sister takes the loss very hard," whispered Meliu, leaning close and pretending to kiss Noran's ear. "Please be careful with your words."

Murmuring that he would be, Noran looked at Allenya. She bore the signs of a woman in much distress, worse even than she had been when he had rescued her from Magilnada. Only once before had he seen her so pale, her eyes so hollow and dark; in the days after that rescue when she had learnt of the death of her son, Jutaar. After learning of that news she had shunned all company for three days; even Ullsaard had been banned from her presence. When her self-imposed incarceration had ended, she had spoken kindly to Noran, after hearing of his intent to leave Ullsaard and return to Geria.

Noran had said nothing to her of the reason for the parting, and she had been too deep in her own grief to ask much of it. The truth was that Noran would never be able to explain to anyone that Ullsaard had bartered half of his remaining life with the sorcerous Lakhyri in exchange for the extension of Noran's existence. In Geria, Noran had almost forgotten the debt he owed to Ullsaard for that; a debt he had not been comfortable to bear. Now that Ullsaard was slain, Noran was not sure how to feel. Part of him was pleased that Ullsaard would never miss those years of life he gave away. The other part of Noran was angered that he would never be given the chance to repay that debt.

"Come, sit by me," said Allenya, gesturing for a servant to bring a chair. Another attendant moved Meliu's seat to make space, while Ullnaar looked on with an amused expression.

"I must decline the invitation, as kindly made as it is," said Noran. He met the gaze of Urikh, who was seated once more, looking pleased that Noran had caused no scene. The smugness faded as the herald continued. "I would have words with the new king, in private. I would know details of the manner of his predecessor's demise, and have questions regarding the manner of my journey here."

"I would be happy to see my herald," said Urikh. "In the morning, perhaps?"

"I think you should talk to him now, brother," said Ullnaar, happy to make trouble for his older sibling. "In fact, the two of you should feel free to converse plainly before all of us. Is that not right, Luia?"

The king's mother had been sitting demurely to the left of her son throughout Noran's arrival, neither smiling nor disapproving. Only now did she look at the herald directly, eyes slightly narrowed. Noran wondered how much influence she had over Urikh, and whether it had been her suggestion to have the herald brought to the palace by force.

"It is too much for me to listen to that dreadful story again," said the queen. She wiped her mouth with the edge of the table cloth and stood up. Looking down the table, she extended a hand to Meliu and then to Allenya. "Come, sisters, we should leave our menfolk to talk of this grim matter without our tears to distract them."

"You will leave us as well," said Urikh, looking at his brother.

"I think I will stay," replied Ullnaar. "One or both of you may wish to have legal counsel."

"I am your king, and I am commanding you to leave us." Urikh's voice was rising in volume as his temper shortened. He glared at the guards and servants around the hall. "All of you, get out. I will speak with my herald alone."

"Let your brother stay if he wants to, Urikh," said Meliu, stopping to glance back at Noran and the king. The way she spoke put Noran in mind of an aunt asking her nephew to look after an infant cousin while the adults had business to discuss, and he could see that her maternal tone infuriated Urikh, despite the king's attempts to conceal his irritation.

"He is heir now, after all. He needs to learn how these things work."

Unseen by his mother and aunts, Ullnaar grinned, and Noran could imagine the annoyance of Urikh at being treated like a child, forced by his mother's sister to look after his younger sibling. The king's jaw clenched as he bit back whatever venomous reply had sprung to mind.

"I am king, not a child," said Urikh, his tone measured once more. "I will be left alone to speak privately with Noran, and that will be an end to the matter. There will be many other opportunities for Ullnaar to observe the functions of court first hand."

"And what if I refuse to leave, brother?" Ullnaar was testing the king, baiting him for a response, but Urikh was wise to the ploy; years of bickering had taught both siblings the best way to deal with each other.

"I will have you locked up by the Brotherhood," replied Urikh, and Noran could see in the king's eye the determination to see through such a threat. The herald darted a warning look at Ullnaar, but the young lawyer-to-be had his attention fixed on the king.

"The empire will not suffer rule by a tyrant, brother," Ullnaar said, his expression losing its humour. "You cannot threaten everybody, remember that."

Ullnaar turned away but Noran paid attention to Urikh, seeing the king's fingers fidget with his sash for a moment. The moment passed and the king's expression hardened. He looked as if he believed that threatening a whole empire was quite possible.

The two men stood saying nothing while the hall was emptied of family and staff. When everybody else had left, Urikh gestured towards the food-laden table.

"I understand that your journey may not have been entirely

comfortable," aid the king. "If you are hungry, please help yourself."

Noran was hungry and glanced at the food, but he would not be distracted and waved away the king's offer.

"You have me arrested and dragged here, and now you think you can offer hospitality?" snapped the herald. "Why? What purpose could it serve to bring me to the palaces, other than to open old wounds? You are a cold man sometimes, Urikh, but I never thought of you as actually cruel."

Urikh listened to Noran without reaction, his face immobile. When the herald had finished, the king nodded, as if in acknowledgement of Noran's complaints.

"It is not cruelty that brings you here, but necessity," said Urikh. "I cannot leave the palace at the moment, and it is imperative that I speak with you."

"A letter of invitation is more traditional than an armed guard," said Noran. He regretted his words a moment later when the king stalked towards him, jabbing a finger at the herald.

"You would not have come if I had invited you," said Urikh, striding up to Noran. "Whatever happened between you and my father has not been settled, that much was clear. I do not know what you have been doing in Geria, but you have not been paying attention to the talk in the streets. If you had done, you would have known of Ullsaard's death long before I sent word for the news to be brought to you. I thought that your friendship with my family, the patronage shown to you by my father, would have been bond enough to bring you to the capital earlier, but time is running out and so I resorted to more brutal methods. That was not my fault, it was yours."

"I do not understand your intent," Noran confessed, shaking his head. "I am a poor ally, if that is what you are after. My father still possesses most of the wealth and influence of my family. It is his support you should seek."

"I already have his support," said Urikh. The king turned away and stalked back to the feast. He snatched up a cup and swallowed a mouthful of the contents. Urikh's hand was shaking slightly as he put the cup down and turned to look at Noran, leaning back against the edge of the table. "There is something that you alone can do for me."

"Time is running out for what?" Noran asked, catching up on the words of the king's tirade. "What can be so urgent?"

"Ullsaard is not dead," said the king.

The words took a moment to settle into Noran's brain. When he had been told of his friend's death, he had thought it the most shocking thing he could have heard; he had been wrong. Unable to comprehend what he had just been told, he listened dumbly as Urikh explained.

"Ullsaard is not dead, and he has returned to Greater Askhor, or will try to do so soon," said the king. To Urikh's credit, he did not try to meet Noran's gaze, but looked up into the dome above the hall. "I am already dealing with the immediate problem that poses to me, but I have a far more insidious issue to contend with. That is where I need you."

"You took the Crown whilst Ullsaard is still alive? Are you mad? Do you know what he is going to do to you?"

"He is going to do nothing," said Urikh. The king gave an exasperated sigh. "Let me make this simple. My father may be alive for the moment, but that is not going to continue for long. He will be apprehended shortly, if he is not, in fact, already dead. The rumour of his return, that is another matter entirely. I have already taken steps to spread the myth that he is not the real king, but an impostor. When his body is brought here, you will act as witness to the fact that the man is not Ullsaard, but someone claiming his name. You were his best friend, and you have nothing to gain by falsehood, so the testimony you give will be accepted and my version of events will prevail."

"If I have nothing to gain from falsehood, why will I lie?" Noran thought he knew the answer already, but it was better to hear it from the lips of Urikh himself.

"You will help me, because if you do not it will cause heartache and shame for my family. In turn, I will kill you."

"What if I do not care whether I live or die?" asked Noran. It was not an idle question and Urikh could see from the herald's expression that this was the case.

"I will also kill your family, and perhaps even Meliu," Urikh replied quietly. There was regret in the king's voice, but no shame. Though Noran had been expecting such a reply, Urikh's pragmatic attitude was like a dagger in the belly, sending a twist of pain through the herald's gut. He saw a calculating look in the king's eye that sent a chill through him. "Do not think to test me on this. I will have my way, and I will be king, but it is better that we make this as painless possible for the empire and the people we love."

Noran had always known of Urikh's ambitious streak, and it was not much of a surprise that he had usurped his father. What confused Noran was that Urikh seemed to be doing such a bad job of it.

"Why did you not simply have Ullsaard killed before taking the Crown?" said the herald. "I know that would not be easy, but it must have been a better alternative than this tapestry of lies you are now forced to weave."

"The time of the empire as you know it is coming to an end," said Urikh, and Noran saw the twitch of cheek and fingers he had noticed earlier. It was nervousness. "If I had not taken the Crown when I had, another would be here now and I and all of my family would be dead. I have... allies who make demands of me. If Ullsaard must die to protect the empire and my family, I will pay that price."

Noran had no idea who these allies might be. The king believed everything he said, and it was clear from the look in his eye and the surety of his voice that he believed he was doing the right thing. A man who believed he had no alternative was possessed of a certain kind of desperation, and Noran recognised this in Urikh.

"Who am I to argue with the king?" said Noran, and he meant what he said. "If Ullsaard needs to die to save the empire, and *my* family, I will lie for you."

III

The cart shuddered over cobbles and Ullsaard guessed that they had passed into Askh. He lay bound by hand and foot in the back of a covered wagon, a gag between his teeth. For most of his incarceration he had been tied only by the hands, but now that they reached the heart of the empire Asuhas and Anglhan were not taking any chances.

You can take heart that we are not yet dead.

"Only because Anglhan and Asuhas want to present me alive to my son, hoping for greater reward," growled Ullsaard. Though his words were muffled by the gag, his intent was known to Askhos. Ullsaard spoke out loud only because it allowed him to keep his thoughts separate from the spirit of the man inside his head. When they communicated without words, Ullsaard felt himself bleeding into Askhos, losing sense of himself. Whether this was because of the broken connection with the Crown, or whether Askhos was trying to exert more influence over the king Ullsaard did not know; he was not going to risk losing his independence to find out.

On the long journey from Menesun the dead king had been an occasional companion, though his insights had been limited and advice undesired. The closer they came to Askh, the more Askhos seemed to strengthen, and for the past eight nights Ullsaard had experienced vivid dreams in which he had walked amongst the stars with his ancestor. He was not sure why this would be the case, when Askhos' tie to the Crown had been severed.

It was never the Crown, Ullsaard. It is merely a window to the place where I continued. The strength of my presence depends upon the Grand Precincts of the Brotherhood. It is a bridge, or a door if you like, to those otherworlds of which I have spoken. The closer I am to the precinct, the easier it is to project myself from the place where I dwell.

"But your sons – you within your sons – conquered an empire, taking you far from Askh."

The coronations always took place at the Grand Precincts, where my power was at its strongest. The moment they placed the Crown on their heads they were pushed aside, allowing for my will to enter. Once I was inside their bodies, the Crown was irrelevant, until another son became king.

"If I had been born before Kalmud, I would have been the true heir, and the Blood would have been strong enough for you to take over me, right?" Ullsaard felt the dead king's agreement without words. As well as the length of time Askhos was able to manifest increasing, the bond between the two kings grew more intimate with proximity to the Grand Precincts. In the dreams there had been moments of communion, during which Ullsaard had found it difficult to tell if he was with the founder of the Empire or *was* the founder of the empire. Memories were becoming blurred by Askhos' spirit being forced to linger within Ullsaard's physical form.

The past is irrelevant; the possibilities of what might have been are of no concern to us. The uncertainties of the future are enough to occupy our endeavours. Most importantly, and most pressingly, how do you plan to escape from this wagon? I know that you have been waiting for us to be brought to Askh, biding your time. Now is the time to act.

"I can think of a lot of words that describe Anglhan, but sloppy isn't one of them," said Ullsaard. He pulled at the rope binding his wrists. The knot was tight, above his hands where his fingers could not work the binding. This rope was tied to the cord that bound the king's ankles, and in turn was looped around a ring riveted into the front board of the wagon. Ullsaard pulled, straining his arms. His right shoulder throbbed, weakened by past wounds that had left scars on the surface and in the muscle. Ullsaard was still a strong man, but even with his feet braced against the board holding the ring there was no give in wood or metal or rope. With a grunt, he gave up. "No, I don't think I'll be getting off this cart until I'm meant to.

"Stop fidgeting," said one of the legionnaires on the driving seat. "Don't make me come back there."

Ullsaard lapsed into immobility, inhaling deeply through his nose to catch his breath. His only hope was if his captors did not want to carry him from the wagon; they would have to free his legs to let him walk. Yet even if he did have a chance to bolt for freedom, what good would it do?

Better to be free than a prisoner.

"Better to be a prisoner than dead," replied Ullsaard. "As you said, perhaps Urikh wants me alive. If I try to escape, Anglhan and Asuhas would prefer me dead than on the loose in Askh."

Yes, I heard them instructing the guards as well. They will kill you rather than let you get away. Your ears are mine, do not forget.

"So it seems that the best option, the only option, is to wait and see what happens." Ullsaard hated the words even as he said them. For too long he had been on the back foot, responding to the deeds of others rather than imposing his will on the situation.

A gong nearby attracted his attention and he listened to the pattern and count of the strikes: second of Duskwatch. They had come into the city not long before the gates were closed at Low Watch, which meant that it would be dark when they arrived. Ullsaard concentrated on their surroundings, sensing that they had moved from cobbles to flat paved roads. That meant they were at least a mile inside the city.

He had seen from their previous stops that there were only three wagons in their small convoy. Asuhas was travelling without his usual guard and the men of the Twenty-first were out of uniform, so as to attract as little attention as possible. Anglhan and the governor were trying to keep their visit as low profile as they could, and Ullsaard had only counted ten men accompanying them. Even so, ten men were too much opposition for one man, bound as he was. Ullsaard's only real hope was of attracting attention in some way that would not be noticed.

Judging by the increasing incline of the wagon, they were on a steepening hill, probably approaching the Royal Mound. That meant either Maarmes, the palace or the Grand Precincts. He did not know which.

Maarmes is too public. Though they could probably hide us away in one of the disused underground training pits, it is less secure than the palace. My choice, if I were detaining us, would be the Grand Precincts. There are many cells in which to lose us and it is safe to assume that Lakhyri is in league with Urikh and knows of your continued survival. Nobody escapes from the Grand Precinct.

"This is all Anglhan's fault."

Your grasp of our predicament is overwhelming, Ullsaard.

"Not just here and now, you dead bastard. Ever since Anglhan turned on me and tried to take Magilnada for himself I've been one step behind every event. The delays in Salphoria, the appearance of Erlaan and the Mekhani, all of that has kept me away from Askh, and given Urikh time to plot his moves. Anglhan is moving against the Brotherhood now though, so it must be the palace we're heading to."

You overestimate your son's capabilities. He is being an opportunist, and in moving so quickly he has left weaknesses to be exploited.

"And you know what those weaknesses are? You know that I am not able to tie my thoughts into the sorts of knots needed to work out these political riddles. Noran used to guide me in those sorts of matters."

Yes, I am constantly remembering how you tried to be subtle by leaving the legions behind. I wish you had just marched back with the whole army and caused a great big mess. That would have been preferable to this. Regardless, let us consider what we are up against. We know from the report of Captain Gelthius that Asuhas and Anglhan have their own goals in mind, which are separate from the Brotherhood. It is the Brotherhood that appears to be Urikh's main instrument of power, so it is possible to conclude that Asuhas and Anglhan's deception of Leraates is also an attempt to deceive Urikh.

"I suppose if I can trust Anglhan for one thing, it is to place his own objectives above everybody else's. Asuhas is an idiot if he thinks he has the upper hand over that slimy toad." Ullsaard had tried hard not to let his imprisonment get the better of his mood, but the closer he came to their final destination, the more hopeless his situation seemed. Bitterness swelled in the king, shoving aside the grasping fingers of sadness. He would not go meekly to his fate. "Maybe we'll get lucky and they'll kill each other in an attempt to claim sole credit for my capture. We'll slip out while they're busy."

Your sarcasm has some truth to it. Finding some way to divide your enemies further would be prudent. Unfortunately, we have nothing to offer, no power to bargain with and so no leverage to apply to the cracks in their alliances.

The creaking of the axles took on a different tone and the wagon swayed heavily to one side for a short while. Ullsaard concluded that they had moved onto the cambered road of the Royal Way, and had turned left at the Royal Mound; Ullsaard had assumed rightly and they were headed for the palace.

Both fell silent, knowing that they were less than half a mile from their destination. Time was about to run out. The wagon carried on for what felt like more than a half mile, and then stopped. Ullsaard could hear clanking chains.

The supply gates at the back of the mound.

Ullsaard had a vision of large double-gates, heavy enough to need a water-driven counterweight to open. They did not rest on normal hinges, but were arranged on a bronze rail to slide aside, even more secure than the main entrance. A broad tunnel behind led directly into the depths of the palace where vast kitchens and servants quarters sprawled. He had not seen these things himself and knew them only from the memories of the spirit residing inside his skull. It was an unsettling experience and he shook his head as if to clear away the alien thoughts.

The cart jarred into motion again, the wheels banging over the raised rail, jolting Ullsaard from his horror. Only a few heartbeats later, the wagon stopped again and the king heard the drivers jumping down from the board. The flaps of the cart cover were thrown back and three legionnaires approached. They were in a cavern-like space, lit by naked torches. Shadows were long, dancing in the flicker of the flames, and the fumes from the brands made it darker still. The thin smoke made Ullsaard cough, reminding him of the day he had been captured. He glared at the warriors of the Twenty-first as they pulled down the tailgate, letting the board swing down on wooden hinges. One of the men rested his spear against the back of the wagon and clambered aboard, while the other two waited to either side.

The soldier came up to Ullsaard, produced a knife and quickly sawed through the bindings on the king's ankles.

"Up," said the legionnaire, waving the point of the dagger towards the back of the wagon. Ullsaard rolled to his knees and was then able to push himself to his feet. He staggered a step, but the soldier made no move to help the king as he stumbled into one of the timbers holding up the frame of the cart's roof.

Ullsaard eyed the spear left resting against the tailgate. The man with the knife was behind him, the other two soldiers distracted as another wagon rumbled past, Anglhan peering out from the covered back. With his mind's eyes, Ullsaard pictured what he would do. A kick would take out the soldier on the right, and the one of the left was standing close enough for Ullsaard to jump onto him from the cart. Ullsaard's breathing started to quicken and he felt the Blood pulse in his body, sending a surge of power to his limbs. He was older than his captors, but was a powerful runner. Three quarters of a mile, that was all he had to manage. He'd be down into the city proper, and despite the cold weather someone would be on the streets. There was always a chance...

The image faded as the clanking of chains heralded the closing of the gates. There would be no mad dash for freedom. Anglhan huffed and sweated as he lowered himself down from the other cart, his red, round face the last thing Ullsaard saw before a sack was placed over his head.

He was trapped.

IV

Voices raised in heated argument woke Noran from his doze on a couch beside the fireplace in his apartment's reception room. Urikh had allowed him to take up his old residence, though the interconnected rooms seemed empty and quiet without Neerita, and he even missed Anriit's company. He opened his eyes and sat up as he heard the clatter of the bead curtain across the door. A soldier in the livery of the First entered, the white stripe in his helmet crest denoting the rank of second captain. Behind him loitered the head of the household servants, one of Ullsaard's former men, Ariid.

"I am sorry, but he insisted on entering," the steward apologised with a forlorn flutter of a hand towards the soldier.

"The king demands your presence, herald," said the captain. "You are to come with me."

"It's an hour after Howling, what business can the king have that cannot wait until tomorrow?" Ariid asked as Noran got up. The herald echoed the question with his look.

"The imposter masquerading as King Ullsaard has been apprehended," said the captain.

It took a moment for the true meaning of the man's words to sink in. There was no imposter, it was a rumour fabricated by Urikh, so the only explanation was that Ullsaard had been brought to the palace. Noran scrutinised the soldier's expression but saw only obedient honesty.

"Very well, take me to the king," Noran sighed. He looked at Ariid as he passed. "Please convey an invitation to Allenya and Meliu to meet me here in the morning. I am sure they would like to have the matter of this unpleasant impersonation settled firsthand from me."

Another four legionnaires were waiting for Noran when he left his apartments. They escorted him in silence through the passages and halls of the palace, heading towards the Hall of Askhos. Coming to the great door of the hall, they knocked and awaited the call of the king. Opening the door, the captain waved for Noran to enter but did not step through himself.

The first thing that Noran noticed was how slender Urikh looked sitting on the throne. His predecessors have been much larger of frame, and even in his failing years King Lutaar had been a larger man than the current incumbent. Noran saw the Crown on Urikh's head, and realised that the new king had been wearing it constantly.

There was nobody else in the hall. The black marble walls, inscribed with the names of all who had fallen in service to the legions of Greater Askhor, made the vast chamber seem smaller. Noran's footfalls echoed dully as he approached the throne. The Crown intrigued him, and he tried to remember what Ullsaard and Lakhyri had told him in the half-dream of his fever coma. Noran had thought he had seen Askhos – in fact Ullsaard had said as much, and Lakhyri, he had been the founder of the Brotherhood. The Crown was key to this, Noran knew, but he had not listened very well to Ullsaard's attempt at an explanation. All Noran could recall was that Askhos had once used the Crown to achieve a sort of immortality. The herald wondered if the same was happening again. Was the man sitting on the throne really Urikh, or a puppet of a dead king?

"You sent for me," said Noran, with a short bow. "Now I am here. Where is Ullsaard?"

"I no longer require your services," said Urikh, in the same flat tone he had used to threaten the herald. "Men loyal to me have delivered up my father, whole and intact."

As the king spoke, three men seemed to appear out of the wall behind the throne. A small door, hidden by a pillar, closed with a click. Noran recognised all three men. The first wore black hood and robes and his face was sallow, thin and carved with disturbing patterns and symbols. This was Lakhyri, who was now High Brother and had been the architect of Noran's escape from Magilnada. The second was a small, intimidated-looking man whose eyes were fixed on Lakhyri: Governor Asuhas. The third brought a curl to Noran's lips and a clenching of fists; the blubbery form of Anglhan Periusis.

"The company you keep has not improved, Urikh," said the herald, sneering at the newcomers. He used the king's name, subtly reminding him of the lifetime of acquaintance between them. "I remember when you were young; your friends had your better interests at heart. Now you surround yourself with sorcerers, liars and traitors. I hope you are not entrusting the future of the empire to these creatures."

Urikh seemed more amused than angered by Noran's accusations. He turned in his throne and nodded to the new arrivals.

"You come at an opportune moment," said Urikh. "I was just informing my herald of the change of circumstances that have rendered redundant his continued participation in my schemes. He has not yet learned what is to become of him."

"Have you decided yet?" said Anglhan. "I think I may have a use for him. Or, I should say, I can think of a use for him that you might have. As your herald."

"I would rather be killed than have a treacherous pig-fucker like you as my saviour," snarled Noran. He turned his attention back to Urikh. "Is Ullsaard alive? Where is he?"

"My father is alive for the moment, but that is an inconvenience that will not last for much longer," said the king. The words were spoken archly, but Urikh's gaze was wandering, searching the upper reaches of the ceiling as if looking for something. Noran could not stop himself looking up, and though the hall was not brightly lit – a dozen lamps on chains hanging from the ceiling – it did seem that the shadows above their heads were thicker than expected.

"Anglhan should tell you the new plan, as he devised it," continued Urikh.

"My thanks for your indulgences, King Urikh." Anglhan's smile was as greasy as oil as he waddled up to the throne and lowered to one knee. His gut almost touched the ground as he leaned forwards to kiss the arm of the throne; a Salphorian abasement that had never been adopted by the Askhan kings.

With deference made, no doubt as false as the rest of the former governor's behaviour, Anglhan heaved himself to his feet with a wheezing breath and stuck his thumbs into his belt.

"Everything turns nicely into a full circle, my friend Noran," announced the Salphor. "Ullsaard was slain in battle, but thanks to the efforts of Governor Asuhas and the soldiers of the Twenty-first legion, his body has now been recovered. You will, of course, stand testimony to this course of events. In fact, in order that the empire be allowed to pay proper homage to their fallen king, his body shall be taken to the provinces and displayed for all to grieve over."

"You are going to parade Ullsaard's corpse around the empire as proof?" Noran looked between Urikh and Anglhan, not sure which of them disgusted him more. "Look, I shall proclaim whatever you wish me to proclaim, there is no need for this insult to be heaped upon a dead man. Urikh, think of Allenya and your brother."

"It will be harsh on them I admit," said the king, looking genuinely upset. "To see a loved one hacked and stabbed, in death an ugly thing that carries none of the beauty of the man as he was in life. It will be a hard moment to stand there with those he has left behind, but when they are convinced, it shall secure my claim to this Crown. None will dispute my right to it."

After approaching the throne, Lakhyri had stood as still as a statue. Now he stirred, tilting his head slightly to one side. So immobile had he been, Noran was shocked by the sudden movement, and all eyes turned towards the High Brother.

"We delay for no reason," said Lakhyri. He glared with golden eyes at his fellow conspirators, and each of them was unable to meet that unnatural gaze. "We also speak unwisely of plans not yet come to fruition. When Ullsaard is dead and the rumour of it becomes truth, we shall be content."

"I shall arrange it immediately," said Anglhan. Receiving nothing but silence in reply, the Salphor nodded and shuffled back towards the hidden doorway. He disappeared behind the column and was gone.

"You spoke of being chancellor?" Urikh said, looking at Asuhas, but with the occasional glance towards Noran, making a point. "This is the reward you seek for bringing Ullsaard to me?"

"I would serve in Askh, as a prime legislator, yes," said Asuhas. "Being governor is too fraught with peril in these times. I no longer wish to be a playing piece in the game of kings."

"A wise choice," said Lakhyri, laying a skeletal hand on the governor's shoulder. Asuhas shrank back from the wizened priest. "Plans are in motion to disband the role of the governors. The Brotherhood will assume direct control of the provinces."

"They will never allow a move against them," said Asuhas, earning himself frowns from Lakhyri and Urikh. He laughed nervously and shrugged. "What do I care, eh? If you want to get rid of the governors, it is of no consequence to me. Not if I am to be chancellor of Askh."

"Or, like your peers in the province, if you are dead," said Urikh. "The governors will not say a word about their new position, because they will not have a chance. Word has been sent to the blackcrests. By decree of the king, all of the governors will be dead within days."

"But, you do not have to kill me," said Asuhas.

"I think you misjudge your company," Noran called out with a bitter laugh. "You are vain and ambitious, Asuhas, but you have never been ruthless. What did you call it, 'the game of kings'? Your new playmates play this game far more seriously than you, and you have just lost."

"But I do not want to be a governor, that was our agreement," said Asuhas, stepping away from Lakhyri, hands held up to defend himself. "I will never speak out against you."

"Chancellors are as redundant as governors, I am afraid," said Urikh.

With a wordless yelp, Asuhas turned and started to run towards the door. Noran was not sure what happened next, but it was like a glimpse of a nightmare made real.

The Hall of Askhos seemed to darken. The lamps dimmed though their flames did not flicker nor grow smaller. The shadows around the ceiling shifted and became a tenebrous mass that was suddenly animated with life. Dark tendrils snaked down towards Asuhas, tripping him as he ran. More shadowy coils extended from the darkness above, snatching up the governor by his limbs and throat.

Noran did not want to look up; every fibre of his being screamed at him to keep his stare locked on the impassive expression of Urikh as the king watched Asuhas being lifted into the air by prehensile shadows. Despite this, despite the shriek of animal instinct warning him not to, Noran raised his eyes; just a fraction enough to see what was above him.

There was not just darkness above. Translucent, yellowish points, multifaceted crystals that shone like stars in twilight. Noran realised that they were eyes, dozen of them. They regarded everything in the hall, reflecting the figures below, the thousands of names of dead men on the walls, and the glitter of each other. Some watched Noran with horrifying intensity, even as he was aware that other eyes were looking at Lakhyri, Asuhas and Urikh. Transfixed by those eyes Noran felt his flesh stripped away, his innards, the core of his being and his thoughts laid bare before those inhuman stares.

The shadows seemed to be ribbed and ridged, the glimmer of the faded lamps catching on bony protrusions, dangling

lash-like appendages and pale ropes of sinew. Rope-like ten-
dons tightened and the shadows darkened and thrashed.
Asuhas was lifted up into the central mass of the shadow, and
Noran thought that he could see the ceiling through the terrifying manifestation; the tiles of the wall and the spars holding
up the roof were visible behind the creature.

Slithering, barbed tongues solidified, extruding from toothless
maws spread around the monster's impossible form. These rasp-
ing feeder tendrils caressed Asuhas' flesh. He did not scream, but
gave a moan of ecstasy instead, more disturbing than any blood-
curdling howl of agony. As the tongues moved over the governor,
his skin disappeared, revealing fat, and then the tongues moved
faster, exposing twisted muscle and sinew and then bone. Layer
by layer Asuhas was stripped away, his blood becoming a cloud
of vapour that was sucked into a pulsating, puckered hole.

Noran's dinner rushed up from his gut. He bent double,
vomiting up the contents of his stomach. Twice more he
retched, interspersed with moans not of pain but of despair.
Even as he dry heaved, his stomach clenched tightly around
nothing, a tiny part of Noran's mind was thankful for the rebellion of his body; at least he was no longer looking up.

"Now you understand fully why I must be obeyed," said
Urikh. Through squinting eyes, Noran gazed at the king. Urikh
looked frightened but was trying to act bravely. Noran wanted
to laugh; there was no hiding the truth from that inhuman
glare. It did not matter what Urikh pretended, his monstrous
master would know his innermost secrets.

"What have you done?" Noran whispered, but Urikh did not
hear the question.

V

The wounds that lacerated Ullsaard's corpse were ugly, his
chest and gut marked by three long cuts. Allenya reached out

a hand towards her husband's body but stopped short of touching him. She wanted to trace those bloody furrows that had been slashed across his unmoving form, dark against the deathly pallor of the skin. His cheeks were sunken, and she was thankful that his eyes were closed, so that she did not have to look into their lifeless stare.

She had no more tears to shed. The reality of his body gave her no release. Like Ullsaard, she felt nothing. War had taken her son and her husband, and their absence left an emptiness inside her that could not be filled. She had grieved, grieved so hard it had brought her to the edge of madness, but as she looked at the pallid remains laid on a covered table in the Hall of Askhos, she told herself that it was just meat and bones.

"This is not my husband," she said.

"Yes, yes it is, sister," said Luia. Allenya felt her hand grasped by Luia's but she could not take her eyes from Ullsaard.

"No," said Allenya. "This is just the carcass of what he was. Ullsaard is not this cold lump of flesh."

"He is a memory now," said Ullnaar, who stood by his father's feet, eyes averted. "This is not how we will remember him."

"Speak for yourself." Noran's tone was full of bitterness and he darted hateful glances at Urikh, who sat on his throne, staring down at his family as though watching petitioners making their pleas. Now and then he looked up at the ceiling and his expression changed to one of worry. "I will be sure to fix this sight in my mind for the rest of my life."

"War makes us all ugly," said Luia. "In life as well as in death. Ullsaard knew that and he chose to live the way he did. It was not likely that he would die in peace of old age."

"How can you be so cold?" snapped Allenya, snatching her hand away from her sister's. "He was your husband! The father of your son, no less. Do you not owe him the decency of remembering that?"

"He was those things, yes, and much more." Allenya saw no tears in Luia's eyes and her limbs did not tremble as did Meliu's as she hugged herself beside the bier, but Ullsaard's eldest widow saw for a moment torment in her sister. There had been little love between her husband and Luia, but they had found their role for one another and respected each other, in private if not openly.

"I am sorry, my words are harsh and unwarranted," said Allenya, taking up Luia's hand again. "We mourn his passing each in our own way."

"Enough of this morbid display," announced Urikh, stepping down from the dais of his throne. "We shall arrange a funeral feast in two nights' time and we can then say the proper words of passing to our departed king, father and husband. It does none of us well to remain here and stare at what has become of him."

"I will remain a moment longer, with your leave," said Noran. Urikh nodded and led the family down the hall. As she passed, Allenya laid her hand on Noran's shoulder and squeezed it.

"Do not be alone tonight," said the queen. Misunderstanding her meaning, Noran glanced at Meliu, who had not spoken a word since they had been told of the arrival of Ullsaard's remains. Allenya shook her head. "With friends who are like family to you, I mean."

"I make no promises," said Noran.

Allenya nodded in sympathy and then followed the rest of her family from the hall, her steps heavy as she walked on leaden legs, her heart feeling like it was being crushed in a clawed fist.

She did not mark anything of the walk back to their apartment, and she murmured words of consolation and parting to her family when they arrived, seeking silence and solitude in her chambers. She called for Laasinia to bring spiced wine and a compound that would aid sleep and then sat by the window. It was mid-morning on a grey, rainy day and beyond the walls of the palace grounds Askh was going about its business. Allenya had persuaded Urikh not to yet make any pronouncement on the return of Ullsaard's body. Such an act would begin a fresh round of visitations from concerned nobles and merchants alike, all seeking to convey their condolences to the royal family for their loss. With the exception of a few, most would have never known Ullsaard, and their sycophancy would have been too much to bear again at this time.

So the capital and the rest of the empire went on without a care of the passing of its former ruler, and Allenya sat by the window looking up at dark clouds gathering over the city.

"King Ullsaard is dead," she whispered.

She heard the door open and did not turn around, expecting it to be Laasinia. A cough attracted her attention and she looked towards the door. A young boy in the livery of a junior herald waited there, his small helmet clasped under one arm.

"Your pardons, queen, but I have a message for you from Noran Astaan," said the youth, proffering a covered tablet. Allenya beckoned to the youth and he brought it over and laid it on the table beside her chair. With a bow, he left and Allenya sat staring at the sealed wax message.

She did not open it until Laasinia had come and gone, leaving a steaming ewer of wine and a cloth bag of dried leaves. Waiting for the wine to cool a little, Allenya read the missive from Noran.

The tablet dropped from her fingers from shock and the queen stared at the fallen slate for some time, not believing what she had read. When she had recovered her wits, Allenya scooped up the tablet and placed it inside the sash that belted her robe. She summoned Laasinia with a call and made ready to leave the apartments.

"Where are we going, queen?" asked the handmaid as Allenya fastened a shawl about her shoulders and slipped her feet into a pair of stiff-soled slippers.

"To meet an old acquaintance," replied the queen.

VI

The table in front of Anglhan was littered with plates, on which there was little left except bones and scraps. Letting out a satisfied belch, he dipped his fingers in a bowl of water, dried them on the tablecloth and lifted up a goblet of wine. Just as the liquid reached his lips there was a knock at the door.

"Enter!" Anglhan lowered his wine back to the table as the door opened and Queen Allenya stepped into the dining room. Surprised, he almost knocked over his chair as he stood up. "I was not expecting a royal visit, my queen."

"I thought it would be better to come unannounced," said Allenya. She stopped on the other side of the table and her eyes swept the room, brow wrinkling with distaste as she saw the remains of the banquet on the table. "I see I have interrupted your celebratory feast."

"Celebration, Queen?" Anglhan felt nervous all of a sudden, the Queen's stare more intense than anything he had been subjected to by anyone else. He reached out for his wine but his fumbling fingers knocked over the goblet, spilling red across the table.

"You eat game and fowl and drink unwatered wine while my dead husband lies on a bier in the Hall of Askhos. Ullsaard is dead; I would think you find that cause for celebration."

"Not at all, my Queen, not at all," said Anglhan. He stepped to the end of the table, hands outstretched in a gesture of innocence. "Ullsaard's death would be very inconvenient for me, as well as a tragedy for the empire."

"Save your lies!" Allenya snarled. She snatched up a small clay dish and threw it at Anglhan. It went over his head and smashed on the wall behind him, marking the ochre paint with splashes of red sauce and rags of chicken skin.

"I swear, Allenya, you have me wrong," said Anglhan. Panic set in when the queen picked up a carving knife from the table and stalked towards him. "Wait a moment, let's not be stupid."

"Murderer!"

Allenya hurled herself at Anglhan, knife raised in her fist. He fended away her first swipe, earning himself a scratch across the back of his hand. She lunged again, and he stepped back awkwardly, crashing into his chair. Impeded, he could not dodge the next cut, which sliced across his left cheek just below the eye.

"Stop, you're making a mistake!" Anglhan cried, backing into the table. The cut on his face stung all the more as tears rolled down his blubbery cheeks. "Stop!"

"Bastard son of a whore's arse!" Allenya shrieked, stabbing down at Anglhan's chest. He slid along the table to his right, the blade in catching him in the shoulder. "Pig-fucking killer!"

Again and again Allenya slashed and stabbed, some of her wild blows going wide, others grazing and slicing Anglhan's flailing arms as he sought to back away. In desperation he grabbed a platter and swung blindly, hoping to knock the knife from her hand. He really did not want to hurt the queen, not now, not when he was so close to getting what he wanted. Killing her would ruin everything he had worked so hard to bring about.

The tray connected with the side of Allenya's head as she bent to slash at his groin. With a gut-shrivelling clang, it glanced from her skull and sent her down. Allenya hit the floor, head bouncing against the bare wood.

"Oh shit, oh shit," gasped Anglhan. "Oh shit, I didn't mean…"

Ignoring the blood streaming from his own wounds, Anglhan bent over Allenya. The side of her face was already swelling up into a bruise and the skin was broken just above her eye, a surprising amount of blood streaming down her face. There was a glazed look in her eyes.

"Black knockholes of the spirits," Anglhan muttered as he grabbed the table with one hand and pulled himself back up. He looked over the crockery and utensils, looking for something he could wrap in cloth to make a compact bandage for the wound in the side of the queen's head. "Spirits can go fuck their mother's ears for all they've done for me. What have I done to deserve this?"

Searing, hot pain lanced along his spine as he bent forward to reach for a half-full cheese bag. Roaring, he turned as quickly as he could, sending Allenya sprawling again, the knife ripped from the wound in Anglhan's back.

"What have you…" The strength went from his legs and he stumbled to his knees, fingers gripping the tablecloth as he fell. Plates and dishes and trays crashed on the floor around him, flinging pieces of meat and fruit peelings across the floorboards.

Allenya steadied herself and advanced with purpose, the right side of her face a mask of blood. There were spatters on her pale blue dress. The knife was daubed with crimson in her hand and Anglhan watched as a droplet of his blood fell from its tip to the floor. It landed in the spilt wine with a tiny splash.

Fear robbed Anglhan of speech as Allenya plunged the knife into his chest. He felt metal on ribs, ripping through fat and muscle. With a moan, he collapsed sideways, crushing bowls underneath him. He knew he was going to die. Blood was pouring from the wound and his breathing was already becoming difficult; a lung had been punctured, he was sure.

"Ullsaard's alive!" he managed to gasp. He pressed a hand to the hole in his chest and felt blood bubbling through his fingers. He looked down as best he could and saw red froth. It was definitely a lung.

"What did you say?" Allenya stood over him, bloodied knife in hand, eyes wide in a smear of red.

Anglhan choked and spat up blood. He was no soldier or surgeon but he knew he did not have long. Looking up at Allenya he had a choice to make. He could take his secret to the grave and Ullsaard would die anyway, or he could tell his killer the truth so that she could save her husband. Did it really matter, he asked himself? Ullsaard had been a butcher and a bastard and had killed thousands by his actions. What did Anglhan owe it to the man, or his wife, to save him now that all profit was lost? No revelation could not stop him dying.

"What did you say about Ullsaard?" Allenya looked scared now. Anglhan tried to laugh but he could not. His chest felt tighter and tighter and knew that soon he would not have enough breath to speak. If he was to say anything he would have to say it now.

"It's fake," he rasped, every word an agony. "Some drugs, superficial cuts and colourings. Ullsaard's alive. I crafted that. I was going to be... It doesn't matter."

He coughed more blood and it felt thick in his throat. Allenya dropped the knife and knelt beside him. She leaned closer to hear his words.

"He needs antidote, before... Before he stops breathing for real."

"Where? Where is the antidote? Where is he?"

It was too hard to speak. Anglhan managed to prop himself up on one elbow and pointed to the door that led to his bedchamber. Summoning up what strength and courage he had left, knowing that his last moments were going to be in agony, he drew in a ragged half-breath.

"Money belt, secret lining. One pinch, hot water. "

"Where can I find him? Where is he?" Allenya grabbed Anglhan's face in both hands as she demanded the answers. Her eyes were locked on his.

"Still in the Hall of Askhos." He hoped to see gratitude in her face, to hear her say she was sorry for what she had done. Darkness was beckoning but Anglhan held on, waiting for the thanks or the apology. The room started to slowly spin but he focussed on Allenya's face, desperately searching for some hint of compassion or sorrow at his demise. He saw nothing but hardness and disgust. The knife was in her hand again and he looked at it despairingly, hoping she would read his desire that she ended his misery quickly.

"There will be no swift death for you, you traitorous piece of shit. Perhaps you did not kill my husband, but you certainly held me hostage and ordered my son killed," Allenya whispered in his ear. She pressed a hand to the wound in his chest, the pressure causing a wave of agony to flood through him. With the last moments of sensation Anglhan felt the blade sliding up his thigh until it pierced a testicle. He could not feel the pain, but the shame bit harder than any physical sensation as she sliced away his genitals. "You are less than a man; you are a glutton, a thief and a coward. Die with the pain and humiliation that you have earned."

It was too much. Her scorn was the last thing Anglhan knew as he reached the end of his strength and death took him.

VII

Noran was not sure where the pool of blood stopped and the puddle of wine began. One hand clasped over his mouth in horror, he walked cautiously around the dining table, fearing that he would find Allenya's bloodied body. He had been delayed by a chance encounter with Urikh, and had hurried to the rooms held by Anglhan fearing the worst. Though he could not see Allenya, seeing the fat man's corpse flopped on the floor the nobleman realised that the luxury of time had been robbed from them.

"Allenya?" he called out, trying to pitch his voice so that he would be heard but not so loud that it would carry into the corridor where a passing servant might hear the commotion. The nobleman looked at the floor and saw a trail of bloody footprints leaving by one of the doors. At least Allenya was still in the apartment.

"We have to get this to Ullsaard." The queen emerged from the adjoining room with a wide leather belt. There was blood drying on her face and matting her hair, and her dress was drenched with red. The pouches of the money belt spilled gold askharins onto the floor but Allenya paid them no attention. She had a knife and was cutting open the woollen lining, throwing the belt to one side, she held up a small leather packet. She talked in a short, breathless way that betrayed excitement. "Ullsaard is not dead. Anglhan used drugs to induce a coma. This will bring him back."

"I know," said Noran. "The marks on the body were shallow cuts made to look worse. That is why I was going to meet you here, to arrange our departure."

"You knew? Why did you not mention in your message that Ullsaard was alive?"

"Would you entrust that sort of knowledge to a palace courier?" Noran took the pouch from Allenya and looked at Anglhan's corpse. "Anglhan had told me what he had planned before Ullsaard was brought out for the viewing. Seems a pity for Anglhan that I was distrustful."

"Pity would not have saved him," Allenya said grimly, stepping past Noran to head for the door.

"Wait!" Noran cried out, grabbing Allenya by the wrist, stop-

ping her. "You cannot walk the palace like this. Let us see if
we can find some cloak or coat to hide you."

Noran noticed that Allenya was starting to grow paler. He also
saw a bruise on the side of her head and realised that Anglhan
had not fallen without striking back. Shock and the blow to the
head were beginning to take their toll on the queen. Her expression became distant as he led her back into the bed chamber.

"Sit there," he said, pushing her gently onto the end of the
bed. There were several chests along one wall – evidently un-
packing had not been one of Anglhan's priorities. A quick
search produced a thick shirt that was large enough to be a
coat for the queen. There was little to be done with the bloodied hem of her dress, but a green cloak with a cowl served to
provide cover for her bloodstained face.

"He said that we have to act soon," Allenya mumbled as
Noran pulled her up and started to help her into the oversized
garments. There was a distant look in her eye. "Ullsaard will
stop breathing for real, he said."

"All is in hand, Allenya, trust me," said Noran, throwing the
cloak around her shoulders and pulling the hood over her
gore-matted hair. She looked at him for a moment, focussed
once more. "I will get you back to your apartments and you
must get everybody ready to leave immediately."

She nodded slowly and Noran felt relief. It was short-lived.
The lie had convinced the queen that all was in hand, but the
truth of the matter was that Noran had no idea how Anglhan
had planned to restore Ullsaard or smuggle him out of the
palaces. It was the middle of the day and Urikh would be busy,
but there were many other people around the palace.

He helped Allenya out of the bedroom and towards the
door, but then the queen stopped.

"What is the matter?" Noran asked, fearing that ordeal she
had been through was taking too much of a toll.

"I have a better plan," she said, smiling weakly at him. "It is too risky for me to walk the palace, so go to my apartments and send Meliu to me here. Have her bring fresh clothes. Nobody will disturb me while I wait."

"Aye, that is a better plan," admitted Noran. He wondered whether to confess the lack of the same for Ullsaard but decided the queen's state was too fragile to risk news of setback. "When I have sent Meliu, I will attend to Ullsaard."

"Very well," said Allenya. She undid the clasp of her cloak and threw it to the floor, before unbuttoning the shirt and tossing that over the corpse of Anglhan. Pulling a chair from under the table, she sat down, back straight, hands in her lap. "Go along now, Noran, let us not tarry."

No, let us not tarry at all, he thought, heading for the door.

"Stay safe," he said, looking back just as he was about to leave the dining room.

Allenya nodded calmly in reply.

"You as well. Bring my husband to me, Noran."

The nobleman could not find it in his heart to make a promise that he might have to break. With a forced smile he left, and headed for the royal apartments, desperately wracking his brains for a plan.

VIII

Meliu sat watching Allenya closely. Washed and dressed, her sister had regained her air of grace, but Meliu could tell there was turmoil below the surface. It was hard for all of them to comprehend. Urikh's betrayal was bad enough, though Noran had babbled something about the king not being in total control of himself, but the back-and-forth of Ullsaard being alive then dead, dead then alive again was almost too much for the youngest of his wives to take in.

Sitting next to her on the couch in the greeting room,

Ullnaar squeezed his mother's hand, offering physical reassurance. Meliu smiled at her son, so proud of what he had become. Lean and handsome, with golden locks the girls were all queuing to run than fingers through, and a brain to match. Perhaps too much of a brain, she thought. Always with a smart word or sarcastic remark ready, Ullnaar had offended more than one noble family in the city by spurning their daughter's approaches.

"So, is there any girl I should know about?" she asked, trying to take her mind off the current situation. Waiting had never been comfortable to her, and knowing that both Noran and Ullsaard were in danger made it an agony to simply sit in the royal apartments and wait for their return.

"One or two," said Ullnaar, flashing a heart-melting smile. "None yet that warrant a mother's scrutiny."

"They all warrant that, be sure," said Allenya. She smiled weakly and Meliu knew that she saw the likeness of Jutaar in Ullnaar's features, though the two could not have been more different in personality. A tear glimmered in Allenya's eye but did not grow enough to spill onto her cheek. "You never know when you might miss the girl that is best suited for you, simply because you look at her with a man's eye and not a woman's."

"Yes, tell us. Who are these girls who are not yet important enough that you choose not to introduce them to your mother?" said Meliu.

A knocking at the door saved Ullnaar the need to make excuses. Both Laasinia and Ariid were on hand, and the chief maid and steward arrived at the door simultaneously, jealously guarding the threshold of the apartment as much as an ailur protecting her cubs. Ariid stopped a step short and waved for Laasinia to open the door.

"Good, you are all here then," said Noran breathlessly as he hurried through the door. He glanced back to the corridor.

Meliu's mood improved dramatically at his arrival and she stood up, her stomach quivering. "Come on, no dawdling."

Noran was followed into the chamber by four legionnaires, bearing on a litter between them the body of Ullsaard. Meliu turned her eyes to the ceiling as the mutilated body was brought past. Even though she knew, by word of Noran, that the king was not truly dead, she could not look at the wounds that had been cut upon his flesh.

With Allenya and Ullnaar to either side of her, Meliu followed the legionnaires into the back of the apartments, to a sitting room overlooking the Maarmes circuit. The shutters had been pulled back from one window, letting cold air and weak winter sunshine into the room.

Under Noran's instructions, the soldiers laid Ullsaard down upon the low table in front of the fireplace. Only now was Meliu able to look at Ullsaard, her gaze locked to his face. He seemed as white as a corpse, eyes sunken, lips cracked and skin peeling.

"You can wait out by the door," said Noran waving away the legionnaires. When they had gone, his voice dropped to a whisper and he knelt beside Ullsaard. He produced a pouch of dried leaves. "I need hot water and a cup."

With a shuddering gasp, Allenya knelt beside her husband and laid her head on his linen-shrouded body, her ear to his chest.

"We are too late," she moaned quietly. "I hear no heartbeat, no breath."

Meliu wondered if the whole story was a cruel joke by the dreadful Anglhan; a spiteful raising of hopes to complete his victory over Ullsaard and his family. She did not voice such concern, but grabbed Ullnaar's hand in hers for reassurance. Her whole body was trembling with nerves and she felt faint. She forced herself to stand straight, not wishing to sit down and appear weak in front of the others.

"It will be all right," said her son, though his expression was grim as he concentrated on Noran. There was tightness around the young man's eyes. "Life would have to be shallow enough not to be noticed by the Brothers that prepared the body. I trust he will be restored."

Laasinia returned with a jug of hot water and a clay cup, while Ariid hovered by the door, attention split between Ullsaard and the legionnaires just beyond the door leading out of the adjoining chamber. Noran handed over the packet of leaves with a slight shrug. The handmaiden prepared a tincture with deliberate precision, measuring out a pinch of the drug between her fingers and then stirring it into the jug for some time. She looked apologetically at Allenya.

"I do not know the exact quantities, my queen, but I hope this will be sufficient."

She poured some of the antidote into the cup, which she then handed to Noran. The noble raised the cup of hot liquid to Ullsaard's lips. He poured as best he could, until greenish fluid ran from the corners of the king's mouth. Sitting back on his haunches, Noran watched Ullsaard's face, as did everyone else in the room.

Meliu wanted to scream with the tension; Ullnaar's grip on her hand was painfully strong. She realised her fingernails were digging into the back of his hand and he accepted the pain without complaint. Relaxing her grip, she suppressed a laugh. She could feel the mania creeping up on her; the energy of fear that propelled her from one drama to another. She had to control herself. The legionnaires were from the First, loyal to the king alone. Anything amiss would rouse their suspicions and they would report what was happening to Urikh. Nobody could know that Ullsaard was being restored.

With a wheezing breath Ullsaard opened his mouth.

"Hush," warned Noran as those in the chamber voiced surprise, relief and excitement. Meliu had to stop a shriek from escaping, clamping her mouth shut so that she could utter no exclamation. She took a few steps towards Noran as the noble stood, and placed her hand on his arm, her expression conveying her thanks even as her voice could not.

She returned her gaze to Ullsaard and found that his eyes were open. Focus came slowly, and then his stare roved around the room, settling on Noran's face as he bent over the king.

"Hello, old friend," Ullsaard whispered. "I've been expecting you."

IX

There was a strange echo inside Ullsaard's heard each time someone spoke. The words rang dully around his brain, trying to fit into some kind of meaning. He glanced out of the window and saw that it was still daylight – he had been "dead" for less than half a day. Still it felt as if he had been buried in the ground for some time and then dug up. His mouth was drier than Mekha and his flesh itched all over with a body-wide rush of pins and needles that made his skin flush.

"It worked? It worked." Noran seemed almost as insensible as Ullsaard, mouth opening and closing with astonishment. Meliu was holding the noble's arm, but Ullsaard looked past her and saw Ullnaar. The king's son was grinning and shaking his head.

"Ullsaard." Hearing the voice of Allenya filled Ullsaard with a surge of happiness. The king turned his head and his gaze fell upon his eldest wife. His eyes were crusted and his vision blurry, but she looked beautiful in a dark blue dress, her black hair let free to fall about her shoulders.

Blinking to gain some focus, he could not quite work out her expression. There was joy there, but also anger flashed through in her eyes.

"I'm sorry," croaked Ullsaard. He reached out a trembling hand, barely having the strength to lift the shroud that was laid across his body.

"Do not ever leave me again," said Allenya, snatching her hand into both of hers. The words were snarled, filled with desperation. "Do you hear me, Ullsaard? You are never to leave me again."

"I promise," said the king, smiling weakly. "I will never be leaving your side again. Whatever happens."

Ullsaard pulled Allenya closer, putting a hand to the back of her head as she bent over him, her cheek next to his.

"I was so alone," she whispered. He felt moisture on his skin from her tears. "So frightened."

"Never again," he promised, stroking her hair.

"This is all very nice, but we have to get you out of here," said Noran, laying a hand on Allenya's shoulder.

"What do you mean?" asked Ullsaard. With a grunt and a wave of dizziness he pushed himself into a sitting position. Allenya was there in a moment to hold him up as his head span. "I'm going nowhere. Give me a few moments and I'll be ready to confront Urikh."

"No!" snapped Noran. Everybody except Ullsaard glanced instinctively at the door, alarmed by his raised voice. The herald released himself from Meliu's grip and looked at Ariid. The steward shook his head.

"They are arguing about tonight's watch rota," reported Ariid.

"Good," said Noran, the effort of keeping calm visible in his strained features. "Ullsaard, you have to get out of here. You'll be killed if Urikh thinks you are alive."

"Not if I get to him first," said Ullsaard. His strength was returning slowly and he swung his legs from the table. Meliu came and helped her sister, the two queens providing support as the king pushed himself unsteadily to his feet.

"That will not work, Urikh has protection," said Noran. Even in his semi-confused state Ullsaard could sense that Noran was not telling the whole truth. The herald could not meet Ullsaard's gaze and he fidgeted with the hem of his tunic.

Recollection came back to Ullsaard and he realised there was someone missing from the room.

"What happened to Anglhan? I didn't think he would keep his word, but I had no choice but to trust him."

"I killed him," Allenya said quietly. Ullsaard saw no remorse in his wife's face as she made this admission.

"Good for you," replied the king, patting her hand. "That saves me the trouble. Now, Noran, there's something you aren't telling me. What did Anglhan say to you?"

"It doesn't matter, just trust me. You do not want to go after Urikh, especially not when you are so weak. He is in league with Lakhyri and has unnatural allies. You have no way of combating them."

Mention of Lakhyri gave Ullsaard something to think about. The king closed his eyes for a moment, seeking any presence of Askhos. There was nothing, and Ullsaard hoped for a moment that his near-death state had perhaps been too much for the spirit of the dead king to endure. That hope fluttered away as Ullsaard opened his eyes and saw the horror hidden behind Noran's eyes. Lakhyri had done something terrible, that much was certain.

With a jolt of fear, Ullsaard remembered what had been done to Erlaan. The king grabbed Noran's tunic and pulled him closer.

"Urikh, he is... changed?"

"No, no, not that," said Noran, grabbing Ullsaard's shoulder. "No, he is not like that creature locked up in the Grand Precincts."

"Is he still locked up?" demanded Ullsaard.

"I do not know," confessed Noran. "I have not seen him, and he is a difficult sight to miss. If he had been seen abroad there would have been panic and I have heard nothing of the sort."

Whatever it was that had Noran so scared, the nobleman was not about to indulge Ullsaard's curiosity. It would be easy to dismiss Noran's fears as the concerns of a lesser man, but there was a look in his eye and a catch in his voice that per-suaded Ullsaard to follow his friend's instincts. If he had learnt one thing in the last day of being dead, it was that sometimes you just had to trust others.

"I'm guessing your plan isn't to simply walk out of here," said the king. A gust of wind through the window reminded him of his own nakedness. Ullsaard looked at Ariid. "I don't suppose you've kept any of my clothes?"

"No, king, I am afraid that I have not," said the steward with an apologetic look. "Perhaps Herald Noran…"

"Won't fit, even if I have lost a little bulk this last year," said Ullsaard. To emphasise his point, he flexed his chest, pectoral muscles and shoulders bulging.

"I… I have something," said Allenya.

She took Ullsaard's hand and led him out of the sitting room and through the adjoining feast chamber. Turning right, they passed into a long corridor with several doors and passages branching off. Allenya stopped at the first door on the right and led Ullsaard through the beaded curtain that covered the arch.

The king found himself in a bedchamber and he glanced at Allenya, wondering whether she had missed him so much that she wanted to bed him now. He had to admit to himself that as pleasant as that proposition seemed, he was neither in the mood nor fit physical state to comply.

Fortunately the dilemma did not materialise; Allenya moved to one of the partitioned cupboards along one wall and pulled aside the curtain to reveal a stand with a suit of armour on it, complete with kilt, sword and spear arranged on a rack behind it. It took a moment for Ullsaard to recognise the suit; an ailur's head in portrait sculpted on the curve of the abdomen, the deep blue cloak fringed with white fur. It was the armour he had been presented when he made second captain, given to him by Allenya's father for their wedding.

He glanced at Allenya and saw that her eyes were glistening with tears, her whole body shaking. He took her up in a tight embrace, kissing her cheeks and neck, mumbling apologies and promises. They were interrupted by a terse whisper from Noran outside the door.

"Apologies for breaking up the reunion again, but these legionnaires are going to get suspicious. I suggest we go out into the gardens, jump a fence or two and then find a group of petitioners to tag onto to leave by the main gate."

"All right, don't start fretting now," replied Ullsaard, pushing himself away from Allenya with considerable reluctance. He looked at the armour and thought about Noran's plan. "It's not exactly inconspicuous is it?"

"Better than being naked," said Allenya. She smiled mischievously and ran a hand over his exposed chest. "In some ways, at least."

With Allenya's help it did not take long for Ullsaard to slip into the armour. There was an oval bronze mirror on a stand on the opposite side of the bed. Ullsaard turned to look at himself and barely recognised the man he saw in the reflection. He had lost weight it was true; the armour would probably not have fitted the Ullsaard who had taken the Crown from Lutaar. His hair hung past his shoulder and his beard hid a pasty face and reached his chest.

"Fetch Ariid, and have him bring soap and a blade."

Allenya departed and shortly after the steward appeared,

with a steaming bowl, a bag of fragranced soap flakes and a curved blade for shaving. Ullsaard sat on the end of the bed.

"Take off all of the beard, and shorten the hair a little," said the king, looking at the stranger in the mirror.

Ariid worked deftly and confidently, removing nearly a year's growth from Ullsaard's cheeks and chin. He teased out the knots in the king's hair with one of Allenya's combs and then cut it straight just short of shoulder-length. Ullsaard regarded the results in his reflection and nodded with satisfaction. The look did not suit him at all, but it was very different from the short-haired, bearded face on the coins of the empire.

"Right, even my mother would have to look twice to recognise me now," said the king, standing up. With a gesture he sent Ariid to fetch the sword, which the steward belted around Ullsaard's waist. With his helmet on he looked like he could be any captain in the legions and as such he felt that he could wander the palace as freely as he wished. For a moment he wondered if he would be able to get close enough to Urikh to draw his sword on his son, but the veiled warnings Noran had made concerning the current king's "protection" dispelled the thought. It would be better to get out of Askh and reconsider his options, rather than force the issue. There had been a degree of luck in his survival so far and the reunion with Allenya reminded the king what it was he was risking.

"Come on, let's go," said Ullsaard, striding back into the chamber where his "body" had been laid. He had just rejoined Noran and the others when there was a commotion from the entrance hall; the sound of armoured men standing up hurriedly.

"What are you doing here?" Luia's shrill tone travelled through the apartments carrying with it all of her scorn. Ullsaard heard muffled replies.

"She won't leave Urikh," said Allenya, grabbing Ullsaard's arm.

"I thought that she was out for the rest of the day," said Meliu, panic written on her features.

"What do mean, you have brought Ullsaard's body…" Luia's voice trailed away as she stepped into the chamber. She looked at the empty shroud. Her eyes swept past Ullsaard without stop to fall accusingly on Noran first and then on to Allenya. Finally recognition registered and she looked back at the man in the captain's uniform, eyes widening with shock, her lips parting.

"How? What has…" Luia fumbled for the words and then gave up. She rounded on Allenya. "What have you done? Urikh will be furious!"

Luia took a step towards the door, obvious in her intent to call the waiting legionnaires. She opened her mouth but Meliu's fist connected with her chin before Luia could utter a word. Luia crumpled to the floor, as Meliu stepped forwards nursing her right hand. She glared at her unconscious sister.

"Oh shut up, sister," snapped Meliu, imitating Luia's sharp tone and rubbing her knuckles. A bruise was spreading across Luia's chin and Meliu flexed her fingers with a pained expression. Meliu noticed the astounded gazes of the others on her and smiled self-consciously. "Come on, we have all wanted to do that for a long time. I know I have."

There was a concerned inquiry called out by one of the legionnaires. The soldiers had been waiting some time and Luia's barrage of insults on arriving had not increased their patience.

"We had best leave," said Allenya, the first to recover from the surprise. She grabbed Meliu's wrist. But the youngest queen pulled free.

"You have to go, but I will stay here," said Meliu. She held up a hand to silence Allenya's protest. "Those legionnaires are not going to wait long until they can return the body to where it is supposed to be. Laasinia and Ariid will not be able to stop them, but they will be reluctant to defy a queen. I will keep them occupied so that you can get out of the palace; Urikh will have you hunted down as soon as he realises that you are still alive."

"I do not agree," said Allenya. "It is not safe here."

"Go, sister," Meliu said quietly. She looked at Ullsaard and then back at Allenya. "If you remain here, Urikh might well use you against our husband, as Anglhan did."

"But what of you?" said Ullsaard.

"We both know what controls your heart," replied Meliu with a wan smile. She looked at Noran and the smile strengthened. "Urikh also knows that, and Luia for all of her faults would not see me harmed to get at you."

"I will stay too," said Ullnaar. He stepped up beside his mother and laid a hand on her shoulder. "Mother is right. The Brotherhood will have the city gate closed as soon as they know that you are trying to get away. The more time we can delay that discovery, the better your chances of escaping."

"Urikh will know that you know I'm alive," warned Ullsaard. "He'll see that as a threat."

"Lakhyri too," said Noran, with the same ominous undertone in his voice that Ullsaard had noticed earlier. "Even if you trust Urikh not to do anything harsh, I do not think the High Brother has any regard for you. This may persuade him that you are too much of a nuisance to keep alive."

"I will take care of that," said Ullnaar. "A letter to my tutors will ensure that Urikh cannot move against us. They already know that all is not well in the palace, and even if they do not have the legion muscle of the Brotherhood the Colleges can still make life difficult for the king. Half of the nobles in the city attended the Colleges. No, if Urikh wants to keep a lid on your survival he cannot announce a general hue and cry. His own secrets will be his downfall."

"I like you," said Noran, slapping the youth on the arm. "I do not know where you got that devious brain from, because it certainly was not your father."

"He is not such a brute, you know," said Ullnaar, winking at his father.

"Good, well now that we're all agreed that I'm not a simpleton, can we stop talking and get moving?"

Ullsaard shook Ullnaar's hands and then gently moved him aside so that he could embrace his mother. Meliu returned the hug half-heartedly and Ullsaard looked closely at her as he stepped back. She returned his gaze, but he could tell from the twist of her body and tilt of her head that she was thinking about Noran.

"You are wasted on me, I am sorry," said the king, kissing her on the cheek. "Thank you for everything."

Meliu said nothing, but she nodded a fraction and dipped her eyes. A moment later she held a hand out to Noran, who took it and kissed her palm.

"You know I could stay…" suggested the herald, but Meliu shook her head and pulled him into a closer embrace.

"Look after my husband and sister," she said. "And look after yourself too."

Ullsaard was getting impatient now. The farewells were not only eating up precious time, they made it seem as if they would never come back again. He was not in the mood for such defeatist thoughts and tugged at Noran's sleeve.

"He'll be fine," the king told Meliu. "We have to go now."

And with no further word, he strode through the apartments to the sun room at the rear. Sliding the bar from the double doors, he opened them with a single thrust, revealing a path that wound down between low hedges into the main gardens of the palace. Further down the hill he could clearly see the Grand Precincts. He stepped out without hesitation;

behind him Allenya swept a cloak and hood over her shoulders and head as she followed, Noran close on her heels.

X

A familiar scent drifted into Erlaan-Orlassai's chamber a few moments before his visitor arrived: incense and decaying flesh. Lakhyri. There was something else as well, the smell of sword oil and perfume. The high priest had been spending time with Urikh again, and his blackcrest legionnaires.

"What news from the palace?" Erlaan-Orlassai asked as Lakhyri stepped into the room.

"Bad news," replied the high priest. "We have been betrayed. Ullsaard still lives."

"You have too many kings, Lakhyri: perhaps it is time that you stopped playing them against each other," said Erlaan.

He had spent a long time thinking about what the priest had promised, and his own place in the schemes of the Temple. He had drawn several; conclusions that were not to his liking and this latest announcement sealed the true heir's feelings on the matter. He stood up, hunched inside the small room but still towering over the high priest.

"I will take matters into my own hands," announced the Prince. He gently pushed Lakhyri to one side with a clawed hand and moved towards the door, stooping to fit under the wooden lintel.

"You cannot go out!" Lakhyri stepped in front of Erlaan-Orlassai. "You will be seen."

"I do not care if I am seen," replied the Prince. "You assured me that I will rule this empire one day. There is no reason why today should not be that day. It is time for these pretenders to be shown their place."

"It is not yet time," said Lakhyri. "There are other preparations to be made for our masters."

"You are wrong," said Erlaan-Orlassai. "Do not forget the sense that you gave me. I feel the presence of the Eulanui, I know they are here in Askh. You delay for the sake of it."

"No!" Lakhyri bared yellowing teeth. "All must be in order for the masters, or the consequences will be terrible. They will take what they are not given. The Brotherhood's precincts are nodes to the Temple, you know this. Stability must be restored and Salphoria brought into the empire properly."

"That will still take many years," said Erlaan-Orlassai. "Why would I wait for so long?"

"With a willing workforce and the support of a king the people can accept, we can have precincts in every major Salphorian town by midsummer. There are twenty thousand blackcrests ready to march, and the legions of the governors will soon be ours too. If you reveal yourself you jeopardise everything we both hope to achieve."

Erlaan-Orlassai did not like the tone of the high priest but the message of his words struck a chord in the Prince's thoughts. For all that Lakhyri's argument made sense, his logic was little salve to the frustration the Prince felt.

"I need to be out of this place," moaned the true heir. "For some time I have seen neither moon nor sun, nor felt fresh air in my lungs."

"Years?" Lakhyri's sneering grimace was a lash to the Prince's pride. "I spent centuries in the Temple, away from this world and its pleasures and pains, in order that our masters were served properly. Many there are who have spent their whole lives not knowing of moon and sun. Your incarceration is a small inconvenience."

"Not for me," replied the Prince, angered by Lakhyri's dismissive words. He reached out with taloned fingers and wrapped them around Lakhyri, engulfing his head. "I could crush your skull now and be free of your spiteful presence."

"And you would never be king of Askh," the high priest replied, voice muffled by Erlaan-Orlassai's palm. "You need me."

"Even so," said the Prince, releasing his grip, "I will not remain here any longer. If I am to hide, it will not be beneath these old stones, but under an open sky."

Lakhyri stepped out of the way as Erlaan-Orlassai made another move towards the door. The Prince squeezed his way into the corridor and looked to the left and right. A startled Brother stood transfixed at the end of the passage to his right, mouth agape.

"If you wish to stretch your legs, I have a suggestion," Lakhyri said from behind Erlaan-Orlassai.

The Prince smile at the transfixed Brother, but revealing his razor-sharp teeth set the man to flight rather than comforted him. The patter of the Brother's receding footsteps echoed through the corridors.

"At least wait until tonight," said Lakhyri, squeezing past the enormous prince. "If you wish to leave the Grand Precincts then you can do us both a service. Hunt down Ullsaard and slay him."

The suggestions sent a gush of happiness through the Prince. He turned his bestial face towards the high priest.

"Kill Ullsaard? Finally you want me to cut down that dog?" Excitement and expectation rose inside the Prince in equal measure. "That is no price for freedom, it is a reward."

"He cannot have got far," said Lakhyri. The high priest started to walk and Erlaan-Orlassai paced beside him, taking slow strides, back bent and head twisted within the confines of the passageway.

"He will head for the Greenwater. I will need a ship."

"You think he will reach Narun before you can catch him?"

"I think that he does not need to head to Narun," replied the Prince. The corridor made his voice loud in his ears and he winced slightly before continuing in a softer tone. "Ullsaard will avoid anywhere where the Brotherhood is strong or where there are legionnaires in numbers. I cannot scour the wilderness for him, but the might of Askh can. When I have left, sweep Askhor between the city and the Wall. Send word to the precincts to expect me. I will travel by night, as you say."

"You assume that he will travel to hotwards? His heart has always been in Enair."

"And that is why he will not return there. He ran to Enair when he overthrew my grandfather, he will not do the same again. Ullsaard is well aware of what would be predictable."

"What else will you need?"

"My armour and my weapons. They were taken when Ullsaard shamed me."

"They can be found. The Greenwater covers a long distance: how will you know where he has stopped?"

Erlaan-Orlassai looked down at the high priest and saw himself reflected in the man's golden eyes; a hulking, brutish thing that filled the corridor. The reflection smiled with dagger-teeth, and the Prince's golden eyes flickered with their own light.

"I can smell the Blood, you know. When you brought Ullsaard to this place I could sense him immediately. I heard the chatter of the Brothers that the old king was dead, but I knew they were wrong. His vitality lingered. I kept my tongue, though I wanted to find him, to complete the job you thought you had done, but you did not include me in your schemes. I thought perhaps the faking of his death was your idea. Had you done so, I would have told you that he was still alive. Even now his spoor hangs heavy in the air. He may have a head start on me, but he will not stay ahead for long."

Lakhyri smiled; a reptilian expression devoid of mirth.

"You will kill him when you find him."

"Yes, and when I return I will kill Urikh and take my place

as leader of the greatest empire in the world." Lakhyri's smile disappeared as quickly as it had come while Erlaan-Orlassai rubbed his hands together, his palms making a sound like stone scraped across stone. "If you try to stop me, I will kill you, priest, and anybody else that stands in my way. Be ready for my return, I will not wait long for my coronation."

TEMPLE

Dust sprinkled from the blocks of the ceiling, catching the yellow light that seeped through the window of the chamber. Laid with his hands on his chest, Eriekh felt the tremor of the Temple and the trickle of particles on his arms and opened his eyes. A patina of tiny motes obscured the swirls and runes carved into his tanned flesh. He saw a crack, as thin as a hair, jagging across the stone above him. He frowned and sat up, looking at the walls and floor. The blocks had shifted, almost imperceptibly but he could see it. Hundreds of years had passed while he had dwelt in this cell and nothing had changed since the moment he had arrived; not until now.

He was not surprised when another near-naked figure appeared at the door. It was the other hierophant, Asirkhyr, and his expression was one of dismay.

"You felt it also?" said Eriekh, rising from his plain stone bed.

"All felt it," replied Asirkhyr. The skin of the second hierophant was flushed, not with fear but a lingering effect of his time in Greater Askhor. While Eriekh had refrained from indulging in mortal pursuits – eating, drinking and fornication – Asirkhyr had happily made the most of his time away from the Temple and was now showing the effects. His stomach bulged a little over the white of his loincloth and there was a vitality to his skin that was seen only in the young acolytes freshly brought from their homes.

A shrill cry of joy echoed along the corridors, but both hierophants barely registered a response; the feeding of the masters had become commonplace in recent times. Now and then a young member of the order would fall prey to the half-material creatures that dwelt in the shadows between worlds. Some were fortunate to succumb in their sleep.

The pattering of bare feet on the stone caused Asirkhyr to turn as Eriekh stepped out of his chamber. Naasadir, one of the upper order, hurried towards them, arms hugging his chest tightly in fear.

"Come quickly, come to the Last Corpse," said Naasadir, beckoning with a skeletal hand. "It changes. There is a visitation."

The hierophants followed at a swift walk when Naasadir turned and headed back along the corridors. They descended into the depths of the Temple, to the main chanting hall. Barely five score of worshippers remained of those who had once filled the hall with their sibilant whispers of supplication and binding. Those that were still alive knelt in a circle around the Last Corpse, a jet black altar stone that bulged with the unnatural shape of inhuman bones.

Until the present crisis, the Last Corpse had been largely inert, taking form only when infused with the spirit of one of the Eulanui. Now it was moving subtly, and seemed to Eriekh to be growing. The bones – a disturbing web of spines and limbs and vertebrae and jawbones – were parting and straightening. The changes were subtle; as with the disturbance of his chamber, Eriekh could see this only from centuries of familiarity and a sense that something was amiss.

"We must speak with Lakhyri," said Asirkhyr. "We try

everything we can to appease them, to ask for patience, but they do not listen."

"I think this is beyond Lakhyri's reckoning also," said Eriekh, glancing at Asirkhyr and then Naasadir. He felt the slightest tremble of the Temple again.

COMING. SOON.

The thought-message blared through Eriekh's thoughts, sending him to his knees, hands clamped to the sides of his head. The shock of his fall jarred him from the disorientation that threatened to overwhelm his thoughts.

Eriekh looked around, eyes moving first to the Last Corpse, but there had been no manifestation. The thought-message had come direct from the Eulanui, on the other side of the veil that kept them from the mortal world.

"I have a fear," he said, grabbing Naasadir's wrist to pull himself to his feet. "I fear we have been deceived for a very long time."

"Deceived by whom?" asked Naasadir.

"Our numbers are growing few," said Asirkhyr, deep in thought. "The masters manifest themselves more frequently even as our channelling of power to them grows weaker. They seek more sustenance."

"No," said Eriekh. "The Temple has not been providing energy for the masters, but it has fuelled the barrier that keeps them from the world of men. The barrier is failing as the Temple fails. For all of this time, I think that Lakhyri has been seeking to keep the Eulanui at bay, not sustained."

"If that is the case, we must warn him," said Asirkhyr. "He must be able to do something."

"Why would we do that?" said Eriekh. "It seems as though Lakhyri has betrayed the masters in his attempts to keep them from seeking purchase in the mortal world. Is this not the goal for which we have strived these many centuries? The masters are almost here! You cannot be allowed to stop them."

"We are not ready for them," said Naasadir. "They will consume everybody in their hunger. The web must be completed before they cross over."

"A task too long to finish now," said Asirkhyr. He looked at Naasadir, his eyes flickering momentarily towards Eriekh. "The more they feed, the greater the strength of the masters and the fewer of us to keep them away. The Temple is doomed."

"No!" Eriekh seized Asirkhyr by the throat, both hands wrapped tight. "You cannot interfere!"

The two hierophants toppled to the slabs as Asirkhyr threw a clumsy punch at his attacker. Eriekh gritted his teeth as he forced every ounce of effort into strangling his foe, while Asirkhyr lashed weak blows against his opponent's shoulders and head.

Something struck Eriekh hard in the back of the head. As he rolled to one side, his grip loosened, he realised it had been Naasadir's heel.

"Not you too," gasped Eriekh. "Are you traitor also?"

"All living things will be destroyed if we persist," said Asirkhyr. "They were meant to be enslaved to our will, not devoured. We have failed."

Naasadir, naturally taller and stronger than Eriekh, seized the hierophant by the arms and hauled him to his feet. Asirkhyr shook his head and rubbed a hand across his reddened throat. Around the group the other worshippers continued their incantation, moving back and forth as they lowered their heads to the ground and regurgitated mantras that they did not understand. A couple of them looked up at the disturbance.

"See sense, Eriekh. There can be no victory in oblivion," said the priest. "That was not our purpose."

"It is victory for our masters; that is all the purpose we need," snarled Eriekh. Asirkhyr's treachery appalled him and he looked away.

"What do you propose?" asked Naasadir.

"I do not know what to do," said Asirkhyr. "Take him and bind him while I think."

Eriekh opened his mouth to shout more accusations, but Naasadir's arm clamped around his neck, elbow under his jaw. Unable to speak and barely able to breath, Eriekh was dragged from the shrine room.

APILI, OKHAR
Late Winter, 213th year of Askh

I

Frost encrusted the vine terraces but there was no snow, not this far to hotwards. Unlike Menesun, Ullsaard's villa at Apili was a working concern. A vast tract of grape-growing estate was attached to the cluster of buildings, from which wine was shipped out across the Askhan Empire and had even made its way as far as Carantathi. Originally the lands had been intended for Urikh as a gift on reaching his twenty-first birthday, at the insistence of Luia, but Ullsaard's eldest son had become more involved in commerce than wine-making and so the estate had been run for Ullsaard's benefit by a man called Houran. The income had been useful during the lean times of Ullsaard's Mekha campaign, and there was good hunting in the forests that lay further to dawnwards. There had been a time when Ullsaard had thought of retiring here. The weather was warm, but not as dry as Maasra, and Okhar was a well-established, peaceful province.

All of that had changed when he had taken the Crown. The capital had been his home, albeit only briefly before his war against Salphoria, and thoughts of coming to Apili had faded.

He had never expected that he would arrive here as a fugitive from his own son.

He was convinced that they had given any pursuing forces the slip for the moment. Leaving Askh, they had turned dawn-wards at Noran's suggestion and headed for the coast. Taking ship to hotwards, they had crossed through Maasra and come to Okhar from hotwards, ignoring the Greenwater altogether. This route had taken considerably more time than a ship on the river, but Ullsaard had put his faith in discretion rather than speed and it seemed to have worked; nobody paid much attention to a man and his wife and retainer – Noran had not been too happy at his part of the subterfuge – travelling hot-wards to spend the winter in warmer lands.

The manager, Houran, had been surprised by the arrival of the estate's owners. Seeing the sense of not asking too many questions, Houran had welcomed Ullsaard, Allenya and Noran into the main house and quit his chambers to take up resi-dence in one of the guest apartments. That had been only an hour earlier.

Ringed by hills, Apili was more of a traditional Askhan villa than Menesun. The complex comprised eight buildings, one of them the major residence with an outbuilding of stables and storage rooms, two guest apartments and the rest dedicated to the winery. Everything was built on a single storey, with high ceilings and wide windows framed with heavy wooden beams. There were no fireplaces or chimneys except in the kitchen. Warmth in these colder times was instead provided by heated water passing through pipes beneath the tiled floor. It was a pleasant, ambient heat and Ullsaard waited for Allenya with bare feet gently warmed by the clay floor.

His armour was piled in one corner of the room, the king dressed only in his kilt. The cold breeze from the window was refreshing rather than bitter, and the darkening evening sky was calming to his nerves. The calls of birds roosting in the bare branches of the orchard that lay between the main villa and the winery added to the scene.

It was almost possible to forget how desperate the situation had become, but Ullsaard could not quite leave behind his woes, not now. Urikh would be seeking him for certain. Apili was a distance from Askh, and the nearest Brotherhood precinct was at least eight miles, but it was also an obvious place to look. There were several dozen men and women on the estate but they were not fighters, and there was no wall to defend. And, besides, even with legionnaires and a more fortified position Ullsaard had not been able to hold out at Menesun. Any feeling of respite was temporary. While winter held, it would be safe enough, but spring came fast in these climes and Ullsaard knew that soon he and Allenya would have to move on.

"You look pensive, my love."

Ullsaard turned at the sound of Allenya's voice. She entered the bedroom, the fragrance of her bath oils drifting across to meet Ullsaard. She wore an open-fronted blue dress, bangles and anklets of silver flashing in the light of the lamp. Her hair was unruly, still damp, and hung in dark curls about her shoulders.

"You are beautiful," said Ullsaard as she sat on the edge of the bed.

"And you are… different," laughed Allenya. Ullsaard stroked fingers across his shaven chin and smiled.

"A temporary change," said the king, sitting on the bed next to his wife. "I think it makes me look younger."

Allenya regarded him with her head tilted to one side, a smile playing on her lips. The smiled faded and she looked away.

"What is it?" asked Ullsaard. Allenya had been distant on their journey from Askh, but the king had thought it only the turmoil of their flight that had weighed on her thoughts. She had seemed distracted rather than angry or upset.

"I see more of Jutaar in you, without the beard," she said, looking at the floor.

"I am sorry," said Ullsaard. "I know that we did not have time to grieve together when he was killed."

"I always knew that time for both of us would be precious when I married you," said Allenya. Her voice was quiet, and her hands trembled in her lap. "But I thought that we would be together when it was important. You managed to come back to Askh for the birth of your son. What was so important that you missed his death?"

"I had a war to wage," said Ullsaard, reaching out to touch Allenya on the arm. She drew away from his fingers. Even as he said the words he knew they sounded empty. How could he explain the drive that was inside him; the frustration that he had felt at the setbacks inflicted upon him by Anglhan? "I avenged our son. Magilnada was razed."

"I avenged him!" Allenya stood up and glared at Ullsaard. The king shrank back from her vehemence. "You destroyed a city but the man who was responsible still escaped. You thought only of Salphoria and your conquest. I needed you, Ullsaard. I needed you so much and you were not there."

Words failed the king as he tried to think of some way to make amends, but all he could muster were excuses for his actions that were better left unsaid. He stood up and tried to embrace Allenya but she stepped away, tears falling to the tiles.

"It has been so long since we have lain together," Allenya said, her voice becoming quiet again. "You left me in Magilnada, unfulfilled. What was I to think? Other soldiers take their wives on campaign, but not you, not the king."

"It is dangerous..."

"And yet families follow their fathers, whether they are

legionnaires, captains or generals. You would not have me, and you left me to become a bargaining tool of that filthy pig."

Ullsaard was helpless against the accusations. It had been the presence of Askhos in his thoughts which had forced him to leave Allenya behind. How could he explain that he would not share her with the shade of a dead king?

"And then when we were reunited, our son dead, what did you do? You packed me away to Askh so that you could continue your war. And I waited for so long for you to return."

Allenya was shaking, every limb quivering, her breath coming in gulped gasps. She paced back and forth for a few steps and then launched herself at Ullsaard, battering her small fists against his chest and shoulders.

"You died! You died, you ungrateful bastard! You went away and were never coming back!"

Trying not to hurt Allenya, Ullsaard caught her arms and pushed her away, but she wriggled free and slapped him across the face. Startled, he shoved her, throwing her onto the bed.

"I'm sorry," he said, taking a step after her with a hand outstretched. Allenya rolled over, turning her back to him. "I am here now. I did not die. I am alive, and I'm here with you."

"Not to me," Allenya sobbed. Her shoulders heaved as she cried, her hands rucking the blanket in her fierce grip. "I was told you were dead. I saw your body. All of those cuts."

He sat on the bed behind her and placed a hand on her head, striking her hair. She glanced back at him, tears streaking her face.

"I saw your corpse, Ullsaard and I knew that you were dead."

There was nothing to say. Ullsaard could not change what had happened and words were meaningless. He pulled Allenya to his chest and cradled her in his thick arms, her face buried against him. She tried to pull away but he would not let her, his embrace firm but not tight. He bent his neck and kissed her hair.

Her sobs continued for some time. Ullsaard did not speak, but simply held Allenya close, feeling the wetness of her tears on his skin. When finally her crying subsided, she looked up at him, eyes reddened, and she looked as beautiful to him as when she had entered the room.

"I'm sorry," she said, and Ullsaard could not stop a laugh.

"You have nothing to be sorry about, my love," he said, stroking a hand over her cheek. "I am sorry, for all of the misery that I've heaped on you these past few years."

"But I would not have it any other way," said Allenya. "I should not blame you for the lies of others."

"But I was not there with you, and you are right that I should have been," replied Ullsaard. His eyes began to fill with tears as he thought of what he had missed. "If I had been a father and husband first, Jutaar might not be dead. I should not have made him first captain. He wasn't ready. He would never have been ready, but I needed someone I could trust with Anglhan. I sent him to be betrayed. I should have known better."

It was Allenya's turn to comfort Ullsaard, as the heartache of his son's death clenched tight in his chest.

"He always wanted to be a soldier," said his wife, sitting up so that she could lay her head on his shoulder and speak softly in his ear. "He was so proud of you."

"And I of him," said Ullsaard. "He always tried to make me proud and I never acknowledged it. I never told him how happy it made me to see him in breastplate and cloak."

Bowing his head, the king allowed Allenya to sooth his troubled thoughts, her hand moving up and down his back with slow strokes, easing the tension from his muscles. When his eyes were drying, he kissed his wife on the cheek.

"Tell me again how Anglhan died," he said.

"I stabbed him in the heart and cut off his balls," Allenya replied, and Ullsaard smiled. "He died begging and crying, in return for killing our son."

"I love you." Ullsaard kissed her on the lips.

"I love you too." Allenya placed her hand on the back of his neck and pulled him towards her, kissing him in return.

The taste of her, the warmth of Allenya's presence, sent energy through Ullsaard. His member was erect almost immediately, pressing against the leather of his kilt. For a moment a thought flickered into his mind: of Askhos. He dismissed it, knowing that he could not hold back any longer. He felt nothing of the dead king's presence and he needed to be with Allenya, fully and unconditionally.

She was pulling aside the front of her dress with one hand, grabbing Ullsaard's wrist in the other so that his hand moved to her exposed breast. He caressed it gently, holding back the ferocious desire that was threatening to engulf him. Their kisses became longer, tongues touching, hands exploring each other's bodies as if for the first time.

Ullsaard quivered as Allenya reached under his kilt, her fingers brushing along the length of his manhood. He twitched and squirmed as her hand engulfed him, massaging slowly from the base of his cock to the tip. He pulled away from her kisses and lowered his head to her breast, tongue circling the nipple before his mouth clamped around it. Her moan of pleasure caused his erection to stiffen even more, pressing almost painfully against the inside of his kilt.

Unable to restrain himself any longer, Ullsaard pushed Allenya aside, so that she lay twisted, her upper half on her front, backside rising up towards him. Pulling up her dress he savoured the sight of her pale buttocks, gently patting them before slipping his hand between her thighs, fingers probing wet hair and then finding entry.

Manoeuvring one leg between Allenya's, Ullsaard slipped his manhood into her, pushing slowly until his whole length was inside. He gritted his teeth as she squeezed tight around him, sending a pulse of pleasure up his shaft.

"I can't..." he growled, pulling out and pushing into her once more before his orgasm exploded through him, every drop of his love and grief and desire flowing from the end of his cock into his wife. The climax felt as if it would never stop, spurt after spurt, every shuddering moment gripping his entire body.

He slumped over Allenya, engulfing her with his bulk. He did not know how long he lay there, unable to reason or sense anything other than the warmth that suffused him. After an age he rolled away onto his back, eyes closed. Allenya followed him, placing her head on his chest, her finger drawing circles on the inside of his thigh.

"I did not mean to finish so swiftly," he said, looking at Allenya. "I didn't mean to use you."

She smiled and her hand moved between his legs, stroking his balls. To Ullsaard's amazement, his member twinged in response, starting to harden again.

"Do not worry, my love," Allenya said, the words coming between kisses on his body that moved down toward his groin. "I will make sure I get what I need as well."

II

When finally Allenya and Ullsaard were sated by their love-making, the king slipped into a calm slumber. A dream came swiftly, of Askhos' mausoleum-cave in the other world that the dead king inhabited. Askhos sat on a wooden stall beside the stone slab of his tomb and looked surprised at Ullsaard's arrival.

"I did not expect to return here," said the First King. "I thought this place dead to me."

"It is," replied Ullsaard, sensing something different about the place. He looked out of the entrance and saw dark hillsides with a clear, starry sky above; the landscape of Okhar. "It is my memory of this place, not the original."

"You seem unusually happy considering your situation."

"Allenya and I have got to know each other again," said Ullsaard, smiling at the thought.

"Enjoy the moment while it lasts, Ullsaard. Your troubles will be waiting for you in the morning."

"They will, which is why I will wake shortly and fuck my wife again, to ensure that I make the most of this night." Ullsaard looked for somewhere to sit. He noticed a bench along one wall of the cave, carved from the stone itself.

"That was not here before," said Askhos as the king sat down.

"I think I have learnt something from you in the time you have spent in my head. This place, the world of my dreams, is alongside that one of which you speak. I can control what happens here, just as you used to. When Lakhyri took me through the dreamworld to Noran, something... something meshed with me. I can feel it, in the Blood, connecting me to you, to this place."

Askhos looked at the king with surprise.

"I do not think it is your understanding that increases." The First King paused and looked around, though his gaze was distant, not looking at the contents of the cave. He frowned as he focussed on Ullsaard once more. "Yes, as I suspected. The veil is thinning."

"Veil?"

"There are worlds within worlds within worlds. On and on, entire universes within other universes. The veil is a barrier, a reality that keeps them apart. Only in essence can we cross between – your dream self, here and now, for example. Physical things, our bodies, worlds, are kept separate. Something is breaking the barrier, coming from the otherworld to our reality.

The thinning of the veil enables you to extend your will into the dream-sphere."

"What does that mean? What is trying to cross over? And what happens if the veil is torn?"

"All good questions," replied Askhos, perturbed by his own pronouncement. "I do not know for sure the right answer, but my guesses are all bad. Only Lakhyri can really tell us what is happening."

"He is in Askh, out of my reach for the moment."

Askhos stopped again, becoming frozen for a short while, during which Ullsaard felt the slight touch of the dead king fluttering through him, searching his memories. With a blink and a shudder, Askhos returned.

"I see, things are even worse than when our minds last touched. I am glad I missed out on the faking of your death, which seems a singularly unpleasant experience. What made you trust that Anglhan would keep his word?"

"Desperation," Ullsaard replied with a sigh. "I had no choice but to believe him when he said he intended for me to survive. The alternative was to die. I cannot think that he had my best interests at heart, but he saw me as his best means to regaining power. It would have been stupid to get myself killed just to spite his ambition."

"And now what do you plan to do?"

"I am not telling you," said Ullsaard, standing up. He grinned at Askhos' frown. "I do not trust you any more than I would trust your brother, or my son. I have no guarantee that you have not been the architect of my misfortune all this time. You have shown me the stranger underside of the world, and told me of how things can be in different locations and yet the same place, and messages can be sent across the world in a moment. How am I to know that you do not collude with Lakhyri?"

Askhos opened his mouth to reply but Ullsaard wagged a finger and the dead king's lips clamped shut.

"See? I am in control here. Always you have sought to use me for your purposes, and that will not continue. I am done with you."

Ullsaard turned his back on Askhos and walked out of the cave, feeling the mute protests of the king following him. Now that he had one less thing to worry about, Ullsaard could concentrate on more solid matters: retaking Askh and bringing his son to account for his actions.

III

Scratching his belly and yawning, Noran walked out of the guesthouse and into the courtyard of the villa. The air was crisp, as was the frost underfoot, but the low sun was bright, catching the rime on the edges of the roof tiles. Ullsaard was sat on a circular bench around the trunk of a leafless tree, a stylus in one hand and a folding wax tablet in the other. The king's face was a mask of concentration as he wrote, pausing every few moments to cock his head to one side and review his progress.

The gravel underfoot betrayed Noran's approach up the path and Ullsaard looked up. He raised the tablet to his brow to shield his eyes from the winter sun.

"Nice of you to join me," said the king. "I think I just heard third bells of Low Watch."

"There has not been a night passed since we left Askh that I was not awake to see the dawn, until this morning. I am entitled to some rest."

A look of guilt passed across Ullsaard's face, and Noran had known the king long enough to guess that it was not for past inconveniences that Ullsaard felt ashamed.

"What do you want?" Noran asked, his mood souring quickly.

"I need you to take a message to Anasind for me," said the king.

Noran looked at the tablet in Ullsaard's hand, unable to believe what he had just heard. He shook his head.

"I am not going to Carantathi for you."

Ullsaard laughed, genuine surprise on his face.

"I wouldn't ask you to! Anasind has been marching all winter, he should reach Ersua about the same time that you get there."

"I am not going to Ersua for you, either," said Noran. He sat down next to his friend. "Understand me, I did not turn up in Askh for your benefit, and I helped you escape only because of the past we share. I want nothing to do with this new war of yours."

"Really?" Ullsaard seemed more amused than irritated by Noran's declaration. "You would rather Urikh was king than me? You want the Brotherhood to rule the empire in his name?"

Urikh was not the problem, Noran thought. He had seen the things that the king had bargained with and wanted no part of opposing such power.

"I am heading hotwards, to Cosuan perhaps. I am getting out of the empire and if you were a smart man you would too. There is nothing left to fight for."

"You know that I will not give up without a fight. I have been wronged, and whatever Urikh thinks he is doing, all he is achieving is Lakhyri's will. I cannot allow that."

"Urikh is an idiot," Noran blurted before he could stop himself. He clamped his teeth together to stop himself saying anything further.

"Why do you say that?" asked Ullsaard. "He has us outmanoeuvred, that's for sure. Well, he has until my message gets to Anasind."

"It doesn't matter," said Noran, standing up. He crossed his arms, defiant to the king's suggestion. "I am not going with any message to anybody. If I am caught, I will have my throat slit, or worse."

"It was Urikh that had you dragged to Askh, do you think he will simply forget about you?" said the king.

"He will have other matters on his mind, I am sure of it. He is about to discover that power borrowed rarely lasts long."

"You think Lakhyri will move against him? If so, that's all the more reason to make sure we're ready to strike."

"Stop saying 'we' and 'us', Ullsaard! You assume that I am with you. You always assume that I will back you. Not this time. No, not this time." Noran took a few paces back and forth and then looked imploringly at the king. "I am scared, Ullsaard. You are not pitching yourself against a… against a natural power this time."

Ullsaard sat back and placed the wax tablet on the bench beside him. His gaze lingered on Noran for quite some time while the king seemed to be making a decision.

"You saw something, didn't you? At the palace."

"What makes you say that?" replied Noran. He regretted answering with a question of his own – simple evasion that even Ullsaard recognised as such. The king leaned forward, arms resting on his knees.

"Something strange? Not of this world?"

"Strange does not cover it," Noran said with a sigh, admitting defeat. It did not matter if Ullsaard thought him touched in the head, he had to tell somebody what he had seen in the Hall of Askhos.

"It was a beast of shadow, but not there really. It… devoured Asuhas. I mean, it swallowed him up, every fibre of him, every drop of blood. I have…" Noran could not describe what he had seen. It was making his heart race and his gut twist just thinking about the horrifying experience. "It was something I never want to see again. You cannot fight that, Ullsaard. Come away with me, and leave Urikh to his folly."

"What about Meliu?" growled Ullsaard, eyes narrowing. "You would abandon her."

Noran shrugged and looked apologetic.

"I am not a hero, Ullsaard. She had her chance to come and she chose to stay, for your benefit, rather than leave with me. Her priorities are clear."

"And you thank her for protecting us by deserting her?" Ullsaard rose to his feet, fists clenching at his sides. "What kind of man are you?"

"One that very much wants to stay alive," said Noran, but he could feel his resolve wavering. Last night, in the brief moments in bed before long overdue sleep had swept over him, he had been adamant that he would stay a few days only and then he would get out of Greater Askhor. The shadow that eats men haunted his dreams, and he was not going to sacrifice himself to such a fate for anybody. Now that Ullsaard mentioned Meliu, Noran saw her sweet face and he hated himself for the decision he had already made.

"There are other messengers," he said, the lameness of the excuse plain even to Noran. He spoke the words but without any conviction.

"It is you that I trust," said Ullsaard. "Or I thought I did. Perhaps I should just let you go. You can run away and we'll stay and fight to protect what's important to us. Enjoy the rest of your life on your own."

Noran shook his head and laughed, bitterness fuelling his words.

"You do not fucking own me, Ullsaard! You are not even king any more. Why will you not leave me be?"

"Because I need you," snarled the king. "Because who else do I have?"

"Oh, so I am your only choice? Thank you for the confidence."

"The things that will control the empire if Lakhyri is not stopped do not care for men and women. Meliu, Urikh, Luia, Ullnaar; they will all die."

"Urikh threatened my family with that thing," said Noran. "They could all be dead already for all that I know."

"Nonsense, we both know that a threat carried out loses its strength." Ullsaard looked sharply at Noran and the nobleman felt even more uncomfortable than when the king had looked to raise his fists against him.

"What is it?" Noran did not like the predatory gleam in Ullsaard's eyes. "What are you looking at?"

"Is that it?" demanded the king. "Has Urikh turned you against me with his threats? Maybe I cannot trust you anymore. Perhaps Urikh has managed to take away something I never thought I would lose."

"Now you are talking nonsense, Ullsaard. I am still your friend. If I was Urikh's man, I would not have helped you escape." The look had not passed from the face of Ullsaard and Noran threw up his hands in defeat. "As you would have it, then so be it. If you cannot trust me, let me go. I will leave, today, and you will not have to worry about me any more."

Ullsaard's expression softened and the king gently shook his head.

"We cannot do this," he said. "If we divide, we will lose everything. Do you think that you could run far enough to get away from Lakhyri? Do you think you can escape your nightmares? Yes, I see that you know what I mean."

"And staying with you will give me that, will it?"

"I know that if you turn away you will wonder if it was the right decision for the rest of your life. I know that you did not wish it, but we are bound together now. My life is your life."

Noran looked away, silently cursing his friend. Why would Ullsaard bring up that piece of history now? Noran started to walk back towards the guesthouse.

"One message and one favour," Ullsaard called out after him.

Noran stopped and looked back. If he agreed, Ullsaard would let him leave. Once he was away from the villa he could go wherever he wanted. If he chose to flee to Cosuan, that would be his choice. Looking at the king, Noran realised that Ullsaard was not stupid. The king knew as well as Noran that he had no way of making Noran stick to his word; except their shared past and their friendship.

"You are a bastard," growled Noran, turning back. "Why did I ever like you?"

"I need you to tell Anasind to make for Narun," said the king, accepting Noran's tacit capitulation without comment. "Only the legions with him are to be trusted. Any other legion that gets in his way is to be destroyed."

Noran approach Ullsaard and held his hand out for the wax slate.

"I assume that you have written this down," Noran said. "Do I really need to know the details?"

"This?" Ullsaard held up the tablet and looked at it as if shocked. "This contains orders for Anasind to head hotwards and seize Geria. It would be a damn shame if somehow you were to run into some Brother or legionnaire and accidentally allowed it to fall into the hands of my enemies."

"Ullnaar was right, you are a much more devious bastard than I give you credit for," said Noran, taking the message slate from the king. "What makes you think that Urikh will believe it?"

"Because he has to," said Ullsaard. "He must believe that Anasind is arriving with all of the legions, because that is exactly what he does not want to happen. An all-out war will put him at a serious disadvantage. He has gambled that I would not sacrifice Salphoria to regain Askh, but he has not counted on my reaching an accord with Aegenuis."

"Aegenuis? What has he got to do with all of this?"

"My own gamble," said Ullsaard, sitting down again. He adjusted his kilt and looked up at Noran, slightly shamefaced. "If I have him wrong, then Aegenuis will be dead and Anasind may have difficulties leaving Salphoria, or my conquest will have been for nothing and the gains lost to Askh. But I don't think so. I am a good judge of character. I think that Aegenuis will keep Salphoria from boiling over in the absence of the legions. Either way, I need Anasind and the army to march on Narun, and Urikh to believe he is heading for Geria."

"You know that I could take all of this to Urikh," said Noran. Ullsaard nodded solemnly and smiled half-heartedly.

"Fortunately you are not as foolish as my son. You could go to Urikh and curry favour for a short while, but he will want more and he will still own you. Either get your family to safety or see Urikh and Lakhyri defeated, those are your only options. You know that one bargain with a poor ally will lead to another and another. That was Anglhan's mistake too. They all keep trying to attack me from positions of weakness, using borrowed power: Magilnada, my family as hostages, the governors and the Brotherhood; none of them really control the empire."

"And from where does your power come from? What makes you so unassailable?"

Ullsaard clapped his hands to his knees and stood up. He stepped up next to Noran and lay an arm, across his shoulders, pulling him close.

"I have the legions, my friend; brutal, direct and unstoppable. As soon as I had the legions, Askh was mine, and it has been ever since. Urikh is about to find out that a few provincial garrisons and some blackcrests do not make an army. When I meet up with Anasind and get my soldiers back, my son is going to pay dearly for his oversight."

Ullsaard broke away and strode back towards the villa, leaving Noran dumbstruck. That was Ullsaard's plan? The legions? He looked down at the tablet in his hand and remembered that Ullsaard had started out with one legion, the Thirteenth, and from that beginning he had taken the empire in two years. When he had become king, he had vowed to conquer Salphoria. Even with the treachery of Anglhan and the invasion of a Mekhani army, it had taken Ullsaard only two more years to deliver on his promise.

The legions really were the key to Ullsaard's success. The man who controlled the legions controlled the empire.

SANNASEN, OKHAR
Late Winter, 213th year of Askh

A dog barked close at hand, in a yard beyond a high wall to the right of Erlaan-Orlassai. Its noisy reaction to the Prince's presence was taken up by other canine guardians across the neighbourhood. The giant cursed the curiosity that had brought him into the settlement; for many days he had avoided all sign of civilisation as he had tracked Ullsaard. Yet it had been too much to pass by this town, with its smells of spiced food and tantalising firelight. The bark of the dogs was harsh in his highly sensitive ears and he could hear shutters being opened and door latches being lifted.

The darkness was almost total, the moon and stars obscured by thick cloud, but to Erlaan-Orlassai the low wooden buildings were as clear as if it was noon. The glow of a lamp increased beyond the wall, signifying a door opening, and he padded further along the street to avoid investigation. It was almost Gravewatch, and he knew he was wasting time, but he had spent so long in the dungeons of the Grand Precincts that his lust to be near life was overwhelming. Though there were people woken by the dogs close at hand, he could hear the snores from other houses. The high-pitched call of bats echoed along the short road and black shapes flitted overhead.

Stopping by a dark, shuttered window, he paused and listened. Heavy, somnolent breathing came to him from inside; three people, one of them much smaller. A man, woman and young child, he realised. Laying a hand against the crude timbers, he felt the warmth of a dying fire through the calloused skin of his fingers, his nose caught the scent of the smoke drifting through the slats of the shutters.

"Who's there?"

The call came from about fifty paces behind him and he glanced back to see a small patch of yellow light spreading from a gateway. The man's shouting would rouse others and though he could soothe their fears with his rune-gifted speech – as he had done the captain and crew of the ship that had taken him from Askhor to Okhar – it was better to avoid confrontation. In that respect, Lakhyri had been correct. Travelling by night had meant that he had been unable to catch his quarry, who had the benefit of moving by light and dark. Yet he was closing in, he could feel it. Long strides and unhindered by encounters, Erlaan-Orlassai could cover dozens of miles between dusk and dawn before finding some copse or tree or cave to conceal himself during daylight.

He moved on, although not so swiftly that his war harness would make any noise to give away his presence. Reaching a corner, he turned into another street, which was as dark as the one he had left. Behind him, closer to the market square, torches were on the walls and a handful of watchmen walked the rounds, to guard against thieves and to quieten drunkards, but out here there were no sentries.

The Prince stopped beneath the branches of a tree overhanging another garden wall. The houses here, though basic by Askhan standards, were solidly built and well-appointed. Traders and craftsmen he guessed, judging by the smell of tanned leather, oil and metal. In the morning would they

chatter about an apparition in the night, or would the disturbance he had caused go unremarked as the people got on with
their lives? They seemed so innocent now, unaware of the
great events that were rocking the empire they thought they
knew so well. Urikh had done a masterful job of making his
succession seem legitimate, almost reluctant. With the Brotherhood to back him, he was the new king in law and in fact.

But Erlaan-Orlassai had been to the Temple and knew
something of the world into which Urikh was moving. It was
not a world of normal men, but of different, gifted individuals
like himself. When the time was right, and that time was coming soon, the people would need a leader stronger than a
mortal man, and Erlaan-Orlassai would be their saviour.

Even as he considered his future, a melancholy settled upon
the Prince. He lowered to his haunches, back against the stone
wall, and rested his arms on his thighs. The time Erlaan-Orlassai had spent in the Temple had seemed to creep past, but
even so he knew that he was no more than twenty summers
old. He still had not experienced so much of what he had expected as a prince of the Blood. Lakhyri and the priests had
given him an enchanted tongue that would make his words
fall softly on the ears of any maiden he wished to woo, but
would he ever find a woman that wanted to be with him as
he was, without coercion or trickery?

There had been much to think about, whiling away the days
in the Grand Precincts, and the thought of what he had allowed Lakhyri to do to him troubled Erlaan-Orlassai's mind.
He recalled taking the last of the life-force from his ailing father, and driven by anger and guilt he had been happy to find
some way to strike back at Ullsaard.

Even now the recollection of that name, that face, made Erlaan-Orlassai's heart race, but not with the ferocity he had felt
even a short season ago. Without Lakhyri's venomous words,

the fire of the Prince's passion grew faint, a glowing coal rather than an inferno. Erlaan-Orlassai was aware enough of his new situation to realise that his enmity was fuelled in no small part by jealousy. Even when he had been a captain in Ullsaard's army, the boy Erlaan had wanted the power and charisma of the general. Now Lakhyri had given him more physical power than any other man in the empire, and yet here he was skulking through a town pining after a life he could no longer have.

Straightening, Erlaan-Orlassai closed his eyes and tried to sense the presence of his quarry. He could feel no lingering scent of the Blood, and concluded that Ullsaard had not passed this way. The trail was growing colder with each night, and Erlaan-Orlassai knew that unless he stumbled on some surer spoor soon he would be searching blindly for the man he hunted.

There were other ways to find someone, those that did not rely on preternatural senses. The Prince still had his mind and he tried to use it as he loped towards the edges of the settlement, trusting to speed rather than stealth as his armour clinked and his feet splashed through puddles in the dirt road. Ullsaard was not the sort of man to keep running. Despite the adversaries ranged against him, the former king was vain enough and stubborn enough to believe that he could still re-take his throne. He would seek a position of safety to gather his strength and plan his strategy.

Long strides taking him out into the fields that surrounded the town, Erlaan-Orlassai wracked his brains for some insight into where his foe might be. It was the one organ that the priests had not been able to improve, when heart and lungs and bones had all been bolstered by their inscriptions, the soft pile of mush between his ears was no greater than it had been before his ordeal.

Something ahead of him bolted across the lane, startled by his sudden approach. There was almost no light here at all, but the Prince saw a deer leaping over a fence before disappearing into the gloom. Like all men carved by Lakhyri, he did not need physical sustenance to survive, but the thought of freshly roasted venison stirred a hunger in his gut.

Erlaan-Orlassai set off after the stag, jumping over the fence with ease. The smell of wet fur, sweat and dung left a drifting trail in the air that was as easy for him to follow as footprints in fresh snow. He could hear the thud of the deer's hooves on the cold-hardened dirt.

He quickened his pace, but before the rush of blood, the thrill of the chase became overwhelming, a memory sprang up in the Prince's mind; of Ullsaard telling him about the hunts he had been on before the march to Mekha. Slowing to a stop, all thoughts of the deer gone from his head, Erlaan-Orlassai tried to work out why that memory had come to him at that moment.

He was hunting, of course, but there was something else, something about Okhar that the general had mentioned in passing.

The memory was hazy, but Erlaan-Orlassai smiled as he recalled a place that Ullsaard had mentioned during a hunting story: Apili. The former king had one of his villas there, somewhere in the hills to duskwards near the border with Nalanor.

That would be a good place to take up the hunt.

THEDRAAN, ERSUA
Early Spring. 213th year of Askh

I

A crowd of people and wagons packed onto the road to hot-wards, the clamour of their shouts and the braying of abada disturbing the calm, sunlit morning. Many on foot abandoned the road to stream across the fields in small groups – families and co-workers carrying what belongings they had rapidly gathered in sacks and on their backs. Like an infection, the fear had spread towards Thedraan in the early hours of the morning, brought by reports from farmers to duskwards and coldwards of thousands of fires burning in the night.

Most thought it was the Salphors, coming to take revenge for the sacking of Magilnada and the invasion of their lands. It was not a leap of logic for those who had lived their lives under constant threat of ambush and attack by the hillmen of the Altes. Few barely believed that Askhan armies had made it as far as Carantathi, and the jump to fear as soon as a sizeable body of men was sighted – even allowing for exaggeration by frightened farmers – was as likely as any other conclusion.

There were some who believed otherwise, who stood on the streets and balconies jeering those who were fleeing for their lives. Most were the older generation, who had lived in and around Thedraan when it had truly been under threat of Salphor attack, before the building of the Brotherhood Precinct and the legion barracks that had propelled the town's growth and prosperity. These stalwarts proclaimed the fires to be the victory pyres of the returning legions, come back to Ersua to declare their triumph.

There were a handful of men who knew the truth, and one of them watched the people pouring from Thedraan with a pensive expression. He stood in the uppermost chamber of the precinct building of Thedraan, watching the people of the town evacuating in their desperate, haphazard way. The disorder served his purpose, spreading fear and uncertainty, ensuring that those loyal to Ullsaard would not receive warm welcome further into the empire. Even now, Leraates was looking for some way to manoeuvre the current circumstances into an advantage for himself.

Those who had remained behind were closer to the truth than those who had run away, but they did not realise that the worst of both theories was about to engulf them. The legions were certainly coming back. They were not coming to celebrate. His blackcrests had encountered them three days' earlier. Though the Brother was not sure of exactly where he stood in the current situation, he was certain that Asuhas had betrayed him, sending him into Salphoria on a pointless search for Ullsaard. Anglhan was most likely serving his own or the governor's agenda too. It seemed unlikely to Leraates that they were for Ullsaard though, and so he deduced that his encounter with the lead elements of General Anasind's army was coincidence rather than intended by his former conspirators.

Turning about in the uppermost chamber of the precinct, Leraates looked out of the window to coldwards, where the dark stain of the approaching army bled across the horizon, spreading along roads and twisting paths towards Thedraan.

There was a significant part of the senior Brother that wanted to flee with the panicked townsfolk; a part that was growing in influence as he watched the legions advancing on the town.

"Why do we stay?" asked Brother Addiel, who stood at the curtained archway at the bottom of the flight of steps that led into the observation room. Normally a young Brother like Addiel would not have been allowed into these levels, and he edged up the stairs as far as he dared, peering over the lip of the floor with wide eyes, trying to see what was worth be so secretive about. He would be disappointed – the observation chamber, right atop the pyramid, was only useful to those with the sight of the augmented, something even Leraates did not possess. When the masters came, their marked servants would be able to see each other across the distances of the empire, able to keep watch on vast swathes of land. For the moment, other than a stone table at its centre, the room was empty and uninteresting.

"Would you prefer to run?" asked Leraates, turning to look down at Addiel. He beckoned his inferior to continue up the stairs and waved a hand towards the throng of refugees when Addiel reached his side. "There will be clothes unattended you could take. Throw off your robe and become one with the masses."

"The armies of the usurper will clearly wish us killed," said Addiel. The youth walked to the high, shutterless window in the dawnwards wall. He leaned out over the sill, his voice dropping to a fear-filled whisper. "I am not so young that I don't remember the last pogrom, when he deposed King Lutaar."

"And you went into hiding then, yes?" Leraates was beginning to tire of his followers' naiveté. While it made it all the easier for them to be manipulated, their beliefs were slow to change at times, and the fear and loathing in which most held Ullsaard was almost insurmountable. "You think to do the same again?"

Addiel looked over his shoulder at Leraates and nodded.

"Our legionnaires have abandoned us," said the young man. "Only two score of them remain to protect us."

It was a matter of some disappointment for Leraates that the vast majority of his blackcrests, over four hundred men, had decided to abandon their Brotherhood commanders. Leraates did not know what rumour had spooked them so much but word had quickly spread back to the camp from the pickets and come first light the following day, almost all of the army had melted away. Captain Taarik and his inner cadre had remained to escort their charges back to the nearest town, which had happened to be Thedraan. The soldiers stood waiting in the square outside the precinct's main doors, though they were hardly likely to lay down their lives for the men who had taken shelter in the building.

"It might seem the wisest decision to depart, but I cannot concur," said Leraates. He joined the youth at the window and looked out, noting that the lead column of the incoming army was about ten miles from the outskirts of the town. Another tendril circled to duskwards, like a shepherd's boy sent by his master to corral the flock.

"Only those with something to fear, something to hide, would flee from the armies of the king." Leraates laid a hand on Addiel's shoulder and smiled. "If those soldiers were to come upon us on the road or in a meadow, they would wonder why we run from our appointed place and duties. Now we are merely Brothers in our precinct, tending to the business of the empire."

"There was whisper that the usurper is not really dead," said Addiel, fingers gripping the sill tightly.

"We cannot be held accountable for the mistakes of others, we have acted in good faith," Leraates assured his companion. He saw the golden glitter of several Askhos icons at the head of the marching army. "Go now, to the others on the lower levels, and tell them to assemble in the counting room. I will speak to them there and we shall prepare a suitable reception for General Anasind, heroic conqueror of our Salphorian foes."

Addiel nodded, but glanced back as he reached the steps.

"You are sure that we will not be judged at fault?" asked the youth.

"General Anasind is a man of reason, and with him will be several first captains of the legions. They are not in the business of slaughtering their own people on a whim, Addiel. Take my assurances to the others and wait for me as I have instructed."

When the boy had departed, Leraates returned his attention back to the encroaching army. He had little experience of Anasind in person, but he knew of him considerably. Though a diehard supporter of Ullsaard, the general would not assume the Brotherhood to be corrupt or at fault. Unless Ullsaard's recall to his troops had contained explicit instructions to treat the Brotherhood as hostile, there was every chance Anasind would continue on towards Askh to settle the matter with King Urikh, rather than waste time with a small place like Thedraan.

If Anasind was of a mind to prosecute some vendetta against the Brotherhood, Leraates was prepared for that also. Bearing such an eventuality in mind, he left the observation chamber and headed quickly down the steps. He would have to use all of his powers of persuasion on his fellow Brothers to keep them from betraying their guilt to Anasind and his captains, but before then he would spend a little time with the unexpected visitor who had been waiting in Thedraan for his return.

II

Thedraan echoed to the tramp of thousands of sandaled feet and the clink of wargear. Street by street the men of the

Thirteenth and Fifth legions spread through the town, securing every doorway, window, cellar entrance and yard. At the forefront of the advance into the town was general Anasind, First Captain Donar of the Fifth walking beside him. The two knew each other well from long years on the campaign road together, and neither felt like saying anything as their troops seized Thedraan.

With icon bearers and a bodyguard of several hundred men, they reached the main square, dominated by the ziggurat of the Brotherhood precinct. A line of legionnaires with black-fronted, golden-rimmed shields and jet black crests stood across the steps leading to the double doors of the building. An officer with a black sash across his breastplate stepped forwards, shield on his left arm, spear in his right hand.

"Do you want me to talk to him?" asked Donar. "You are a general, after all. You should have us inferiors do the talking for you."

"I don't remember Ullsaard ever doing that," replied Anasind. "I think I can speak for myself, but thank you for the offer."

More companies peeled away to the left and right as the general and his entourage strode across the cobbles of the square. Here and there a shout sounded from a side street or upper floor of a building, and there were bellows of protest and shrieks of shock from the inhabitants that had chosen to stay. Anasind stopped about a hundred paces short of the precinct steps and waited; if the blackcrest captain had something to say, he could approach the general. If not, Anasind was not going to go any nearer until the building was completely surrounded.

A small group of robed and cloaked dignitaries emerged from a three-storey building to Anasind's right, to be intercepted by a group of legionnaires from the eighth company. Voices were raised in demand, but Anasind had been very specific in his instructions and the merchants and nobles were escorted back into their meeting house at spearpoint.

While this was going on, the leader of the blackcrests realised that he would have to make the first move. Anasind felt a few spots of rain falling on his face and bare arms as the captain made his way across the square. Glancing up, the general saw clouds gathering upwind, promising a fiercer downfall to come. The wind was picking up too, bringing a chill edge to the air.

"Captain Taarik," said the officer, touching the haft of his spear to the brow of his helm in salute. The man was quite old, at least forty-five summers and likely at least ten more. His left eye was stitched shut and a scar ran across the bridge of his nose and down his right cheek, pale against weathered skin. The man had no beard, but moustaches grew to his chin either side of a thin-lipped mouth, in the style of old Ersuan chieftains. Judging by the man's height, perhaps two finger-widths less than Anasind, and the captain's darker flesh, Taarik had a Nalanorian ancestor somewhere along the bloodline.

"I am General Anasind, of the Thirteenth. Where is your commanding Brother?"

"Brother Leraates and his associates are in the precinct, general," said Taarik. Anasind thought there was something familiar about the man's voice, but could not quite place it.

"And why do you stand on the steps as if to bar my progress?"

"I am duty-bound to protect the men and premises of the Brotherhood, and so until you declare peaceful intent I must hold the precinct clear." Taarik's formality did not cover his nervousness. The captain spent more time looking at the soldiers fanning out to other parts of the town than he did their commanding officer.

"How many men do you have, captain?" asked Donar.

"Just these, first captain," replied Taarik. He waved a hand to indicate roughly seventy men waiting on the steps.

"We have eighty thousand," Donar said quietly, leaning closer to Taarik to ensure his point was heard. The captain glanced at Anasind, perhaps for confirmation, and the general nodded. Blinking, Taarik straightened and fixed Anasind with an impassive stare.

"I answer only to the Brotherhood and the king," Taarik said stiffly. He was obviously a veteran, as were the men who had stayed to protect the Thedraan precinct, and Anasind was becoming more certain that he had seen the man before.

"Which legion did you serve in, Taarik?" said Anasind.

"The Tenth, general."

Anasind nodded as he absorbed that piece of information, but it was of no help to his memory.

"Have we met before, captain?" he asked, unable to shake the nagging familiarity. "Where do I know you from?"

"Askh, general." Taarik sighed. "You would have seen me then, the night before we took the city."

Anasind nodded again but could not place the encounter any better for Taarik's explanation. The general shrugged and pointed past the captain towards the precinct.

"I am a general with the authority of King Ullsaard, and if you do not dismiss your men they will be killed."

"King Ullsaard is dead." Taarik looked nonplussed, perhaps thinking that Anasind had not heard the news. "Killed in Salphoria, general."

"What you have heard is wrong, captain, or worse you have been deliberately misled," Anasind said patiently. He harboured no desire to butcher the blackcrests just for doing their duty, and wanted to give Taarik every opportunity to see sense.

The captain looked around again and Anasind did likewise, seeing that there were nearly ten companies in the square now, more than one and a half thousand men. They held a line to the left and right of the general, arranged two companies deep facing the precinct.

"You have done everything you can," Donar said, patting Taarik on the soldier in paternal fashion though the captain was clearer his elder. "Honour satisfied, duty done. Tell your men to walk away."

"How would you like to be a captain in a proper legion again?" said Anasind. "We are always looking for good officers in the Thirteenth."

"I am too old," replied Taarik. He looked back at his men. With a solemn expression, he lowered to one knee and presented his spear to Anasind. "But not so old that I don't value the years left to me. I cannot stop you entering the precinct, and I would not throw away the lives of my men. That they have stayed this long proves their courage."

"And no man will be punished for doing his duty," said Anasind, waving for Taarik to stand up, allowing him to keep his spear. "If you wish to remain after we depart and take up your protection of the town again, I would appreciate it, as would the rightful king."

Having seen the capitulation of their captain, the remaining men of the blackcrests started to move away from the precinct steps, a few at first, the rest joining them after a few moments' consideration. When the way was clear, Anasind raised a hand to attract the attention of the company captains. The rain started falling more heavily, pattering from the armour of the assembled soldiers, splashing from the dark cobbles. With a wave towards the precinct, Anasind sent his men forward. The square resounded to their purposeful tread as company-by-company they advanced on the ziggurat. Anasind had ordered that the building be taken without harm befalling any of the Brothers or others inside and the captains were doing their job well, ensuring

that none of their men became carried away by an un-
seemly rush.

The doors were not barred and the men of the first company
up the steps entered without pause, and soon lines of soldiers
were gathering while others took up position around the
building to stop anybody from slipping away.

When nearly half of the companies had entered, the steps
were cleared, allowing the first prisoners to be brought out.
Brothers in their black robes filed out of the doorway, eighteen
of them. These men were quickly surrounded by soldiers and
separated, each company taking a few prisoners away and passing them from one group to another until the Brothers were
held apart on the side of the square furthest from the precinct.
Anasind watched all of this without comment, pleased to see
that no violence had been necessary.

The first batch of Brothers was followed a while later by several legionnaires escorting two men. One had the robes of a
Brother, the other was dressed in a shirt, tunic and kilt. Unlike
the other prisoners, these two were brought hurriedly towards
the general. As they approached, Anasind saw the flash of a
silver mask beneath the hood of the Brother, but it was the
other man that attracted his attention. Anasind's astonishment
made him call out.

"Noran? What are you doing here?"

III

Leraates had decided that his best policy was to say as little as
possible. He would answer the questions put to him as honestly
as possible – without implicating himself in the deception of
Ullsaard's death – but would volunteer no further information.
It was timely that Urikh's herald, Noran Astaan, had arrived
shortly before the Brother had returned, bearing important
news concerning Ullsaard's next moves. There had been just

enough time to communicate with Lakhyri to warn of the legions' return and to receive confirmation that Noran was under the sway of the current king. Having passed on the orders that Noran intended for Anasind, Leraates knew that there was no more he could do for the cause and every effort of his was now steered towards ensuring his continued survival.

"You are a welcome sight, general," said Leraates, bowing his head. "Too long has Greater Askhor been without its leaders."

The general ignored the Brother and focussed his attention on Noran Astaan. The two were well known to each other, and Leraates was curious to see if the herald still held Anasind's confidence.

"A sentiment I echo," said Noran, extending a hand in greeting. Anasind gripped wrist-to-wrist with the herald, somewhat hesitantly. He then smiled and stepped closer, slapping his companion on the back. Noran darted a smile at Donar. "Good to see you too, First Captain."

"Likewise," said the general. "I feared you might be caught up in all of this somehow, but I am pleased to see you still alive. Ullsaard's always favoured your advice."

Hidden behind his mask, Leraates smiled briefly. He cast his gaze downwards the moment Anasind turned towards him.

"What of this man? Can you vouch for him?" Leraates looked at Noran, but Anasind continued before any answer was given. "I received warning from the king that the Brotherhood is being influenced by Urikh and the Brothers are not to be trusted."

"A sad truth, for most of them," said Noran, causing Leraates' breath to catch in his chest. The Brother flexed his fingers in agitation and darted another look at the herald through the eye slits of his mask. Noran appeared flippant, but as the herald's gaze passed over Leraates the Brother saw just a flicker of movement; a hint of a reassuring wink. "This is Brother Leraates, and he has been most helpful in combating the scheming of Urikh, Asuhas and others. If not for his actions, Ullsaard would have been waylaid the moment he reached Ersua."

Anasind raised his eyebrows at this testimony and looked searchingly at Leraates, not entirely convinced. If Noran misspoke now, he would condemn them both, but the herald continued almost glibly.

"I do not know what Ullsaard sent to you, I was not with him at the time, but there is a lot I have to tell you. Did you know that Anglhan survived Magilnada?"

"Anglhan's alive?" Leraates let out a slow breath as the attention of the general moved back to Noran.

"Not so much these days, but he was around for a while," said the herald. "We really have a lot to catch up on, we cannot waste any more time." He started to walk past Anasind and then stopped. He fished into his tunic and brought out the wax tablet with Ullsaard's orders and handed it to Anasind. "Your commands from the king. We need to discuss them in private, though."

Noran continued to step forwards, and the general moved with his progress, turning his back to Leraates. It was simple thing, but the Brother admired the easy manner in which Noran could manipulate the attention of those around him with a word or gesture. His family held hostage to guarantee compliance, Astaan was a valuable ally to have.

As he had hoped, Leraates saw his future brightening again. With Noran's approval, he would be accepted into the counsel of the general. The road to Geria was well known and Urikh had enough time to move his loyal legions into position to prepare an appropriate welcome for the returning legions of Anasind.

APILI, OKHAR
Early spring, 213th year of Askh

I

From a wooded hillside overlooking the villa, Erlaan-Orlassai gazed down at the lair of his prey, considering his options. The men and women tending the vines had returned to their cottages, and he could see no armed men patrolling the grounds of the house. He had not seen Ullsaard during the day he had spent watching, and the lack of guards made the Prince wonder if the sense he had of the Blood nearby was to be trusted.

He put aside his doubts and set off down the hill; the only way to be sure would be to enter the villa. He skirted along the edge of the terraces, easily climbing over the low walls that separated the vineyard from open country. There were lamps in the buildings, glowing through the gaps in the shutters, and as he neared the grounds of the villa another window lightened ahead of him in the main house. Effortlessly vaulting a hedgerow, he entered the gardens.

The scuff of a boot on gravel caught his attention and he froze, looking to his left from where the noise had emanated. Light spilled across a paved area from an opening door and a man stepped outside. The man pulled on a heavy coat – the spring nights were still cold – and started across the courtyard.

Sensing an opportunity, the Prince sped quickly behind the man and clamped a massive hand across his face. Grabbing the back of his coat, Erlaan-Orlassai easily lifted the man from his feet and pulled him back into the shadows. The captive's struggles were fruitless against the Prince's inhuman strength though his flailing feet caught on the Prince's armoured legs with a dull thumping.

"Be still or I shall snap your neck," whispered Erlaan-Orlassai. The man went limp, immediately cowed by the words that came from the Prince's sigil-inscribed tongue. "That is better, my friend."

Releasing his grip on the coat, Erlaan-Orlassai stayed out of sight behind the man for the moment, still covering his mouth – the shock of seeing the Prince's altered body would work against the effect of his enchanted words.

"I am going to ask you questions and you will answer them," the Prince said quietly. "You will not call out or turn around."

The captive nodded dumbly and Erlaan-Orlassai released his grip.

"What is your name, friend?"

"Houran. I am Houran, the estate overseer."

"Good, then you will be able to tell me what I need to know. Is Ullsaard here?"

"Yes, the king is here. He arrived about twenty days ago."

"And where is he now?"

"The main bedroom is on the corner," said Houran, pointing towards a wide window beside a set of double doors leading onto the main courtyard. "He retires early and wakes at dawn."

You can take a man out of the legions, Erlaan-Orlassai thought, but you can never take the legions out of the man.

"How many soldiers does he have with him?" asked the Prince.

"None, there are no soldiers here," replied Houran. "I thought to hire some men from the town but he said not to; that it would attract attention."

This was good news indeed. Erlaan-Orlassai gently laid a hand on Houran's shoulder. The man flinched at the touch and made the mistake of glancing down, seeing the claws and extra knuckles of the Prince's digits.

"Wh-what manner of man are you?" he gasped. His body started to tremble but the lingering power of the Prince's words stopped him from looking back.

"I am your master, Houran. You will return to your home, go to bed and not wake until morning. If you remember me at all, it will be as if you dreamed our encounter. Do you understand?"

"This is a dream? Yes, that must be so. I am in bed and dreaming."

"Return to your slumber now, friend." Erlaan-Orlassai gave Houran the slightest push, propelling him back towards the open door. He watched, ready to pounce and silence the man in a fatal fashion, but Houran tottered back to the threshold, paused and then stepped inside. The door closed quietly and Erlaan-Orlassai set off at a run, heading straight for the bedroom of Ullsaard.

He reached the door and carried on another two steps, stopping by the windows. Crouching to hold his ear against the slatted wood, he listened for a few moments. He could hear footsteps padding back and forth across bare boards and the rustle of cloth. The footfalls moved out of the room briefly and he waited, taking slow deep breaths to calm himself. The sensation of the Blood was strong and he was sure it was Ullsaard making the noise. When the footsteps returned, the Prince straightened and reached out, his arms long enough to stretch from one edge of the window to the other.

Seizing the wood, Erlaan-Orlassai applied his considerable

muscles, ripping both shutters from their mountings in one motion. Tossing them aside he looked into the room.

Ullsaard was standing over a low cupboard, naked but for his sandals. The former king turned, eyes widening as Erlaan-Orlassai clambered through the window, and it was then that the Prince noticed the sword in Ullsaard's hand.

"I thought I heard someone," said the usurper, springing at Erlaan-Orlassai, the point of his sword spearing towards the Prince's throat.

The giant met the blade with the vambraces on his left arm, as his right hand gripped around the hilt of his own blade. Ullsaard was unbalanced by the powerful parry, but he turned his potential fall into an awkward roll as the Prince pulled free his sword.

Crouching, Ullsaard lashed out at the Prince's groin, but the blade caught only the beaten bronze on his thigh. Erlaan-Orlassai swung his sword at his opponent's head, missing by a hair's breadth as Ullsaard ducked back. The usurper's blade came up to meet the Prince's next thrust, but the force of the blow sent Ullsaard's sword flying from his grip.

Backing up, the former king stopped as he reached a curtained wardrobe. Erlaan-Orlassai grinned, showing rows of pointed teeth.

"You should have killed me while you had the chance," said the Prince, bringing back his sword for another swing.

Ullsaard dived forwards under the blow, wrapping his arms around the Erlaan's Orlassai's thigh. The grapple was perfectly timed, hitting the Prince's leg as he shifted his weight, and it was enough to send him backwards. He fell onto the bed, crashing through the frame in a spray of splinters. Lashing out with his other foot as Ullsaard dodged back, Erlaan-Orlassai caught the usurper in the side and he felt ribs giving way under the impact. With a yelp of pain, Ullsaard flopped to one side, grimacing.

As Erlaan-Orlassai pulled himself from the wreckage of the bed, Ullsaard came at him again, driving the heel of his foot into the Prince's face. The blow would have floored a lesser man, but its only effect on the warped prince was to split his lip. In retaliation, Erlaan-Orlassai reached out and snatched hold of Ullsaard's wrist. The Prince flexed his muscles, nearly pulling the arm from the socket as he sent Ullsaard across the room to land in a heap against the wall beside the door. Blood pumped from a cut on the former king's brow and he grabbed hold of his injured shoulder with his other hand.

A look of fear passed across the usurper's features, sending a thrill of excitement through Erlaan-Orlassai. He let his sword fall from his grip and raised up both fists.

"Do you remember a promise I made to you?" asked the Prince. Ullsaard groggily shook his head. "I said I would rip you to pieces. I said I would tear off your balls and feed them to you. I think it is time I was true to my word."

Erlaan-Orlassai took a step forward and Ullsaard held up a hand, teeth gritted. It had been disappointingly easy and the Prince did not wish for the end to be too swift. He stooped and grabbed Ullsaard's ankle, lifting him from the floor.

"Where is your army now, Ullsaard?" Erlaan-Orlassai threw Ullsaard like a doll, sending him crashing into a cabinet. The door split under the impact and Ullsaard flopped to the floor, more blood pouring from his broken nose.

The usurper wiped his hand across his mouth and flicked blood away from his fingers. With pained grunts, using the remnants of the cabinet as support, he pushed himself to his feet. He grinned, showing blood-flecked teeth.

"Come on then, you big bastard," said Ullsaard, holding up shaking fists. He swayed from side to side, his face a crimson mask. "You and me, right now, Maarmes-style. I'll stop holding back if you will."

The man's insolence even in the face of death was infuriating. With a snarl, Erlaan-Orlassai launched himself at his foe, fist poised to smash his head to a pulp.

Ullsaard dropped and rolled at the last moment, avoiding the fatal blow. The Prince punched through plaster and stone, driving his arm through the wall up to his elbow. Erlaan-Orlassai struggled to pull his arm back, and heard laughter behind him.

"I'll kill you!" roared the Prince, ripping a hole the size of a man's body from the wall as he wrenched his arm free. He turned to confront his foe, expecting Ullsaard to be making a bolt for safety. Instead, the former king stood in the middle of the room, feet apart, with the Prince's immense blade gripped in both hands.

"And now I have your sword, you fucking amateur."

A scream caused both fighters to turn.

II

Allenya screamed again, a wild, primordial sound of terror. She let the belt in her hands drop to the floor and raised her hands to her head as she shrieked again, eyes fixed on Ullsaard's attacker. Her robe had fallen open, revealing the curve of her thighs, and the patch of dark hair between them. A breast came into view as the robe slipped further, falling away from her shoulders.

"Get out!" yelled Ullsaard, turning his attention back to Erlaan, bringing up the point of the heavy sword. "Run!"

The twisted prince was no immediate threat though, as transfixed by Allenya's appearance as she was by his. His grotesque features were a mask of shock and Ullsaard was reminded that the monstrous warrior was barely more than a youth. The king knew he should attack now, while the Prince was distracted, but feared that if he moved he would be break the trance that had bewitched his foe. The sword Ullsaard held was too cumbersome for him to wield properly, his breath was short in his lungs and his shoulder was a knot of burning pain; his incredible opponent would finish him in moments and it had been pure bravado that had propelled the king to pick up the blade.

"Aunt Allenya?" The words were spoken softly, almost reverentially. Just as it had the first time, hearing Erlaan's voice issue from that fanged mouth was deeply disturbing. Ullsaard remembered the boy the Prince had been. As an infant he had been fond of sitting with Allenya when she did her needlework, while she made up stories for the scenes she created with canvas and thread.

It was if the youth's words seeped through Allenya's horror. Her expression moved back and forth between horror and confusion as she tried to comprehend what she was seeing. Ullsaard had never spoken of his war with the Mekhani, not in detail, and had certainly kept Erlaan's survival as secret as possible.

"What has happened to you, Erlaan?" Allenya's confusion resolved itself into pity. She looked at Ullsaard, her glare admonishing him as if he had somehow inflicted this fate on the Prince.

"He attacked me," Ullsaard found himself saying in his defence, though it sounded like the excuse of a child.

As if reminded of his purpose in coming to the villa, Erlaan looked at Ullsaard and snarled. Allenya whimpered and stepped back, causing the Prince to physically flinch. Now it was Erlaan's turn to show bewilderment as he looked between Ullsaard and his wife.

"What are you doing here, what has happened to you?" Allenya said, recovering her composure. She pulled her robe across her body and stepped up behind Ullsaard, seeking protection.

"I am to be king," said Erlaan. A look of anguish passed across his rune-scarred features. Golden eyes blinked quickly and then the frown returned. "It is my birthright to be king, and Ullsaard has taken it from me."

"I spared your life," said Ullsaard. "This is how you repay me?"

"You took me captive and shamed me," replied Erlaan. Bony fingers curled into fists and Ullsaard moved himself directly in front of Allenya, but she stepped around him.

"You knew he was alive?" she asked.

"Not at first," said Ullsaard, glancing at his wife for a moment before returning his gaze to the man who wanted him dead. "It's complicated."

"I am the true heir, Ullsaard," growled Erlaan. "My grandfather and father are dead. The Crown belongs to me."

Ullsaard narrowed his eyes as he considered his options. His head was throbbing, his ribs were sending stabs of pain into his chest and his arm was going numb. The fact that Erlaan was not battering him to death was a boon in itself but the Prince was on edge, and Ullsaard had seen the rage that could take hold of him; the wrong word could set off another wild attack.

"You would never have become king," Ullsaard said slowly. He lowered the point of the sword to the floor, though he kept his grip as tight as he could around the thick hilt. "Nor your father before you."

"It was my right as heir to the Blood," said Erlaan.

"It was no right, it was a curse," said Ullsaard. He glanced at Allenya, realising what he had to say. She looked at him with a perplexed expression, making it even harder to do what had to be done. "The Crown was tainted, an artefact fashioned by Lakhyri."

"What taint? What has Lakhyri to do with the Crown?"

Ullsaard answered, the words coming in a stream as he unburdened himself of the terrible secret he had kept for three years. He spoke of Lakhyri and Askhos, two men seeking im-mortality – one in spirit, the other in body. He told them of the making of the Crown and the curse laid upon it to deliver up each generation of Askhan kings to the control of Askhos.

"Three years ago, almost to this day, I placed the Crown upon my head and Askhos became part of me," said the king. "I did not know it then, but he tried to take me, as he would have taken your father, and as he would have taken you. You were just a vessel, of no value other than a working heart, functioning limbs and brain. Even in your altered state, that was the fate Lakhyri had in mind for you. He is using you, just as he is using Urikh."

Ullsaard watched Allenya's reaction turn from disbelief to belief to true understanding, her expression becoming more and more alarmed as realisation crept up on her. She looked at Ullsaard with something bordering on disgust, and took a shuddering breath.

"All of this time," she said, backing away. "Is that why you abandoned me? That is why you pushed me away?"

"Allenya, I could not share you with him," Ullsaard said. He wanted to reach out to her, but would not let go of the sword while Erlaan was a threat.

"These are lies, concocted by you to save your life," said Erlaan.

"How?" snapped Ullsaard, letting the frustration of three years fuel his words. "How will these lies save me? Will they turn into a spear and shield for me? Why would I invent such madness?"

Erlaan shook his head and looked away, rubbing an inhu-man hand across his brow.

"No, it cannot be true," said the Prince, but there was no conviction in his words. He glowered at Ullsaard but his chest was heaving, not from anger but agitation. "I must… I will find the truth. The empire will be mine."

Erlaan ran towards the window and leapt out with a loud grunt. Ullsaard dragged himself across the room in time to see him leaping over a wall before disappearing into the darkness. The sword dropped from his fingers with a loud clatter and he fell to one knee.

"I need a surgeon," he muttered, turning to where Allenya had been standing but he was alone in the room. It seemed somehow fitting. He closed his eyes and concentrated, but he could sense nothing of Askhos, banned from the king's conscious thoughts though still locked inside his mind somewhere. Using the sill to help, Ullsaard pulled himself up to the window and called for Houran.

He really did need a surgeon, and quickly.

MARRADAN, ERSUA
Spring, 213th year of Askh

I

The frantic clanging of a gong woke Gelthius. He rolled over and sat up on his bunk, pushing away his thin blanket. Around him the other men in the prison dormitory were rousing from their slumber, groans and complaints breaking the early morning stillness. From the bed beneath Gelthius, Muuril put out his legs and pushed himself onto the bare stone floor. The lower bunk now vacated, Gelthius swung over the side of his bed and lowered himself to the ground using the edge of Muuril's cot as a step.

The dorm housed forty men in twenty double-bunks, with barely enough room between each for the prisoners to fit. There were no windows except for a few grates in the ceiling that had been letting in light, rain and snow in roughly equal measure since Gelthius' incarceration had begun. Directly above the prison chambers was the drilling space of the barracks and occasionally a witty legionnaire would ensure an abada stood over the gap, to let a stream of pungent piss into the cell.

It was dark through the openings, and the gong was not the wake up ring of Dawnwatch, but a more insistent, alarmed clamour. There was light from the doorway as lanterns moved past at quick intervals, carried by legionnaires mustering from the company barracks adjacent to the prison. There were a few men at the door calling out to the passers-by for information, but their shouts went unanswered.

Knowing that it was unlikely that he would be left in peace to go to sleep again, Gelthius pulled on his kilt and tunic and fished out his sandals from the open-topped box at the end of the bed. Muuril and most of the others were also getting dressed, expecting the worse. It was not the first time Captain Lutaan had called out the companies in the middle of the night for surprise drill. Even though they were in the punishment battalion, the men of the Thirteenth and the miscreants of the Twenty-first would be expected to turn out in due course to take their place in the muster.

Soon enough, a gaggle of blackcrests appeared at the door, shining a lamp through the narrow grille of bronze bars. More figures appeared behind them and Gelthius was struck by how many soldiers there were when the door was opened – at least twenty.

"Stand by your bunks!"

The order was snapped out and the men in the dorm complied, though not with the vigour and pride they would have once shown. When each pair of men was standing beside their beds, four blackcrests came in, two of them with their spears ready and shields held up, two with spears and lanterns.

Much to Gelthius' surprise, the guards were quickly followed by Captain Lutaan. He had his sword belt on, his shield slung on his back and a spear in his right hand; Ullsaard's golden spear. There came a barely audible growl from Muuril but the sergeant said nothing out loud.

"This is not a drill or a punishment," Lutaan said sharply. "Scouts have returned with warning that an army of Salphors is marching on Marradan. I need every man to defend the city.

All of you swore oaths to fight in the legions to protect the empire. Today, despite your transgressions, I will hold you to your oaths. As laid down in the code of the legions, from the Book of Askhos, each of you has the choice to fight, earning commutation of your sentence, or you may submit to summary execution. If you agree to accept the king's pardon, you will be subject to full legion law once again and if you are found derelict in your duty or otherwise insubordinate, mutinous or cowardly you will be summarily executed. Any infraction of the legion code will be punished by death."

"Which sort of shit do you prefer?" whispered Loordin from the bed behind Gelthius'. "Sheep shit or cow shit? It's all the same when it's on your foot."

"Shall I accept it that all here are willing to fight?" Lutaan paused for a moment and there was silent agreement from everybody in the dormitory. "Good. You will form an ad-hoc company with the rest of the prisoners; one hundred and twenty men. Captain Caaskil will be your commander. Muuril and Gelthius will be the officers, all other rank positions to remain as before incarceration."

With this bare statement delivered, Lutaan turned on his heel and strode from the chamber, soon replaced by the squat, broad form of Captain Caaskil, a thirty-year veteran of the legions with a hook for a right hand and more scars than Gelthius had seen on anybody. He had been the drill officer throughout their imprisonment, and Gelthius was actually pleased to be fighting under him – many of the Twenty-first's officers were untested and undertrained.

"You heard the first captain, fall in," barked Caaskil. "Muuril, Gelthius, get here."

The two men of the Thirteenth approached with brisk steps and stopped a couple of paces form the officer, rapping their fists to their chests in salute.

"You've had good experience of butchering these Salphor cunts, don't let me down," said the captain, seemingly oblivious to the fact that Gelthius was, in fact, also a Salphor. He raised his voice to address everybody in the dorm. "Fall in, two lines, to report to the armoury. You have your shields and spears back, lads. Don't fucking dishonour them again."

II

Though Caaskil's company was under strength, it contained a fair number of veterans from the Thirteenth and was positioned to hold the flank on the right-hand end of the line as the Twenty-first Legion formed up in the dark. Coloured lanterns were used to denote the mustering areas and in the gloom Gelthius could see kolubrid-riding messengers moving back and forth between the companies as Lutaan tried to get his line in order before the Salphors arrived. Bodies of men marched out, armour and spearpoints gleaming in red and green and blue and yellow, depending on where they were gathering.

The noise of the army was louder even than the sound of people evacuating their homes just a few dozen paces behind the line. Lutaan had made the brave, or possibly duty-bound decision to protect the whole city – Marradan had a wall to defend the inner reaches where the palaces, precinct and nobility were found, but it had outgrown those defences several years before. Gelthius approved of the decision, not only for the sake of those whose homes would have been sacrificed to the Salphors, but also because it would force the enemy into a decisive attack. One way or another, the Twenty-first would have to be beaten tonight; no drawn out sieges. With the empire is such disarray, there was no guarantee of aid from the other cities or provinces had the enemy been given the chance to encircle the city to starve the people of Marradan.

That the enemy were attempting a night attack spoke either of brilliance or utter stupidity. Gelthius knew from personal experience that most Salphors liked to raid other tribes after dark, but it was a long stretch from a few hundred men descending on neighbours' pastures and farms to executing a full battle in the pitch black. The defenders of Marradan had been taken surprise by the approach of the Salphorian army, but even the Twenty-first, now bloodied at Menesun, were more organised than your average Salphorian raiders.

"This is a bit of overkill for some hairy bastards that have come down for a bit of fun," remarked Loordin. "How many of them do you think there are?"

"About ten thousand, give or take a few hundred, the scouts said," said Caaskil, emerging from the darkness having overhead the legionnaire's question. "We need you pig-worriers because the Twenty-first is only four thousand strong."

On hearing this, Gelthius started to have second thoughts about taking sanctuary behind the city wall. His face must have shown his concern, as a cruel smile twisted Caaskil's lips.

"Don't worry yourself, Second Captain Gelthius." Caaskil put sarcastic emphasis on Gelthius' rank. "If we each kill two men, we'll win. On the other hand, if you want me to slit your throat now and save your friends the trouble, then just speak up."

"These ain't my friends, right enough," answered Gelthius. "Free country peoples, I reckon. I wonder what's got them so heated up they think they can come into Ersua and have a go?"

"Not a question to be asked now," replied Caaskil. "Don't know, and I don't care. Feel free to take some prisoners to ask later, if you like. Let me know if you see anyone you recognise."

Realising that any meaningful discussion with Caaskil would be fruitless, Gelthius simply nodded and lifted his spear in salute. Sensing that the Salphor would not give him any further sport, Caaskil moved on towards the back ranks, speaking to the men from the Twenty-first, ignoring those who had been taken from the Thirteenth.

It was not chance, Gelthius realised, that the front ranks were filled with prisoners from the Thirteenth. Not only were they the toughest fighters in the company, they would be the first to fall.

After shifting position twice more, as the line extended further duskwards to respond to the latest reports of the scouts sent into the night, the prisoner company finally found themselves about three hundred paces from the outlying buildings of Marradan, with the rest of the army stretching out at an angle to hotwards and dawnwards. A brief calm settled on the legion and Gelthius felt again the sense of foreboding that had marked the beginning of every battle in which he had participated.

It did not help that this particular struggle seemed entirely pointless. He was, by oath, a man of the Twenty-first. But Captain Lutaan, this city and this enemy, meant nothing to him. At least the Thirteenth had saved him from Aroisius' rebels and he had felt some comradeship with them; Ullsaard had also favoured him and was worthy of his service.

"What's the point?" muttered the captain.

"We're still Thirteen, all the way to the bone," replied Muuril, sensing Gelthius' mood. The two of them had hardly swapped words since the episode when they had been clearing the snow; they had nothing to say to each other except such communication as was required for two men sharing a bunk bed. "I'm fighting for you and Loordin, and the rest. I fought for the general and the king, but first always for the man behind and next to me."

Gelthius looked at Muuril and could not stop a smile.

"The man next to me will be Captain Caaskil," said the Salphor. "Want to change places?"

"We'll see everybody right, don't worry," said Muuril.

The two of them fell silent again, made awkward by the threat of sentiment. Fortunately distraction was not long in coming. From between the buildings on the outskirts of the city, catapults hurled balls of twine and tar into the air, inside each a small flask of lava. When each missile crashed down, several hundred paces from the city, the balls exploded into flame, lighting the battlefield. Another salvo followed shortly after, spreading a line of fire almost half a mile long in front of the waiting legion. Between the flames advanced the Salphor warriors, beneath banners of tattered cloth, round wooden shields held up, axes and spears in their hands.

"That's Aegenuis' colours," exclaimed Gelthius, pointing his spear at a large shaft at the middle of the army from which fluttered four ribbons, alternating red and green. "We could be in trouble. Captain Caaskil!"

The company commander heard his name being called and returned to the front rank with a few more words of encouragement to his men.

"What?" he demanded

"You have to send word to Captain Lutaan. This is the king's army. Aegenuis' own army."

"So?"

"If the king leads, there will be more than ten thousand warriors around," said Gelthius, picking his words carefully. He did not want to sound frightened, but in truth he was. "Aegenuis is a canny commander; if the other men haven't been counted you can bet they're not far away."

Concern appeared on Caaskil's face and he called out for a messenger. Moments later a kolubrid rider came around from the back of the company. Caaskil stomped away to converse with the serpent-borne messenger. When the captain paces away, Gelthius heard a whisper from behind him. He could not make out was said and turned around to Loordin, who was the second-ranker.

"Play dead," Loordin said again, his voice barely audible.

"What?" replied Gelthius.

"Oh, for fuck's sake," said Loordin, rolling his eyes. "Ask Muuril. Pass it on."

Confused, Gelthius turned to the sergeant, keeping his voice quiet.

"What does 'play dead' mean?"

Muuril was taken aback and he glanced over his shoulder at the ranks behind before answering. Leaning close to keep his voice low, he explained.

"It's an old trick of Ullsaard's. When the company captain falls, the rest of the first few ranks start to go down as well. The enemy step over them to get at the rest of the ranks, thinking they're dead, and when the call's given, them that's pretending get up and attack them from behind."

"And what good will that do?"

"Just do it," said Muuril. Captain Caaskil had finished talking to the kolubrid messenger and was returning to the company. "If that cunt-hole Caaskil goes down, you go down just after."

"What if I really get cut down?" said Gelthius, not sure whether Caaskil was part of the plan, or if he was meant to be genuinely killed. Gelthius was not convinced that the Salphors would simply ignore a man who went to ground.

"Then you're not going to fucking care, are you?" Muuril replied quickly.

When Caaskil had taken up his place in the front rank, Gelthius readied his spear and shield. He felt the presence of Loordin behind him as the rear ranks packed in. Ahead, the Salphors were organising into warbands, the men of each tribe gathering around their leaders. Skirmishers with bows ran ahead of the main line, moving in the shadows cast by the lava fires. Though they were silhouetted against the flames, they had little chance of seeing their targets; Lutaan had ordered the lights of the city and the mustering lamps put out where possible and so the Askhan legion was all but invisible in the night.

The catapults and spear-throwers started the battle, launching bolts and showers of fist-sized rocks at the Salphors. The Twenty-first had barely enough kolubrids for their messengers and so the task of forcing the enemy into an attack fell to the war machines. As bronze-headed shafts plunged through their ranks and stones rained down on them from above, the Salphors edged closer and closer. The shouts of the war-leaders could be clearly heard along the line, urging the archers to move in and loose their missiles at the engine crews. The skirmishers were understandably reluctant to get too close to the Askhan phalanx. Gelthius translated this debate, much to the amusement of Caaskil and the others around him.

"I don't like it, not this," said Gelthius, still looking ahead. "This ain't right."

"What's the problem?" said Caaskil. "Afraid for your friends?"

"They're too bad, even for Salphors," said Gelthius, unable to articulate his worry any better than that. He could not shake the feeling that the army in front of him were being terrible on purpose, perhaps to ensure that they were the centre of attention. "Why do they keep advancing? Why not pull back and wait for dawn to even the matter?"

"Don't fret, I sent word to Captain Lutaan about what you said," replied Caaskil, his mood becoming sincere. "If it is Aegenuis and he's got another army out there, it'll be spotted before they can do any damage. Right now, we have ten thousand Salphor bastards in front of us. Concentrate on them."

The Salphors seemed convinced that their weight of numbers would carry the battle; despite all experience and past battles to the contrary. Under attack from the engines and their skirmishers all but useless, the Salphorian chieftains withdrew the archers and called for the advance to continue. The bowmen melted back into the warbands, swapping bows for knives and spears.

"All quiet!" came the hushed command from the company to Gelthius' left. "All quiet!"

The legion had not being make much noise before, but as the order was obeyed, every man standing as still as possible to minimise clank of wargear, an unsettling silence descended. The grunts and shouts and tread of the advancing Salphors were the only sounds to be heard; even the war machines had stopped their bombardment to conceal their positions.

Afraid to blunder straight into their waiting enemies, the Salphors slowed their advance. Gelthius glanced up and was pleased to see a cloud-filled sky. There was not a patch of starlight to be seen, and the glow of the sliver of the moon cast barely a shadow.

From the left, quite some distance away, a shout broke the stillness: an order for a company advance. Spears crashed once on shields, ringing back from the buildings behind the line. The Salphors responded, drifting towards the noise, away from Gelthius. The enemy were bunching up, getting in each other's way in the darkness, losing the advantage of their numbers as they tried to find their enemies.

Something pale appeared in front of Gelthius and he almost jabbed with his spear as a half-naked figure resolved from the gloom. The boy was only thirteen or fourteen summers old, one of the messenger corps.

"Captain Lutaan wishes the companies of the right to advance by one hundred paces. Quiet as you can, he says."

After hearing Caaskil's acknowledgement, the youth vanished again, navigating his way back to the command staff by some means unknown to Gelthius.

"Slow pace, keep steady," whispered Caaskil. The order was passed back from rank to rank. Gelthius felt Loordin's shield press against his back as Caaskil raised his arm, barely visible even to Gelthius beside him. The captain's hand came down and Gelthius took a pace, counted one-two, took another pace and so advanced into the darkness. The clink of harness could not be prevented, but for a body of more than a hundred men, the company made almost no noise, and Gelthius was not sure if the other companies to his left were advancing at all. He had to trust that Lutaan was not hanging the former prisoners out like bait, as he had the companies advancing more audibly on the far left of the line.

They had made seventy-five paces when Gelthius heard the rustling of grass ahead. He thought it was the wind, but then something flickered across one of the fires, no more than fifty paces ahead. More followed, and he realised there were warriors directly in the path of the advancing company. To say something to Caaskil would be to reveal their position.

It did not matter, a moment later a shrill war shout cut the air and the ground ahead seemed to rise up into a thicket of barbed spears and double-bladed axe heads. The Salphors had kept a second line of warriors hidden, advancing on hands and knees after the first, and Lutaan had ordered Caaskil straight into them.

"Lock shields!" Caaskil barely had time to roar the order before the Salphors were on top of the company. As the company stopped and closed up, Muuril's spear flashed out from beside Gelthius, its tip plunging through the long beard of a charging warrior, punching into his throat. Protected by Caaskil's shield, Gelthius jabbed with his weapon, the point crashing against the bronze shield boss of the Salphor directly ahead of him.

Almost undone by the surprise of the attack, the company could do little except receive the charge, catching weapons on shields and absorbing the momentum of the Salphors. Gelthius saw yellow sparks soaring into the air above the men in front of him, and realised that they were flaming arrows being shot from behind the Salphor attack. Though each was nowhere near as bright as the tar fires launched by the catapults, there were several hundred flashing overhead.

By luck rather than judgement, the advance of the company had brought them much closer than the enemy had suspected, so the fire arrows arced overhead and landed some distance behind. Gelthius and the others, and their attackers, were still shrouded in darkness, save for the odd glitter of firelight from a spear tip or raised axe. Sound was a far greater aid than sight, and Gelthius heard thousands of bellowed war cries as the Salphors launched their all-out charge against their now-visible opponents. His instincts had been right, in a way: the initial ineptitude of the Salphor attack had been a ruse.

Captain Caaskil was an experienced fighter and so was Muuril, and between the two of them Gelthius barely had a foe to face. He concentrated on keep his shield up to protect Muuril's spear side, and ramming his spear in the general direction of any Salphor that managed to get past Caaskil's vicious jabs. In the darkness it was hard to tell how many more foes were coming, and Gelthius could feel the rank stretching out, more distance growing between him and the men to either side, as warriors from the back ranks fed into the front to counter the overlap of foes to either flank. The inexperienced warriors of the Twenty-first were trying too hard to push into the fight, adding pressure from the rear ranks that meant those in the second, third and fourth ranks were forced to step forward too quickly as legionnaires fell at the front.

A particular burly Salphor with a red mane of hair and bushy beard smashed aside Muuril's spear with his shield and swung high with a long-hafted axe, forcing the sergeant to duck back as Gelthius tried to raise his shield against the blow. At the same time, Caaskil stepped forwards to drive his spear into the shoulder of another warrior, and the gap between the two captains widened even further. The axeman saw the opening and plunged towards it, swinging for Gelthius' face. Gelthius was forced to barge into Muuril to avoid the axe head whistling just past his nose, and then the front rank disintegrated.

Half-turning away from Gelthius, the Salphor hefted his axe at Caaskil's back, his blade biting into the captain's exposed neck between body armour and helm just as Gelthius' spear plunged into the exposed armpit of the axeman. As more warriors plunged into the fray, ignoring the front rankers to get inside the reach of the spears of the following ranks, Gelthius could feel the cohesion of the company fracturing. He had drilled enough to know what a solidly manoeuvring formation felt like, and the warriors at the back short on battle experience were committing the fatal crime of backing away at just the moment the rear ranks were supposed to shove those men in front to regain the momentum of attack.

Catching a sword blade on the bronze band beneath the head of his spear, Gelthius felt something grab hold of the hem of his jerkin. Powerful arms pulled him down and he cried out in alarm as he came crashing down on top of Muuril.

"Play dead!" the sergeant spat, the words almost lost in the cacophony of the fighting. Muuril's hand shifted to grab Gelthius' spear hand, pinning him to the ground. All around him, the men of the Thirteenth were falling, some with blood flowing from wounds, others, as far as he could tell, only mimicking their less-fortunate comrades.

With the front ranks of the Askhan company faltering and falling, the Salphors came on with renewed determination. Gelthius ground his teeth as a Salphorian warrior stood on his leg, stepping over the supposedly dead and wounded to hack and slash at the soldiers of the Twenty-first. Another boot caught Gelthius in the side of the head and he stifled a cry of pain.

He had thought it madness when Muuril had offered brief explanation, but in the chaos and darkness both the Salphors and Askhans were paying no heed to the men that had gone down; there were living foes to worry about. The fight continued to rage above Gelthius and out of the corner of his eye he saw the remnants of the company being forced back. Those who had been appointed sergeants did their best to reform the ranks and hold position, but there were too many Salphors. Amongst the angry shouts and hoarse moans of the wounded Gelthius heard cries of alarm.

It was impossible to see the first of the men running, as they peeled away from the rear rank, leaving those in front to the unkind attention of the Salphors. The withdrawal was fast becoming a retreat and teetered on the verge of rout.

"Now," growled Muuril.

Gelthius did not hesitate. He pushed himself to his feet and retrieved his spear and shield as the others of the Thirteenth did likewise around him. Some of the Salphors must have heard the commotion behind them, but their warning shouts were silenced as the suddenly resurrected legionnaires surged into the back of the Salphorian warband. Gelthius rammed the point of his spear into the chest of one of the warriors that had turned at the noise, sending the man toppling back into his comrades.

Muuril led the charge, his spear snapping on an upraised shield. He batted away a thrust from a Salphor and used the splintered haft of his weapon to batter the man in the side of the head. Gelthius finished off the downed warrior with a speartip to the man's gut while the rest of the Thirteenth legionnaires cut into the Salphors with ruthless ferocity.

Caught unawares, a score of Salphors had been brought down before they realised their dire position. The fighting was close and frenetic, the legionnaires using shields as much as their spears. Finding himself without a foe for a moment, Gelthius saw a discarded axe half-hidden beneath a corpse in front of him. Dropping his spear, he picked up this weapon and launched himself at the Salphors with a furious howl, swinging the head of the axe into face of a man driven back by a lunge from Loordin.

His arm aching from the effort, Gelthius fought on, blood spilling down his thigh from a cut opened up by a wild sword blow, his right eye closing up where the rim of a Salphorian shield had caught him on the cheek. Panting and snarling like a wild animal, Gelthius hacked down another Salphor and almost fell over the man's corpse.

It took him a moment to realise that all but a handful of the Salphors were dead. He caught glimpses of some running into the darkness. There was no sign of the prisoners from the Twenty-first; they must have fled the fight when the Salphors had turned on the men from the Thirteenth. The surviving Salphors were surrounded and quickly butchered and calm descended.

The sounds of the ongoing battle could be heard from the direction of Marradan, and by the light of the fire arrows Gelthius could see the long lines of the spear companies holding like a wall against the crashing waves of Salphorian warriors. Although it was impossible to be sure in the darkness, it seemed to Gelthius that they were alone. There were moans from wounded men around him, but he could not see whether they were Salphor or Askhan.

"Thirteen to me," rasped Muuril, plunging the ragged end of his spear into the face of a fallen Salphor, ending the injured man's misery.

Those that could do so gathered around the sergeant, twenty-seven in all. Four others managed to drag themselves to the small muster, nursing grim wounds. Gelthius saw that one of the casualties was Gebriun. His face was split from left eye to chin and blood pumped from a cut under his right arm.

"Legion code," muttered Muuril, drawing his knife from his belt.

Gelthius' heart sank when he realised the sergeant's intent. The Salphor looked down at Gebriun, who was barely conscious, the flap of flesh and skin that had been the left side of his face hanging down to the collar of his blood-soaked tunic.

Knowing that it was a mercy, Gelthius bit his lip and brought the axe down on to the back of Gebriun's neck, chopping deep into bone. Gebriun collapsed and lay still. All of the strength drained from Gelthius' body as he watched the other mortally wounded legionnaires being despatched with knife and sword. He let the axe drop from his weak grasp and settled to his haunches, still sucking in deep breaths from his exertions.

Muuril appeared next to him and grabbed him under the arm to pull him upright.

"Looks like we have an opportunity, captain," said the sergeant.

It took a moment for Gelthius to understand his meaning, looking dumbly into the darkness. They were alone. There was nobody from either side that could see them in the night.

"Shouldn't we help protect the city?" someone asked from the darkness. "We can't let those filthy Salphors take Marradan."

"There's not enough of us to make a difference," replied Muuril. "Look at it this way. If the Salphors win, we're fucked. If they lose, we're stuck with the Twenty-first. I don't know about you lot, but that's a fool's choice."

There were murmurs of assent and no further objections raised. Someone asked where they should go.

"There'll be bands of Salphors to duskwards, win or lose, so I say dawnwards," said Muuril. "Unless anyone has any better suggestions?"

None were forthcoming and the sergeant turned to Gelthius. "If that's all right by you, captain?" said the sergeant.

"Dawnwards, right enough," said Gelthius. "Let's get moving before anyone comes to find out what's happened to us."

III

By dawn, Gelthius and the rest of the Thirteenth's survivors from the company were miles away from Marradan. The morning light revealed evidence of a quiet exodus during the night, with many fresh foot prints and wheel ruts on the road heading away from the border with Salphoria. Word had spread of the Salphor attack and people had abandoned their homes overnight, so it was that they had come across an abandoned farm as the red tinges of daylight had crept over the horizon. From this temporary shelter, Gelthius could see a smudge of darkness in the sky above Marradan: the smoke of fires.

"You think the Salphors won?" he asked Loordin, who stood beside him at the door.

"Nah, that's just from the fires set during the battle," replied the legionnaire, raising a cup of watered wine to his lips. He drank deeply and smiled. "I think Lutaan has managed to pull off his second victory."

Mention of Captain Lutaan brought unwelcome memories of Menesun, and it was in this frame of mind that Gelthius moved away from the door and back into the kitchen where Muuril and about a dozen others were finishing a stolen breakfast of eggs and bread; Gelthius had no appetite. The rest of the men were scattered through the building and the attached outhouses, some of them still snoring heavily in their sleep, most awake but unwilling to make a move just yet.

"What now?" asked Muuril, looking for Gelthius to provide an answer. The captain shrugged in reply and picked up the cup of water he had left on the table.

"It isn't up to me, is it?" said Gelthius. He looked around at the other men. "I'm not a captain, not now. I wasn't a captain before, so don't treat me like I am. Every man can do whatever he likes, right enough."

"We're still legionnaires of the Thirteenth," said Muuril. A couple of the men beside him nodded but the sentiment was far from universal amongst those in the kitchen. Their reluctance brought forth a deep frown from the sergeant. "We are still legionnaires of the Thirteenth. We are sworn to the king until he releases us from oath."

"He's more than likely dead," said Gelthius. Muuril stood up, tossing his spoon down onto the table with a snarl.

"You don't know that. We have to find out. I'm not leaving him to the mercies of Urikh and those other bastards."

"You want to attack Askh and get him back?" said Loordin, stepping in behind Gelthius. "Feel free, but don't expect me to come with you."

Muuril looked pained at his friend's desertion and turned to the other soldiers.

"I've had a look myself, that ain't no city burning, which means Lutaan will figure out that we didn't die in that battle when they collect the dead."

"He's got too much to think about to come after us," said Loordin. "With Salphors prowling around getting funny ideas, he's not going to worry about a couple of dozen escaped prisoners. I'm heading to Thedraan to pick up the family and then heading coldwards. War's kicking off again, with the Salphors, and with all the mess Urikh has made of everything you can bet they ain't going to be easy to stop. Marradan's just the start, I'd say."

"I'd head to Salphoria to find the rest of the Thirteenth, but that's out of the question," said one of the others, "not with them barbarians getting ideas of attacking Askhans."

"The king needs as many good men as he can get," Muuril said, his demeanour defiant against the opinions being voiced.

"The king can suck my cock," said Loordin. "I followed his father but I owe nothing to Urikh."

"Not him, Ullsaard," said Muuril. He waved a hand at them and turned away. "Fuck the lot of you. I'm not just going to lie down while those cunts Urikh and Aegenuis fight over my empire."

Gelthius laughed at the sergeant's choice of words.

"Anyone would think you was king, the way you talk," said the Salphor.

"I might as well be," said Muuril, looking back as he headed for the door into the rear yard. "Seems any bastard can call himself king these days."

There was silence as the sergeant left, and the men in the kitchen looked at each other, some of them ashamed, most amused or simply apathetic. It had been a long night and Gelthius shared their weariness. Despite his words, he felt their gazes lingering on him, expecting a final decision. They were waiting for leadership and, legion or not, they thought it would come from Gelthius.

"We need eyes out on the road," said the Salphor, pointing at Loordin. "Take four men with you and head a little ways back towards Marradan. You see anything of the Salphors or the Twenty-first, you come running right back."

"Didn't I just say I was through with this?" said Loordin. Gelthius gave no reply, but stared hard at the man. "All right," Loordin said. "Just for now, but when we're safe and away from here don't think I'll be following your orders then."

Loordin rattled off a handful of names and the chosen men left with him. Having already taken the lead in organising the remnants of the company so far, Gelthius felt the expectation of the other legionnaires increasing. They were looking at him, alert and ready for orders. He stifled a sigh and a yawn.

"Right enough," he muttered before taking a deep breath. "Whether we're staying or going, sticking together or splitting, we'll need more than just our battle gear. I want foraging parties to scout around and get us bags, sacks, fodder, food, carts and whatever else you can find."

Pleased to have purpose, the men nodded their acknowledgements and left with a scraping of chairs and muttering. Once he was on his own, Gelthius slumped into a chair at the table and put his head in his hands.

"There's gonna be a whole lot of folks need something to look up to soon enough." Gelthius looked up and saw that Muuril had returned, his face and arms wet, hair slicked back with water. "Whole empire's falling apart."

"And you think we can put it back together?" said Gelthius. He shook his head and lowered his hands to the table. "Two dozen soldiers ain't going to save the empire."

"We're from the legions, we stick together," said Muuril, sitting opposite the captain. "I've been thinking."

"Save us from your thinking," said Gelthius.

"Hear me out. Best place to head is for the Greenwater, right? Maybe head down to Cosuan, or jump off somewhere along the way."

"I suppose so."

"So let's head to Narun, get a ship and be on our way," Muuril continued. He was not a sly man and Gelthius could tell that there was something other than a river voyage on the mind of the sergeant.

"Narun? Just a few days from Askh, right?"

"If we hear anything about Ullsaard while we get there, we'll be in the right place. If not, then I'll leave you be. It's a busy road, nobody will notice a few more legionnaires. Come on, what do you say?"

Gelthius considered the sergeant's proposal. It had merit. All of them had been locked up for a season and more and knew virtually nothing of what had been happening in the wider empire. It would certainly be wise to head dawnwards, away from any Salphor attacks; away from Captain Lutaan. Narun made as much sense as anywhere else in that case.

"We give everybody a choice, right?" said the captain. "If they don't want to come, they don't have to."

"No, fuck that," said Muuril. "We're either Thirteenth or we're not. At Narun we'll give them the choice."

"That's a long walk, with disappointment at the end of it," warned Gelthius.

"If we learn Ullsaard is dead for sure on the way, I'll leave you to decide what you want," promised the sergeant.

Scratching a stubbled cheek, Gelthius thought some more. From outside came the noise of chickens being rounded up and the thump of men breaking in barred doors on the outhouses. A lifetime of legion rules had ingrained obedience into them, but if they decided to turn on Gelthius there was nothing he could do. He was uneasy with Muuril's stubbornness, and there was something to be said for Loordin's plan to go to his family in Thedraan.

Thinking of his family made Gelthius sigh heavily. If the empire was collapsing, he wanted to be with them, but if there was a chance he could help them more by aiding Ullsaard – however unlikely that seemed – then did he owe it to them to put his personal feelings aside and seek out the rightful king? As a Salphor he was not naturally filled with loyalty to men of lofty position, and Ullsaard had done things that had angered Gelthius considerably; on reflection Ullsaard had done better by Gelthius than worse, and perhaps deserved to be given a chance.

"Right enough," said Gelthius. "Narun it is, unless we hear anything sooner. After that, you're on your own."

GERIA ROAD, NALANOR
Late Spring, 213th year of Askh

The wooded hills of Nalanor seethed with armed men moving between the trees overlooking the paved road that headed straight as an architect's ruler towards Geria. From the road all seemed as normal, but just half a mile behind the tree line, three legion forts housed the warriors of the Second, Fourteenth and Seventeenth. Company-strength patrols moved back and forth above the road, watching for the approach of the enemy; seventeen thousand men awaited the call to fall upon their unsuspecting foes.

So far the waiting troops had seen nothing more than farm carts and trade caravans; a phenomenon that concerned the council of Harrakil, appointed General by King Urikh. With his fellow first captains, Naadlin and Canaasin, the general looked down at the stretch of road from a vantage point overlooking the Gesian River.

"No refugees, no panic," said the general, arms folded. "If Anasind's men were moving along the road, I'd expect there to be some sign of their advance."

"We have outposts at each crossing twenty miles up and down the Gesian, if they try to come from hotwards or cold-wards," replied Naadlin. As the most experienced of the three, his words carried weight in Harrakil's thoughts. The commander of the Second pulled off his helm and wiped sweat from his wrinkled face with the sleeve of his tunic. "We'll have at least four days' warning to pull back to Geria if need be."

"I'm with the general," said Canaasin. "We've been here ten days already, and sent patrols up the road each day. If Anasind is coming directly from Thedraan he should have been here by now. Are you sure they are coming for Geria?"

"It makes sense," said Naadlin. "Take Geria and you can throttle the trade up to Narun, and that means strangling Askh too. The information from the Brotherhood was precise."

With a doubtful grunt, Harrakil moved out from the cover of the trees, stepping into the glare of the sun. With his back to the morning light, he looked duskwards along the road and saw nothing but the occasional abada-drawn wagon and traders with hand carts. If Anasind and the legions returning from Salphoria were coming for Geria they were not arriving that day. He growled to himself, feeling that Urikh had made a mistake. He did not want to admit such a thing in front of the other captains; his position as general depended upon them having faith in the new king. It had been a struggle to convince them that Anasind was a rebel in the first place.

"I don't know how, but Anasind has got the drop on us, I'm sure of it," said Canaasin. "We should move to defend Geria directly."

"That means taking our troops back across the Greenwater, severely limiting our reach," argued Naadlin. "Anasind could march past thirty miles away and we would not be able to respond in time to stop him turning coldwards."

The conflicting views of his companions did no help Harrakil's mood as he rejoined them. He grimaced as he considered the decision he had to make.

"The labours of command," said Naadlin, smiling at the general's discomfort. "That's what you get for being the king's favourite."

Harrakil said nothing. The position of general had been given to him in return for his continued loyalty, but it was clear from the attitude of his fellow captains that it did not guarantee respect. Harrakil suspected that Naadlin and Canaasin were only with him because it offered a break from tedious garrison duty in Maasra and Okhar.

"Three more days," announced the general. "If Anasind and his army are not here in the next three days, he is not coming at all. Nobody takes that long to march from Ersua, even if they have crossed all of Salphoria first."

"So what do we do if he doesn't come?" asked Naadlin. Harrakil knew what the next question was going to be; he had been avoiding asking it for several days now. It was a question for which the general had no answer. "If Anasind doesn't want Geria, where is he?"

NARUN, ASKHOR
Late Spring, 213th year of Askh

I

The capture of the massive docks and wharfs of Narun was proceeding nicely, according to the stream of reports being brought back to Anasind by his second captains. Several warships had been seized ten miles to hotwards by Donar and the Fifth, creating a blockade to stop any ships heading downriver towards Geria. Three nights of forced marching had taken Meesiu and the Third across the Greenwater at Caarfin, to create a barrier between Narun and the Wall, preventing any communication with Askh. Meanwhile the Eighth, Thirteenth, and Sixteenth had marched into the city itself. Isolated and faced with three battle-hardened legions, the men and soldiers of the Brotherhood had capitulated without a fight.

All in all the advance had been pretty bloodless. It seemed that Ullsaard had been right that the Brotherhood had the means to warn Urikh of an attack on Geria and Noran had played his part well. The bulk of Urikh's forces were far away, leaving only the men of the First to defend Askh itself.

There were some scuffles and arguments with ship's captains and crews as the thousands of legionnaires fanned out through the intersecting quays and bridges, boarding the ships at berth and commandeering boats and galleys to be taken out to the ships lying at anchor in the middle of the massive artificial lake. It was to be expected that there would be resistance, and Anasind had told his men to be restrained if possible. A few hotheads had tried to weigh anchor and get away, but they had soon turned back when the war engines in the twin forts at the mouth of the Greenwater had fired warning shots into the river; any ship trying to leave would be sunk by the massed batteries meant to defend the wharfs against attack.

In fact, the whole campaign had gone so smoothly Anasind was at a bit of a loss what to do next. Noran had insisted that Ullsaard would send word of the next part of his plan, but the general knew that it would be difficult for the king. Short on men that could be trusted, Ullsaard had been neatly isolated by Urikh and the Brotherhood, and it had only been the foresight to bring back the legions that gave the true king any leverage at all.

Having set up a command post in the warehouses attached to the King's Wharfs, Anasind stood on the roof terrace of the ship master's house, offered an unparalleled view of the city. He had dismissed the latest of the heralds bearing word from the captains moving through Narun, and was alone with Noran. There had not been much opportunity for the two of them to speak candidly, what with the swift march and the constant presence of lower officers.

"What do you think he wants us to do next?" Anasind asked, resting his arms on the wooden rail of the terrace. Noran had found a jug of watered wine and two goblets and offered one to the general, which was accepted gratefully. It was hot, unseasonably so for Narun, and the liquid brought a moment of refreshment. "It will not be as simple as taking Askh, will it?"

"No, it will not be that simple, not this time," said the herald.

There was something in Noran's voice that hinted at fear, but Anasind had never considered his companion to be cowardly.

"What is wrong?" asked the general. "What am I getting myself into?"

Noran shook his head and downed the contents of his goblet.

"Nothing that we need to worry about just yet." Anasind could hear the forced bravado. "Let us just clear one hurdle at a time."

"But you know something that I should know of, I can tell. Ullsaard trusts me, you know that. So can you."

"It is not trust that is the issue, general, it really is not," replied Noran, placing the half-empty jug on the rail next to Anasind. "Anyway, to the matter in hand. You are right that the First and the taking of Askh is not the biggest obstacle to overcome. To be honest, once the people of Askh see that Ullsaard is alive, I think he expects the city to surrender itself back to his rule. Urikh's reign is based on the flimsiest of lies, when you think about it. The Brotherhood is another matter."

There was that flutter of uncertainty again, and Anasind could not ignore it.

"It is time that the Brotherhood's power was curbed, but they will accept that," said the general. "They can cause problems, but despite everything they will see that a return to stability is the best option for the empire."

Noran looked at Anasind for a long time, saying nothing. He refilled his goblet but did not drink from it.

"Do you remember the man who came with Ullsaard before we took Magilnada?" asked the herald. "The one with the golden eyes?"

"I could not forget him, even though I wish I could," replied the general. "The new High Brother, yes?"

"Yes. A man called Lakhyri, though I use the term 'man' loosely. He is using Urikh as a puppet, and I think it is his desire to dispense with kings entirely. He has already forced Urikh to dismiss the governors and he seeks for the Brotherhood to control the empire directly. He would set himself up as ruler in place of the Blood. Or that is what I believe."

"He will find that a task beyond his resources," said Anasind, turning to face Noran, one elbow resting on the rail, cup in hand. "They have no military strength, and the few legions that follow Urikh will soon be brought back into line. If they think they can choke us with a withdrawal of their services as they tried before, they will find Ullsaard less forgiving. I think it is the Brotherhood that will find itself surplus to the empire's needs, not the king."

"They have other, less tangible powers at their disposal," said Noran, picking his words with visible care. The noble turned his eyes to dawnwards, his gaze moving to something in the far distance. "I think I see now something of their purpose. Since the birth of the empire they have crushed the old beliefs, teaching us that there is nothing in the world save for the mortal and physical. They have lied to us."

Anasind laughed, but it was from nervousness not humour.

"You sound like a Salphor, talking about spirits and otherworldly forces."

Noran turned on him with a fierce look, one hand gripping the rail tightly.

"I have seen things that have no mortal explanation. You have witnessed it too, if you would open your eyes to it. You remember the plagues and snows that beset you when you fought against Lutaar? What of my recovery from a never-ending sleep? Did you not consider how that was possible? What did you think of a man with eyes of gold? These are not natural things, and I have since encountered far worse."

A chill trickled through Anasind despite the warm sun. To mask his unease he took a swig of wine and waved a hand to encompass Narun.

"Their power cannot be so strong if they let us walk into the greatest docks in the empire without resistance. If they are not bound by mortal limits, why is it that they did not see us coming?"

"You do not believe me?" Noran shook his head. "The Brotherhood have done their job well."

"In Salphoria our foes called upon the spirits to aid them, but the Salphors fell to our spears and swords all the same. Do not take offence, but I think that you have not recovered from your ordeals and your mind is prey to simple tricks and malign suggestions."

"I wish that you were right," said Noran. He shrugged. "Better to believe my own thoughts unsafe than to acknowledge that which I have seen as truth."

A commotion in the street below drew the attention of both men and Anasind leaned out over the rail to see what was happening. A handful of soldiers were approaching along the street, calling for the legionnaires in their way to clear a path. Anasind recognised Donar in the knot of men striding towards the command post, surrounded by a cadre of legionnaires. Beside the first captain walked a large man, clean-shaven and with hair hanging to his shoulders. The face was unfamiliar but there was a strut to the man's step and a confidence in his bearing that struck a chord in the general's mind.

"Well, that is one less question to vex us," Noran said with a laugh.

"What do you mean?"

Noran pointed at the stranger with Donar and grinned.

"The king has arrived."

II

Ullsaard entered the building and found Anasind hurrying down a stairway, Noran just behind. The surprise of the general was evident in his expression, but Ullsaard was happy to see a familiar face. After recent tribulations, both political and domestic, the sight of Anasind filled the king with a joy he had not known for some time. Anasind's presence signified a shift in the fortunes of the king, and heralded the conclusion of the whole sorry affair that had engulfed Ullsaard and the empire. Before Anasind could say anything, Ullsaard stepped up and threw an arm around the general, slapping him on the back as they embraced.

"I've never been so happy to see another man," Ullsaard said with a grin, stepping back. "That and the thousands you've brought with you."

"I am equally happy to see you alive and in good spirits, my king," said Anasind, reeling slightly from Ullsaard's greeting.

Looking around, Ullsaard noted an absence.

"Where is Aegenuis?" he asked, expecting the Salphorian king to be close at hand, as he had instructed. Anasind's smile faded and Ullsaard's mood darkened quickly. "Why is he not here?"

"In order to move swiftly to your aid, I had to make a fresh bargain with Aegenuis," Anasind explained, looking away. The general waved towards a curtained doorway and led Ullsaard into an adjoining room. Within was a small room, furnished with low couches and a table strewn with tablets and slates. "His son, Medorian, escaped the failed attack against us and had been rebuilding support amongst the Salphorian chieftains. It would have taken more time and men than we had to spare, so I impressed upon Aegenuis the need for him to restore his authority."

"You left him?" Ullsaard could not quite believe what he had heard. "My orders were specific for a reason. What is to stop Aegenuis making peace with his son and turning against us?"

"It was an impossible situation, Ullsaard," said Noran, standing by the doorway. Ullsaard turned and the noble flinched under his glare but continued. "I agree with Anasind's choice.

There is no point keeping Salphoria if you lose Greater Askhor, is there?"

As much as it pained him to admit, the two of them had a point. Acknowledging this, he patted Anasind on the shoulder.

"You did the right thing," said the king, provoking obvious relief from the general. "I knew the risks I was taking by calling you back, and we'll just have to deal with the shit that follows. And if we are lucky, Aegenuis and Medorian will tear each other apart, making it easier for us to regain control when we are done with Urikh."

"If we are really lucky, Aegenuis will crush Medorian and hold to his word," said Noran. His eyes roved around the room seeking something; something he evidently did not find as he sighed and returned his gaze to Ullsaard. "I left the wine on the roof, otherwise I would offer you proper welcome."

"Wine can wait," said Ullsaard. He called out for Donar, who slipped through the door past Noran and strode across the room to stand beside Anasind.

"Are we all acquainted again?" said the first captain. "What next?"

"Narun will be secured before nightfall, and all proof suggests that Urikh's legions are far to hotwards," said Anasind. "We will have plenty of time to prepare defences for their return."

"No, I'm not wasting time," said Ullsaard. "The time to strike is upon us and we must hit hard while there are no other distractions. We will take Askh and bring down Urikh, and that serpent Lakhyri too if we can find him. I am out of patience. The Brotherhood will be brought to heel once and for all."

A worthy goal, I am sure. How do you plan to achieve that?

There was a mocking tone to Askhos' question, but the point was valid.

"The majority of the Brotherhood are loyal to the empire, and when we have removed Lakhyri from his perch they shall

return their loyalty to me. The Brothers across the empire follow the instructions of their superiors, and so we shall install
a High Brother who is aligned to me."

"I do not think there is a man you could trust with such
power, not now," said Noran.

"What do you intend to do with Urikh?" asked Donar. "I
know he is your son, but…"

*Noran is right. You place a great deal on the shoulders of whomever
you pick.*

Rubbing his temple, Ullsaard tried to separate the conversation in the room with the commentary in his head. He looked
between Donar and Noran and attempted to answer both
questions at once.

"Urikh will be punished, do not think that he will escape retribution, but he is not wholly to blame for this. Without Lakhyri
and the Brotherhood he can do little real damage. His mischief
will cost him dearly, but it is Lakhyri that we must get rid of."

Easily said, but more difficult to enact.

"Lakhyri is not without protection," Noran said, glancing
with concern at the two first captains.

"Such protection does not extended to immunity from a
spear," said Ullsaard, tiring of his companions' questions and
arguments. "Debate will not resolve this, only action. Anasind,
have your men ready by Low Watch tomorrow. We march on
Askh without delay."

TEMPLE

Terror and chaos reigned. Blood slicked the floor of the main chamber and bodies lay all about the Last Corpse. Asirkhyr looked on in horror as the handful of surviving worshippers continued their struggles, divided in loyalty between the hierophants. Eriekh had called out damning accusation to the followers and some had risen up in his defence; others had come to the aid of Asirkhyr and fighting had broken out. The Temple was devoid of weapons and so both sides had throttled and bludgeoned with hands and feet, bashing each other's heads against walls and floor, breaking bone and choking life with grasping fingers.

Drawn by the bloodshed, the Eulanui had gathered, their presence pouring from the Last Corpse like oily smoke, coalescing above the mayhem, feeding on the life-force of the dying and the dead. Asirkhyr watched now as the last few men slipped in the crimson puddles, grappling and snarling, spurred on by a vehemence possessed only by the truly faithful.

The Last Corpse was swelling with power, soaking in the blood that trickled against its base, its aura darkening the room so that the hierophant could only dimly see the thrashing, flailing limbs of the Eulanui as they absorbed the meat and

337

bones of the fallen. The shadows were deepening with every passing moment, substance given to the insubstantial.

Eriekh lay at Asirkhyr's feet, his face a ragged mess, his blood smeared over flagstone and brick. That blood stained Asirkhyr's arms up to the elbow and he still trembled with the primal, feral joy of smashing his enemy's head against the floor with his bare hands. He had never been a violent man, but the whispers of the Eulanui had urged him on, fuelling blow after blow. Now horrified calm gripped the hierophant as he backed away from the carnage, turning towards the passageway that led to the lower levels where he would be able to displace himself into the Grand Precincts of Askh.

Something gripped his ankle and he turned to find Eriekh still lived, bony fingers wrapped about Asirkhyr's leg. Hate-filled eyes stared up at him from the ruin of the hierophant's face, and bloodied lips peeled back to reveal crimson-flecked teeth.

"You have doomed us." Eriekh's words were barely more than a whisper, but his grasp was tight with insane strength as Asirkhyr tried to free his ankle. "You have brought the masters' wrath down upon us."

Asirkhyr kicked out, driving the heel of his foot into Eriekh's face. Twice more he stamped on the hierophant's head and Eriekh's grip grew limp.

Looking across the chamber, Asirkhyr realised that Eriekh had delayed him long enough. The Eulanui had finished feasting on the others and circled above, skittering and clambering over the ceiling and walls, clusters of tenebrous tentacles gathering around him. A strand of darkness extended down from the ceiling and touched upon his shoulder, almost loving in its gentle caress. Pleasant numbness flowed through Asirkhyr's body and all thought of resistance fled his mind as more feeder-tendrils latched onto his withered skin.

His heart beat once more, and then his body collapsed into nothing, every particle of his essence absorbed by the nightmares his folly had brought forth.

ASKH
Early summer, 213th year of Askh

I

This time there were no legions to bar Ullsaard's path. The captain commanding the garrison on the wall, on being confronted by the true king and five first captains of the legions, had opened the gates without hesitation, and two days' more marching had brought Ullsaard's army within sight of the capital. The last time he had marched on Askh with intent for battle he had been forced to kill one of his oldest friends; the prospect that he might have to dispense the same fate to Urikh filled him with a grim mood.

Nearly thirty thousand strong, the column stretched for several miles along the road. Icons of Askhos glinted at the head of each legion when the sun broke from the scattered cloud, and helmet crests fluttered in the strengthening wind. The tramp of the legionnaires marching in step reverberated across the countryside, giving warning to the farmsteads and trade posts dotted along the road that the rightful king had returned.

Some folk came from their homes, shouting cheers of encouragement and praises to Ullsaard, but most stayed indoors, peering fearfully from windows and doorways as rank after rank after rank of soldiers marched past. Rumour of turmoil had been rife for a long time, and the arrival of the army increased worry rather than set minds at rest. Here in the heartland of the empire, Urikh's tyranny had been well-masked. Answering directly to the king, the people knew little of the banishment of the governors, and cared even less.

"I see accusation in their eyes," remarked Ullsaard as he strode past a small group of farm houses, a man and two women watching the progress of the legionnaires from the shadow of a barn. Behind them clustered a trio of children, all of them too young to properly remember the last time Ullsaard had come to Askhor with an army.

"It will take longer to repair the damage wrought by Urikh than it did for him to inflict it," replied Noran. "Askh was once a bastion of civilisation and peace and you have overturned that. Memories are short-lived concerning the bounties of Salphoria that flowed into these lands, but will long remain of you bringing hungry soldiers."

Salphoria was still a sore issue with the king and he said nothing, though he looked to Anasind not far ahead with his command staff. Ullsaard knew that he had unfinished business with Aegenuis, and though he did not hold the general at fault for his decision, he would have preferred that the Salphorian leader had remained under close watch.

"I know that you are reluctant to discuss the matter, but have you considered what you will do with Urikh?" Noran asked. The herald had become more obviously distressed as they came closer to the city, his nerves bringing his talkative nature to the fore. "He is still the heir of the Blood, regardless of what he has done. And princes of the Blood are thin on the ground these days."

Ullsaard grimaced, reminded of Jutaar's death. Thoughts of succession were far from his mind and in his irritation he snapped back at Noran.

"Perhaps you should give more thought to your own affairs before delving into mine. What is your intent towards Meliu?"

This time it was Noran's turn to make a sour face, reminded of matters he had been avoiding.

"Well?" said Ullsaard. "When I have the Crown again, do I dissolve her position as my wife and release her to you?"

"I am divided on the subject," Noran admitted. "Meliu would make a fine wife and I have deep affection for her, but we lay together in a moment of passion and I do not know if I would be the husband she desires. Also, I am still wed to Anriit. There are complications."

It was clear to Ullsaard that Noran had concerns he had not voiced and the king was in no mood to accommodate the noble's half-truths.

"It's not like you to worry yourself over the legal niceties of marriage. The fact that you fucked my wife proves that. Take her as your mistress if you want."

"If it were that simple," Noran said with a sigh.

"By nightfall I plan to be at the palace, you need to make up your mind quickly. When Urikh is in our custody and Lakhyri slain, I will have to head to Salphoria again, to settle matters with Aegenuis and reinforce our rule there. I am not staying around for you to make up your mind. Meliu is devoted to you as she once was to me, and she is both forthcoming in her affections and beautiful. What more could you want?"

"A lover that did not once share the bed of my best friend?" Noran said, the words quiet and thoughtful. "A lover that will not remind me of yet another thing I have taken from you in my selfishness?"

Noran's confession would have made Ullsaard laugh in better circumstances, but the king was aware that his friend's conflicted thoughts were in part caused by him. Before Ullsaard could reply, Noran continued.

"I had found happiness with Neerita, and she was to bear me a son, but that was not to be. It occurs to me that you seek to give me one wife in exchange for the one I lost to your friendship."

With a growl, Ullsaard grabbed the sleeve of Noran's tunic and dragged him from the road to stand beside a low wall. The following company of legionnaires glanced at their king as they marched past, but the shouts of their captains returned their attention ahead.

"You still blame me for Neerita's death?" snarled the king. "Is that why you fucked Meliu? To take from me what you thought I took from you?"

"If it was as simple, I would be glad," said Noran, dejected. He pulled himself from Ullsaard's grasp. "I once had a life of my own; a loving wife, estates, wealth and happiness. Now I am dependent upon you for the smallest kindness. That is not friendship, it is servitude. If you were not king, what would you have to offer me? And if you were not king, I am not sure I would follow you."

Noran's words were like a punch in the gut, knotting up Ullsaard's stomach and causing him to take a sharp breath. He fought against the urge to lash out, to strike his friend for such disloyalty. Clenching his fists, the king instead turned away.

"I have never demanded anything of you," he said, causing Noran to laugh.

"Not in word, but by expectation. Why, only this spring you cajoled me into travelling all the way to Ersua for you, putting myself in danger for the purpose of deceiving Urikh. Did you once consider the hazards I would face? If my tongue and wit had failed me, I would be made prisoner by the Brotherhood, or worse. I delivered your message and misled Leraates, and for what? Have I had any thanks or reward for it? As a friend you are ungrateful, and as a king you have nothing to offer but empty promises."

"When I regain the Crown, you can have any rewards that you desire," said Ullsaard turning back to his companion. "One of my wives is yours, if you desire her. Wealth? I will empty the coffers of the empire for you. Position? The empire stands with no governors, or perhaps you would prefer the rule of a Salphorian province? Do not question my generosity. To be an ally of the king is no small thing. Perhaps it is you that is fucking ungrateful."

"Fuck you, Ullsaard," Noran said through gritted teeth, face flushing with anger. "You take everything and give nothing. You are a conqueror in heart as well as deed. You wish to possess everything for yourself, and all others exist to serve that ambition. At least Urikh is honest about his ambition, and his threats were openly made. Even now my family stands in danger, and you would have me lay them to sacrifice for your benefit. Do you know how easy it would have been to become his man? All the things you promise me were his to grant as well."

"You are wrong," said Ullsaard, stung by the herald's words. "I have stayed true to those closest to me."

"You betrayed Aalun and killed Cosua. You dealt with a toad like Anglhan at my expense and against my judgement. You gave Urikh power and money, and were bought off by Lakhyri's promises of loyalty. That has turned out so well for you."

"Then why the fuck do you stay?" asked Ullsaard, slumping against the wall, his anger becoming sadness as the truth of Noran's accusations settled in his thoughts. Amongst the turmoil in his mind, the king was reminded that it was he that had made Jutaar first captain, promoting him beyond his measure when blinded by the desire to see his son succeed. He swallowed hard, grief threatening to take him. "Why didn't you turn on me and serve Urikh?"

"Because I have seen what power Lakhyri truly serves, and through him they are Urikh's masters also. You are an unmitigated whore's cunt sometimes, Ullsaard, but you have always been your own man. The thing that I saw in the palace had a hunger that I cannot explain. I felt its power and its desire. It was... inhuman. You will grow old and die and pass on your rule to another, as was meant to be. Askhos, these strange creatures that placed him and Lakhyri above us all, they cannot be allowed to control the empire."

Ullsaard considered these words carefully, convinced by the bitter words of Noran that his insights were deeply felt and the opinion voiced based on true conviction. If what the herald said was true, Urikh was not the greatest of the king's concerns.

"A handful of years ago, I would have thought you a fucking madman," said Ullsaard. "Now I have a dead king living in my head, I have travelled through dreams to wake you from a deathly sleep and given to you half of my life-force. I have seen in Erlaan the nature of the powers Lakhyri entreats. This is not the world of men as we once knew it, but you must trust me. I will give every drop of my blood to keep the empire safe, whether from Urikh or darker powers."

The king reached out a hand. Noran looked at it, his gaze moving between Ullsaard's outstretched palm and his determined stare. The herald shook his head slightly and Ullsaard thought that his friend would walk away.

"You are a fucking arrogant, bullying arsehole of a man, Ullsaard," said Noran, gripping the king's wrist as Ullsaard's fingers tightened around the arm of the herald. "But at least you are a man."

Still grasping his friend's wrist, Ullsaard looked to dawnwards and the pale smudge of Askhos on its distant hilltop.

"Did I tell you how I single-handedly killed a behemodon?"

the king said with a lopsided smile. "I don't care where they're from, these shadowy cunts have got more coming for them than they bargained on. I'll make them wish they'd never set eyes on my fucking empire."

II

The news that an army approached, possibly led by King Ullsaard, had started panic in the palace. Like a parchment touched by fire, the fear was spreading to the rest of the city. The gates had been closed and companies from the First and the Brotherhood's legion were stationed across Askh, enforcing a curfew decreed by Urikh. In the palace, soldiers guarded every doorway, and the servants scurried about their business with fearful glances at the black-crested legionnaires patrolling the corridors and hallways.

Lakhyri had other concerns as he pushed open the doors to the Hall of Askhos. Within, he found Urikh and Luia deep in conversation. The king looked up as Lakhyri approached.

"Where have you been?" Urikh demanded, rising from his throne.

"Attending to the security of the city," Lakhyri replied. "Sit down."

Urikh looked as though he would argue, but a whispered word from Luia made him comply with the high priest's demand. The king's mother looked at Lakhyri with narrowed eyes as he approached.

"You intend to wait for Ullsaard's assault?" she said. "If I thought you were an idiot I would be concerned, but I know that you are not. Word comes that Ullsaard has five legions with him, so what defence do you have against his attack?"

Lakhyri ignored her and addressed his next words to the king.

"I am told that you attempted to leave the palace," said the high priest. "It is not safe for you."

"I will not be caught like a rat in a trap, no matter what you caution against," replied Urikh. "Nor will I surrender calmly to my father's judgement. You assured me that Ullsaard would be dead, and now he is here, seeking my head upon a spear. You have failed me."

"It is you that have failed," rasped Lakhyri, dropping all pretence of servitude. Acceding to the king's foolish scheming had been a bruise to Lakhyri's pride and now that the moment of truth was swiftly approaching, he could bear the charade no longer. "Do not forget who it was that placed you upon that throne, boy. If not for your interference, Ullsaard would have been upon his pyre a long time past. I told you what had to be done, but you would not listen."

"It was you that thought Anglhan was suitable to the task," replied Luia.

"A criticism that does not hold greater weight for being voiced so frequently," said the high priest. He turned his golden gaze upon the queen and she took a step back, alarmed by the hatred in his eyes. "You mistake your place in the new order that will rule the empire. Be thankful that I still require one of the Blood as my figurehead, to ease compliance to my wishes. Your continued presence is a salve to resistance, not a necessity."

"Was it not you that came to me, asking for my aid?" replied Urikh. "I remember well the day that I first lay eyes upon you, while my father still waged war in Mekha. You told me that you would see me upon the throne of the empire and the Crown of the Blood upon my head." Urikh reached up to the gilded iron at his brow. "You warned me to be patient, and I was. As you promised, the rule of Lutaar failed, but then you placed my father upon the throne instead. Still you assured me that my time would come soon, but I watched as you raised up Erlaan, creating a half-Mekhani mongrel beast to take my place. They would destroy each other, you claimed, and the path would be set for me to ascend to my rightful position. My father failed you, and Erlaan failed you, but I held on to my desire and have delivered what they could not."

"A tool long kept on the shelf only remains useful while its work is unfinished," said Lakhyri. "I was sent to you by the masters, and I found you, nurtured your pride and gave you coin and influence. The promises I whispered were nectar to your ambition, and you fed deeply upon it. My brother, with Aalun and Ullsaard, even Erlaan, were too focussed upon each other that they did not see the weaver working at the loom. All that has passed, not without delay or setback, has been as I desired. When I needed you, I used you. Hope that I do not need to replace the tool with one sharper and more fitting to the task."

Possessed of a similar temperament to his father, Urikh did not take this bald statement well. The king rose from the throne again and took hold of the collar of the high priest's robe.

"You are a weak, pathetic thing, Lakhyri. I may not be the warrior my father is, but I have enough strength in my grip to throttle the life from you."

Lakhyri grinned, baring yellowing stubs of teeth.

"Would that I needed to draw breath like some pitiful mortal creature, your threats would have foundation."

"A spear or knife, then," suggested Luia. "Perhaps you would find immortal existence more testing without your heart or throat."

"Do not waste time with this misplaced bravado," said Lakhyri. He felt the presence of the master coalescing in the hall; a drying of the air that he had become accustomed to during many long rituals. Luia gasped and raised a hand to her mouth as the Eulanui seeped up from the tiled floor, becoming corporeal as it spread out gangling limbs and sinuous fronds.

"Perhaps you wish to beg for my protection?" Lakhyri asked as Urikh freed his grip and staggered back to the throne, stepping around an uncoiling tendril. The king looked to make some cutting remark but held his tongue, fear outweighing spite.

COMING.

The thought-message thundered through Lakhyri's brain, flaring with pain behind his eyes. Luia fainted from the mental assault, to fall draped over the arm of the throne. Hissing, Urikh attended to his mother, face flushed with pain.

"Yes, my master, soon we will have prepared the way," the high priest gasped.

The Eulanui continued to grow darker, the shadow of its body deepening. With rune-tainted vision, Lakhyri could see the sinews and muscles warping into existence, layering over contorted bone and cartilage. It reminded him of the awakening of the Last Corpse, but there was no such altar-node through which the master could manifest.

"What is it doing?" snarled Urikh as snake-like appendages slithered across the hall, stretching from one wall to the next. Like some grotesquely hideous octopus pulling itself from its lair, the Eulanui heaved it bulk across the veil between realities. Eyestalks swivelled, crystalline orbs regarding Lakhyri, who saw himself reflected in a thousand mirrored facets.

"It is too soon, master," said Lakhyri, falling to his knees. "There are still precincts to build, to extend the weave of your power. There is not the energy to sustain you."

COMING. NOW.

III

Only scattered cloud broke the blue sky and the white walls of Askh were bathed in afternoon light. Half a mile from the city, Noran caught the glimpse of sunlight sparkling from

helms and speartips on the ramparts of the curtain wall but he
had no idea how many men still protected the city. Contrary
to Ullsaard's hope the gates were closed; there had been no
uprising in support of his return. There was more than duty
and high reward keeping the men of the First and the blackcrests at their posts, of that the herald was certain. Urikh was
not a man to inspire loyalty with speeches and charisma, so it
had to be fear that drove the soldiers to muster against the five
legions deploying for battle around the city. Whether that fear
was spun by spiteful words from Urikh – perhaps claiming that
Ullsaard would see the city sacked again and all within slaughtered – or had a more sinister origin was impossible to know.

"Desperate men fight hard," said Ullsaard, seeming to guess
Noran's thoughts.

"Perhaps if you offer mercy they will see sense," replied
Noran. "I would wager what little I have left that Urikh has
them convinced they have no alternative but to fight."

The king stared at the city, considering this advice. He nodded to himself and his lips moved in speech, though Noran
could not hear the soft words spoken. To anyone else it would
seem that Ullsaard had lost grip on his mind and talked to himself, but Noran knew that such a conclusion was not quite the
truth. He recognised the signs that the king was conversing
with the spirit of dead Askhos. Noran wondered what counsel
the ancient king gave, but whatever it was it appeared to tally
with Noran's recommendation.

"We will send embassy, and maybe there will be someone
at the gate willing to parley," said Ullsaard. Noran knew well
the look in the king's eyes and realised suggestion had been
taken as consent to perform the task.

"Are we sure they will accept the peace of parley?" said the
herald. "Nervous men do stupid things. I do not want to be
spitted by a bolt."

"That's always the risk," replied Ullsaard. "I'll come with you if you think it'll help."

"No, that would only make it more dangerous. Some smart legionnaire might decide that killing you would save us all a lot of grief. I will take Anasind and a guard of men."

"Thank you," said Ullsaard, surprising Noran. The king noticed his astonishment and shrugged. "What? Your words on the road have finally sunk in. I should not take your service or your friendship for granted. Don't make me change my mind."

"Of course not," replied Noran, bowing formally. "To hear praise spill from your lips is the greatest reward I seek, my King."

"Piss off, you sarcastic bastard," said Ullsaard, though his smile softened the words.

With a more sincere nod of the head, Noran left the king and sought out Anasind, who was overseeing the dispersal of the army around the walls. He passed on the king's intent to seek peaceful accord with the soldiers at the gates and soon was striding towards the city at the head of fifty men, the general walking beside him.

"Do you think they will listen, really?" asked Anasind.

"I actually have no idea," replied the herald, "but it must be worth the effort. Too much Askhan blood has been spilt over this city these last few years, it would be better to seek less violent resolution."

"Your eloquence is already showing," said Anasind, laughing. "What man could hear your entreaty and resist?"

"I cannot say for the effect on men, but I can assure you that it has served me well with women for many years," replied Noran, grinning broadly.

There was activity on the towers and rampart of the gatehouse as the delegation approached. Noran stopped within shouting distance, the legionnaires forming up around him and Anasind to provide protection against attack. Noran was always slightly envious of the dedication of the common soldier, willing to place himself in harm's way for their betters; it was a trait he did not share with them often.

Askh stretched across the Crown of a high hill and from his position Noran could see the summit stretching up beyond the walls; the Royal Mound that held the palace and the Grand Precincts of the Brotherhood. He wondered if Urikh stood looking back at him, perhaps surveying the army spreading like a gold and red sea around the city. Did Lakhyri stand atop the pinnacle of the Grand Precincts, sneering at Ullsaard's resistance?

The wind was growing chill and the clouds thickening overhead when a man with the crest of a second captain came to one of the embrasures on the rampart.

"I am Captain Geert, who are you?" he called down. He had the manner of the nobility, groomed for an officer's position in the First since he was a child. Noran was used to dealing with such men. "What do you want?"

"You have the privilege of addressing Noran Astaan, herald of Ullsaard, rightful king of Greater Askhor. We seek to resolve the dispute between the king and his son, and I can assure you that no retribution is intended towards those misled by the Prince's deceptions."

"Assurances from Ullsaard carry little coin in this city," Geert replied. "There are widows and orphans who remember the last time he came to Askh to seek an audience with a reigning king."

"Urikh seems to have found himself a zealous spokesman," Noran muttered to Anasind. He raised his voice in reply. "And the promises of Urikh are worth a piss in a pot against five legions, my friend. No harm is intended to the city or its people, but Ullsaard is not a man renowned for his patience. Open the gate and put aside resistance. Your dedication to your duty will be rewarded by the true king once he has settled matters with his usurper son."

"It takes one usurper to know another," said Geert.

"Perhaps you should talk to him, one military man to another," Noran suggested, taking a step back and looking to Anasind. "Make it clear just how fucked he is if he resists."

As Anasind took several steps forward Noran shivered, as though a cloud had passed across the sun and brought sudden coldness. The herald looked up and saw that the sky above the city was darkening, the clouds growing thicker and blacker as he watched. He shivered again, but it was not the temperature that caused it.

"Wait," he said, grabbing Anasind's arm to pull him back. "This is not good."

The general looked up, following the herald's gaze.

"A storm gathers, that is all," said Anasind. "It should not delay the assault."

Noran could tell that this was no natural storm. The thunderheads gathered quickly above, lightning starting to flicker through the darkness. There were quiet mutterings from the legionnaires around Noran.

"Silence!" barked Anasind.

"We should withdraw," said Noran. He could see Geert and the others on the gatehouse looking up as a deafening peal of thunder rumbled across the city.

"The storm will dampen the spirits of the defenders, it is of no concern," said Anasind.

"What storm have you seen that seems bound by the confines of a city's walls?" said Noran, pointing to dawnwards and duskwards. It appeared as though the dark clouds formed almost a perfect circle, following the boundary of Askh's curtain wall. They were slowly spinning, their heart centred above the Grand Precincts of the Brotherhood. "And why is there no rain?"

"I..." Anasind's voice failed as lightning forked down from the cloud, striking the summit of the Brotherhood's building. Half-blinded, Noran blinked hard and through the after-image of the strike he thought he saw a pale yellow sky filled with wisps of strange colour.

"We need to go," Noran insisted, though his legs did not seem to agree with his head as he stood rooted to the spot, staring at the spectacle unfolding over the city. Armour jingled as the legionnaires started to take steps backwards, giving voice to alarmed whispers despite their commander's order.

The herald watched as the Grand Precincts shimmered, a dark shadow spreading down its levels from where the lightning had struck. More flashes of light tore the sky, but they were like no lightning storm Noran had seen; each bolt streamed slowly from the whirling cloud, ripping through the air to leave blazing rents in reality.

The Grand Precincts were almost encased in blackness that pulsed with the fury of the storm raging around the summit of the Royal Mound. The creeping darkness seemed to seep across the divide, burrowing into Noran's chest, its freezing touch clasping around his heart. Flocks of birds streamed up from Askh, cawing and shrieking, accompanied by the howls of dogs and screams of women and children carried over the wall by the wind.

"Run," said Noran but his feet would not obey him.

Lightning of all colours flared across the sky, emanating from the Grand Precincts, not the clouds above it. When Noran's sight returned, the Grand Precincts had disappeared. In their place stood a seven-tiered ziggurat of weathered sandstone. The sky around it pulsed with ochre energy, drawing in the power of the storm. The sky churned, the blue of the summer giving way to yellow and green and purple, falling like a veil over the hideous temple.

The shadows engulfing the ziggurat started to fracture, spilling sickly yellow light from within. From its tip burst forth a stream of what at first appeared to be black smoke. In moments the billowing cloud resolved into many-limbed monsters formed of darkness and glinting eyes. Like spiderlings erupting from an obscene egg they spilled down the sides of the building, first dozens, then scores, then hundreds. Tentacles lashed as the monstrous beings propelled themselves down the mound and into the city.

"What are they?" yelled Anasind, eyes wide and wild.

"Just. Fucking. Run!" each word torn from Noran in a scream until he was finally able to follow his own advice.

IV

Fire burned through Ullsaard from his toes to the top of his head, painful and exhilarating at the same time. The Blood coursed through him, feeding on the tears between his reality and the otherworld. Through the shadow and cloud he saw the same starry gulf that surrounded Askhos' tomb and knew instinctively that he was looking through a gaping wound into the half-dreamt realm he had traversed with Lakhyri; the parallel existence of nightmares where Askhos still dwelt.

Breaking from his trance, the king looked to his left and right and saw the companies of his army turning to run. The men were filled with a primal, unreasoning terror.

"Stand and fight!" Ullsaard roared, unsheathing his sword.

He turned about, but there was nobody behind him – even the brave Thirteenth were set to flight by the horror unfolding across Askh. A hot wind washed down the hillside, bringing the stench of decay and death with it. Ullsaard choked on the stink.

You cannot fight them.

Ullsaard watched as the unnatural creatures clambered over the palace and descended from view into the city.

"I'm no coward," he said.

These are the Eulanui, the masters that Lakhyri serves. You cannot hope to defeat them. You cannot stay.

The noise of running men was as loud as the thunder that had instigated the rout. Ullsaard looked around desperately for any that would fight beside him, but we he was alone. He saw Donar and the standard bearer of the Fifth off to his left in a knot of legionnaires; the first captain was waving for his men to retreat.

There is no battle here. Do what you must to survive and restore your army. Take them with you or they will scatter to the winds.

Askhos' words sunk into Ullsaard's whirling thoughts. He had to turn rout into orderly retreat or all would be lost. The creatures that had emerged moved awkwardly on spindly limbs, and had yet to reach the wall of the city. There was yet time to restore order.

"Rally to me!" he bellowed, lifting his sword high. Ullsaard glared at the city for a heartbeat longer and then turned from it, running to catch up with Donar. "Rally to me and withdraw to the Wall! Rally to me!"

Hearing his king, Donar stopped and turned, aghast at what had happened. Grabbing a nearby musician by the collar of his breastplate, the first captain snarled something at the man. The legionnaire raised his horn to his lips and sounded the signal for rally and retreat, repeating the notes again and again. The order was taken up by others across the Fifth and spread through the legion and then to the others.

Horn calls reverberated all across the hills of Askhor, as Ullsaard reached Donar. Whether they would be heeded, the king did not know, but he had to trust that a lifetime of training and discipline would overcome blind fear.

This was not a battle he could win, but Ullsaard was certain he would have an army to fight another, when the time and place were right.

PARMIA, NALANOR
Early summer, 213th year of Askh

I

It was difficult for Ullsaard to remember how it was to be ignorant of the true nature of the world. For some years had he suffered the intrusions of Askhos into his thoughts and through veiled hints and threats from the dead king Ullsaard had gained some measure of understanding of the otherworld, or so he thought. Even prepared as he had been to the darker truth of the empire's existence, it was hard to reconcile a lifetime's surety against the unnatural events of Askh.

For his subjects, who had for generations been taught the very opposite of the truth, the realisation that there existed things beyond mortal comprehension bordered on cataclysm. A full third of his army had been unaccounted for when finally the legions had mustered again at Narun. There were those who had fled in unreasoning panic, and those who had deserted during the march duskwards to seek out family and perhaps to hide from the horror of what they had witnessed. It was only Ullsaard's uncompromising attitude and constant attention that stopped the army from fracturing altogether.

Even so, it was hard to offer encouragement to Anasind and the other officers in the face of what they had witnessed. Some coped better than others, but all were shaken by the experience. Faced with admitting the truth that the whole history of Greater Askhor was a lie and that he had misled his followers since taking the throne – an admission that would tear apart his fragile command – Ullsaard instead feigned ignorance when questioned.

Rumour had travelled even faster than the army, with deserters fleeing into the empire with outlandish tales. Narun had been in uproar, and stories were rife of the king's defeat at the capital, though details were few. Ships bearing these wild accounts had already fled hotwards along the Greenwater; each telling of the story magnifying the claims and the terrors that would be unleashed.

It had been wise to put more distance between his shocked soldiers and the site of their horror. Parmia offered some measure of sanctuary, being far enough away from Askh to allow order to be restored, yet close enough for the army to strike again if possible.

The king hoped that the routine of the daily march would reinforce the discipline of the legions, but as the twenty thousand men that had retreated from Askh made their camps around Parmia there was still an air of panic in the companies.

"It is too much for them to understand," Noran told Ullsaard in the evening after reaching the town. As on campaigns before, the king dwelt in a great pavilion at the heart of the Thirteenth's encampment, and the two of them discussed the situation over a sparse dinner.

"If I tell them the truth, do you think they would understand more?" replied Ullsaard, his tone making it clear that he did not think this was the case.

"It is an opportunity," said Noran. "Unless you can act quickly, this setback will become an utter defeat. You must speak out and spread the news as you wish it to be known. To leave this to the panicked chatter of others will serve no purpose. In a way, this is the best thing that could have happened."

"Really?" Ullsaard plucked a chicken leg from his plate and waved it like a baton as he spoke. "Creatures from a world we have been in ignorance of have invaded the empire and the king has been sent scurrying from his capital. That is good news?"

"At least the real foe is revealed," said Noran. "By speaking the truth you can rally the legions and the people against Lakhyri and Urikh. This is a war you have already been waging for years, and with the right telling it becomes a tale of a brave general who tried to rescue the empire from these inhuman foes."

"And admit that I have lied to everybody that trusted me along the way." Ullsaard took a bite from the chicken and continued with his mouth half-full. "Who would believe me now?"

"People do not believe what is true," Noran said. He took a mouthful of wine, studying the king. "You must make sure that they hear what you want them to hear. Your overthrow of Lutaar was for the good of the empire, because you suspected that he was betraying the people he was meant to rule. You are not an usurper – you are a liberator. Those who doubted your motives for becoming king now can be given good reason to back you."

Ullsaard considered these words as he finished his meal. Pushing away his plate, he leaned forward and rested his arms on the table.

"It is not enough to talk about the past," said the king. "Terror, real terror at something the people have never seen before, is going to engulf the empire. That will bring division, not unity. I must show that there is another way; that this is an enemy that can be defeated. Actions speak louder than any story I can tell."

"You put yourself in an impossible place, Ullsaard." Noran refilled his cup and offered wine to the king, who declined with a shake of his head. "Until you have wider support, what victory can you offer the people? Where will you fight?"

"Not Askh, that's for sure," said Ullsaard. He rubbed his chin. "I can't confront this enemy directly, not yet. I've no idea if we can even fight these creatures, from what you've told me and Askhos' hints."

"No word from the dead bastard on this?"

"Nothing since Askh. Anyway, we have to curb their power somehow, and the only way I can see for us to do that is through the Brotherhood. The precincts are linked to this somehow. The one here at Parmia was deserted before we arrived, so plainly the Brotherhood know something of what is happening. There must be those amongst their ranks that will join with me now that their true purpose is revealed."

"Make the Brotherhood the enemy?" Noran thought for a moment, lips pursed. "I like that idea. Talk of evil shadow creatures from another place will just feed the terror, but the Brotherhood is something tangible, something people can understand. Yes, I can see that working. Easier to turn against the black-robed bastard that has taxed you all of your life and made you labour for the empire than fight against some distant, unknowable threat."

"It is a fine thought, but I don't have the first idea how to make it happen," admitted Ullsaard. He had spent the last days working hard just to keep his army together, with no time or energy to spare for planning his next move.

"You can leave that to me," said Noran. The herald stood up, seeming purposeful. "A war against the Brotherhood is something I can foster. All you have to do is set the example."

"Oorandia," said the king. "The city has fallen in favour and power these last decades, but it still has the largest precinct outside of Askh. If the capital is beyond us, Oorandia will do. I'll have Anasind start the preparations for the march tomorrow. It's fine to have the general populace in uproar against the Brotherhood, but the first hearts I have to win are in my own army."

Noran left the king to his thoughts. It was not just his men Ullsaard had to motivate; he needed a focus for himself. It was perhaps a delusion to think that a strike against the Brotherhood would make any real difference in the war that was about to be waged, but it was something to concentrate on. Ullsaard knew himself well enough to admit he was better with something physical, something achievable to work towards. Seizing Oorandia would give him that purpose.

II

Though there could be no such thing as normality in light of the recent events, but the news that the king was preparing to move against the enemies of the empire brought some measure of stability to the army. The withdrawal from Askh had seen much baggage lost and so legionnaires and officers were kept busy foraging and commandeering what supplies they could for Ullsaard's fresh offensive. Noran spread the word that the Brotherhood were being held responsible for the nightmares unleashed at the capital, playing on old prejudices and rivalries that existed between the legions and the Brothers.

Two days after arriving at Parmia, Ullsaard was visited in his pavilion by Anasind. The general was uneasy and wasted no time in explaining the source of his distress.

"Our hotwards scouts report a column moving up the Greenwater road," said Anasind. "I am awaiting a confirmed report, but it has to be Harrakil and the legions that intended to ambush us. We are in no state for another battle."

"Given everything that's happened, I don't think we could get the men to fight another legion anyway," Ullsaard replied. He pulled his helm from where it had been hooked on the back of his chair and continued talking as he walked towards the entrance of the pavilion. "It would shatter any faith the men have in me if I ask them to raise their spears against a legion when it is plain there is a more pressing foe to face."

"What do you intend?" asked Anasind, falling in beside his king as Ullsaard stepped into the open. "We must head hotwards if we are to reach Oorandia. We cannot avoid a confrontation."

"We can't avoid the legions under Harrakil, but we can avoid a fight," Ullsaard said. "Have a guard assembled. I'll be heading out to meet him."

"He is Urikh's man," warned Anasind. "Remember what happened at Menesun."

"I can be very persuasive, when I try. Continue with the preparations for the march on Oorandia. I will be back before nightfall."

Seeing that the king would countenance no argument, Anasind selected a guard company from the Thirteenth and accompanied Ullsaard to the hotwards gate of the fortified camp. Despite Ullsaard's confidence, the general felt it necessary to issue one further warning as the contingent formed up outside the palisade.

"I may be the general, but this is your army, not mine," Anasind said, keeping his voice low so that the men could not hear his concern. "If you do not return, I cannot continue the campaign in your place. I am not you, Ullsaard."

"No, and that's to your credit," replied the king. He gripped Anasind's arm in a gesture of reassurance. "I'm coming back. Just have the army ready to march as soon as you can."

The weather was fair and the journey hotwards not unpleasant. Ullsaard enjoyed being away from the camp, though he was careful to guard his tongue as he chatted with his bodyguards. It was a little past the start of Noonwatch when they encountered kolubrid outriders. The patrol turned back towards the advancing column as soon as they set eyes upon the companies marching down the road, giving Ullsaard no chance to announce his presence or send word to Harrakil of his intent.

So it was that a force several thousand strong arrayed itself across the road ahead, spreading out where the highway crested a rise. Ullsaard counted the icons of three legions spread across the line and knew that he had made the right choice. Even if Harrakil could not be turned from Urikh, the other first captains might listen to the true king's demands.

No delegation came down the road, so Ullsaard was forced to march into the middle of the waiting legionnaires, as was no doubt Harrakil's intent. There was much activity when Ullsaard ordered his guard to hold their ground and walked the last two hundred paces alone; kolubrid messengers raced back and forth along the line and the king saw the first captains coming together under the icon of the Seventeenth.

"I seek words with Captain Harrakil," Ullsaard called out, stopping twenty paces from the front rank of the army. "You know me by my voice, so come out and talk to me like a man."

Three men emerged from the company and Ullsaard recognised them all: Harrakil, Naadlin and Canaasin. This gave him hope for he had fought alongside the latter two. He raised his hand in greeting, looking at each of the three men in turn.

"Fuck me, you really are still alive," said Naadlin, who was of the same generation as the king.

"You're an idiot for doubting it," replied Ullsaard, and his words were not delivered as a jest.

"I am General Harrakil," said the man at the centre of the trio. He was middle-aged, with a square jaw and dark eyes. "I take it from Captain Naadlin that you really are Ullsaard."

"You can keep your posturing, Harrakil, it isn't impressing me. If you want to keep that rank of general, which Urikh doesn't have the authority to give you, I would listen more than you speak right now."

"I am willing to hear your entreaty," said Harrakil, but his words lacked confidence. Unconsciously, the other two officers moved apart, leaving the general standing on his own.

"I am the king. I don't entreat, I fucking command. And you're a captain, so you fucking obey." Ullsaard waited until Harrakil reluctantly bowed his head. The king had some sympathy with the other man. Like many he had tied his fate to a lie and had been forced to follow it through to its conclusion. Ullsaard was reminded of his own actions when he had unwittingly been drawn into the scheme of Prince Aalun, which had pitched him onto the road leading all the way to this point. Even so, there had to be consequences.

"I am hoping that you've heard word of my muster at Parmia and are seeking to add your forces to my army, general," Ullsaard continued. "Is that the case?"

Harrakil glanced at Canaasin, who shrugged, and then at Naadlin, who had a lopsided smile on his face. The would-be general nodded once, acknowledging his circumstance, and raised a fist to his breastplate.

"If it pleases my king," said Harrakil, with a look of relief and gratitude. Ullsaard's opinion of the officer improved considerably at that moment; lesser men would have tried to negotiate or salve their wounded pride. "We have heard some disturbing tales on the road. We were not sure what course of action to take."

"The stories are probably true," said Ullsaard, earning looks of shock form the three men. "Urikh has got himself up to his neck in shit, and it's going to spill into the whole empire. I can't be looking over my shoulder at you three while I dig him out, so tell me plainly whether you want to follow me or not. I'm not in the mood for sanctions and finger-pointing right now, so if you aren't prepared to swear your oaths to me again, leave. I will think worse of you, but that's all the punishment you'll suffer. If you want to stay, then I'll take you at your word. Either way, you're all good captains and I need your men."

All three men nodded their agreement, overwhelmed by Ullsaard's forceful honesty.

"What do you wish us to do?" asked Canaasin.

Ullsaard was not sure of an answer immediately. It crossed his mind that three more legions might give him the strength to take the war directly to Askh, after all. He dismissed the thought. There were sound reasons for taking Oorandia first, both for the future strategy and as a boost to the shattered morale of his men.

"Have your legions make camp here," the king told them. "My army will be along in a day or two."

"You're heading hotwards?" Naadlin was clearly surprised. "I thought you'd be heading to Askh."

"Already tried that. It didn't work out too well," said the king. "This time I'm going to try something else."

From their expressions, Ullsaard could tell that the captains were not satisfied by this answer, but they were sensible enough not to push the point.

"You strike me as a sensible man, Harrakil," Ullsaard said. "And though my son is a vain, ambitious shit, he is not stupid. You can keep the title of general. For now. Don't give me reason to regret it."

"I will repay the honour, my king," said the commander of the Seventeenth, though Ullsaard sensed some disapproval from Naadlin and Canaasin.

"You were happy to accept his command when Urikh was in charge," the king said, glaring at the other two first captains, who looked away from his hard gaze. "You were willing to turn against the other legions, and I don't care what your reasons were. Don't think for a moment I'll forget that any time soon. I expect all three of you to work fucking hard to make that memory fade."

Ullsaard allowed his words to sink in before he turned away. Out of sight, the king grinned to himself. Three more legions gave him a fighting chance, he was sure. His buoyant mood evaporated quickly as he walked back towards his bodyguard.

He had been confident at the walls of Askh too, and that had not turned out as he had hoped.

III

Gelthius carefully placed his shield and spear on the ground and stepped back from them. The rest of his company – if two dozen bedraggled legionnaires could be called such – followed his lead. Around them, the bellows-bows of the kolubrid patrol were unwavering, ringing the men with bronze-headed shafts. The patrols' mounts bobbed their heads and hissed, scales glistening in the evening sun. The shields slung behind their intricate saddle-seats bore blue lacquer and silver bosses; men of the Third.

"Where are you heading?" asked the patrol's leader.

Gelthius glanced at Muuril, thinking it better that the question was not answered with a Salphorian accent.

"Narun, if it's your business," said the sergeant. This was greeted with coarse laughs. "What's wrong with that?"

"You picked a fucking bad time to desert, Twenty-first scum," said the patrol captain. "And you're definitely heading the wrong fucking way if you want to stay out of trouble."

"We're Thirteenth," said Loordin. He nodded down at the discarded wargear. "We was just borrowing those for a while."

"I'll bet," said the captain. He shouldered his bellow-bow and the other riders relaxed too.

"It's true," said Muuril. "In fact, I'm the King's Companion. We got split from him at Menesun."

"Is that fact?" The captain leaned over in his saddle, amused, looking at the ragtag group. "And you've walked all this way from Ersua to find him, have you?"

"Pretty much," said Loordin. "We got a bit delayed on the way, you see."

"I'm not sure what to do with you," the captain said as he straightened.

"Is he still alive?" asked Gelthius. The captain's words had provided no answer to the question that had been in every man's mind since they had set out seen Ullsaard dragged out of Menesun. "The king, I mean."

"Which one?" joked one of the riders.

"Ullsaard, of course, you fucking arseholes," said Muuril. The patrol raised their weapons again as the sergeant stepped towards the captain. "Do you know if King Ullsaard is alive or not?"

"Yes, Ullsaard's still alive. He's just about to leave Parmia," said the captain. Gelthius was not sure whether he welcomed the news or not, but there were smiles and laughs from many of the others. The patrol leader waved for his men to back off. "You got here just in time, I reckon. You must be Thirteenth, for sure."

"Why's that?" said Gelthius.

"Haven't you heard? Askh has been overrun by giant fucking spiders, the Brotherhood want to rule the world and the whole empire is falling to pieces. Only men from the Thirteenth would be fucking stupid enough to walk into that and be happy."

IV

The return of the Menesun survivors had brought a talismanic boost to Ullsaard's army, not least to the king himself. Noran had watched as Ullsaard had greeted each of the twenty-five men with a salute and a shake of the hand. They had been led around the camp of the Thirteenth like conquering heroes, receiving a personal triumph that matched in enthusiasm any received by a general returning to Askh, if not equalling such parades in grandeur. Ullsaard seemed especially pleased by their arrival; more than could be explained by an appreciation of such an example of loyalty and determination.

"It must be because they are just as stubborn as you," the herald remarked over a cup of wine in the king's pavilion. "You think you can turn all of your army into men like that."

"No, not in the time I have," replied Ullsaard. "That sort of pig-headed loyalty comes from years of shared battles. But you are right, I am very happy to see them alive. Almost as happy as they are to see me, it seems."

"Do not try to tell me it is for sentimental reasons," said Noran.

"It is, in part." Ullsaard shrugged and smiled. "Men like Muuril are rare. And Gelthius? He was a landship slave when I found him, and now he is probably the match of any second captain under my command. It genuinely makes me happy knowing they are still alive."

"And yet?"

"Their return has made me realise something, which I'd forgotten," said the king. "Put your faith in men and they'll put it in you." He shook his head. "No, more than that; much more than that. Adversity makes heroes out of the most normal of men. Those warriors have been at my side through the worst times I have had. They grumbled, they moaned, and even though they must have felt betrayed at Menesun, they came looking for me because they thought that I would lead them right. It's not that I know with men like that following me I can't fail. With men like that following me, I can't let *myself* fail. I have to do everything in my power to repay that loyalty and trust. I am the fucking king, my friend, and the empire looks to me."

"All very nice, but what does that really count for? You always say that actions are better than words. What are you going to do to prove that to everyone?"

"I'm going to save the empire. And you're going to help me."

"Of course I am," Noran said with a sigh. "And how am I going to do that, this time?"

"Sorry, but you'll have to go away again," said Ullsaard. "If we are going to stand any chance against those creatures Lakhyri has summoned, we're going to need something more than just flesh and bronze. We're going to need something much more than that. Pack for a long journey, you'll be heading to Maasra."

"Maasra? What is so strong in Maasra?"

Ullsaard smiled. The king's good humour had the opposite effect on Noran. The herald dreaded the king's reply, and was not disappointed.

"Nemuria," said Ullsaard. "I need you to go to Nemuria."

Shuddering as something darker than the night shadows stalked across the gardens, Luia closed the shutter and turned back to her sister. Meliu half-lay on a couch, her head resting on Ullnaar's shoulder.

"She wishes to hear nothing you have to say," said Ullnaar, clasping his mother's hand.

"Stop being childish," snapped Luia. "This is no time to be pretending that you cannot hear me."

"There is nothing that comes from your lips that is not a lie or spite," murmured Meliu. "It was the same when we were young."

"All is not yet lost," said Luia, sitting opposite her sister. "Ullsaard still lives."

"I am sure he has no thanks for your part in his escape," said Ullnaar.

"I am sorry," said Luia, folding her hands in her lap.

"Sorry?" Meliu straightened and tucked a stray lock of hair behind her ear. "You helped Urikh overthrow Ullsaard and you brought these hideous… these hideous *creatures* to Askh. There is no apology you can offer to make amends for that."

"No, I suppose not."

Luia fell silent for a moment, hearing the telltale skitter and scratch of a Eulanui moving past the window. She tried not to think about what had happened since their arrival but there was little else to occupy her mind; an existence spent for the most part hidden away with Urikh in her son's apartments. Occasionally Lakhyri would summon the pretender king to make a proclamation, but the noble and wealthy courtiers dragged in to hear such pronouncements cared not that the words came from one of the Blood. They knew clearly who held the reins of power in Askh these days, and it was not Urikh.

The Eulanui – Luia had heard the high priest use the name on several occasions – were like a stain on the city. They prowled the streets and alleys just as they prowled the corridors of the palace. There were tales that people were going missing, but Luia did not know what had happened to them. Urikh was terrified, though he could not admit it. He and Luia had been standing at a window when the Eulanui had arrived, and watched in horror as the ancient temple had manifested in the grounds of the Grand Precincts. That terrible edifice towered over the palace, and the storm that had brought it forth seemed to have raged forever. The city had become a place of hot winds and energy-sapping dryness, and every night Luia had nightmares filled with the shadow-clothed creatures that had come to possess the world of men.

"You do not have to stay," Luia said, when the Eulanui had passed. She did not know whether the creatures could hear as a human hears, but they certainly understood Lakhyri's entreaties and praise. For all she knew they could look into the deepest part of her mind but she was past caring about herself. If her thoughts would betray her, she would face her fate like the queen she always knew she deserved to be.

"The city is sealed," said Ullnaar. "If the gates were not barred, fear of the things that haunt the streets are imprisonment enough."

"Not all passage is barred," Luia explained. "Members of the Brotherhood come and go, and there are still some patrols sent out to keep watch for attack. We have allies that would see both of you safe."

"Allies?" Meliu raised an eyebrow and Luia understood her sister's doubt.

"A captain in the First who has made acquaintance with my bed more than once," the queen admitted. "And will do so again if he sees you safely outside the walls of Askh."

"You trust him?" said Ullnaar. "What does Urikh think of this?"

"Urikh does not know," said Luia. "Lakhyri has him locked in perpetual dread. We can no more look to Urikh to solve our problems than we can anybody else."

"Ullsaard will do something," Meliu said. Her loyalty was sickening at times, like a puppy's adoration for its master, but on this occasion Luia kept her scorn inside.

"Yes, Ullsaard will do something, but until then we must look to ourselves to ease our woes."

"You did not answer my question," said Ullnaar. "Do you trust this man?"

"I trust that his cock hungers for my kind attentions and his desire to fuck a queen is undiminished by the experience of it," Luia said briskly. "This evening I promised him greater delights than he has yet experienced, in return for conveying you to safety."

"If he has the means of escape, it must be more than lust for your cunt that keeps him in this city," said Ullnaar.

"There are other reasons for his loyalty," Luia replied, ignoring the jibe implicit in her nephew's tone, "his three children and two wives being the greatest. There are some that have abandoned their families given opportunity, but many who return to their duties, hoping that their service will see their families spared whatever horrors others will face."

"If it is your bed that seals his compliance, you must remain to give payment," said Meliu. "I cannot see why he will let you get away with debt outstanding."

"I am not going," said Luia. She had made the decision the previous night, as she had suffered the captain's clumsy pawing and pounding. "It is for the two of you only that I have negotiated passage. You must be ready at Gravewatch, when he will oversee a caravan of supplies entering the city. Another group goes out to bring food from the farms, and in one of their wagons you will be hidden from discovery."

"Why?" said Meliu, suspicious as ever of her older sister's motives. "Do not pretend it is out of feelings for me and Ullnaar."

Luia bit back an insult, hurt by the accusation. She had known Meliu would not trust her but it did not matter. Seeing her sister and nephew safe was her sole concern that night.

"Urikh needs me, so I must remain behind," she said, ignoring the question. "Nobody else will protect him."

"You think you can protect him from these invaders?" Ullnaar laughed bitterly. "Have you some power not yet demonstrated?"

Luia offered no reply. It was not from the Eulanui that Urikh needed protection, nor from Lakhyri. The greatest threat to Urikh's future was currently Urikh himself. Luia wanted to be free of distraction so that she could concentrate on his well-being.

"I will come at Gravewatch, be ready," she said standing up. "When you are out of the city, you should head for Enair. Pretaa will take you in."

As Luia strode towards the door, Meliu called for her to wait. She turned to find Meliu on her feet, tears in her eyes.

"Keep yourself safe, sister," said Meliu. "And thank you."

The urge to return and embrace Meliu was almost overwhelming. Since childhood they had been opposites and the years had widened the divide, but they were still sisters. Urikh was too obsessed with himself to be any comfort and Ullsaard had considered Luia little more than an inconvenience once she had been the first to provide him with an heir. The thought that she might seek comfort in the arms of Meliu, even just for a moment, burned inside Luia, but she could not bring herself to indulge that weakness. If she held her sister now, would she be able to let go and see her removed from the palace? Would her sister's love provide solace from the catastrophe her son had unleashed? She could not afford to find out; Urikh and the empire depended upon her being strong.

"Just be ready," said Luia. She left with more haste than dignity, before she changed her mind.

OORANDIA, NALANOR
Midsummer, 213th year of Askh

I

The smoke rising from the centre of Oorandia and the cheering mobs that greeted the king as he advanced through the suburbs of the city were testament to whatever it was Noran had done before leaving for Nemuria. On reaching the Brotherhood precinct he found the doors broken from their hinges and the slit windows blackened with soot. The smoke came from a fire at the centre of the square flanked by the precinct and the homes of the local worthies.

Legionnaires held back small crowds at each of the intersections leading into the square and the shouts of the inhabitants continued to decry the Brotherhood.

"Find out what they've been burning, and secure what's left of the precinct," Ullsaard told Meesiu, whose Third Legion was accompanying the king. Anasind and the rest of the army were forming a cordon around the city. "Try to find any intact records."

The clamour from the protesting citizens was such that Ullsaard crossed the square to the nearest street and ordered his soldiers to let him through. The crowd was a few dozen strong and backed away as the captain leading the company holding the road barked for respect to be shown to the king.

"Go back to your homes," Ullsaard said. "Announcements will be made in the morning."

"What about our money?" one toothless old worker demanded, waving something at Ullsaard. "The precinct vault's all locked up."

"What have you got?" said Ullsaard. He stepped forward and took the small piece of bronze the man was holding. At first he thought it was a coin, but not any denomination he had seen before. On one side was the image of a Brotherhood precinct, rising up on four tiers. It was then that Ullsaard recognised the markings on the other side – a tax token. They were used by legionnaires in lieu of real coin whilst in camp, and could be exchanged at Brotherhood precincts to claim pension every quarter-year. When a legionnaire was signed to retirement he was given enough tokens for ten years.

"Where did you get this?" Ullsaard demanded, as the old man made a grasp for the token. "Who gave it to you?"

"You did!" someone called from further into the crowd, followed by laughter.

"A Brother gave it to me, as sure as you're standing here," said the old man. "Bounty of the king, he told us."

"The Brothers weren't honouring it, and when one of them confessed that they had deposed the king, we took matters into our own hands," said a short woman who was elbowing her way to the front. She bobbed awkwardly in front of the king and looked up at him hopefully. "We're going to get our money, right?"

The mood of the people was already starting to turn sour as Ullsaard looked over the crowd. They looked at him with a mixture of expectation, concern and surprise.

"Yes, you'll get your money," Ullsaard told them, knowing that to say anything else was to invite a riot, which he had not the inclination to deal with. "I am here to administer the payments. Return to your homes and wait until you are called for. This is Greater Askhor, where we do things in timely and orderly fashion; I'll not have you scrabbling around like Salphorian pigs in shit."

Though they were being told they would have to wait, the people received this speech with a ragged cheer and some clapping. Only an Askhan could take pride in bureaucracy if the alternative was to be considered a barbarian.

Ullsaard handed the token back to the old man and sent him on his way with a smile and a slap on the shoulder.

"Make sure they disperse," he told the watch captain as he returned to the square. He spied Anasind with Meesiu and strode over to the pair of officers. They fell silent at his approach.

"What can you tell me about pension tokens?" the king asked his general. Anasind smiled and shrugged.

"Noran said it was best not to bore you with the details. Anyway, we raided the Brotherhood stores in Parmia and had the camp forges make up some more. I gave Noran thirty men as couriers, heading all over the empire with the same story. The king has ordered a payment to every citizen in the empire. People are already worried about the removal of the governors, and this gives them more to get aggravated about. Noran thought this would make the people more inclined to believe the Brotherhood were the enemy." Anasind jabbed a thumb towards the soot-stained precinct. "Never stand between a citizen and his tax rebate."

"He's a cunning fucker," said Ullsaard, smiling and shaking his head. "How many of these tokens are there?"

"Each man we sent out had about three thousand, give or take," said Anasind. "Noran thought that once word started to spread, folks wouldn't wait for the tokens. Across every province, the Brotherhood are about to become everybody's target."

"And did Noran suggest how we would fulfil the promise he made? The same mob that turned on the Brotherhood will be coming for us if we don't settle up."

"He said if your coffers were too shallow to hold the balance, at this time of the year every Brotherhood precinct should be bulging with the half-year taxes."

"Excuse me, my king," said Meesiu. "If there's some money to be handed out, my legion hasn't been paid since we left Salphoria."

Ullsaard turned back to Anasind, brow creased.

"The men haven't had their coin since the winter? Did you forget or something?"

"There is little coin to give," said the general. "You left me in the middle of Salphoria with winter closing in. I cannot create tin or silver from thin air."

"You risked desertion and mutiny all the way to Askh. I know that a legionnaire will march if he is waiting for his pay, but how did you get them to follow you for so long?"

"I made them a promise in your name," said Anasind. He drew himself up and met the king's gaze without wavering. "I gave the men rights to final campaign."

"You offered them all pension rights at the end of the fighting?" It was another of Askhos's old strategies to wean the legions away from their original tribal commanders; to offer all pay and privileges of a pensioned soldier at the end of the current campaign, regardless of time served. It was a drastic measure that meant whole legions would retire at the same time, and one Ullsaard was sure he would regret.

"It is amazing what men will do, what they will face," continued Anasins, "if they think the biggest payday they have ever seen is at the end of it."

"We can't lose," said Meesiu, earning himself a scowl from the king. "Look at it this way, king. If we beat Urikh and those spirit-monsters, you'll be more than happy to reward the men who did it for you. And if you lose, you're not going to be around to suffer the consequences."

II

Opening his eyes, Ullsaard heard voices at the entrance to the pavilion. Lying on his cot he listened as the sentries explained that the king was asleep and should not be disturbed. He heard Anasind claim that Ullsaard would wish to be woken, and the legionnaires submitted to the general's will. Pushing himself from the bed, Ullsaard wrapped his kilt around his waist and belted it before stepping through the curtained doorway into the main chamber.

Anasind was just entering and stopped as he saw the king emerge from the bedchamber.

"A visitor for you," said the general, stepping aside to allow another to enter.

It was Allenya, a dark blue shawl around her shoulders and head, followed swiftly by two legionnaires hauling a travelling chest between them.

"Husband," she said formally.

"Wife," Ullsaard replied, his happiness at seeing her punctured by her cold demeanour.

They said nothing more as the legionnaires placed the chest in one of the side chambers and left. Anasind darted a worried glance at his king, sensing that this was not the reunion hoped for when Ullsaard had despatched a company to Apili to bring Allenya to the army. Ullsaard nodded his gratitude and the general departed.

"We have much to talk about," said Allenya.

"Let me get you a drink," said Ullsaard, moving to a table of jugs and cups alongside one side of the chamber. "Wine? Or I can have something hot brought from the kitchens."

"I am not thirsty."

When Ullsaard had left Apili he had been destined for Askh and a confrontation with Urikh. He had hoped to send for Allenya to join him at the capital once the matter had been dealt with. He had also hoped that the distance that had come between them following Erlaan's attack would have been narrowed by separation, but it appeared that this was not the case.

"It is safer for you to be with the army," Ullsaard said, wanting to breaking the silence. He had said as much in the letter he had sent with the soldiers. "If Erlaan returned or Lakhyri learnt of your whereabouts it would be dangerous at Apili."

"Your concern for my wellbeing is welcome," said Allenya. "I am tired."

Despite her words, Allenya made no move from where she was standing just a few paces from the pavilion entrance. Ullsaard guessed her meaning.

"I shall have another cot brought in, if you do not wish to share my bed tonight," he said, heart heavy.

"I would not wish to inconvenience you," said Allenya. Her flat tone was infuriating, but Ullsaard kept his temper in check, knowing that harsh words would not help to close the gulf that had opened between them.

"There is nothing I can say that I have not already said." Ullsaard moved to his large campaign chair and sat down. He gestured to one of the smaller chairs beside it. "Please, come and sit and talk to me like a wife to a husband."

"If that is your wish," she said, taking a few steps forwards. "You are my husband and king, after all."

"Stop it," said Ullsaard, unable to bear the accusation in her eyes any longer. "Tell me what is wrong and I will attempt to make it up to you."

"You really do not know?" Allenya dropped the veil of enforced formality and clenched her fists at her sides. "I spoke to you of being abandoned and hopeless, and what was your response? You left Apili without me. You promised I would never be from your side again and yet only a day passed before you were gone. What am I to think of that?"

"I did not know that we would be apart for long," Ullsaard replied, leaning towards her in the chair. "You heard what happened at Askh? I am glad you were not there to see such a thing."

"Glad?" Allenya's voice rose in anger, causing Ullsaard to wince at his choice of words.

"I brought you here, didn't I? To be with me."

"An afterthought, I am sure. To keep me safe and ensure that your enemies do not use me against you."

"Not at all," said Ullsaard. The accusation stung because there was some truth to it, but Ullsaard knew that it was desire for his wife's companionship and concern for her safety that had moved him to act. He stood up and approached Allenya with arms open, palms held up in pleading. "I need you with me, my love."

"Once more your words and deeds say different things." Allenya took a step back, away from the advancing king. "When dawn comes and your lust has been satisfied, will your whim change? Will you decide that an army on the march is no place for a queen?"

"No!" Ullsaard took quick steps and grabbed Allenya's arm as she tried to avoid his embrace. The shawl slipped to the floor from her shoulders. "This is my final campaign and I need you beside me."

"What do you mean?" Allenya ceased struggling against his iron grip. "Why would this be your last campaign?"

"Because I don't expect to win," Ullsaard answered, his voice a whisper. Speaking the words brought clarity to the fear that had been gnawing at him since the catastrophe at Askh.

"Even if I defeat Urikh and the foul monsters he has enslaved himself to, I cannot be king any longer."

"If you lose, it will be because you are dead," said Allenya. A tear slid down her cheek and she raised a hand to his face. "I cannot bear the thought of it."

Ullsaard lifted his hand and rested it on her cheek. He bowed his head and placed his brow against hers as she stepped into his embrace.

"I need you," he said. "I have never been so afraid; afraid for you, afraid for the empire and all of us."

"But you are still the king, and the strongest of us all," said Allenya. "I am sorry. I thought to quash fear with coldness, but I cannot sit in judgement for your deeds. It is the thought that I will lose you that keeps me awake at night, not dreams of the empire burning. The empire will lose only a king, I will lose a husband. You do not have to be king. I am sure we could slip away, perhaps head coldwards or duskwards, far from the evil of Lakhyri."

"If I were such a man, you would not love me," said Ullsaard. Allenya sobbed and buried her face against his bare chest. "Fuck the rest of the empire, but I have friends and family that will be killed or made slaves if I fail."

Pulling back, Allenya smiled through her tears. She stroked a hand down Ullsaard's arm and looked at him with an affection he had not known for some time.

"Let us sleep," she said. "Tomorrow brings its own challenges, but so does every dawn bring new hope."

"All I can do now is wait," said Ullsaard. "I have set a fire in the empire to burn down the Brotherhood, but I don't know if the flames will spread. For the moment, there is nothing else I can do."

"What is your intent?"

"Urikh and Lakhyri will know where I am soon enough, and they will come for me."

"Then we should move on."

"No, I want them to come. I will draw them onto me and spare the rest of the empire their cruelty while they seek to dispose of me. In fact, I'm counting on it."

"You offer yourself up as bait? Is that wise, my love? Do not look for death, even though you are prepared for it."

Ullsaard pulled his wife close again, smelling the fragrance in her hair and feeling the warmth of her against his skin.

"I've always tried to stay one step ahead of the pyre, but wisdom is the bitch of desperation. These otherworld bastards are going to learn that desperate men make for dangerous enemies."

NEMURIAN STRAIT, MAASRA
Midsummer, 214th Year of Askh

I

The wind had not yet turned to coldwards and summer's grip still held firm along the coast of Maasra. A break in the cloud allowed the weakening morning sun to reach the bireme Noran had hired two days before. The noble moved to the port rail, out of the shade of the mainsail to catch what warmth he could. From this position he could see out across the Nemurian Strait to the smoke-shrouded horizon. He had not mentioned his intent to land on Nemuria when he had approached the ship's captain, Haukin Maanam, but he had heard that Maanam was something of a maverick and would dare the ban. Noran had a fortune to spend, after all, to persuade the captain that it would be worth his while.

That would be only the first obstacle to overcome. Noran was not convinced that even if Maanam was willing, the Nemurians would allow any human ship to approach their island. There was, Noran decided, a good chance that they would be sunk or attacked or otherwise stopped from reaching the opposite shore.

It did not matter, the simple truth was that the Nemurians might prove vital to Ullsaard's defence of the empire and

Noran was not about to turn back just because circumstances might turn difficult, even lethal.

Noran remained at the rail while the crew busied themselves on the ship and quay, casting off the thick ropes and hauling at the lines of the sail to bring it into trim. Three men leaned on the tiller arm as the ship started underway, guiding the bireme away from the dock.

Wondering if he would see any part of the empire again, Noran glanced back across the ship to Askhira, and the sight jogged a memory of when Ullsaard had been making his claim for the Crown and Askhira had been home to his fleet. In the end the fleet had been nothing but a huge feint, drawing the defenders of Askh away from the Wall to the coast.

Noran was forced to consider that his mission to Nemuria was also a diversionary tactic. Certainly there was little enough chance of success, but his presence in Askhira would surely have been noted and reported by the Brotherhood. He had laid low as best he could, but the Brothers had ways of knowing things, just as they had strange ways of communicating across the length and breadth of the empire. It was entirely possible that Ullsaard had no confidence at all that his emissary to the Nemurians would succeed, but that the act of trying to establish contact with the Nemurians was part of a greater plan, timed to inconvenience Urikh and his unnatural allies.

It reminded the nobleman of how much Ullsaard had changed. He remembered a time on another ship, on the Greenwater, when Ullsaard had been asking about the nature of politics. A smile crept across Noran's lips as he also remembered Ullsaard's pledge to stay out of politics altogether. It made Noran reconsider everything he had known about the man who had befriended him in Askh so many years ago.

Ullsaard had been made first captain of his beloved Thirteenth and had come to Askh to receive orders from Lutaar, and to receive the praise of his sponsor, Aalun. Noran had no doubt that Ullsaard had been genuine at that time, and his claims to have achieved his ambitions truthfully spoken, but all the while he had unknowingly been a child of the Blood. How much had the Blood been responsible for Ullsaard's rise to power? Had it been driving him for his whole life, and secretly affecting those around him, projecting his innate power in a way that others could feel but not identify?

A quiet word from a sailor moved Noran away from his place at the rail, so that rope could be stowed. The nobleman moved to the aft deck, where Haukin Maanam was overseeing his crew. The captain was about the same height as Noran, and a little younger. His black hair was cropped short – unusually short for a sailor, Noran thought – and his open shirt revealed a tattoo of a reclining harlot across his lightly haired chest. She held a snake in her arms, which wound up around Manaam's throat and under his ear, so that its forked tongue seemed to lick at his right eye from the captain's cheek. It was an impressive piece of body art, and was matched by numerous smaller images across his arms and stomach.

"Fair wind for coldwards," the captain said, glancing up at the sky. "We'll make the Askhan coast in four days, I reckon."

Noran was not sure whether to speak now about their true destination, or wait until they were further out to see. If he spoke now, Maanam could easily turn the ship about and put back into Askhira; if he waited too long they would waste time heading coldwards and be forced to travel back against the wind to reach Nemuria. He was not sure whether days were so tight yet, but Noran had no desire to eke out this journey for longer than necessary.

"Captain, there is something I need to discuss with you," said Noran, speaking quietly. "Concerning our route, I mean."

"Really?" There was a disconcerting half-smile on Manaam's lips. "What would that be?"

"I apologise, but I may have misled you somewhat when I told you it was my intent to travel to Askhor." Noran found a piece of dirt under the nail of his right middle finger. He fetched out his knife and began to pick at it intently, avoiding the gaze of the ship's captain.

"Is that right?" said Maanam. "And why would you feel the need to, er, mislead me about our destination?"

Noran ceased his fidgeting and looked the captain in the eye. The nobleman took a deep breath, preparing himself for scorn or derision.

"I need to get to Nemuria," he whispered, glancing at the men manning the tiller.

"I see," Maanam said slowly. The captain looked to his left and right conspiratorially and nodded. "Well, we best go down to my cabin for the rest of this discussion, hadn't we?"

"I'm willing to offer you triple the rate..." Noran realised that Maanam had not objected outright. "Of course, down in your cabin. Yes, after you."

He followed Maanam down to the main deck and then under the aft deck. The captain's cabin was located right at the stern of the ship, running almost the full width of the ship. A cot was attached to the port hull and a table and chairs affixed to the floor on the starboard side. A chest of drawers formed a chart table in the middle, but there were no maps on display.

Along the aft bulkhead, small windows overlooked the white froth of wake cutting through the waves. Peering out, Noran saw the coastal buildings of Askhira almost directly behind them, the bay of the harbour curving to the left and right along the shore. It struck him as odd that they were putting out directly into the strait for what was normally a run along the coast to Askhor.

Realisation dawned as Noran thought about this and Manaam's casual attitude to the change of plans.

"You already knew we were going to Nemuria!" he said accusingly, turning to confront the captain.

Maanam shrugged, laughed and leaned against the edge of
the table.

"It was not the greatest of mysteries to solve," said the captain.
"When I told you the price for heading up-coast, you didn't
even haggle a tin about it. That told me that you were expecting
to pay a lot more than you were saying. Also, I can tell by your
luggage that you've come from Okhar. Nobody travels all the
way from Okhar to Askhira to get to Askhor; you travel right
up the Greenwater and go via Narun. The only place worth
going to from here is Nemuria."

"I stand humbled by your deductions," grumbled Noran. "Although, I must point out that only a fool would travel to Narun at
the moment. All right, but I have to tell you that I am not planning
at stopping at the one-mile limit. I mean to go to Nemuria itself."

"That will certainly cost you extra, but you can afford it, I'm
sure." Manaam's smile faded and he tapped a finger to his chin
for a few moments. "The thing that will cost the most, though,
is having to move away from Askhira."

"I don't understand," said Noran. "I do not expect you to
wait for my return. You are free to do what you wish once you
drop me off on the island."

"I have something to show you," said Maanam, nodding towards the door.

The captain led Noran back to the gangway outside his cabin
and produced a long bronze key from a pouch at his belt. He
opened a small door to their right and ducked inside the room.
Noran followed him in. What he discovered caused the nobleman to straighten in surprise, crashing his head against a deck
beam above.

"Shit!" Noran snarled, clapping a hand to the back of his head. "What is he doing here?"

Sat on the pile of blankets, a small stool with a candle stub on it beside him, was a young man in the black robes of the Brotherhood. There was a thick bruise on his temple and his right eye was blackened. He looked up at their entrance, the slim volume of the Book of Askhos open in his lap. The Brother's good eye opened wider as he recognised Noran.

"That's the one," the Brother exclaimed. He tried to get to his feet, but Maanam laid a hand on his shoulder and kept him down. "That's Noran Astaan! Captain, I will forget my rough treatment and you will be richly rewarded if you return to Askhira immediately."

"Meet Brother Hasdriak, an unintentional stowaway," said Maanam. "The funny thing is, he came to me yesterday, warning that some agent of the rebellion might approach me and ask for passage to Nemuria. He reminded me of the ban and said I would be well paid for any information."

"I see that you have already decided not to accept his offer," said Noran. "Thank you."

"Never liked the Brotherhood, and certainly don't like them without Governor Kulrua keeping them in check." As he spoke, Maanam grabbed the collar of Hasdriak and hauled him to his feet. Noran saw that the Brother's hands were bound with thin rope, and the pages of the Book of Askhos shook in his nervous grip. "I just needed to make sure it was you he was talking about."

Pushing Hasdriak in front of him, Maanam marched up to the deck, Noran a couple of steps behind. Those crew that could see what was happening stopped in their work to watch Maanam guide Hasdriak to the rail. The captain drew a knife from his belt and sawed through the Brother's bindings.

"That's Askhira back there," said Maanam, pointing aft at the town that was now nothing more than a smudge of white against the green and grey of the coastline. "Have fun getting back."

Noran watched as Maanam tipped the Brother over the rail, Hasdriak's cry of fear ending with a loud splash. The Nobleman stepped up to the rail and saw Hasdriak floundering amongst the waves as he swept aft, his heavy robes dragging him down. Moving aftwards, Noran continued to keep his eye on the flailing man, who managed to wriggle out of his black robes, but was being repeatedly forced under by wave after wave.

"He cannot swim," Noran said, turning back to Maanam.

"Then he shouldn't have set foot a ship, should he?" replied the captain. "Bastard Brotherhood have no business on my deck."

Noran looked again for the drowning man, but saw nothing save the blur of his robes drifting further and further astern.

"How much does that cost me?" he asked, when Maanam stepped up beside him.

"Pretty much everything you've got," said the captain. "You're the one who doesn't want bringing back, so we'll just keep those chests of yours, eh?"

Looking around, Noran saw the hardened expressions of the crew; not one of them seemed shocked or saddened by the callous murder of the Brother.

"When my informants told me you were a maverick, did they, by any chance, actually mean to use the word 'pirate'?" Noran asked, his voice a whisper.

"And smuggler," Maanam replied with a grin. "Good job you came to me first. Who the fuck else is going to be able to take you across to Nemuria without the Brotherhood and the scalies knowing, eh?"

II

They had turned hotwards after another hour, taking the wind onto the port beam and making good speed down the Maasra coast. Maanam informed Noran that the approach was best made at dusk, from hotwards. The weather seemed set fine for the rest of the day, and so Noran dozed on the aftdeck in a folding, canvas-backed chair that Maanam brought out of his cabin for the nobleman's use.

When the sun was not far above the dark line of the coast, the captain ordered the ship to come about, to make their run-in towards the Nemurian coast.

"The ban hasn't really changed anything," Maanam explained as they made good speed across the waves, the main sail full and the men at the tiller holding hard on a course that seemed set for the centre of the smoking isle ahead. The smoke of the volcanoes made silhouettes against the dark blue of the approaching night, and Noran could see how one might easily slip into the shadowy fog unseen. "There's been folks hiding out in coves and caves on Nemuria since before our great-great-grandfathers were born."

"You are not Maasrite though, are you?" said Noran. Despite his name, Maanam was too tall and well-built to hail from Maasra.

"Mother was, so learnt the trade from her father," replied Maanam. "Other half of me is Ersuan. Father was a brick trader. Boring as anything, he was. Spent all my time on grandpa's ship, and learnt the little nooks and crannies on both coasts where the Brotherhood and the scalies don't look."

"So you've done this a lot, yes?" Noran was feeling more reassured about the unsavoury company he had accidentally chosen.

"A few times," said Maanam. He took a few steps towards the main deck and shouted orders to the crew to bring the mainsail to half-mast. When he returned, Noran noticed the tension in the captain's face.

"How many times?" the nobleman asked. "How many times to Nemuria?"

"A few," growled Maanam. "Don't piss your kilt, I'll get you there safe as you like. Of course, what you do when you get there is your business. We normally leave stuff we don't want found and come back for it later. Nobody ever stays there; least, none that intends to."

"What does that mean?"

"You can be as wily as you like, sometimes the Nemurians might catch you inside the one-mile limit."

"And what happens then?"

"I haven't got a clue," said Maanam. "Nobody's ever come back to tell, have they? You just go missing."

"Or perhaps they just got lost and swept out to the ocean," said Noran, but he knew he was grasping for straws of comfort. Maanam did not deign to give a response to such speculation.

They sailed hotwards, the dusk on their left enough to light the waters, but just barely. No lamps were lit and the crew moved quietly about their tasks, no voices raised in command.

"Coming up to the one-mile limit, I reckon," said Maanam, scratching his ear. The dark, jutting rocks of the Nemurian coast were highlighted ahead by a ruddy light reflected off surf and spray. Maanam looked left and right, perhaps gauging his position from the peaks that disappeared into the night sky. Further inland some of the mountains were topped with halos of fire, lighting the clouds from below.

It was stunning and equally terrifying to Noran, who realised that he was within a half-hour of setting foot on Nemurian soil. He had no idea what he was going to do when he got there, or how he would get back, if at all. The Nemurians would be just as likely to slay him out of hand for trespassing against all agreement as they were to listen to his talk of woe concerning the Askhan Empire. Even if he had a chance to speak to someone in authority, the pirates were going to take all of his money, Noran was pretty certain of that. The Nemurians were mercenaries, and he would have nothing to pay them.

Realising this, he approached Maanam, who was in quiet conversation with the tillermen.

"Ease over starboard, aiming for the cleft between the hills there." Maanam turned as he heard Noran's feet on the wooden deck. The captain smiled, but without any genuine humour. "Not long now, we'll have you on-shore soon enough. I'm not a heartless man, you can have a sack of clothes and such."

"I need one chest of coin," Noran said softly. "I have to hire Nemurians, after all. One chest. You can keep the other three. Believe me, that's more askharins than you have ever seen."

Maanam seemed to think about this, and put his hand across Noran's shoulders. The two of them walked to the aft rail, guided by the captain's step.

"You have yourself in a bit of a fix, Noran Astaan," said Maanam, leaning his free arm on the timber of the rail and looking down into the water. His voice was quiet. "You see, there are lots of rocks in the water here, and a ship can be holed in moments. And I only have the one boat and none of the men are wanting to risk getting capsized in the heavy surf. I just don't think you'll be wanting to carry too much baggage."

"You have lost me, captain," said Noran. "If you cannot get the ship to shore and you will not take me over on a boat, how am I supposed to get there?"

"This is why you I need to hang on to all of your chests, you see," said Maanam. "You can't swim with them."

He grabbed Noran's belt in both fists and hefted the nobleman over the aft rail, his laugh following Noran down until he crashed into the water, driving all of the breath from his body. Noran bobbed on the waves for a few moments, the sound of his own splashing louder than the pirate's guffaws, until the wake of the ship dragged him under the surface.

III

The sound of waves crashing on rocks brought Noran to consciousness. He felt water lapping at his feet and sharp rock beneath him but was too weak to move. Gulls made their raucous calls overhead and he realised that day had come, the light seeping through his eyelids as clarity returned.

He opened his eyes and rolled to his back with a grunt. The sky was smeared with grey clouds of ash and smoke. Raising his head a little, he looked down at his feet. He was lying on a shelf of rock that sloped down to the sea, the water washing closer as the tide came in. With no clue as to how far up the slope the sea would encroach, Noran summoned up what strength he had to push himself to a sitting position.

He had no idea how long he had been in the water, or lying in a daze upon the shore, but the sun was still low, casting golden light on the waves. All he could recall was the desperate pounding of his heart and the fire in his lungs as he had struck out for the forbidding shore of Nemuria. He could not remember reaching sanctuary, but the burning of his arm and leg muscles stood testament to his struggle against the swirling currents.

The first rule of survival, he told himself, is to survive. That much he had achieved, but he was stranded on an isle of the Nemurians, without coin or even clothes to change for the sodden garments that clung to his body. He was in violation of the edicts of the Nemurians, and though he had escaped a watery grave there was little to hope for in his immediate future.

"Best not get washed out again," he said to himself. The ache of his limbs turned to sharper pain as he pushed himself to his feet and plodded a few steps up the slope. A jutting rock provided support while he caught his breath, sucking in air through gritted teeth. His right arm was fearfully painful and he looked at it, seeing a stain of blood soaked through the linen of his shirt. He tentatively pulled up his sleeve, revealing a gash from wrist to elbow. It was not deep, but the salt of the water sent surges of pain through him as he examined the wound. He still had a knife at his belt and stripped away the sleeve to make a rough bandage. It provided little comfort, but he hoped it would be some protection.

Becoming aware of a ravening thirst, he looked around.

The slope was part of the footing of a mountain that soared up into the sky overhead, smoke billowing from its peak. Off to his left, further inland, he saw wisps of steam issuing from vents, and pools that bubbled like cauldrons hung over flames. The horizon was blocked off by more volcanoes. The air was thick with the stench of rotten eggs, but further up the side of the volcano he could see low bushes and thin-trunked trees. Where there was vegetation, there was water, he reasoned. He pushed himself away from the support of the rock.

He took a faltering step, summoning up reserves of endurance he had not tapped since his escape from Magilnada.

The sound of small pebbles tumbling drew his attention to his right. What he had taken for a rock about fifty paces away started to expand, rising up from the ground, its shadow lengthening towards him. A club-ended tail unfurled, thudding to the ground as the Nemurian stretched to its full height, nearly half again as tall as Noran and three times as broad as him. What he had seen as grey stone flexed, revealing itself to be dark scales, and two yellow eyes opened.

Noran's first instinct was to run, but there was nowhere to run to, and the Nemurian would have easily outpaced him even if Noran had been in the prime of fitness. Seeing that escape was not only impossible but counter-productive to the goal that had brought him to the island, Noran drew the knife from his belt and laid it on the ground before raising in his hands in what he hoped was the universally accepted gesture of surrender.

"Take me to your leader?" he suggested.

The Nemurian plodded across the slope with long strides, tail swinging and bouncing behind it. Noran could not stop himself taking a step back as its shadow engulfed him. It stopped at the knife and looked down. The Nemurian reached out with delicate, slender fingers and picked up the blade. It examined the knife for a few moments, turning it one way and then the other.

Noran realised that the creature did not wear the armour and kilt he associated with the Nemurians and glanced between its legs before he could stop himself. He was glad that he was not confronted by some inhuman phallus, but only a stretch of light scales that disappeared between the Nemurian's thighs.

"Do you understand me?" he asked.

"The waves warned of your coming," the Nemurian replied in a lisping accent. Noran had never spoken to one of the creatures before and was surprised by its gentle tone. The eyes that regarded him, slowly scanning from toes to face, did not seem angry, but he was not foolish enough to believe a Nemurian's expressions would mirror those of humans.

"I hope they said good things about me," Noran joked. He started to shiver, but whether it was from fear or the shock of his ordeal in the sea he did not know.

Slitted nostrils widened as the Nemurian sniffed heavily. It reached out, handing the knife back to Noran. The herald took this as a good sign and smiled as he took the weapon, shoving it back into its sheath with fumbling fingers. The Nemurian's fingers grasped Noran's shirt and he pulled away out of instinct. The creature made a sound like two stones rubbing together and reached out again, tugging at the wet linen.

"The sun brings life," it said. Noran tried to remain calm as it gently stripped him of his shirt and then tugged at his breeches.

"Right, wet clothes, of course," said the herald, taking a few steps backwards. "I can take care of that."

Conscious of the Nemurian's inquisitive gaze on him, Noran unbuttoned his breeches and stepped out of them, rebuckling his knife belt around his naked waist. The wind was warm even this early in the day, and as he took off his ragged sandals Noran could feel the heat of the rocks on the soles of his feet. He stopped shivering almost immediately, with the warmth of the sun direct on flesh. Trying not to feel too self-conscious about his nudity in front of his alien host, he pointed to his chest.

"Noran," he said. "Noran Astaan. From Askh."

"Stranded fish," said the Nemurian, which Noran thought was a strange name, until he realised the creature was talking about him.

The Nemurian laid a hand on his shoulder, with surprisingly light touch for such a large figure, and pointed up the slope. There were several more Nemurians standing there, about two hundred paces away. Iron gleamed in the sun, a sight much more familiar to Noran. He told himself that he would not have received such a gentle welcome if the Nemurians planned to kill him anyway, but he could not help but wonder as he looked at the armoured figures waiting for him. His brief contact had already shown that the Nemurians did things very differently to Askhans.

With an insistent but tender push, the Nemurian set him up the slope. He took a few steps and looked back.

"Thank you," said the herald. "For whatever that is worth."

"The stones decide," came the enigmatic reply.

IV

Noran's return to wakefulness was accompanied by the soft slap of leather and a gentle swaying motion. He did not remember falling asleep, and nor did he remember being picked up by one of the Nemurians, but that was plainly the case. Judging by the close smell of metal and tanned hide, he was being carried in its arms like a child. Though it was not the most dignified way to travel, he was pleased to rest his tired limbs and made no move that would betray his woken state. Opening one eye a crack, he looked down upon a vast lake, ringed by verdant slopes. Strangely shaped rocks jutted up from amongst the foliage, on which had been painted brightly coloured patterns. Curves of stone arched over the treeline like bridges, and from them hung what could only be described as enormous nests made of entwined branches and broad leaves, each spacious enough for several dozen men to lie in comfort.

He also saw more Nemurians, clambering up the rock bridges and swinging along ropes from one nest to another. They moved with a grace that was far from their lumbering strides on land. Out on the lake, large flat-bottomed boats bobbed on the waves, and he could see nets draped through the waters between them. Moving his head slowly, opening his other eye to peer past the thick arm of the Nemurian, he saw that the lake stretched for more than mile behind him, ringed by volcanic upthrusts.

The Nemurians were talking, or so he assumed from the half-whispered syllables and grunts that passed between them.

He was also surprised to hear the bleating of goats nearby, heard against the noise of the wind in the treetops.

The Nemurian stopped and lowered him to the ground, its green eyes regarding him critically.

"I think I can walk," said Noran. He looked up and saw that it was nearly noon. He remembered nothing of the morning passing, but it was clear they had travelled at speed for some distance.

"We have come," said the Nemurian. "The stones beckon."

The creature stepped aside and Noran saw that they had come to a large cave mouth. Something glittered with pale green light within and he could see the outlines of more Nemurians, settled on their haunches.

A strange hooting call overhead drew his attention and he looked up to see a lattice of ropes strung between the slope above the cave and a pinnacle of rock. There were several Nemurians of different sizes but all smaller than those he had encountered – infants he guessed – hanging from the ropes, looking down at him with curious gazes. Some of them used their tails as extra limbs, swinging from one rope to another with the ease of monkeys despite their size. Several pointed and made more whooping noises. Noran had the suspicion it was laughter and placed his hand over his exposed genitals out of instinct.

"I am a man-speaker." This pronouncement came from the cave entrance. The Nemurian who made it did not wear armour or kilt, but around its neck hung a long scarf of twisted leather strips studded with a king's fortune in diamonds, rubies, sapphires and other precious gems. Its scales were pale grey, with flashes of dark blue across the shoulders, the face a deep purple colour around bright green eyes. "Nok'ka is an acceptable term of address."

"Noran Astaan, of Askh," said the herald, bowing his best courtly bow, which somewhat lost its dignified purpose as he swept his hand away to reveal his dangling private parts. Covering them again quickly, Noran rallied his nerve. "A man-speaker? I thought that many Nemurians learned the tongue of Askhor."

"The words are not difficult for us, but the thoughts behind them are rare, approached by only a few." The Nemurian beckoned Noran to approach. "A man-speaker gives voice to your thoughts so that the mind of the rocks is known."

"Um, you lost me with that last part," said Noran, approaching with short steps. "The mind of the rocks?"

"Forgive, but it is a rock-thought that does not translate well."

"Would you pass my thanks to the one that carried me?" said Noran. He stepped into the shadow of the cave mouth and his skin prickled at the sudden coolness. "Also, I would be very grateful if you had perhaps a blanket or something?"

"Your thanks would not mean anything to Ok'kak'ka. She finds reward in the duty of the rocks and it is sufficient. For you we have prepared your arrival. Food and water, and coverings for your flesh. Be following me."

Walking into the cave just a step behind Nok'ka, Noran saw that the glow within came from jagged veins of stone set into the walls. After a few strides the air grew warmer again and through an arched opening he saw a red glow. He looked for a moment and saw the ruddy light shifting slowly, but not the flicker of fire. He was not able to investigate further as Nok'ka led him across the hall-like cave towards a small bundle of cloth lying on a rock shelf. Taking up the bundle, Noran discovered it was a loose smock of wool, soft to the touch. He slipped it on, tucking it through his belt, reminded of a child's garment. On the floor next to the outcrop of stone were two bowl-like mats of woven reed; water in one and seared fish on another.

He drank first, careful not to splash his new robe with the water, and then wolfed down the fish, which had a slightly acrid taste but was not unpalatable. Nok'ka watched him silently, hands clasped across its belly. Something the man-speaker had said struck Noran.

"You said 'she' finds reward? The one that carried me, I mean."

"I am also of the female," said Nok'ka. "I am understanding it is difficult for humans to be understanding, but there is little in our forms to differentiate the mothers of the rock from the sons of the rock. It is being of little importance. Are you fed well?"

"Enough for the moment, thank you," said Noran, his stomach already feeling tight from the generous helping of fish. He suspected he had swallowed a lot of saltwater and thrown up at some point, for his gut felt tender. "I must also thank you for your welcome. I had been led to believe that Nemuria was a place inhospitable to my people. The one-mile ban, and all of that, you see?"

"You are confusing our sensible treatment with the kind regards of welcome," said Nok'ka. "The stones have yet to speak on your behalf. Your man-thoughts are misleading you."

Realising that he had certainly misread his situation, Noran swallowed hard. The isle seemed peaceful, and Nok'ka certainly showed no ill intent, but he could not help but recall stories of the things Nemurians did in battle; smashing bones and crushing skulls, ripping off limbs and pulling out organs. It was hard to marry such savage tales with his docile surrounds, but he was suddenly wary again.

"The one who on the shore said I was expected," Noran said, hoping that this was a sign to his credit. "The waves spoke of my coming?"

"A ship was seen, that is all," explained Nok'ka. "My people are not usually seeing the separate parts of the world as men do. A ship is the sea. A city is the rock. A bird is the sky. Your ship was easily seen coming close to the island. Urki was waiting to see the intent of those on the ship."

"Well, I've come for your help, if that is not yet clear. I had gold to pay for your services, but the pirates – the men on the ship – took it from me."

"This we will be discussing with the stones," said Nok'ka. "Be coming with me."

They walked back to the cleft in the wall that Noran had seen earlier, and passed into the red light. There was no sign of artifice to the walls, the corridor being nothing more than a cleft in the fabric of the rock that broadened out after less than fifty paces.

The source of the light was a deep gorge that split the cave floor ahead, from the depths of which poured heat and redness. Somewhere beneath the cave, a fire river flowed its light reflecting from crystal deposits in the cave roof. On the very lip of the precipice were three standing stones, or more precisely three piles of large stones painted with more of the shapes and symbols Noran had seen out on the lake shore.

A handful of Nemurians crouched around the stones, their heads covered in leather cowls adorned with gems that glinted in the light of the fire river. A collection of stones was set before each of them, every pebble with a single painted symbol upon it. Noran recognised an eye on one as Nok'ka brought him closer. Another looked like a triangle with curved sides, which might have been a mountain, while a third seemed to be marked with a cloud. Of the others, he could not make any guess.

"Are these your rulers? Am I to make my offer now?"

"It is man-thought to be speaking of rulers and offers. The time for bargainings has passed."

"I can get more gold," Noran said, "if that is the problem. Help us and I have the treasuries of the empire to give to you."

"The empire of the Askhans is finished." Nok'ka's statement hit Noran like blow to the gut.

"Not with y–"

"Gold is of no value with no men to be returning it to," Nok'ka continued. "The night-sky-walkers have returned. We are facing the choice again."

"What choice? Again?"

"It is being of consequence to us alone."

"Not bloody likely," said Noran, feeling that he was being treated like a child again. "You say the empire will fall and it is only *your* problem?"

"It is man-thought to be hearing without listening. Attend, Noran Astaan." Nok'ka placed a hand on Noran's shoulder, the insistent pressure urging him to sit down, though not unkindly. He sat with his legs crossed, hands in his lap. Nok'ka lowered to her haunches in front of him, hands resting palm down on the uneven floor of the cave.

"Long is the memory of the rocks. The night-sky-walkers came before, when the lands you call empire were belonging to the people of the rocks. On the hot winds they came, with the men of red skin. Great was the war."

"The Mekhani? They are the men with red skin, correct?"

"If that is the calling of them in your words, then yes. One man there was, of pale skin, who had come to us with false words. He stole from us many secrets, many turnings before the coming of the night-sky-walkers. The blood of the mountains that you call lava he took from us, and the telling of the winds and many other things that men would not know by their own thoughts. The night-sky-walkers heard his words and gave him more secrets. The lands of the dust and sands were green and watered, but the one of the pale skin fed the lands to the night-sky-walkers and they drank deep of the essence of the grass and the trees and the beasts."

Nok'ka made a sound that might have been a sigh, or perhaps something more pained.

"Full from their feast, the night-sky-walkers desired more and they painted the red upon the skin of the pale man's warriors, making them mark upon them. Into the cold the red men came and we dug deep, bringing forth the iron to slay them. The night-sky-walkers followed in the wake of the armies and we fought them too. For many turnings we warred with the red men and the night-sky-walkers, and the lands of the hot winds were drained of their life to feed the night-sky-walkers. The rocks were stronger than the wind and we endured, but the pale man escaped us, taking with him the body of the last night-sky-walker to tread upon the rocks."

"Lakhyri," muttered Noran, piecing together what he could from the ramblings of the man-speaker. She may have been versed in the ways of human thought, but her sense of narrative was woefully lacking. Noran noticed Nok'ka was looking at him attentively. "Lakhyri is the name of the pale man. I think. He brings the shadow creatures with him."

"The wind told us this and now the rocks feel their tread again," said Nok'ka. "The men of the setting sun came when we were weak from our war and so we were fleeing, those mothers of rock and sons of rock who had survived the war. The men of the setting sun were too many to fight and we were hiding from them."

"The tribes that came before Askh," Noran said, trying to keep up. "They came from duskwards, but that was centuries ago."

"One thousand, four-hundred and twenty-two times has the sun turned about the world since we hid," said Nok'ka. "When the men of the setting sun built cities and came to us offering peace, we listened to false promises. In guise of battle we searched the world again for sign of the night-sky-walkers but found nothing. The red men lived, but their power was gone. So we believed that our victory had been won. Not so. The lies of the setting sun men return to us. The night-sky-walkers come to the world once more and we face the choice. We hid from the choice, leaving your empire so that the night-sky-walkers would not find us, but you bring the choice with you."

"To fight or to hide," guessed Noran. "That is the choice, is it not? Look, with your help we can beat Urikh and these shadow-monsters. I bet that Ullsaard would even give you some of your old lands back in return for your help."

"Promises are man-thought. Deeds yet to be done have no value. We shall let the rocks decide."

Nok'ka turned her gaze to the Nemurians squatting around the columns. The elders, or whatever the Nemurians thought them to be, started to talk quickly amongst themselves, their soft voices echoing around the chamber.

"On a personal level, if you decide to hide, what happens to me?" Noran asked, trying to appear casual.

"We will kill you," Nok'ka replied without any obvious malice. "Or we will not. The rocks will be telling of your fate. The night-sky-walkers are seeing the man-thoughts easily. It is danger to let you leave, but the people of the rocks do not punish innocence. Rock-thoughts are not for the night-sky-walkers to see. You know of the choice now, so from you the night-sky-walkers perhaps learn again of the people of the rocks."

"Oh good," Noran said weakly. "I thought it might be something like that."

"Be still with words now, for we must be listening to the choice of the stones."

Noran started to bite a fingernail, wishing he had some wine to soothe his nerves. The stone watchers were still talking constantly, but now and then one would pick a pebble from his or her pile and toss it towards the standing stones. The ping of their contact and clatter of their landing on the cave floor punctuated the discussion. As more and more pebbles clattered from rock, the Nemurians stood up and pointed, drawing lines with pointing fingers between the symbol-stones. When the last stone had landed, they fell silent for a moment, stepping back to sweep their gazes over the pattern thus formed.

"Is that it?" asked Noran. "Throw some pebbles around and the answer will be given to you?"

"The rocks are knowing," Nok'ka replied sharply. "The rocks were once suns, and those suns once other rocks. They are the sun and the world and the stars and the moons. What knowledge can we be having that they do not?"

This made no sense to Noran at all, but he felt the irritation of the Nemurians at his interruption. The stone-hurlers were all glaring at him from across the cave. He raised a hand in apology and they started talking again, each one taking a turn to interpret the meaning of the symbol-stones. There seemed to be some kind of consensus and the Nemurians moved across the cave picking up their pebbles. One of them, with a diamond as large as a fist set into an iron collar around his neck, gestured for Nok'ka. The man-speaker approached and they talked briefly before she returned to Noran.

The herald stood up, trembling in anticipation of the Nemurians' decree.

"The fire will consume the rock," Nok'ka said.

Noran waited but there was no further explanation. He ran through the words again, turning them over in his mind, trying to figure out the meaning. Nok'ka turned and started back towards the crevice leading out of the chamber. Noran was glad that he had not been killed yet, but that did not seem to indicate anything of his future life prospects.

"Wait!" Noran called out. Nok'ka stopped and looked back. It was impossible to tell if she was sad or happy with the decision. "The fire will consume the rock? In simple man-thought, with man-words, what the fuck does that mean?"

OORANDIA, OKHAR
Midsummer, 213th year of Askh

I

Since the time of Askh there had been an accepted informality between an Askhan king and his generals. As he lowered himself to both knees, Lutaan wondered why Urikh thought himself better than all of his predecessors, but he was not about to voice any objection. The newly-appointed commander of Askh's army could see the shapes of Urikh's creatures moving in the twilight; the same twilight that had swathed Askh and followed the army as it had marched hotwards to Oorandia. By the latest ringing of the watch it was an hour after High, the middle of the afternoon, but the storm clouds that swathed the sky turned everything to a dusky red. At night lightning of different colours flickered above, and the men huddled in their tents while the things of shadow prowled the camps.

Urikh sat on his throne, which had been placed upon an ornately carved palanquin that had to be carried on the backs of four abada and needed twenty men to lift and lower it. Golden icons were fixed at the four corners of the platform, bearing not the face of Askhos as had been tradition since the founding of the empire, but a gilded resemblance to the new king. There had been no complaints voiced against the change, not when

the creatures allied to Urikh had been sighted issuing forth
from the capital to join the army, following the captains of the
First who had brought the decrees of the king to Lutaan and
the legions he had assembled. Black-robed Brothers, many of
them as terrified as the soldiers it seemed, kept their eyes and
ears alert for any sign or word of dissent. Legionnaires that had
been brothers in battle for years watched each other with suspicion, willing to offer up long-held comrades in return for
diverting accusations of treason from themselves.

Lutaan risked a glance up at the king, but Urikh had yet to
acknowledge his general's presence. The empire's ruler wore
the Crown on his head and black robes threaded with precious metals. His hair had been bleached white – or so Lutaan
thought, though he had heard whispers that terror had paled
the king's hair on the first night of the shadow-creatures' arrival. The king was speaking with the golden-eyed husk of a
man that led the Brotherhood. Urikh's mania was disturbing
to witness, but Lakhyri's presence brought hushed dread
wherever he appeared, always accompanied by at least one
of the shadow-monsters. There was one of the things with
them now, a tentacled blot in the gloom, stretched between
the two icon poles at the back of the palanquin. Clusters of
diamond-like orbs met the general's gaze and he quickly lowered his head.

In no hurry to pass on the news he had, Lutaan waited for the
king's word, his eyes averted. At least the day had been quiet.
Oorandia had been almost deserted, except for a few old folk and
cripples unable to flee, abandoned by their families as the darkness had descended upon the city. Those that had fled had been
wise; every town the army had passed through had become a
feast for the shadow-things. Lutaan had suffered the experience
of seeing one of the creatures devouring a family, rendering
them down to nought with lashing, tongue-like appendages.

"You may address me, general." Urikh's sudden voice made Lutaan flinch.

"The city has been abandoned, majestic king." The honorific almost stuck in the general's throat, but he forced out the words, having seen the flayed remains of those punished for improperly addressing the king. "There is no sign of Ullsaard."

"The coward runs from me again," declared Urikh. Lutaan glanced up for a heartbeat, to judge the king's expression. Urikh was most definitely displeased. "He spits in my face and then turns tail like a flea-ridden dog. He tries to turn my people against me, and slays the Brothers that spread the word of my rule, but is not brave enough to face me himself. "

Lutaan knew well it was not the king that Ullsaard did not wish to face. Urikh had never been physically imposing and was now an emaciated, haggard figure who suffered trembling limbs like a man three times his age.

"There was a parchment left in the city, nailed to the charred timbers of a large pyre, my great king." Lutaan did not want to continue, but he knew Urikh would insist on knowing the details and so carried on despite his instinct to stay quiet. It was better not to have the king ask questions if it could be avoided. "We found fragments of black cloth in the ashes. I think they burned the Brothers. It is part of the message."

"A message?" Urikh spoke lightly, affecting only passing interest.

"A letter, magnificent ruler," said Lutaan. He took the roll from his belt and held it up, not looking at the king.

"Read it to me."

This had been the moment that Lutaan had been dreading. He had already seen the contents of the letter and had hoped he would have been able to pass it to the king and then excuse himself. He had also considered giving it to one of the other captains to present, but shame at the notion had forced the general to do the deed himself. He risked a moment of softly-spoken dissent.

"It would be better if you read it yourself, mighty ruler of Askh. I would not trust my poor intonation to convey its proper meaning."

"Read it." The words were said quietly, but there was harshness behind them. Lutaan heard scraping, of something slithering across the wood of the palanquin, and he felt the air turning hotter. He dared not look up, but could feel the air around him saturated with the presence of the shadow-thing. With shaking hands he unrolled the parchment. Clearing his throat, he started to read.

"To my worthless cunt of a son." Lutaan stopped, expecting to feel the touch of a shadow-limb on him or the hiss that Urikh gave when displeased, but instead there was laughter from the king; laughter edged with madness.

"My father has an eloquence that puts the playwrights to shame," said the king. The humour in his voiced died away. "I shall remember such greeting when I see him next. Continue."

"I regret the day my seed spilled into your mother." Lutaan forced himself to concentrate on the written words, trying to rid his voice of emotion or emphasis. He was only the conduit for Ullsaard's insults, not the source, he told himself, but it was hard to focus. "I wish I had fucked her in the arse instead that night. You have been nothing but a disappointment to me. Ullnaar is more intelligent than you and Jutaar was loyal. There is nothing in you worth compliment. I am not surprised that you cannot even fight your own battles, but have become Lakhyri's piss boy. I am heading hotwards to where this all started. Bring all of the soldiers and all of the otherworld creatures you can, because you are going to need them. You had a chance to end this and keep your life. I gave you that because you were my son, but I do not accept you as my son any longer. You are as filthy as a cheap whore's gash and I would wash away the stench with your blood."

Urikh was panting hard, the wood of his throne creaking as he rocked back and forth.

"His words are meant as barbs, to cloud your thinking," snapped Lakhyri.

"Fucking shit-eating mongrel bastard, I will see him die a lingering death, a painful death that will last for a long time." Urikh continued to rave, spilling insults and expletives in a steady stream.

"General, you are dismissed," said Lakhyri.

"What are my orders?" Lutaan asked as he pushed himself to his feet, eyes still on the ground. He dropped the parchment and stepped back, wanting to vomit. He grasped one hand in the other to stop the trembling as he felt the sinuous movement of the shadow-monster just a few paces in front of him. Another wash of hot air felt like tiny claws on the general's skin. "Are we to march?"

"We are going to fucking march, oh yes!" shouted Urikh. "We will fucking march day and night. Ullsaard is a fucking idiot if he wants to fight me. I will show him where the true power in the empire lies now!"

"As you command, noble king, it shall be," said Lutaan. He turned and marched away as quickly as he could, while the king's anger was focussed on Ullsaard. He was met by the other first captains a short distance away.

"How did he take it?" asked Neerdrin, commander of the First.

"If we don't bring that madman Ullsaard's head, we're all dead men, or worse," Lutaan whispered. He pushed past the other officers, desperate for the sanctuary of his pavilion. "Assemble the companies. We march hotwards, to Mekha."

NAKUUS RIVER, NEAR-MEKHA
Midsummer, 214th year of Askh

I

There had been many times when an army on the march had been the greatest thing Ullsaard could imagine. He stood with Anasind and the first captains on a hill overlooking the army as it passed by. Company after company stretched back along the rough track that ran alongside the sluggish river, the column winding its way through the scrub and dirt of near-Mekha. The gleam of the icons, the tramp of feet in unison and the jingle of wargear used to set the king's heart racing, especially when there was sure to be a battle at the end of the march. Hundreds of Kolubrid riders slithered through the sparse grassland to either side while abada hauled a train of thirty lava throwers and dozens of other war engines. Eight legions followed him and it was a force to be reckoned with, a physical representation of power that was unmatched by anything else.

He had once confided in Noran that the thought of politics daunted him, but after years of turmoil and fighting he understood that politics was a very simple thing. Men had ambitions, dreams to achieve, and politics was simply the interplay of these desires, shaped by the power wielded by those involved. Some men had wealth to shower bribes and gifts to supporters, and to pay off their enemies and the vanquished. Some men had a knack for words, working on the desires and prejudices of others to suit their own ends.

Ullsaard had an army.

Wealth could buy loyalty, and influence could sway the minds of the masses, but when everything was rendered down to its basic level, only a fool argued against forty thousand spears.

Armies had marched and conquered at Ullsaard's command for more than a decade, but this time he felt different. This was not a battle to seize the Crown from an ailing dynasty. This was not a conquest to enrich the coffers of the empire and bring barbarian foes under the civilising heel of Askh. This was a war of survival. The empire had been a sham, created solely to make men biddable to the wishes of Lakhyri; a pen for lambs to wait placidly in for their slaughter. The creatures that the priest had brought forth were not rulers, they were predators. They would devour the empire, and every man, woman and child within it.

Ullsaard was not certain he could stop them. He had forty thousand men, but were bronze spears and blades enough to halt the shadowy horde Lakhyri had summoned? The king did not expect it to be enough, not against such an enemy, but he did not share his doubts with his officers. Ullsaard's reputation of never being on the losing side was worth more than promised pensions to the warriors of the army. They believed in him, and in his ability to deliver them victory. It was a belief that somehow was proving stronger than the fear of the unnatural enemy.

It was a belief that could be shattered at any moment, if Ullsaard showed the slightest sign of weakness. The moment he allowed a crack to show in his confident demeanour the strength of his army would be lost and they would slip away into the wilds.

So it was that he stood on the hill with his captains, raising sword in salute to the legions that marched below him, and inside his guts writhed and his thoughts were filled with visions of disaster.

The Thirteenth reached the stretch of track beneath him and raucous cheering rolled up the slope to greet the king. The sight of them, with Muuril marching alongside the icon of Askh – a device that meant so much more than the praise of a dead king – stirred Ullsaard from his grim mood. He raised his shield and sword above his head and let out a bellow from the bottom of his lungs.

"Thirteen!"

"Thirteen!" The replying call sounded across the low hills, along with the crash of spears beating on shields. Ullsaard laughed, dismissing the fears that had clouded his thoughts since retreating from Oorandia. With men like this to fight beside him he might lose, but he would not die meekly.

"My King, troubling news." Anasind's words punctured Ullsaard's moment of joy. "Scouts have reported a force of Mekhani moving towards us from duskwards. We need to break from the march and be ready for attack."

"Not yet," replied Ullsaard, turning away from the spectacle below. He pointed coldwards, where a smear of dark cloud could be seen over the horizon; a storm that had followed them all of the way from Oorandia, gaining on them every night. "We have perhaps three days advantage left to us. I have a battleground in mind that will be to our advantage, but it will be a close-run race."

"If the Mekhani fall on us while in column…" Anasind did not have to explain the consequences. Ullsaard's look reminded the general that he was well aware of the dangers. "As you command," said Anasind. "We will double the patrols to duskwards to warn of the Mekhani movements."

"How far away did the scouts say this army was?"

"A day and a half, from our current position. They are ahead of us though, so we will contact them this time tomorrow if we continue the march."

"I best set out now then," said Ullsaard. Anasind knew the king well enough to stifle a protest. "It is not coincidence that those red savages are coming. I think I know the reason why."

"Do I need to organise a guard?" Anasind was half-turning towards the other captains.

"No, this time I'll go alone. No point putting more men at risk."

"Risk?" Anasind took in a sharp breath. "You admit there is a risk and still expect me to let you go?"

"You mother me more than Cosuas did," replied Ullsaard. "It is not your choice."

The general made no further complaint while Ullsaard reeled off a series of orders to his captains for the encampment that night. He told them to continue directly hotwards the next day, and he would catch up with them on the march. Ignoring their unasked questions, the king put some water and food in a bag and set off down the hill, heading hotwards and duskwards, towards the Mekhani, fording the river a little while later.

He walked for some time, wondering if he was doing the right thing. If the Mekhani captured or killed him, he realised guiltily that he had not said goodbye to Allenya. He never considered the possibility that he would not see her again. Not in all the years they had been married had he ever doubted he would survive to know her embrace at least one more time. Today was no different, and the king decided it was better that he had left without warning. He had been so busy with the ordering of the march and other preparations he had only seen her one day out of every three since leaving Oorandia. With luck she might not even learn that he had gone.

He continued until nightfall, covering more than twenty miles. The hills were flattening into the desert, the vegetation became thinner and thinner with every mile passed. The skies were clear overhead and the stars bright, the half moon seeming almost within reach, away from the lanterns of city and camp.

In the distance he saw a glow of red and a column of smoke drifting across the stars. The fire had been lit on top of a hill, easy to see from miles around. Far from being alarmed, this increased Ullsaard's confidence. He was sure that the fire would be a signal for him, though part of him warned that it could also be the bait for a trap. Either way, there was only one way to find out.

It did not take him long to reach the fire, the flames of which reached high into the air; an obvious beacon. From the foot of the hill he could see a figure silhouetted against the flames, a figure far larger than any ordinary man.

"Erlaan!" The king's shout was swallowed by the darkness but the figure above moved, turning towards him.

"Ullsaard."

With quick strides, the king reached the ring of light around the fire and saw the Prince lit by the flames. Erlaan's armour was in dire need of a good polish, the rivets that fixed it to his flesh showing tarnish and wear.

"Do you want to finish our fight?" asked the king, hand on the pommel of his sword.

"Not yet," replied Erlaan. "But if you do not keep your words civil I will end what was begun at the villa."

"I am pleased to hear that," said Ullsaard, relaxing. "I knew that the Mekhani army was to gain my attention. Well, you have it. What do you want?"

"I want to know what you will do if you win," said Erlaan. The flames glinted from golden eyes and Ullsaard detected sadness in the Prince's voice.

"I haven't thought that far ahead," Ullsaard replied. He low-ered himself to the dirt and sat down, the fire distant but large enough to bring out sweat on the king's face. He pulled a piece of bread from his bag and broke it in half, offering one portion to the Prince.

"I am not hungry," said Erlaan. Metal scraped on metal as he lowered to his knees and sat back on his heels. The Prince sighed heavily. "I have been blinded by my jealousy, Ullsaard. Lakhyri never intended the empire for me, no more than he intended it for you or wishes it to be ruled by Urikh. I thought I would bring the Mekhani back and take it from both of you, but I am too late."

"Of course you were never going to be king," said Ullsaard. "I told you as much at the villa."

"And I thought hard about what you said," said Erlaan. "It is time for me to choose a side."

"The fact that you haven't beaten in my face tells me you have already decided," said Ullsaard, munching on the bread.

"You misunderstand me. I do not have to choose between you or Lakhyri. I choose myself. I shall wait to see which of you prevails in the battle to come, and then I will destroy the victor. It is better that you are alive, to prolong the fighting as long as possible."

"You think I'll lose?"

"I know it."

"So why tell me?"

"Because I do not want you to lose," said Erlaan. He sighed again. "The people will never accept me as their king, will they?"

"The Mekhani don't have any problem with you, I suppose you might grow on the citizens of the empire in the same way."

"The Mekhani think I am the incarnation of the giant that once ruled them; Orlassai, who led them in an ancient war for the Eulanui."

"The what?"

"The shadows from beyond the veil are the Eulanui, Ull-saard. That is the name of your enemies. Well, the name given to them by the Mekhani. The Mekhani have had myths and prophecies for fifty generations telling of my rebirth. My tongue, my lips, form words that they cannot disobey."

"You were saying, about the people of the empire accepting you?"

"I was the heir of the Blood, Ullsaard. It was my right to become king one day. But I have thought of what you said, about Askhos and the true legacy he left to his descendants and I realise that you spoke the truth. I would never have been king except in body."

"I'm sorry. I really am, if that means anything."

Erlaan's right hand formed a fist and Ullsaard tensed, expecting an attack. Instead the hulking prince punched the ground softly, his frustration obvious.

"Fight with me, Erlaan," said Ullsaard, coming to a decision. "I don't want the empire. You can have it, or what's left of it. Truth is, with everything that's happened I doubt there is any empire left; Salphors invading from duskwards, the Brotherhood being pulled apart by angry mobs, legions against legions… You're welcome to it."

"If you lose, do you think they will come into Mekha?"

"I don't know. I only know what you've told me. I think that if the Mekhani once worshipped these things, the Eulanui will probably want them back. But perhaps not. Maybe the empire will be enough."

"You would give me the throne of Askh? Why should I believe you?"

"I'm not fighting for myself this time. I mean it. If you want the empire, you can have it. Even if I win, I'm not staying as king. You can fight it out with everyone else who wants to be my successor. My word as a man of the legions, I swear to you that if you fight with me and we both survive, I will name you as my heir. Fuck, that's about as good a claim as anybody else has."

Ullsaard waited for the Prince's reply, gazing into the flames.

"Do you remember this place, Ullsaard?" said Erlaan, standing up.

"Looks like any other piece of near-Mekha. Why, have I been here before?"

"We sat at a fire down there," the Prince pointed to hotwards, "and you spoke to me about the Blood. We did not know that it was in your veins too. You told me that the quality of the metal determines the worth of the blade forged from it. You also said that I needed to learn when to change events."

"I don't remember," said Ullsaard. He stood up and looked around. In the dark it was hard to be sure, but he accepted Erlaan's account that he had been here. And then the memory returned.

"Fetch me a brand from the fire," he said. Erlaan narrowed his eyes in anger. "Please. It is too hot for me to get one for myself."

"As you asked nicely," said the Prince. He strode towards the flames, into heat and smoke that would have felled a normal man, and returned quickly with a burning branch in one hand. Ullsaard took it and headed down the hill to dawnwards, waving the brand left and right as he scanned across the stubby blades of grass. Erlaan followed close behind.

"Fuck me…" he said, catching sight of the thing he sought in a patch of dirt. He handed the branch to Erlaan and squatted down to dig with both hands, pulling free a smooth stone a little wider than his outstretched fingers. On one side was a crudely scratched rune of the Crown. "It's still here!"

"What is it?" Erlaan bent down, bringing the brand closer to see what Ullsaard held.

"I placed this here on that night. I don't know why I did it."

"The destiny of the Blood, perhaps?"

"Fuck that," said Ullsaard. With a grunt, he slung the rock out into the darkness. He turned back to Erlaan and drew his sword. "Men make their own destinies. Which one do you want to make? Are you going to fight with me or not? If it's the second, I am going to attack you here and now. Just so you know."

Erlaan laughed and pulled himself up to his full height. In the light of the brand the Prince's golden eyes seemed like pools of fire.

"I think you are right. You are the bastard son of a whore and a king, Ullsaard, and somehow it falls to you to be the defender of the world of men. It is not the destiny you chose, but it is the one you have created. I will fight with you."

"Good to have you with me," said Ullsaard, extending his hand.

"And my ninety thousand warriors," Erlaan added, engulfing Ullsaard's hand in a mass of bulging knuckles and curved talons. "Be glad you have persuaded me."

II

Against the bright sun of the desert, even the shadow-cloud of the Eulanui failed to bring night to the day. From his vantage point atop his palanquin, Urikh surveyed his army with pride. By the morning after the next Ullsaard would be brought to battle. If he continued to retreat, the swift advance of Urikh's forces would catch them on the march and the king knew his father would not allow that to happen. The thought of the reckoning being so close at hand made Urikh laugh.

"The red-skinned scum will not help them," he declared, looking at Lakhyri, who had brought the news that a large force of Mekhani had joined with Ullsaard. He waved a hand towards the mass of writhing, black-skinned creatures following in the wake of his tame legions, like goads driving a herd.

"When their gaze falls upon my host they will run screaming for their desert hovels or fall down to their knees to grovel for my mercy."

"*Your* host?" said Lakhyri. The priest turned his golden stare upon the king but Urikh did not care.

"I am still king, and this is my army; the grand army of Askhor. I do not know why you delayed so long in bringing them. Too cautious by far. If you had brought me these allies when you first approached me I would have swept aside everybody without all of the fuss."

"The Eulanui do not serve any but themselves," said Lakhyri, leaning closer. "Without the precinct network carefully harvesting the energy of the world to sustain them, they will devour everything, as they did with the civilisation of Mekha. I was rash then. This time was meant to be different."

"Well, it does not matter, does it? We are where we are."

"If our masters countenance for one moment that we are not wholly dedicated to them, it will be you and I that are consumed. You have lost your mind and should still your tongue before it gets us both killed."

"Look, my idiot general approaches," said Urikh, spying Lutaan and a body of men walking back down the advancing column. "He will complain that the men are exhausted and in no condition to fight, just as he did yesterday and the day before. If he mentions it again, I will have him killed for distracting me with his insubordination."

The king spoke a word to the men leading the abada and his throne-wagon slowly came to a halt to allow Lutaan and the others to approach. Amongst the knot of helmeted men, Urikh saw a familiar face: Noran Astaan.

"What is that doing here?" the king demanded, rising to his feet to jab an accusing finger at the traitor. "Kill him now before he lies to me again."

"A moment, supreme majesty," said Lutaan, falling to his hands and knees in deference. "We caught the herald trying to pass our army last night."

"Do not execute him yet," snapped Lakhyri. "We know he was trying to hire Nemurians. We must know if he was successful."

"Very well, if that is your counsel," said Urikh. He gestured to the guards holding Noran. "Bring him here."

The herald did not resist as he was guided past the abada to stand at the side of the palanquin. This duty fulfilled, the legionnaires swiftly retreated, not once raising their eyes to the platform.

"Hiring mercenaries against me, Noran?" said Urikh. "Just how treasonous have you been? I am sure your funds stretched to a few hundred. Tell me, how many will be joining my father?"

"See for yourself," said Noran. He turned and pointed hotwards. There was a low cloud of dust in the distance, which Urikh had thought to be a small sandstorm. The cloud was quickly lengthening to hotwards, kicked up by the tread of many feet – many, many feet.

"How many?" Lakhyri demanded.

Urikh did not like the sly smile on the herald's lips and repeated the priest's question. Noran pretended to count on his fingers and then shrugged.

"All of them."

III

Lutaan and his legions were doomed, that much was obvious, but the desire to die fighting rather than face the terror of the Eulanui forced them to attack. The shadow-creatures made no move to support the men as they advanced, twenty thousand against more than ten times their number. The army of Ullsaard was spread along a line of hills, the Askhan legions forming the centre, the mobs of the Mekhani out on the flanks where they would not impede the manoeuvring of the phalanx.

The desert-dwellers had brought twelve behemodons with them, and groups of lacertil riders with slings and javelins. The war beasts grunted, bellowed and hissed as the kolubrid riders advanced from the line, predators and prey forced alongside each other by the chains and reins of their respective masters.

Spear throwers and lava throwers were drawn up in batteries, sited amongst the spear companies, two protecting the Fifth and Thirteenth at the centre and another two guarding each end of the line. Crews readied their engines, drawing back the torsion bows of the spear throwers, pumping the bellows of the lava machines.

Into the heart of this, the legions of Urikh slowly advanced, the men dragging their feet from fatigue, barely able to hold up spear and shield. Their narrow-faced icons of Urikh were collected at the centre, where Lutaan led the other first captains and their guards from the back of an ailur.

"Poor bastards," muttered Muuril, standing to Gelthius's right. Beyond the Companion stood the king, next to the icon of the Thirteenth. Ullsaard turned his head as he heard Muuril.

"They made their choice," the king said grimly. "We'll put them out of their misery soon enough."

It did not seem right to Gelthius and he could not keep his opinion to himself. The king was hardly like to punish him for speaking out of turn, not there and then. And if the day went with the king, Gelthius would be glad to live to suffer such punishment as would be due.

"It's not their fault, king," he said. "They got homes and families just like us. Homes and families they had to protect the only way they could, right enough."

"Feel free to offer yourself up to their spears, captain," the king replied. "Or maybe you think you could ask them nicely to... Wait. You might have a point."

The king stepped out of the front rank and turned to call to the right, where Anasind was leading the second company of the Thirteenth.

"Hold position! We're going for a short walk."

The general's response was lost in the laughter of the company as Ullsaard waved for the men to follow him. They broke from the line at a steady pace, a few steps behind their commander. His course was obvious, heading directly for the opposing commanders. Despite the bedraggled appearance of the other army, Gelthius was acutely aware that he was one of only one hundred-and-twenty men marching to face off against more than fifteen thousand.

Lutaan recognised what was happening and his command staff stepped up their pace, moving ahead of the rest of their army. The two contingents met roughly halfway between the two lines, stopping a few dozen paces apart. Lutaan looked uncomfortable perched atop the ailur, awkwardly holding a golden spear in one hand and the gilded links of the reins in his other. The general's mount become more agitated, flicking her ears, swaying her head and pawing the ground while a bass growl sounded against the backdrop of tramping and scuffing steps.

"That's my fucking spear," Ullsaard said. "And my fucking cat!"

"You can have them back," said Lutaan. He tossed the spear down into the dirt and almost fell out of the saddle.

Relinquished of her rider's control, Blackfang surged forwards, almost barging Ullsaard to the ground as she was reunited with her real master. The king scratched her hard under the chin and behind the ears, eliciting a deep purring.

"Good to see you too, beautiful," said Ullsaard. He grabbed the horn of the saddle and swung himself over the ailur's back. "Companion, fetch my spear."

Muuril ran out to retrieve the discarded weapon, returning to place it in the king's outstretched hands before taking his place again in the front rank.

"You army seems to have wandered into my battle, general," Ullsaard said loudly. "I would get them out of the way before they get hurt."

"We will fight for you," called out one of the other captains as Lutaan rejoined them.

"Not a fucking chance. You'll be worse than useless," Ullsaard replied. He turned and pointed to hotwards, beyond his army. "The camps are that way. Be sure to have the fires burning and the wine poured for when the real soldiers return."

It took time for the news to percolate through the weary legions, but slowly by company their line broke apart, dejected men dragging spears behind them, leaving their shields in the short grass so that they did not have to carry them any longer. Ullsaard's company turned about and returned to the Thirteenth while the jeers of the king's warriors ushered out those who had surrendered.

The departing legionnaires quickened their pace, and soon started to run, glancing with terrified eyes over their shoulders. As the army dispersed, the black mass of the Eulanui was revealed, the air dark around them. A hot wind kicked up the dust in the wake of the breaking legions and drove as a wall through the army of Ullsaard.

Gelthius held his shield in front of his face while the sandstorm raged around him, men choking and coughing as the wind swirled and the dust rasped skin. The unnatural gale did not last long, but when the Salphor lowered his shield, black tendrils of clouds were creeping overhead and the shadow army was advancing fast.

IV

The attention of Urikh and Lakhyri was focussed on the battle. Noran eyed the pair of them carefully as they stood next to the grotesque block of bones and black rock that Lakhyri had brought with him. There were a few dozen Brothers around the camp, watching the army of Ullsaard and the Eulanui swarm from the vantage point of the wooden palisade further down the hill.

Nobody seemed to be paying the herald any attention.

With another glance around, Noran hurried between two pavilions, disappearing from view. He headed coldwards, away from the battle, and broke into a jog, not believing his luck. He moved between rows of smaller tents until he reached more open ground around the kitchens and storehouses.

"Running away?"

Noran stopped and looked over his shoulder towards the kitchen tent. Luia stood there with arms crossed.

"Yes," he replied, figuring that he had a good enough head start even if she chose to raise the alarm.

"Be kind to my sister," said Luia. "You will find her in Enair, if you wish to look for her."

Noran was about to continue on but there was something about the queen that made him backtrack a few steps.

"You should come with me," he said. "One way or another, this is not the place to be right now."

"I would not expect you to understand," Luia said to him, glancing up at the summit of the hill where Urikh and Lakhyri could still be seen. "I have to protect my son."

"I think it is a little late for that, Luia. Come with me, I will make sure you are safe."

"No." Luia turned away and started to walk back up the hill, towards the centre of the camp.

"Suit yourself," muttered Noran.

The legion had not finished building the fort when they had been ordered to assemble for the attack. The hills of near-Mekha rose up in front of Nora, and beyond them the more welcoming lands of Ersua. The herald looked back but could see nothing of the battle unfolding. That was probably for the best, he thought, and broke into a brisk walk, heading back towards distant civilisation.

V

The Mekhani were the first to respond. Amplified by rune-scribed lips, Erlaan-Orlassai's voice boomed out across the battlefield and the red-skinned hordes surged forwards. The grunts and hoots of the behemodons sounded out alongside the harsh blaring of war horns. Skirmishers on reptilian lacertils raced towards the oncoming army of shadow, their sling stones and javelins falling like rain into the dark mass; the effect was much the same as the Eulanui poured onwards, ignoring the missiles falling upon their leathery flesh. Scorching hot gusts of air forced the lacertils back, the riders unable to control their mounts as they scurried away from the searing heat.

With a sea of Mekhani warriors streaming around them the behemodons plodded forwards, catapults on their backs launching boulders into the press of swarming black bodies. The rocks thudded into unearthly flesh, cracking chitin plates. A few of the Eulanui were caught directly beneath the fall of the boulders, their black limbs thrashing under the heavy projectiles.

Through the dust and gloom, the king of the Mekhani could see a throbbing miasma surrounding the Eulanui army. Beneath the oil-slick cloud the grass withered and bushes crumpled into nothingness, their meagre life essence absorbed by the flowing horde of monsters. Where a Eulanui fell beneath a plummeting rock or was pinned by a storm of javelins, gouts of energy sprayed out into the seething, invisible morass.

Bellowing his challenge, Erlaan-Orlassai led the charge, a stone-tipped axe in each hand. Whooping and yelling, the Mekhani avoided attacking their gangling foes directly, but swept wide around the flanks of the enemy army. It was their task to use their numbers to swamp the ends of the enemy line, dragging more and more creatures towards them from the centre.

The Eulanui responded to the Mekhani mobs pouring around the sides of their host, groups of shadow-nightmares peeling away to face the threat like a smoke scattering into tufts on a breeze. The ground started to shake, and Erlaan-Orlassai felt a quivering in his gut as the shadow-things roared to each other below the range of even his superhuman hearing. The reverberations intensified as the Mekhani and Eulanui came closer, resonating inside the desert king's head.

Whipping tentacles and scything tongues met bronze- and flint-tipped spears as the Mekhani closed in on the attack. There were no shouts of pain when tendril-tongues lapped at flesh and armour, dissolving through hardened leather and bronze studs, stripping away skin and fat and muscle. Spears scratched against unnaturally tough hide and rang from crystal eye clusters. Flint shattered on bony barbs and bones snapped at the sweep of horn-sheathed limbs.

Erlaan-Orlassai ploughed into the midst of the Eulanui swinging his axes to left and right. Their heads split and their shafts splintered in moments and the desert king tossed aside the remnants of the weapons and laid about with bronze-clad hands and iron-hard talons. In a welter of spewing yellow ichor, the rune-carved warrior tore away coiling appendages and ripped gouges into black flesh.

Over his own panting and the shouts of his warriors, Erlaan-Orlassai could hear cheering; encouragement being shouted by the legions of Askh. Faced with a common foe, the men of Greater Askhor raised their voices in support of their fellow men, calling out praise to their monstrous leader.

Listening to the cheers, a feeling of peace and contentment flooded through Erlaan-Orlassai. Ripping a banded tentacle from a Eulanui, he was filled with hope; hope that even a

monster like him might find acceptance. Fuelled by this feeling, he raked his claws across the thorax of another foe,
gouging deep into unnatural fibre and bone. As ichor spurted
from the wound he saw the slick of life force leaking also. He
drew in a great breath, reaching out with a part of him that
was not flesh, drawing in the power of the escaping energy.
The essence of the Eulanui burnt him, but it was powerful,
causing rune-etched muscles to grow larger, rivets pinging
from his skin as he swelled up, infused with strength.

A tendril looped around Erlaan-Orlassai's throat, its touch
freezing cold. The runes carved into him started to glow with
a golden gleam, shining from his mutilated form. The feeder-
tendril snaked back, steam drifting in wisps from its scalded
skin. The Mekhani commander snatched hold of the limb before it was out of reach, and pulled hard, dragging the Eulanui
into a swinging punch that smashed deep into its writhing innards. Seizing hold of alien organs, Erlaan-Orlassai ripped his
hand free, pulling the creature almost inside-out.

All around him the Mekhani were dying in their hundreds,
but they looked upon their king and were filled with courage.
Like a red spear driving into the sides of their foe, the warriors
of the desert pushed on.

VI

"Ready to the front!"

Gelthius heard the call from Ullsaard repeated along the
long line of the legions as the Eulanui swept forwards. They
were almost within range of the spear throwers and the
shouts of the battery commanders readied the crews of the
war engines.

The Salphor glanced at his king and saw Ullsaard sitting
proud on the back of his ailur, his golden spear raised above
his head, ready to give the signal that would unleash the fury

of the war machines. To the front, Gelthius could see the enemy scrambling and lurching over the uneven ground, forced to climb the slope of the hills. He looked again at Ull-saard, trying to draw some strength from the king's calmness, wondering how a man could look upon the enemy bearing down on them and not show any fear.

With an ear-splitting crash of thunder, red and purple light-ning lashed down from the black clouds boiling across the sky. Lava throwers exploded as their fuel tanks erupted, showering fire and debris over the nearby legionnaires. The shrieks of burning men made Gelthius shudder and he tried not to imag-ine those caught in the blasts flailing around, skin and flesh burning away in the grip of the flammable liquid.

The lightning continued to rage, moving along the line of the legions with deadly wrath. Their ropes severed by the fork-ing energy, catapults and spear throwers tore themselves apart, flinging rocks and shafts and splinters into their crews, tattered cords whipping around like striking serpents. The storm clouds whirled above, the lightning leaving the Askhan war engines as smoking wrecks and still the unnatural tempest did not abate. The lightning crawled across the barren ground and flared through the phalanx. Shields cracked and spears shat-tered, clothes were set on fire and men screamed as the forking energy crackled through their bodies.

The air was growing hotter as the Eulanui approached and the ground was trembling beneath Gelthius's feet. He gripped his spear tighter, knuckles paling. The shaking increased and Gelthius heard the pounding of massive drums off to his right. The companies of the Seventh and Fourteenth made way for the Nemurians as they marched, the crash of their drums matching the thump of their heavy tread.

A lightning strike earthed itself into the rear ranks of Gelth-ius' company, causing those at the front to turn in shock, in time to see after-sparks flaring across the helms and breast-plates of a dozen men, the cries of the wounded drowned out by the thunder of the Nemurian drumbeat.

"Eyes to the enemy!" commanded Ullsaard, pointing his spear towards the advancing black mass, now a hundred and fifty paces away.

Gelthius pulled his shield up a little higher and set the butt of his spear against the ground. Looking at the shadow-things he knew what it was they faced: dark spirits. The Askhans had forgotten, but in Salphoria they had kept alive the tales of the unearthly forces that had shaped the world and continued to inhabit it. He whispered a few words to the spirits of sun and air to clear the cloud, and hoped that today would not be the day the raven came for him. He thought about his family, and realised that he did not know whether they were alive or dead; nor did they know of him.

Like an iron cleaver biting into meat, the Nemurians col-lided with the leading edge of the Eulanui advance. Six thousand of them and more had travelled from their distant isle to fight in the battle, Gelthius had heard, but such knowledge was little comfort to him; if they had come all of that way to take part the consequences of defeat were dire indeed.

Hammers and axes and brutal maces crushed and cut into the Eulanui as the Nemurians steadily pushed forwards. Equal in size to their foes, the scaled giants battered and tore and stomped a gouge into the Eulanui's ranks, but risked being en-veloped by their numerous enemies. Ullsaard clearly thought the same and his voice called out the advance. Dozens of trumpets sounded the order as the king raised his spear once more and then swept it down, its gleaming point directed at the heart of the enemy force.

VII

It was such a familiar noise, the crunch of feet and jangle of armour, but to Ullsaard it had a new sharpness, a clarity he had never noticed before. He felt the beating of Blackfang's heart beneath him, the compression and expansion of her muscles as she carried him towards the Eulanui. Her panting mingled with the rub of leather and scrape of metal.

He could sense the unease of his army, but despite their fear they advanced with him, a solid wall of shields and spears. So far his plan, carefully concocted in council with Erlaan, the legion first captains and several representatives of the Nemurians, seemed to be working. The initial Mekhani assault had drawn out the enemy, splitting them and teasing the mass apart like dough stretched by a baker. The Nemurians had plunged in at an angle, driving forward to meet up with Erlaan and his warriors on the right, effectively cutting off several thousand foes from the main host.

Now it was the job of the Askhans to exploit that divide, the legions on the right following up in the wake of the Nemurians to widen the split, while Ullsaard in the centre and the legionnaires spread far to his left pushed the remaining Eulanui into the Mekhani on the left flank.

The behemodons had reached the battle, wading into the nightmare army with crushing tread and snapping jaws. Thick leathers straps studded with vicious blades and ropes pierced with barbed hooks swung from the flanks of the enormous beasts as they trampled and gored their way forwards. These snares caught in the flesh of the Eulanui, dragging and ripping through the press of creatures. From their howdahs the red-skinned warriors jabbed long spears into their foes and hurled down rocks and javelins.

With all things considered, the king was pleased with what was happening, so it came as a surprise when the enemy did something he was not expecting: they started to retreat.

The legions were still a hundred paces away when the Eulanui withdrawal began. The black spread appeared to constrict upon itself, drawing in its outermost reaches like an octopus pulling in its tentacles, funnelling into an ever narrower mass as it retreated at speed from them advancing spears of the legions. Those creatures surrounded by the Nemurians and Mekhani clambered over each other and their enemies as they attempted to get away, but made themselves easy prey in their bids to escape.

Overhead the cloud was drawing back also. It roiled and swirled as it followed the Eulanui back down into the valley from which they had emerged, growing smaller and darker as it did so.

The Mekhani on the left whopped victory cries and sprinted after the fleeing enemy, but Ullsaard was too experienced to believe the battle had already been won. The Askhan advance continued at a steady pace as the gap between the armies widened.

Heading down from the hilltops, Ullsaard could see that the ground into which the enemy retreated had been turned to parched earth by their devouring presence. Not a shred of vegetation could be seen in a swathe a mile wide stretching into the distance. Seeing this devastation, he was forced to wonder what was left of the empire to coldwards; would there be anything or anyone left to save?

The uneven ground grew steeper as the legions continued the pursuit, leaving Erlaan and the Nemurians to finish off the Eulanui that had been caught. For more than a mile they followed the retreating enemy, encountering more rugged ground, split by wide cracks and broken by jagged rocks. His caution growing, Ullsaard called the army to a halt while he examined his options, leaving the Mekhani to continue racing after the enemy alone.

He could see the half-finished palisades and white tents of Urikh's legions another couple of miles or so ahead, and it was to this place that the Eulanui seemed to be heading. Not understanding what purpose there was for the invading nightmares to defend the encampment of the deserted legionnaires, Ullsaard was caught in two minds. If the legions pressed on swiftly, they might catch the Eulanui before they reached the dubious sanctuary of the poorly-built walls. To do so would be to plunge into something that Ullsaard was not certain about. He had thought he had come for a final battle to decide the fate of the empire, but it seemed his otherworldly enemies might not cooperate for such a dramatic conclusion.

Messengers on kolubrids gathered to hear his commands and he despatched them with orders for three of the legions to remain as a rear guard in case the Nemurians and Mekhani behind could not contain their surrounded foes. The rest of the army advanced again, the line narrowing to only a few companies wide to negotiate the rough terrain. It was not quite a column of march, but it was more vulnerable than a full battle-line, and Ullsaard kept a wary eye on the Eulanui as the army moved forwards. He had been ready to write history in an orgy of blood and fire, but the strange actions of his opponents unsettled him far more than their outlandish appearance and otherworldy powers.

The Mekhani caught up with the rearmost foes when they were less than half a mile from the unfinished way forts; another half a mile ahead of the legions. Some of the monsters turned, throwing out whip-like tendrils to slash away heads and limbs, feed-tentacles whirling, every touch vaporising a red-skinned attacker. The rest of the horde slithered and scrambled through the gaps in the log walls while the cloud over the camp writhed and contorted. It was spread out for half a mile, a bruise on the clear blue sky.

Ullsaard had a sickening feeling of apprehension as the storm span faster and faster, tightening and darkening further

as it funnelled down towards the tents and pavilions. The Eulanui were skittering and lurching around the point of the
tornado's mouth, thousands of them writhing and flailing.
Canvas ripped and ropes snapped, the whirlwind snatching up
debris and dust. The king heard gasps of shock from the men
following him as the distinctive shapes of abadas were drawn
up into the storm like leaves. The lightning returned, crackling
across the cloud rather than forking down, the multicoloured
flashes growing in intensity and frequency as Ullsaard continued to lead the legions on.

With a pulse of power that blinded Ullsaard for a moment,
the cloud imploded into the camp, sending the logs of the palisade spearing out like splinters, slashing through Eulanui and
Mekhani together. A shroud of blackness seeped over the hill
on which the camp had been erected, reminding Ullsaard of
the oily shadow that had spread across the Grand Precincts.
He was not the only one to make the connection and disturbed
whispers and fearful muttering from the ranks behind greeted
the terrifying spectacle.

The Mekhani, much reduced in numbers, did not realise
their peril. They stood and watched in horrified fascination as
the darkness bubbled and writhed, waves and ripples sloshing
across its surface contorting the ground into which it was sinking. More shadows lifted up from the glossy blackness, a pitch
black mist that hid the camp from view.

All fell silent except for the sound of the legions marching.
Sensing they were in danger, the Mekhani started to fall back
from the pulsating blackness; their instincts were right but
their reactions too slow.

The cloud pulsed and roiled, and from its depths the Eulanui emerged again. The multi-coloured flashes of energy
returned to scythe through the fleeing red-skinned warriors.
More and more night-creatures boiled from the dark cloud in

a frenzy of snapping, whirling tendrils and spines. The tide kept growing, engulfing the Mekhani, more Eulanui than had retreated from the battle. And still they kept coming, hundreds more, thousands...

Ullsaard did not need to issue a command to halt the advance. As one the legionnaires of his army stopped in their tracks as a fresh mass of lethal shadow-beasts surged towards them over the blasted wasteland.

VIII

Fingernails drawing blood from her palms, Luia's fists were clenched tightly by her sides as she watched Lakhyri bringing forth the Eulanui.

The high priest was standing behind some nightmarish altar of black stone and bizarrely-shaped bones, his hands upon its top, head thrown back. Lightning coruscated across the dome of the storm that surrounded them. The whorls and lines and shapes carved into his skin had become a web of pure blackness, seeming to suck in the light around him. He chanted a meaningless stream of sounds, darkness issuing from his open mouth like vapour that coiled with a life of its own. The altar block shimmered and writhed in and out of reality, spewing forth a fountain of shadow that created bottomless pools on the bare earth. These pools extruded grasping claws and tentacles, becoming more of the Eulanui, dozens of them every heartbeat.

Luia knew she had to do something, but she did not know what. She took a step forward and was checked by Urikh's grip on her wrist. She tried to pull her arm free as she turned to look at him, but his grasp would not break.

"Look how my army receives timely reinforcements," said her son, but there was a madness in his eyes and voice that she did not know. The lightning gleamed from his pupils, as though a storm raged inside them. Moving her gaze upwards, her eyes settled upon the Crown on the king's head, its gilding reflecting the colours of the flashing energy.

"We must stop them," she said, but Urikh simply shook his head.

Realising that her son was lost to her, she pulled up her arm and sank her teeth into the back of his hand. With a yelp, Urikh snatched his hand away, eyes turning to the queen in accusation. She kicked him between the legs, her sandaled foot connecting hard and Urikh went down like a boar felled by a spear.

Luia caught the Crown as it toppled from its perch, feeling its weight in her hand. With a snarl, she broke into a run towards Lakhyri, the iron Crown held up as a weapon. A newly formed Eulanui saw her and flung out a barbed tentacle that slashed across her face, but drew only blood. Ducking beneath a feeder tendril arrowing towards her, Luia rolled through the dust and came to her feet at full sprint.

Lakhyri was possessed by the energy flowing through him, utterly unaware of anything else happening. Something hit Luia in the back when she was only a few paces from the priest, sending her tumbling. She managed to avoid another lashing limb and pushed herself to her feet, swinging the Crown at Lakhyri's head with all of her strength.

A point of the Crown punched into the side of the priest's neck, blood erupting from the wound to splash across Luia's face, drenching her dress with crimson. She watched Lakhyri fall backwards, black blood spewing from the wound. Any normal man would have been slain instantly, but Lakhyri was far from a normal man. Writhing, the high priest flopped onto his front, arms trembling as he tried to push himself up, hate-filled eyes glaring at the queen. Bubbling black fluid issued from his mouth, staining his naked flesh, running in rivulets along the carved symbols on his skin. He reached out a grasping hand but Luuia stepped back, teeth bared in her scorn.

Lakhyri fell into the dirt, a black puddle soaking into the dry earth beneath him. His limbs twitched and his head jerked as the last of the vile fluid sustaining his existence poured from the wound. Clawed fingernails scratched at the ground, dragging furrows through the blood-soaked mud. Still Lakhyri would not give up his life, turning himself towards the altar with slow determination. One shaking hand outsretched, the high priest heaved himself towards the block of bone and pitch.

His questing fingers flapped desperately just a hand's span from the side of the altar. With a final spasm, Lakhyri collapsed, a last wheezing expulsion of air whistling from his lungs. Luia sensed movement behind her but ignored it, stooping to ensure the high priest was truly dead. His body was unnaturally light as she rolled Lakhyri to his back, gold-flecked eyes staring vacantly, mouth slack.

Satisfaction filled Luia for a moment, before she felt the delicate, invigorating touch of an Eulanui tongue upon her shoulder.

IX

Ullsaard bellowed orders, trying to instil some hope into his legionnaires. With golden spear held aloft, he rode up the line, every word from his lips a defiant curse against the enemy. His impassioned speech seemed to have an effect. Shields were set and spears raised and the line that had been threatening to break solidified.

The king dared not look at the enemy in case his own courage failed him. Instead he fixed his stare on the warriors in the front ranks as he rode past, as if daring them to defy him by running away. When he reached the companies of Donar's legion, he hear talk rippling through the army, surprised shouts sounding out from in front and behind him. Some of the legionnaires were pointing towards the foe, but with expressions of surprise rather than horror.

Pulling on the reins, Ullsaard turned Blackfang so he could see what had caused such a reaction. The Eulanui were no more than a few hundred paces away, but the tide of black washing across the hills was slowing, coming to a stop. The whirling cloud that had birthed them had disappeared, leaving a hilltop that had been scoured down to bare rock. Yet it was not this that had drawn the attention of the legionnaires.

On a ridge beyond where the camp had stood came a broad swathe of colour; blues and reds and greens pricked by the spark of sun on metal. It was a host of men, marching beneath fluttering banners, and beyond the crest of the ridge could be seen wind-filled sails as landships, a score and more of them, trundled into view.

Ullsaard judged the Salphorian army to be at least fifty thousand strong and more were still crossing the crest of the ridge.

Between the Salphors and the Askhans, the Eulanui baulked, unsure which foe to turn against. Ullsaard doubted such creatures knew the meaning of fear, but he hoped they did. He raised his spear again, drawing the eyes of his men to him.

"This is it! The provinces of Askhor lie ravaged, our loved ones slaughtered, our homes destroyed because of these creatures. Now they lie at our mercy. Now we bring down the wrath of Askhor and make them know that these lands belong to men, not their kind. Attack, attack and let not one of the cunts escape!"

X

Ullsaard had known war for his whole life, but the carnage of that last battle was greater than anything he had ever witnessed. Cornered, the Eulanui fought to the last, and fully two-thirds of the Askhans who had marched with him lay dead or were disintegrated by the battle's end. The slain were as thick as the pebbles on a beach, the Salphors' suffering no less a toll from their army. The burning husks of landships struck by unnatural lightning spilled a blot of smoke across the reddening sky, and slicks of lava from destroyed Askhan machines flickered on the bare slopes. The ground was blackened by the filth of the dead Eulanui, their crumpled corpses mounds of darkness that slowly withered in the light of the setting sun.

There were many amongst the dead whom Ullsaard had known, and several he had once called friends. Donar had been split from crotch to throat by a whipping, barb-tipped limb. The sharp-tongued Loordin had lost his head to a slashing tentacle. There was nothing left of Anasind to place on a pyre, the general having been obliterated by the touch of feeder tendrils. Others too, from the ranks and the officers of all the legions whose names would be added to the long roll in the Hall of Askhos. Never in Ullsaard's life had he counted the cost of victory so highly; so high that it felt like defeat. There were few untouched by injury. Muuril was amongst them, the companion caked head-to-toe in the drying ichor of the inhuman dead.

Erlaan-Orlassai had survived too, though he had lost almost all of his warriors. Nearly eighty thousand Mekhani slain, the men of the desert had paid the highest price of all to defeat their former masters. Their warped king approached the survivors of Askh and Salphoria while his followers sent up howls and wails of lament into the skies.

When all was done, what was left of the Askhan and Salphorian armies faced each other across a charnel field, each king standing at the centre of his exhausted warriors. It was Aegenuis who approached first, waving his chieftains back as they made to follow him. Ullsaard dismounted and threw Blackfang's reins to Captain Gelthius, who caught them awkwardly, his left arm wrapped in an improvised bandage from shoulder to wrist.

"Still want me to call you king?" Aegenuis asked as the

two men met a few paces apart. The Salphor jabbed a thumb at the horde of warriors behind him. "We're ready to go again if you are."

"No," Ullsaard replied.

"You'll not be wanting this then?" The Salphorian king turned and waved to his chieftains. Two of them emerged from the huddle, dragging between them the limp form of a man. They dropped him in the dirt and Aegenuis rolled him over with his foot, revealing the contorted face of Urikh. His throat had been ripped out, but in his hand he still clutched the Crown, slicked red with blood. Aegenuis stooped to prise the Crown from dead fingers and handed it to Ullsaard. The Askhan looked at it, and then tossed it back onto Urikh's chest.

"He can keep it; it never fit me anyway," said the king.

Ullsaard laughed as Aegenuis produced a wineskin from under his cloak, took a draught and then offered it across. The Askhan king swallowed a mouthful, recognising the vintage. "This is from Apili?"

"I still had a little left," confessed Aegenuis.

"I don't understand how you come to be here, not that I am ungrateful."

The Salphor's reply was interrupted by the arrival of Erlaan. Aegenuis shied away from the bestial giant, eyes looking to Ullsaard for reassurance. The Askhan king could offer none, remembering Erlaan's threat to destroy the victors to claim the empire for himself.

"Good to see you alive, Ullsaard," said the desert ruler.

"Is it? I'm certainly pleased about it."

"You two have unfinished business," said Aegenuis, "I can see that. I will leave you to to your discussion."

"Stay," said Erlaan and the Salphor stopped mid-turn, gripped by rune-enchanted speech. "You have as much right to divide what remains as anyone. Your men fought bravely today."

"Yes, and many widows and orphans there are tonight in Salphoria because of it," replied Aegenuis, sighing long and deep. "I do not know if the peoples will recover from this."

Ullsaard looked up at Erlaan's face and chose his next words carefully.

"My promise stands," said Ullsaard. "I name you heir to the empire. I cannot guarantee that the people will accept you, but I will not oppose you taking the throne."

"I hold you to your word," said Erlaan.

"I would ask one favour though, for the good of the empire."

"Voice it without expectation," replied Erlaan.

"Give Salphoria back to the Salphors. Greater Askhor and Salphoria have both been brought to the edge of ruin by the ambition of Lakhyri and Askhos. Deny them by forging a new alliance, one of trust, not enmity. I have been a conqueror my whole life, but you could do things another way. An easier way, maybe."

Erlaan turned his golden eyes to Aegenuis. The Salphor shrugged.

"I would speak to the chieftains and ease the anger of these past few years," said Aegenuis. "They are proud, but they will listen, I hope."

"And do you think that a Salphor army can cross into Greater Askhor, attack our cities without retaliation?" growled Erlaan. "You chose to side with Ullsaard today, but only out of self-interest. You sought to take lands from the empire while it was weak."

"Now, about that, I have to explain," said the Salphorian king. "Anasind wanted me to put down the rebellion raised by my son. I caught up with Medorian after he had crossed into Ersua and attacked one of your cities. Marradan, it is called. He flew the family colours, not me. It was then that we heard stories, of Askh overthrown and legions clashing again. There were all kinds of tales, but I knew the truth of them and knew Ullsaard was up to his neck in someone else's shit, as usual. We headed towards the dawn looking for you, Ullsaard, and came across towns that had been wiped out by the dark spirits. Your Brotherhood had not destroyed our knowledge of the spirits, light and dark, and we knew what manner of creature would take whole towns. Everything was left dead behind them. It was not difficult to follow them here. I am glad we arrived in time."

"Just in time," said Ullsaard.

"That's usually the way of things," Aegenuis said philosophically. "So what do you want to do now, Ullsaard?"

The king looked over his shoulder and smiled.

"I'm going back to camp to get my wife and I'm going to have sex with her like this was our last day on earth. Ater that, tomorrow, maybe the day after, I think I'll head down the Greenwater, or maybe see what lies Duskwards of Carantathi."

"Men who eat the flesh of other men, I have heard," said Aegenuis. "You are not staying in Askh?"

"Not a fucking chance," replied Ullsaard, looking at Erlaan. "I just saved the empire. Some other poor bastard can put it back together again."

XI

Listening to Ullsaard giving up his claim to the throne, letting the Salphors simply walk away, made Askhos rage. Yet his torment went unheard; Ullsaard was oblivious to the dead king's ranting.

He realised that he had suffered the very fate of those that he had possessed, driven into a corner of Ullsaard's mind, never to be heard from again, unable to see or touch or smell or interact with any part of the living world.

Askhos's frustrated screams went unheard.

A GUIDE TO THE LANDS
& PEOPLE OF MEKHA

The lands called Mekha by the Askhans lie far to hotwards of the centre of the empire, the region of Near-Mekha bordered by Okhar, Anrair and Ersua. The exact size of Mekha is unknown for the majority of it had never been explored, even by the Mekhani who dwell there.

Mekha is for the most part desert, giving way to scrub in the coldwards region of Near-Mekha, and to equatorial jungles where the Greenwater flows through the dawnwards stretch of desert. Although arid, Mekha is not lifeless and there are many oases where the Mekhani can raise goats and take water.

Natural Resources

Though lacking in flora, Mekha has much dangerous and sizeable fauna. Most noticeable are the behemodons, towering lizard creatures bigger than an Askhan townhouse. The Mekhani build howdahs on the backs of these creatures and use them as beasts of burden to drag huge sleds of stores across the deserts. Some Mekhani tribes live wholly in the howdahs of their behemodons while others use them only as transport.

Another common beast of the desert is the lacertil. These

reptiles run low to the ground and have a knobbled, armoured back and flat bodies. The Mekhani trim spinal growths from these creatures to fit saddles and use them as long-range steeds for scouting and skirmishing in war, and for messengers and trading perishable goods in peace.

The tanned hides of these creatures are used to make armour for warriors, tents, sleds and many other goods. Sinew is used for bows and tent ropes, while the meat is edible, if somewhat stringy. Snakes and smaller lizards form a major part of the Mekhani diet, supplemented by cacti fruit and other succulents found in Near-Mekha. Those tribes that live close to the Greenwater trade fruit and fish with those further from the river, so that the majority of the major trade routes run duskwards to dawnwards.

Peoples

The Mekhani live in a loose conglomeration of tribes, and all Mekhani are identified by their dark red skin – a hereditary trait that the Mekhani people have possessed for several thousand years. There is constant war between these different groups, for resources are scarce and the people of the desert hot-headed and proud.

Each tribe is led by a shaman-chief, a position passed on by an apprentice system rather than hereditary right. They are aided by dynastic chieftains, who carry out day-to day-business, while the shaman-chiefs concentrate on the preservation of knowledge – the legends and myths of the peoples, the hunting grounds and hidden waterways, the bloodlines of the chieftains and so on.

The shaman-chiefs do not marry and any children born to them by their many sexual partners are bastards and forced from the tribe to join another, if they can find one that will accept them. Sexual promiscuity amongst unmarried males and females is expected amongst the Mekhani, although once a partner is found for marriage the commitment is for life. Only married couples are allowed to produce children for the tribe – women who become pregnant before they are married must find a man to marry them or be banished when their child is born, usually to die in the desert. This behaviour ensures that the tribes never become too big to feed or find water for, whilst ensuring that great warriors and shaman-chiefs remain with their people.

History

The Mekhani know little of their history, except that which they maintain in the ancient songs and stories, and these tales vary from tribe to tribe. There are some beliefs that unite the Mekhani together. All the tribes believe that they came from a great oasis called Oogaro, and when they die their bodies fall beneath the sands and their souls descend into Samanoa, the fires that consume the Mekhani dead and dries the waters. All Mekhani know that there used to be a time when they were ruled over by a single king, Orlassai, and no other Mekhani has called himself king since.

Orlassai was the uniter, who brought the tribes of the desert together under the protection of the great night. Though they did not understand the nature of their new masters, the Mekhani were recruited to become the footsoldiers of the Eulanui during one of the incursions made by the creatures into the realm of mortal men.

The Mekhani had an empire even larger than that of Askh, centred on the city of Akkamaro, now lost in the deep desert. It was in Akkamaro that the Mekhani raised a great temple to the Eulanui. The Mekhani under Orlassai fought against the Nemurians, who at that time ruled over the lands coldwards of Mekha. Mekha itself was not the desert it has now become, but was fed by many waterways, a verdant place of life and beauty. It was only the consumption of the Eulanui that created the barren wilderness Mekha is in the present day.

When the Nemurians were victorious in their war and the Eulanui driven from the mortal world, Orlassai disappeared and the empire of Akkamaro faltered. The temple vanished and the city was swallowed by the sands, taking with it the leaders of the Mekhani civilisation. Hunters, warriors and farmers were left to wander the desolation that remained. These itinerant groups tried their best to survive and maintain what they could of the height of their civilisation but as they grew more tribal, knowledge was lost and the battle for survival turned thoughts away from architecture, mathematics and literature. Over the hundreds of years that followed, all Akkamaron culture was lost entirely, save for a few legends.

Every now and then, when the veil between worlds grows thinner, the shaman-chiefs feel the pull of the ancient temple. They led their tribes to the Calling, pulled by an instinct they cannot understand. The Calling is a time of cooperation and peace, which unknown to the Mekhani takes place above the ruins of dead Akkamaro. As worlds move apart once more and the veil grows thicker, the Calling comes to an end and the tribes disperse, returning to their nomadic ways.

GLOSSARY

People

Aalek – Member of the Brotherhood, assigned to watch over Luia in Askh.

Addiel – Novice Brother at the precinct of Thedraan.

Adral – Governor of Nalanor.

Aduris – Legionnaire of the Thirteenth.

Aegenuis – Former king of Salphoria, father of Medorian.

Aghali – Salphor chieftain, advisor to Aegenuis.

Allenya – Eldest of Ullsaard's wives and mother of Jutaar. As matriarch of the family, she is responsible for the running of the household, and tempering the worst excesses of her sisters.

Allon – Governor of Enair. Ullsaard served in Allon's provincial legion before gaining the patronage of Prince Aalun. He later returned for a while as first captain. Jutaar served in Allon's legion.

Anasind – First captain of the Thirteenth Legion, later Askhan general.

Anglhan Periusis – Formerly a debt guardian of Salphoria and owner of a landship. Colluded with Ullsaard in the taking of Magilnada and later governor of the city. When Askhan forces razed the city, the treacherous governor had escaped.

Anriit – Noran's surviving wife, older sister of Neerita.

Ansarril – Askhan chieftain, first Companion to Askhos.

Ariid – Chief servant of Ullsaard's household.

Artiides – Steward of Noran at Geria, former legionnaire of the XVII.

Asirkhyr – Hierophant of the Temple.

Askhan – Collective term for both the native people from the tribes of Askhor and those peoples brought into the empire of Greater Askhor.

Askhos – First King of the Askhans, founder of the empire and sire of the Blood. Charismatic and ambitious, Askhos united the tribes of Askhor and subjugated the surrounding peoples to create the fledgling Greater Askhor. Before his death, Askhos laid down his teachings and beliefs in the Book of Askhos, a tome of law, military organisation and customs revered by many people throughout the empire and rigidly adhered to by the Brotherhood.

Asuhas – Governor of Ersua, co-conspirator of Anglhan Periusis and King Urikh.

Brotherhood, The – A widespread administrative sect responsible for many of the functions of the empire, including criminal law, taxation, trade, infrastructural organisation and the suppression of pre-empire superstitious beliefs. Proselytisers of the Book of Askhos. The upper echelons of the Brotherhood are members of the cult of the Eulanui.

Caaskil – veteran captain of the XXI, placed in charge of the prisoner company when Marradan comes under attack.

Caaspir – Legionnaire of the XIII, employed as runner and herald by King Ullsaard.

Canaasin – First captain of the XIV legion.

Cosuas – A general of the empire of long years and staunch ally of King Lutaar. Son of King Tunaard II and last survivor of the dynasty that ruled Ersua prior to Askhan conquest.

Killed by Ullsaard.

Daefas Maron – Alias used by Anglhan whilst working for Urikh in Ersua.

Donar – First captain of the Fifth Legion, uncle to Lutaan.

Enairians – Native peoples of Enair. Considered dour, head-strong, sometimes rebellious. Enairians are typically of larger build than the other peoples of Greater Askhor and are valued as soldiers in the legions.

Eriekh – Hierophant of the Temple.

Erlaan/ Erlaan-Orlassai – Prince of the Blood, son of Prince Kalmud, grandson of King Lutaar. In his early twenties, Erlaan was heavily warped by the intervention of Lakhyri and his priests and was accepted by the Mekhani peoples as the reincarnation of the Great King Orlassai.

Ersuans – The peoples native to Ersua. In recent generations, Ersuan tribes have interbred with Nalanorians, Anrairians and hillmen from the Altes Hills and so are considered something of a mongrel people in other parts of the empire.

Faasil – Legionnaire of the XIII.

Gebriun – Legionnaire of the XIII.

Gelthius – Captain of the XIII legion. A former fisherman, farmer and bandit of the Linghan people in Salphoria, Gelthius has served as a debtor on Anglhan's landship, joined Salphorian rebels, been involved in the fall of Magilnada to the Askhans, was drafted into the Thirteenth Legion and fought in the overthrow of King Lutaar. He longs for a return to a quiet life.

Harrakil – First captain of the XVII Legion, general to King Urikh.

Hasdriak – Member of the Brotherhood in Askhira, found aboard the ship of Haukin Maanam.

Haukin Maanam – Pirate and smuggler working the Nemurian Strait out of Askhira.

Herikhil – Youth of the Temple sent to Marradan precincts of the Brotherhood. Inscribed with runes of communion that allow Lakhyri to manifest partially through his body to communicate between the precincts.

Hillmen – Catch-all term for various tribes found in the Ersuan Highlands and, more numerously, the Altes Hills. The hillmen come from a mix of Ersuan and Salphorian stock and are known for their fierce territorialism and banditry.

Houran – estate manager and vintner of Apili.

Jutaar – Slain son of Allenya, second eldest of Ullsaard. First captain of the First Magilnadan legion.

Jutiil – First captain of the XII.

Juutan – Captain of the XVII.

Kalmud – Prince of the Blood, eldest son of King Lutaar, father of Erlaan. Infected by a devastating lung disease whilst campaigning along the Greenwater River.

Kulrua – Governor of Maasra.

Laasinia – Chief handmaiden of Queen Allenya.

Lakhyri – High priest of the Eulanui, elder brother of Askhos, architect of the Askhan empire, known to the Nemurians as the Pale Man.

Leerates – Senior Brother.

Linnir – Legionnaire on disciplinary duty from the XXI, attacked by Loordin.

Loordin – Legionnaire of the XIII.

Luia – Second eldest of Ullsaard's wives and mother of Urikh. Wayward, headstrong and adulterous, Luia tests the patience of her husband constantly and owes her continued prosperity, perhaps even her life, to the intervention and protection of her older sister.

Luisaa – An infant, daughter of Urikh, grand-daughter of Ullsaard.

Lutaan – First captain of the XXI, nephew to First Captain Donar.

Lutaar – Previous incumbent of the throne of Askh, incarnation-puppet of Askhos usurped by Ullsaard.

Maasrites – Natives of Maasra, of normally tanned skin due to the sunny climate of their homeland. Some undertake the Oath of Service and have their tongues removed so that they may not speak out of turn to their masters. This has led to the rise of a secret sign language unknown to other peoples.

Medorian – Son of King Aegenuis.

Meesiu – First captain of the III.

Mekhani – Savage desert-dwelling tribes of Near- and Deep-Mekha, with distinctive dark red skin. Dispersed hunter-gatherers that utilise stone weapons and tools. Led by shamanic tribal chieftains.

Meliu – Youngest queen of Ullsaard and mother to Ullnaar.

Murian – Governor of Anrair.

Muuril – Sergeant in the Thirteenth Legion, latterly Companion to King Ullsaard.

Naadlin – First captain of the II.

Naamas Dor – Engineer of the XIII.

Naasadir – Elder worshipper of the Temple.

Nalanorians – The peoples native to Nalanor. As the oldest members of the empire outside of Askhor, Nalanorians are generally staunch supporters of the empire, and seen as traditionally conservative in outlook and politics. The presence of the Greenwater's headwaters means that most Nalanorians are accomplished fishermen and sailors, valued across the empire, and they are also respected for the productivity of their farms.

Neerlima – Wife of King Urikh.

Nemurians – Non-human species that live on a chain of

454

volcanic isles lying off the coast of Maasra. Standing more
than twice as tall as a man, and of broad girth, Nemurians
are heavily muscled, covered with thick scales and pos-
sessing prehensile tails. Extremely secretive, the only
Nemurians known to the people of Greater Askhor are
those who hire out their much-sought after services as
mercenaries. Nemurians are also well known for the skill
in metalworking and the quantity of iron in their weapons
and armour, an element still rare in the empire.

Nok'ka – Man-speaker of Nemuria.

Noran Astaan – A noble of Askhor, sole heir of the Astaan family and royal herald in service to Prince Aalun. A long-time
friend and ally of Ullsaard. Noran lost his youngest wife and
unborn son in a legion camp whilst supporting Ullsaard.
Married to Anriit, lover of Meliu. Rendered comatose stopping an assassination of Ullsaard, granted life through the
intervention of his friend and Lakhyri.

Ok'kak'ka – Nemurian who carried Noran across Nemuria.

Okharans – The native peoples of Okhar. Most populous peoples
of the empire, Okharans are seen as listless and lazy by the
natives of other provinces, and the bountiful wealth of their
province encourages a culture with little love for physical
labour and a deserved reputation of indolence within the
Okharan nobility.

Pretaa – Mother of Ullsaard, former courtesan in Askh and
lover of Cosuas.

Rainaan – Headman of Thedraan.

Rondin – First captain of the X.

Taarik – Captain of the Brotherhood legionnaires under Leraates, veteran of the X.

Thyrisa – Headwoman of Thedraan.

Ullnaar – Son of Meliu, youngest of Ullsaard. Clever and cul-
tured, Ullnaar is studying civic law at the colleges in Askh,

under the tutelage of Meemis.

Ullsaard – King of Greater Askhor, conqueror of Salphoria. Married to Allenya, Luia and Meliu. Father to Urikh and Ullnaar. Haunted by the disembodied spirit of Askhos.

Urikh – Son of Luia, eldest of Ullsaard, former governor of Okhar. As heir of the family, Urikh has spent considerable time expanding his personal assets and influence across the empire. Usurper of the Crown.

Places

Altes Hills – Low mountain range stretching coldwards from the Magilnadan Gap to the coast of Enair. This range forms the duskwards boundary of coldwards Ersua and all of Anrair. Sometimes referred to simply as the Altes.

Anrair – Smallest imperial province, located between Okhar, Ersua and Mekha.

Apili – Ullsaard's estate in coldwards Okhar. Vineyard, winery and villa.

Askh – Founding city of the empire, capital of Askhor, birthplace of Askhos. The largest and most advanced city of the empire, boasting the Grand Precinct of the Brotherhood, the Royal Palaces, the Maarmes arena and circuit and many other wonders of the world.

Askhan Gap – The widest, and only easily navigable, pass in the Askhor mountains. Protected by the Askhan Wall and dominated by the harbour at Narun.

Askhira – Large port city on the coast of Maasra, with a harbour on the Nemurian Strait.

Askhor – The homeland of the Askhan empire, situated in the dawnwards region of the empire, bordered by the Askhor mountains and the dawnwards coast.

Askhor Wall – A defensive edifice stretching the entire width of the Askhor Gap, built in the earliest years of the empire to defend against attack from the neighbouring tribes.

Carantathi – Current capital of Salphoria and former seat of King Aegenuis's court. Lying several thousand miles to duskwards of the Greater Askhor border.

Cosuan – New settlement at the mouth of the Greenwater.

Enair – Most coldward province of the empire, brought into the empire during the reign of King Lutaar's predecessor. A land of strong winds, frequent rain, large marshlands and heavy forest. Enair has no major cities and relies on timber trade and sea fishing for its low income. Birthplace of Ullsaard.

Ersua – Most recent province of the empire, situated dawn-wards of Nalanor and separated from Salphoria by the Free Country. Consisting mostly of the foothills of the Altes Hills, Ersua is now Greater Askhor's main source of ore for bronze.

Ersuan Highlands – A range of mountains that separates Ersua from Nalanor, curving several hundred miles to duskwards between Ersua and Anrair.

Genladen – Ersuan village close to the villa at Menesun.

Geria – Harbour town on the Greenwater, capital of Nalanor, whose quays are owned by the Astaan noble family.

Gesian River – Tributary to the Greenwater in Nalanor, from duskwards of Geria.

Grand Precincts of the Brotherhood – An imposing black stone zig-gurat situated on the Royal Hill in Askh, predating the founding of the city. The centre of the Brotherhood's organisation, it is here that ailurs are bred, the fuel known as lava is created and the great library of the empire – The Archive of Ages – is found. Adjoining the precinct are the highest law courts of Greater Askhor.

Greenwater River – More than seventeen hundred miles long, this is the greatest river of the empire and main route of trade and expansion.

Khar – A meeting place of the Mekhani tribes, razed by Ull-saard at the outset of his campaign in Mekha.

Landesi – Village in Salphoria, populated by a tribe of the Ling-han peoples. Birthplace of Gelthius.

Maarmes – Area of Askh, dominated by the sporting circuits and arena of the same name, where ailur chariots are raced and wrestling tournaments take place. Maarmes is also home to the bloodfields of Askh, where nobles can resolve disputes in mortal combat. All duels on the bloodfields are to the death. Commonly, such duels are over marital disputes; if a marriage proposal is opposed, a noble that kills the head of a noble family undertakes to marry the daughters of that family.

Maasra – Province of the empire situated hotwards of Askhor, with a temperate climate and long coastline. The chiefs of the Maasrite tribes acceded to the empire without battle. They initiated the Oath of Service by cutting out their tongues so that they could raise no opposition to the conquest. Its people are known across the empire for their placid disposition and its wine is considered the best in the empire. Nemuria lies just off the coast of Maasra.

Magilnada – A city founded by Baruun at the coldwards extent of the Altes Hills, in opposition to the rise of Askh. Magilnada has changed hands through many Salphorian chieftains since its founding, until its status as a free and protected city was guaranteed by agreement between King Aegenuis and King Lutaar. Conquered by Ullsaard, it was subsequently razed following treachery by its new governor, Anglhan Periusis.

Marradan – Capital of Ersua.

Mekha – An arid land hotwards of Nalanor and Ersua, divided into the semi-scrub of Near-Mekha and the deserts of Deep (or Far) Mekha. Home to the Mekhani tribes.

Menes River – Waterway of Ersua that flow duskwards from the Menes lake.

Menesun – Ullsaard's estate in hotwards Ersua, granted by right of conquest.

Naakus River – A river in Near-Mekha, considered the border between Greater Askhor and Mekha. Site of Ullsaard's camp during his Mekha campaign and proposed location of a new Askhan settlement in the region.

Nalanor – Province of the empire lying to duskwards of the Askhor Gap and first to be conquered by King Askhos. Consisting of rich farmlands, Nalanor was once the centre of trade of the empire, but as Greater Askhor has grown, the province faces stern competition from Salphorian importers and growing farmlands in Okhar. Despite this, Nalanor is considered the gateway of the empire, as it is linked by the Greenwater to other parts of Greater Askhor and sits next to the only secure route into Askhor.

Narun – Largest harbour on the Greenwater, situated on the border of Nalanor and Askhor. Known as the Harbour of a Thousand Fires due to its many light towers that allow safe navigation even at night. Many decades of construction have made Narun a huge artificial laketown boasting dozens of docks and quays. Almost all trade along the Greenwater passes through Narun at some point on its journey and most of the empire's shipbuilding is centred in Narun. The jewels in the crown of Narun are the stone-built docks of the King's Wharf.

Nemuria – A chain of smoke-shrouded islands situated to dawnwards of the Maasra coast. Home to the inhuman Nemurians, little is known of this realm other than its volcanic nature and richness of iron. Nemuria is protected by arrangement with the empire so that no ship may approach within a mile of its shores.

Nemurian Strait – A narrow stretch of water separating the shores of Maasra from the isles of Nemuria.

Okhar – Province of the empire flanking the Greenwater River coldwards of Askhor and bordered to dawnwards by Maasra, duskwards by Ersua and hotwards by Mekha; of rich farmlands, vineyards, forested uplands and numerous harbour towns. After Askhor, the richest province of the empire, due in large part to its much-prized marble and linen.

Oorandia – Former capital of Nalanor, now mostly deserted but still home to the second-largest precinct of the Brotherhood.

Osteris – Town in Maasra, situated in the parched farmlands in the hotwards region of the province, where the great aqueduct terminates to provide irrigation.

Parmia – City of Nalanor, duskwards of Narun.

River Ladmun – River that runs along the border of Anrair and Enair from the Altes Hills.

Royal Way – The broad thoroughfare running from the main gate of Askh up to the palaces on the Royal Hill.

Salacis Pass – Site of famous battle in the Ersuan Highlands.

Salphoria – Lands situated to duskwards of Greater Askhor, separated from Ersua by the Free Country. Populated by disparate peoples and tribes. Formerly ruled over by King Aegenuis from the capital at Carantathi now conquered by King Ullsaard and made the latest province of the Askhan empire.

Sannasen – Village in Okhar.

Sea of the Sun – The body of water lying to dawnwards of Askhor and Maasra.

Stykhaag – Ullsaard's home village in Enair.

Sulunnin – Town in Enair where the XVI and XVIII legions were ambushed during Enair's conquest.

Thedraan – Ersuan town situated a few miles from the Altes Hills.

Ualnian Mountains – Range in Salphoria, site of Carantathi.

Creatures

Abada – Large herbivorous creature with prominent nose horn, used as a beast of burden throughout Greater Askhor.

Ailur – Large species of cat bred by the Brotherhood as beasts of war and status symbols for Askhan nobility. Possessed of savage temper, only female ailurs are ridden to war, and do so hooded by armoured bronze masks. Known to attack in a berserk frenzy when unmasked.

Behemodon – Large reptilian creature native to the deserts of Mekha. Employed as beasts of burden and war mounts by the Mekhani tribes.

Blackfang – Ailur owned by Ullsaard.

Kolubrid – Large, snakelike beast native to Maasra, employed by Askhans as mounts for messengers and skirmishing cavalry.

Lacertil – Giant reptile used by the Mekhani as mounts.

Lupus – Large, wolf-like beast used by Salphorians to draw war-chariots.

ABOUT THE AUTHOR

Gav Thorpe works from Nottingham, England, and has written more than a dozen novels and even more short stories. Growing up in a tedious town just north of London, he originally intended to be an illustrator but after acknowledging an inability to draw or paint he turned his hand to writing.

Gav spent 14 years as a developer for Games Workshop on the worlds of Warhammer and Warhammer 40,000 before going freelance in 2008. It is claimed (albeit solely by our Gav, frankly) that he is merely a puppet of a mechanical hamster called Dennis that intends to take over the world via the global communications network. When not writing, Gav enjoys playing games, cooking, pro-wrestling and smiling wryly.

mechanicalhamster.wordpress.com

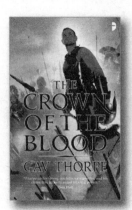

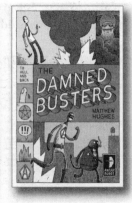

ANGRY ROBOT

WHO NEEDS FOOD?

Own the complete Angry Robot catalogue

DAN ABNETT
☐ Embedded
☐ Triumff: Her Majesty's Hero

GUY ADAMS
☐ The World House
☐ Restoration

JO ANDERTON
☐ Debris
☐ Suited

LAUREN BEUKES
☐ Moxyland
☐ Zoo City

THOMAS BLACKTHORNE
☐ Edge
☐ Point

MAURICE BROADDUS
☐ King Maker
☐ King's Justice
☐ King's War

ADAM CHRISTOPHER
☐ Empire State

PETER CROWTHER
☐ Darkness Falling

ALIETTE DE BODARD
☐ Obsidian & Blood

MATT FORBECK
☐ Amortals
☐ Carpathia
☐ Vegas Knights

JUSTIN GUSTAINIS
☐ Hard Spell
☐ Evil Dark

GUY HALEY
☐ Reality 36
☐ Omega Point

COLIN HARVEY
☐ Damage Time
☐ Winter Song

CHRIS F HOLM
☐ Dead Harvest

MATTHEW HUGHES
☐ The Damned Busters
☐ Costume Not Included

TRENT JAMIESON
☐ Roil
☐ Night's Engines

K W JETER
☐ Infernal Devices
☐ Morlock Night

J ROBERT KING
☐ Angel of Death
☐ Death's Disciples

ANNE LYLE
☐ The Alchemist of Souls

GARY McMAHON
☐ Pretty Little Dead Things
☐ Dead Bad Things

ANDY REMIC
☐ The Clockwork Vampire Chronicles

CHRIS ROBERSON
☐ Book of Secrets

MIKE SHEVDON
☐ Sixty-One Nails
☐ The Road to Bedlam
☐ Strangeness & Charm

DAVID TALLERMAN
☐ Giant Thief

GAV THORPE
☐ The Crown of the Blood
☐ The Crown of the Conqueror

LAVIE TIDHAR
☐ The Bookman
☐ Camera Obscura
☐ The Great Game

TIM WAGGONER
☐ The Nekropolis Archives

KAARON WARREN
☐ Mistification
☐ Slights
☐ Walking the Tree

CHUCK WENDIG
☐ Blackbirds

IAN WHATES
☐ City of Dreams & Nightmare
☐ City of Hope & Despair
☐ City of Light & Shadow